The Riddle at the Revelry

A Cozy Mystery

L.L. Gray

Heroic Rose Publishing

To everyone who finds hope in new beginnings, courage in endings, and love in the moments in between—this book is for you.

Contents

Grab your FREE novella now!

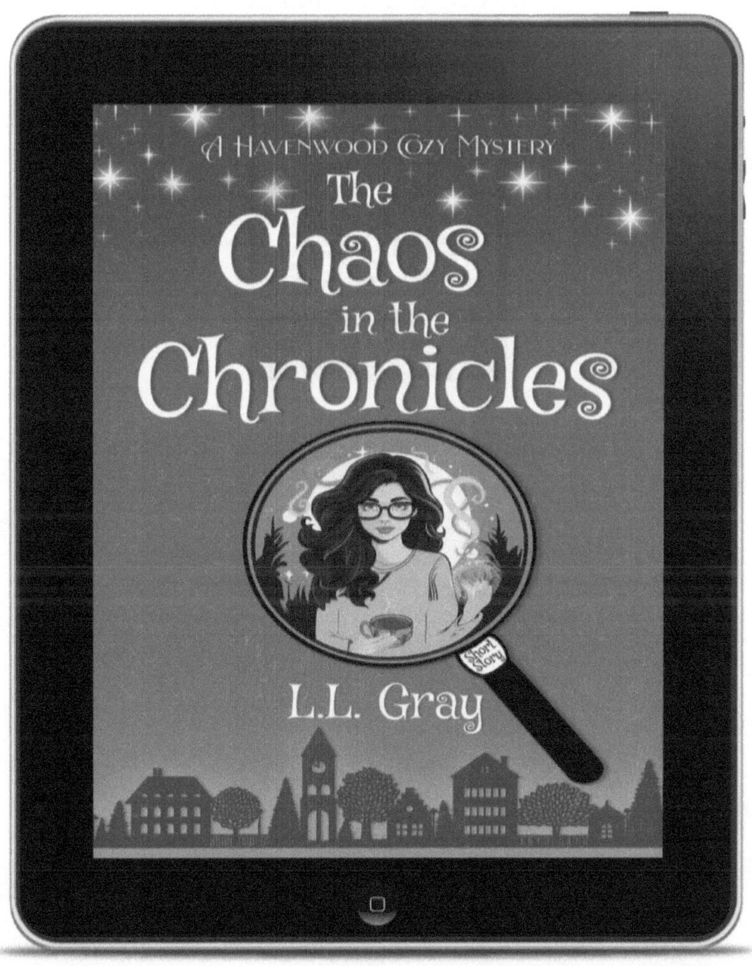

Want a free book?

Of course you do, what madness could possess someone to **not** want free books?
There's no catch - you do sign-up for my mailing list but you can unsubscribe at any time.
There's also no spam.
Ever.
Sign up here to get your free book!
https://www.subscribepage.io/havenwood

Hidden Treasures

THE BELL ABOVE MY bookshop door jangled one last time, announcing the departure of my last customer for the year. I waved as Madame Fontaine hurried out into the chilly December night, her garish red and purple hat soon disappearing out of view.

I dramatically brushed invisible dust from my hands. "Ladies and cats, that's a wrap. The next few glorious days are filled with absolutely nothing to do. I cannot wait," I said with a sigh, collapsing in a nearby armchair I'd set up for bookish browsers.

"Well, not nothing," my best friend, Bella DeLuca, pointed out, passing me a thick slice of her mother's famous peppermint mocha brownies generously sprinkled with crumbled candy canes on top. "We're hosting our annual New Year's Eve bash at the Oasis, and I'm counting on your help setting it up over the weekend."

I bit into the fudgy confection and closed my eyes in rapture as a small moan of pleasure escaped my lips. "I don't know what I can possibly do to help when your mom bakes like this. No one is going to remember me setting out paper plates or trying to straighten the tablecloths once they taste something she baked. Seriously, how does she do it?" I asked around my delicious mouthful.

"Magic," Bella said, a twinkle in her eye. She wasn't being hyperbolic, and we both knew it. Bella's mom, Honey DeLuca, was a brownie. No, not the same kind we were indulging in. One of the fairy creatures often misrepresented in children's books. Honey wouldn't fix shoes, drink all your milk, or play pranks on the local shepherd, but she did have a magical talent for baking. It seemed to me that whatever went into her oven came out a million times better than I could have imagined, and I have an excellent imagination. Every time I tasted one of Honey's creations, I was transported to sugary heaven, the peppermint mocha brownie being only the latest example of her culinary prowess.

Bella interrupted my oncoming sugar rush. "Seriously though, Harper, are you really just going to help me party prep for the next couple days? Are you avoiding something...or someone?"

I felt the heat rise in my cheeks and rolled my eyes. "I'm not thinking about him, okay?"

Bella's grin widened. "Who? Finn or Gabriel?"

"Either. Both." I sighed. "Christmas Eve was complicated enough. I'm taking a break from all of that."

"Well, suit yourself," Bella said, laughing as she took another bite of her brownie. She waved it at me. "But if either of them shows up at this New Year's party, I'm not responsible for what happens."

I gave her a look. "You're terrible."

"I know." She winked and then her eyes lit up. "Oh, speaking of Christmas...maybe we should rope Isadora into helping with the party prep. She hasn't gone back to her special magical academy yet, has she?"

I shook my head. "No, she doesn't leave until January."

"Do you think she'd help? I bet she's fantastic with party planning, what with all the events her family throws."

"Maybe. I'll send her a message now and see if she's free," I offered, grabbing my phone and tapping out a quick message.

Bella nodded. "Speaking of free, can I just say how grateful I am that you're taking some time off and helping me with this party. Mama and Papa let me pick the theme this year for the first time ever. It was a toss-up between an Around the World theme with passports and international food or a Vegas theme, but I went with Vegas. I really want to make sure I pull this off. It has to be amazing, you know? I want the first New Year's Eve party I'm in charge of to be an enormous success. Off the charts. Incredible!

Dare I say, even, legendary!" Bella exclaimed, throwing her arms wide in exuberance.

"I'm in. How can I help?" I asked, not bothering to hide my grin. Bella's energy was infectious, and I could feel myself already getting swept up in her plans.

"Set-up for one. I was kind of hoping you wouldn't mind coming over in the next few days to help me get an idea for the flow of the rooms, refreshments, the whole nine yards."

"Of course! Granny Bea always closed the shop for several days right before the new year to do a reset. After how busy I was leading up to Christmas, I can see why. So, whatever you need in the next few days, I'll be your right-hand woman. How many people are you expecting?" I asked.

"Well, Mama and Papa always invite whoever is staying at the Oasis, but it's never that full this time of year. Other than that, just a handful of close friends and family. Estimate fifty at a minimum. Maybe a hundred max?"

"A hundred people?! Just how big is your family? How do you manage to do all this with guests in the B&B?" I exclaimed.

Bella chuckled. "Mama and Papa like to be inclusive with who they invite. Then, inevitably, Mama goes off the deep end and invites everyone she runs into. As for the guests at the Oasis, they generally like the idea of celebrating but not having to drive anywhere. They gladly join the party. And for those who don't, Papa invested in some magical soundproofing, so there's never a worry there."

"Oh, well, that's good," I said. Magic could be simultaneously cool and useful in ways I never imagined.

"Yeah. Which is why I picked the Vegas theme. Vegas just has a lot more excitement going for it. We can give the guests fake money that they can gamble with and exchange for prizes at the end of the night, not to mention that I've already contacted several businesses around town to contribute to the silent auction. All proceeds of which will go towards the children's wing of the hospital in Havenwood."

"Which reminds me, here's that collection of books I offered," I said, putting my brownie down and grabbing the books I'd stuck behind the counter. It was a newly completed series by one of my favorite indie fantasy authors who I thought definitely needed more fans. The stories were so good!

"Much appreciated," Bella said, popping the last morsel of chocolate into her mouth and wiping her fingers free of cocoa dust before accepting the books.

"Hey! If you're set on doing a Vegas theme, I think I saw some decorations we might be able to use up in the attic," I said eagerly.

Two long white ears poked out of the display in one of my shop's front windows. Luna sniffed derisively as she ran a paw across her whiskers. The white talking rabbit used to be my great-granny's familiar but had decided to stay with me when I inherited the shop. I didn't mind most days, but Luna had a tongue sharp enough to sting and a vocabulary that cut deep when she chose to use it.

"Hoppy horrors! I hope you're not suggesting letting those two imps out again," Luna said, reminding me of the Halloween pranks gone horribly wrong.

I shook my head emphatically. "No, absolutely not. Wizzle and Snicker are with Aunty Agatha. There's no way I want to relive their escapades from Halloween," I said earnestly. The imps had wreaked havoc on Havenwood until I'd managed to stop them by successfully completing my very first magical ritual with some timely help from my friends.

Luna's ear twitched. "What about the wizard? He might not be inclined towards pranks, but he did love to listen to himself talk."

I shook my head. "Wrapped up tight. I learned my lesson about opening boxes. Check the label or ledger first. Then you can choose decorations."

"Good," Luna said, hopping out of her hutch and selecting a delicious-looking piece of cabbage from her bowl. "It appears there may be hope for you yet."

I'd grown used to the rabbit's acerbic grumbling since moving to Havenwood in September. Most days, it barely registered at all. I looked at Bella. "You know what? Why don't we go upstairs and see what we can find for your party in the attic right now?"

Bella's face lit up. "Really? That would be great!"

A pitiful yowl rang out from the other side of the shop, and my large, orange tabby Maine Coon lifted his head from his eighth nap of the day.

Bella quirked an eyebrow at his empty food bowl. "Did you forget to feed him?"

"As if he'd let me!" I chuckled. "No, he's taken to begging for treats, but he really needs to cut back, don't you boy?" I asked, walking over to scratch behind the enormous cat's ears. A deep rumble permeated the shop as Mr. Wigglesworth flopped over on his back with a thump, presenting his tummy for belly rubs. I shook my head in bemusement even as I stroked the long, soft fur.

"He's more dog than cat," Bella observed from behind me.

"Don't I know it. But he's too cute to say no to," I said, flicking him a couple of his favorite tuna treats from the bag I kept near his kibble. He lurched to his feet with a speed that belied his size and gobbled them up almost as soon as they touched the floor.

"Which is how he learned that begging for treats from you works," Luna pointed out. I ignored her.

Bella idly picked up a book I'd left on the small table between the armchairs as I gave Mr. Wigglesworth a proper belly rub. "What's this?" she asked curiously.

I glanced over. "Oh, that's a book of Havenwood's history I received for Christmas from Spellbooks. I haven't read it all yet, but the stories I have read are interesting. It's definitely helping me learn more about the town."

Bella flipped through the pages. "It looks good. What's the best part so far?"

"There was the great blizzard of 1888 which was way worse than the one we had on Christmas Eve this year," I said, referencing the snowstorm that had been a blessing in disguise because it allowed us to catch some jewel thieves. "Apparently, it was so severe that the entire town was cut off. They had to tunnel through the snow to visit neighbors and share food. Imagine the whole town, interconnected by snow tunnels like a fortress."

"I hope they had an epic snowball fight," Bella said with a grin.

"Me too. Also, did you know about the Guild of the Greenwood?"

"No, what's that?" Bella asked.

"It was a secret society set up right here in Havenwood, around the early 20th century made up of environmentalists and artists, all sworn to protect the town's natural beauty and ancient crafts. They met in a secret chamber under what's now the Miller's cottage on the edge of town."

Bella's eyes sparkled as she looked up from the book. "This town's history is richer and more intriguing than I thought, and that's saying something in Havenwood," she mused, clearly impressed. "Mind if I borrow it when you're done?"

I nodded in agreement, giving Mr. Wigglesworth one final scratch. "Absolutely. Maybe there'll even be a recipe from a great bake off or something your mom could try."

"I'm sold. But before that, let's go explore the attic. I bet your granny has a whole bunch of things that would look amazing at the party," Bella said, setting the book down and following me towards the stairs leading up to my apartment and the attic beyond.

Eager to start our attic adventure, Bella and I made our way up the narrow staircase. The air was thick with dust and the scent of old paper, which somehow felt comforting in its familiarity rather than musty. The attic, much like the rest of the shop, was a treasure trove of the unusual and the magical, packed with items that Granny Bea had collected over her many years. Her knack for finding the most extraordinary things was truly remarkable. Thanks to the shop's magical nature, space was never an issue. Spellbooks seemed to expand and contract as needed, defying the usual constraints of physics and floor plans.

"I swear, this place is bigger on the inside," Bella remarked, her voice filled with wonder as she peered around the cluttered space.

"It's one of Spellbooks' many charms," I replied with a smile, laying a hand on the wall. I felt a little vibration as the wood warmed under my palm which was Spellbooks' way of communicating. I grinned in response as we began our search through the boxes and trinkets that filled the room.

We discovered so many interesting things as we rummaged. We were sidetracked by exploring and trying on hats and clothes, but finally I found the box I was looking for, tucked away under a stack of old magazines. I recognized Granny Bea's looping handwriting and craned my neck to read the words.

"*Vegas night*? Perfect," I murmured under my breath. "Look at this!" I called to Bella, pulling the box out and opening it with a triumphant grin. The box was full of neon lights, plastic poker chips, and other Vegas-themed decorations which would be ideal for Bella's New Year's Eve bash. I searched for a ledger which might have a record of any magical items, but when I found nothing, I was fairly confident this was all mundane décor.

"That's perfect!" Bella said, coming over to inspect the contents. "But I'm kind of sad we haven't been able to find anything about secret societies yet. I thought for sure your granny would be part of at least one."

"Well, I suppose if she was, she did a good job on the whole secret front then," I teased.

"Maybe, but wouldn't it be exciting if we discovered something hidden?" Bella mused as she rummaged through the Vegas-themed box.

That sparked a thought. "Spellbooks," I said aloud, glancing at the walls and ceiling, knowing the building was always listening, "any chance Granny Bea had some secrets that might be useful? Or maybe a hidden society she was part of?"

For a moment, nothing happened. I wasn't sure what I expected—Spellbooks never responded in words, but it had a way of communicating that I usually understood. The silence stretched on, and I turned back to Bella, shrugging. "Worth a shot."

Just as I spoke, there was a faint creak and rumble behind me. The picture frame that had been leaning against the wall slowly tipped forward. I rushed over, steadying it before it could crash.

"That's weird," Bella said.

"No, I think that's Spellbooks," I murmured.

Bella moved to have a closer look of the floral painting I held. "What? Is there something in the picture? It's pretty, but I don't see how that has anything to do with secret societies."

"No, not the picture," I said, setting it to the side. "Look here. There's something carved into the wall."

Leaning in closer, I saw what looked like small, intricate runes etched into the wood. They were barely noticeable, worn smooth with time. I snapped a quick photo with my phone, hoping I could maybe enhance the image to better see what was carved there. Curiously, I traced the lines with my finger, and as I followed the runes, my fingers caught on a slightly raised edge.

I paused, feeling the edge more carefully. It wasn't obvious, but not completely hidden either—just enough that you'd miss it unless you were really looking. A small, barely-there groove outlined a section of the panel, almost like a button.

"What's this?" I murmured, pressing my fingers against the raised edge. It gave a little under the pressure, clicking softly as the panel shifted. The wall slid open, revealing a hidden room behind it. I stumbled back a pace, nearly knocking into the picture frame behind me as my breath caught in my throat.

"Okay, that's not weird. That's a hidden room," Bella said, wide-eyed.

I took a deep breath, a grin tugging at my lips. "I guess Spellbooks has its own way of answering a question."

"Whoa," Bella gasped, peering over my shoulder into the hidden space. "What's in there?"

"I don't know. I didn't even know it was here," I said, pulling out my phone and flipping on the flashlight feature. We both leaned in, the narrow alcove dimly lit by my phone. A cool draft swept past, carrying dust into the air and sending a few cobwebs floating away. I sneezed, rubbing at my nose.

"Look at that!" Bella exclaimed in excitement, pointing past my shoulder. I wiped at my eyes before focusing on where she was pointing.

Inside, beneath layers of dust, were several objects, their details softened by age. There was a long-forgotten box with what appeared to be party supplies—glimmering glassware, old-fashioned cigarette holders, feather boas, some beaded headpieces with delicate fringe, and a couple of flasks with tarnished finishes. The items had a vintage feel, not flashy but sophisticated in their own way.

Bella picked up one of the bright, sequined headbands, turning it over in her hands. "This is so cool," she gushed. "What do you think your granny used all this for?"

"I'm not sure," I said as I shifted some of the party supplies to the side. "Granny Bea had some interesting tastes, that's for sure. Why do you think she hid these in a secret room?"

"Maybe she was struggling for storage space and forgot she shoved these things in here," Bella suggested, scooping up another handful of beaded and sequined headpieces.

"Maybe," I allowed, but I wasn't convinced. Spellbooks seemed to have an uncanny ability to ignore the rules to which regular buildings were bound. Granny Bea had more than enough space, even if she'd nearly packed it from wall to wall. So, why did she leave these things in a hidden room?

"I'm taking a load downstairs," Bella announced.

"Right behind you," I murmured. As I turned to go, the beam of my flashlight caught the edge of a narrow box, buried under sequins and boas until Bella's rummaging partially revealed it. Shifting aside a feather boa, I uncovered the small box, worn and nondescript. Inside it were a flask, a pocket-sized notebook, a set of old keys with no obvious purpose, and a handful of other odds and ends. At the bottom of the box, half-buried under a folded handkerchief, a small, faded photograph caught my eye.

I picked it up and brought it closer to my flashlight. It was in the sepia tones that predated color photography, showing the face of a handsome young man with a mischievous, almost knowing gaze. A shiver ran down my spine as he stared out at me, his eyes seeming to follow me as I juggled the box and the flashlight.

"Harper? Are you coming?" Bella's voice drifted up from my apartment.

I shoved the picture back in the box and tucked it under my arm. "Yeah! Be there in a sec!" I called back as I scooped up some of the party supplies we'd found.

"What's that?" Bella asked as I set my load down on the kitchen table.

I held up the small box. "This was in the hidden compartment. Come take a look."

Bella leaned in, rummaging through the box while I turned my attention back to the photograph. In the more familiar, well-lit surroundings, the image felt a little less eerie. Flipping it over, I saw there was an inscription and read aloud.

> *"Benny O'Rourke,*
> *Havenwood, 1924.*
> *Remember, the best secrets are the ones we share."*

Underneath was a series of intricate runes that looked similar to the ones on the wooden panel upstairs.

"Benny O'Rourke?" Bella murmured, leaning in to get a closer look at the photograph.

"Have you heard of him?" I asked, handing her the photo. Bella had lived in Havenwood almost all her life and knew more about the town than I did.

She shook her head. "Not a clue. Was he a relative of yours maybe? Is that why your granny has his photo stashed away in the attic?"

"Maybe, but I've never heard of him either. Although after what happened in September with Thaddeus, I wouldn't be all that surprised if I had more relatives I didn't know about," I said, referring to my first week in Havenwood. I'd moved here thinking I was Granny Bea's sole heir, only to discover I had a second cousin with whom I was competing for the ownership of Spellbooks. Things were pretty tense for about a week, but after Spellbooks officially became mine, Thaddeus moved on quickly, and I hadn't seen him since.

"What do you think 'the best secrets are the ones we share' means? Isn't that a little contradictory?'" Bella asked, her fingers tracing the faded handwriting on the back of the photo.

I shrugged, equally puzzled. "Maybe Benny was a detective?" I asked as I tucked the picture in the small notebook for safekeeping.

"But don't detectives want to bring secrets out into the light?" Bella pointed out. "Maybe he was involved in some of the secret societies around here like that Guild of the Greentree and wanted to bring more people into the fold."

"Greenwood," I corrected her. "Being involved with a secret society would be a lot more interesting. Hmm. 1924. Wouldn't that put him smack dab in the middle of Prohibition? I can imagine that period of history must have made Havenwood an interesting place. Flappers. Speakeasies. Bootleggers. Jazz. All of it!"

Bella's eyes lit up with inspiration, a spark of creativity flashing across her face. "I've just had a great idea! What if we focused on a Prohibition theme instead of Vegas? Don't get me wrong, I like the glitz and glam, but there's something secretive and sophisticated about the '20s, don't you think?"

"Are you sure you want to switch themes? You were excited about the Vegas idea," I said.

Bella shrugged and held out her hands like she was weighing something. "Vegas. Prohibition. Really all that changes is the style of the clothes." She grabbed one of the beaded headpieces. "And if your granny has any more of these upstairs, we should be just fine."

I glanced at the scattered items, my mind already drifting to what else could be hiding in the attic. "Well, if it gets to be too much, I suppose we can always pivot back to the Vegas idea. There's enough upstairs to decorate the Oasis and still have some left over."

Bella nodded. "Yeah, you're right. We'll be fine either way. But honestly, I think a little Prohibition flair could add a fun, mysterious touch. Speakeasies, secret societies...all that hidden-in-plain-sight stuff."

"It would be fun," I admitted, getting swept away by her enthusiasm. Her words triggered something in my mind. If there was one thing Granny Bea loved, it was keeping secrets. My thoughts flickered to the old photograph I'd found with Benny O'Rourke's name. Secrets. Hidden places. Maybe Granny hid more than this old box in the secret room upstairs.

"Either way, we need to get these decorations over to the Oasis," Bella said, nudging a box with her toe.

"You have your car, right?" I asked. Bella nodded. "Okay, why don't you take the decorations we've already found back to your house while I keep searching here for anything else we can use?"

"Do you think there's more up there?" Bella asked, shooting a look at the narrow staircase leading to the attic. "Are you sure you don't want some help?"

I gestured at the boxes we'd already brought down. "These plus the rest of what we already found will pretty much fill up your car. Let's get you packed up."

Bella put her hands on her hips and looked at the boxes. "Yeah, you're right. My car isn't huge."

"I'll keep poking around upstairs to see what else I can find. There might even be something in the history book about Havenwood during the Prohibition era that we could use as inspiration."

Bella's eyes lit up. "That sounds amazing! I'd love it if we could tie some authentic Havenwood history into the party."

I grinned back. "Sounds like we've got our work cut out for us. Let's get this stuff out to your car, and then we can meet up bright and early tomorrow to go over everything and start our planning?"

"That's a terrific idea. How about after the breakfast rush? At least give me time to help Mama get the buffet laid out?" Bella suggested.

"Deal. And I'll bring over any other decorations I can find."

"You really are the best," Bella said, giving me a squeeze. "As long as you're poking around upstairs, don't forget we'll need to find the right costumes for the party. Slinky dresses, statement jewelry, the whole shebang."

"Don't you have an entire closet full of costumes?" I teased.

"Sure, but I've already worn all of those, and your granny always had the best outfits. I guarantee there are some treasures hidden somewhere up here."

"I feel like I'm fueling a budding clothes addiction," I teased.

"Budding? Girl, that ship sailed years ago. Remember, I look better in gold than silver," Bella said with a grin. "If you find some, you should definitely go for something rich, and jewel toned. Something like the ballgown you wore at the Christmas ball but with more beads and fringe."

I rolled my eyes but couldn't help but smile, caught up in the excitement of party planning. "This is going to be amazing. What a perfect way to celebrate the New Year!"

As we hauled the large box of decorations down the stairs and out to Bella's car, I couldn't help but feel grateful for the magical serendipity of finding exactly what we needed, when we needed it. Granny Bea's hidden treasures never ceased to surprise and delight, and Spellbooks always seemed to know exactly what needed to be revealed and when. With the help of the shop, I knew this New Year's Eve bash was going to be one for the books.

whispers of the Past

AFTER BELLA HEADED HOME with the enormous box of decorations and a few smaller ones we'd found, I continued to search through the attic for any costumes that we could use for the party. To my surprise, I found more than I expected, and some even seemed like it would fit Bella's vision to a tee. By the time I was done, I'd pulled out nearly an entire clothes rack of glitzy women's clothing along with two enormous boxes of accessories, including an impressive range of shoes, hats, and oodles of costume jewelry.

I lugged the last of the dusty old boxes down into my apartment, working hard to strategically pivot the largest box on my own so it fit down the narrow stairs. It took more effort than I'd first imagined, and I was sweating by the time I got it through the doorway. I put my hands on my hips, surveying my haul. Bella would be thrilled with all of my discoveries. The clothes looked even more incredible in the bright light of my apartment. A couple of them caught my eye, and I couldn't wait to try them on. Although, I was less thrilled by the sizeable sprinkling of dust which now coated both my apartment and me in a fine film. There also appeared to be at least three cobwebs, which seemed determined to make a permanent home in my wavy hair despite my best efforts to evict them. Looking around, I blew out a breath and then got my bucket of cleaning supplies out, knowing I'd never be able to go to sleep with this mess lurking in the darkness. Costumes would have to wait until both the apartment and I were clean.

An hour later, I'd accomplished both tasks. The cobwebs in my hair had put up a good fight, but eventually surrendered to the combined efforts of clarifying shampoo, a deluge of water, and a good scrubbing. Wrapped up in a cozy robe over my pajamas, I curled up in my window seat overlooking Arcadia Avenue with a cup of chamomile tea, a couple of vanilla almond biscotti left over from Honey's delivery of baked goods this morning, and the book on Havenwood's history, determined to find some juicy tidbits about secret societies or Prohibition for Bella's soiree.

I learned several interesting things about Havenwood. For example, there was an annual pie-baking contest in the 1950s where bakers had to qualify for the final competition round. The top ten bakers were handed a mystery ingredient on the day and tasked with turning it into something delectable. The twist? The ingredient was always magical—diamondfruit, elvish elderberries, wrigglewort weed—you get the idea.

It all went smoothly until a few contestants started pushing for other desserts. That's when things crumbled. The pie purists weren't having it, and the contest fell apart faster than a poorly made crust.

Amid some rather boring stories, there was a chapter dedicated to the annual pet parade, which was apparently still a thing. The owners dressed in themed, matching costumes with their pets and paraded through town. I thought that sounded ridiculously adorable but not at all what Bella wanted for her party.

Another story that piqued my interest was that of the traveling topiary. In the summer, Havenwood used to host a gardener's week with events ranging from produce to flowers. Topiaries were the highlight of the 1973 gardening week, but for all the wrong reasons. The most famous topiary was in the shape of a teapot. Mysteriously, it would appear in a different part of town each day. No one ever admitted to moving it, leading to much town speculation and amusement.

"And that's more about topiaries than I ever wanted to know," I murmured as I turned the page.

Fatigue pulled at my eyelids, but I was determined to find something. I could always fall back on the secret society if I had to, but I wanted to see if there was anything else. I padded to the kitchen to make another cup of tea. My phone buzzed, and I glanced at the message. It was from Isadora, enthusiastically agreeing to help with party planning. I grinned and quickly sent her the details for tomorrow. She responded with a thumbs up and a cheery confirmation. With that sorted, I idly flipped through the pages of the book while I waited for the kettle to boil, looking for anything that was more interesting than pets and plants.

That's when I saw it. I gasped, almost knocking my empty mug off the counter and onto the floor. I had to flip back a few pages until I reached the item that had caught my eye. The title of chapter thirteen was *Benny O'Rourke and the Hideaway Murder.*

Murder was good. I mean, it wasn't *good.* Ever. Never would I condone murder. But as far as getting people engaged in the town's history went, I couldn't think of anything more exciting. Authors, screenwriters, and movie producers built entire entertainment empires on murder after all, so why couldn't Bella use a little to spice up her New Year's Eve party?

Kettle forgotten, I hurried back over to the window seat, thoroughly engaged in the chapter before I even sat down.

In the annals of Havenwood, few stories are as poignant or imbued with intrigue as that of Benny O'Rourke. Benny grew up in Havenwood and lived in the town until his untimely death in 1928. With an inherent charm and a smile that could dispel the darkest cloud, Benny was a local figure who was known to be a good neighbor, always willing to lend a hand and quick with a joke.

Like his father before him, Benny managed the Hearthstone Inn. It was a warm beacon where tales, laughter, and good cheer were abundant. The Hearthstone served as a cozy nexus for travelers and townsfolk alike. After his father passed, Benny became the owner of the Hearthstone on top of being the most charming bartender the town had ever seen. He was the heart and soul of the place. His reputation for good company, better food, and memorable stories over a drink had people flocking to the Hearthstone from all over the state in no time at all.

However, as Prohibition cast its long shadow across the land, many establishments such as the Hearthstone faced an uncertain future without the ability to pull in revenue from selling alcohol. But where others saw despair, Benny saw an opportunity to adapt and thrive. With discerning foresight, he began a new project—the clandestine creation of a speakeasy. A place where he could covertly run an off the books business in conjunction with his legitimate one.

A tunnel, originally built in 1888 as a practical solution to feed livestock during winter storms, was repurposed. With much hard work, Benny created Havenwood's very own speakeasy, aptly named "the Hideaway." According to town lore, he used part of the existing tunnel system to connect the inn to the Hideaway so his illicit clientele could enter the speakeasy without ever arousing suspicion from anyone watching outside. The Hideaway quickly became the *place in Havenwood to go. Under the muted radiance of glowing lights and amidst the rich aroma of illegal spirits, it was a bastion of revelry and defiance against the temperance of the times. Benny's business flourished, as did his pocketbook. It was here, with the strains of jazz music drifting up through the floorboards, that Benny O'Rourke became a town legend.*

The Hideaway was far more than a mere speakeasy for banned drinks, gambling, and dancing. It was an institution, a testament to the resilience of the Roaring Twenties' spirit. A place where the jazz was as smooth as the whiskey and genuine camaraderie was the order of the day.

By all accounts, Benny ran a tight ship, ensuring the secrecy and safety of everyone who entered his establishment. He took great pains to guarantee the existence of the Hideaway remained a secret. For years, the Hideaway thrived under Benny's careful management. Eventually, it became more than just a speakeasy. A thrilling defiance of the dry era. In a very real sense, the Hideaway was the beating heart of Havenwood's underground scene. It was the only speakeasy in town and pulsed with life in a time when joy was rationed like sugar.

And it was all thanks to Benny O'Rourke.

But like all good things, the era of the Hideaway came to an end. One tragic evening, seemingly for the first time in his life, Benny's easy smile, quick wit, and hard work were not enough to save him. That fateful night, the music in the Hideaway died, never to be heard again. On October 25th, 1928, the police found the town's beloved Benny O'Rourke lifeless on the speakeasy floor. He'd sustained a blow to the head and that was ultimately assumed to be the cause of death. However, the events leading to his tragic end remain as mysterious as his trademark enigmatic smile. The Hideaway, once a haven of laughter and music, transformed overnight into the setting of a senseless death.

The news of Benny's untimely passing swept through Havenwood with the swiftness of a chilling winter wind. After Benny's death, the existence of the secret tunnel connecting the Hearthstone Inn to the speakeasy hidden under the barn became public knowledge. Officials combed through the evi-

dence, but, other than Benny's body, there were no apparent clues to be found, not even the murder weapon. With no obvious suspects or conclusive evidence, the police closed the investigation without solving the mystery of what had transpired that fateful night.

After the official inquiry ceased, the townsfolk who loved Benny engaged in an exhaustive search for a possible weapon and pursued any leads they could find. However, the circumstances of his death remained an enigma, leaving the townspeople with nothing but conjecture. Was it a lover's quarrel turned deadly? A crime of passion in the wake of a drunken brawl? Or the malicious act of a business rival who was jealous of Benny's success? Perhaps his tragic passing was simply an unexpected accident.

The case grew cold, leaving the story of Benny O'Rourke as an unsolved puzzle, a piece of local lore whispered about at the same inn he had once proudly run. Today, Benny's Hearthstone Inn still stands, but operates under a different name, its walls echoing the storied past. Unfortunately, the Hideaway never reopened to the public. The memory of the former speakeasy serves as a silent monument to an epoch and a man who epitomized the unyielding spirit of camaraderie and joy. Though Benny O'Rourke's life reached a premature and tragic conclusion, his legacy endures, imbuing Havenwood with a poignant reminder of a bygone era of defiance and celebration.

To this day, the tale of Benny O'Rourke captivates those visiting Havenwood. It's even whispered that Benny's spirit still lingers in the town, perhaps waiting to pass on the secret of that final, ill-fated evening.

I caught my breath as I saw the picture on the last page of the chapter. If there had been any doubt in my mind before, that smiling face erased it.

What was Granny Bea doing with what looked like an original photo of Havenwood's preeminent speakeasy owner, Benny O'Rourke?

A Frosty Morning

I AWOKE BEFORE DAWN, my mind already racing. The gray morning light did little to illuminate my small apartment, but I hardly noticed. I was too excited about the mystery of Benny O'Rourke's untimely demise. I don't know what it said about me that a man's murder almost instantly intrigued me. Maybe I'd been listening to too many true crime podcasts while cleaning the shop, but I couldn't believe I'd never heard about Benny or his speakeasy at any point during my visits to Havenwood as a child or in the past few months since I moved here.

I made a mental note to ask Isadora about the Hideaway when I saw her. Maybe she'd know something, especially with her own involvement in that secret club, the Vault. Given the prominence of her family, she might even know more about Benny O'Rourke than had been in the history book.

Captivated by his story, I sat at my kitchen table, a steaming cup of coffee warming my hands, searching for any additional clues about Benny O'Rourke's untimely death online. It was a mystery that the internet, with all its vast resources, had barely brushed the surface of, leaving me with more questions than answers.

A shiver ran down my spine. I scanned the room, wondering if I'd left the window cracked again last night. Curling up under blankets with a cool breeze sneaking in had become my new routine, but with the temperatures plunging below freezing, I'd been trying to make sure all windows stayed shut. The last thing I wanted was to wake up with frostbitten toes.

I glanced over at the window and groaned. Sure enough, I'd gotten too distracted and forgotten to close it. Typical. I padded over, feeling the icy air nip at my skin as I confirmed the crack. I firmly pushed it shut, muttering under my breath about how easily my mind wandered lately.

Another shiver stole over me, and I realized it wasn't the cold that was bothering me. It was more of the eerie sensation you got when someone was staring at you. Unblinking and creepy. I scanned my cozy kitchen nook, half-expecting to find a pair of eyes watching from the shadows. Had Mr. Wigglesworth crept up the stairs to glower at me because I'd neglected leaving his food bowl full last night? However, there was nothing but the familiar hum of soft music from my Bluetooth speakers and the distant sound of the town stirring to life. No hungry cats or feisty rabbits.

Just me, the cold, and my overactive imagination.

I shook my head, somewhat disappointed with myself. Here I was, jumping at shadows just because of something I'd read the night before. How was I ever supposed to keep up with all the new releases so I could speak intelligently to my customers if one tragic event from decades ago made me jumpy?

What I really needed was to talk this out with Bella. I bet she'd have some fabulous ideas of how to weave Benny's story into her New Year's Eve celebration or possibly even use it as a theme for next year's party. Maybe she could host a murder mystery party where everyone was assigned a unique character ahead of time. That would be really fun and a great way to usher in the new year. Perhaps, if she didn't want to do that, I could have the event right here at Spellbooks. Now, that was a thought...

I shook my head, pulling myself out of the daydream of planning a murder mystery, and glanced at the clock. It was too early to head over to the Enchanted Oasis, especially with the breakfast rush probably in full swing there. Unless I wanted to be underfoot and a nuisance, I had at least an hour or so before I could show up to talk about the party with my best friend.

With time to kill and the mystery on my mind, I decided it was the perfect time to examine the items found alongside Benny's photograph in the attic. Luckily, I'd brought them down with the rest of the things for Bella, so I didn't have to brave the dust and cobwebs of the attic again. I arranged the flask, notebook, and keys on the table in front of me, along with a couple of mismatched buttons, a train ticket stub, and a broken gold chain.

Another quick shiver swept over me as I finished organizing. What was going on? I stood up and checked the windows, but each latch was securely locked from the inside. I ran a hand through my hair, a bit confused.

I knew I'd just paid the heating bill, so that couldn't be it. Maybe the chill was just left over from the window being open earlier? Still, I made a mental note to ask Grimgor, my friend and handyman, to take a look. Maybe the windows needed sealing, or the temperature controls needed adjusting. This was my first winter in Connecticut, and I didn't know how good Granny Bea had been about home maintenance. Sure, Spellbooks was sentient, but the shop couldn't just manifest sealed windows out of thin air.

I grabbed a blanket from the back of the couch and wrapped it around my shoulders before returning to the table and the strange collection of items once more. Contemplatively, I took a sip from my coffee cup and nearly burned my tongue. I looked at the offending liquid in confusion. How could it still be so hot when I was so cold? Maybe I just needed an extra sweater. I grabbed my favorite oversized hoodie from the couch and tugged it on before cuddling under the blanket once more. Finally, warmth started to seep into my bones.

Intent on focusing on anything other than the lingering chill, I reached for the box of things I'd found in the attic. As I flipped through the pages of the notebook, the jumbled mix of letters and numbers caught my attention. My curiosity piqued; I examined the lines of handwritten text more carefully. The pages were filled with a chaotic mix of letters, symbols, and numbers that didn't seem to make much sense at first glance. I squinted at the characters, wondering if it was some forgotten language or just gibberish.

Attempting to understand the writing, I tried Googling a few things to make sure it wasn't just a language I didn't recognize. No luck. Maybe it was a code?

I sat down, grabbing a piece of paper to start working on it like I'd seen done in those crime documentaries. First, I tried the basics: shifting letters, substituting numbers for letters. I scribbled out patterns, checked for common letters or symbols, and even pulled up an online cipher decoder, just in case it was something simple.

But after about half an hour, nothing I did seemed to unlock the pattern. The letters refused to form words, and the numbers didn't translate into anything recognizable. I groaned, leaning back in my chair. It wasn't that I couldn't crack it—it was that I didn't have the energy or focus to keep trying. Whatever message the notebook held would have to stay hidden for now.

Discouraged by my lack of success with the notebook, I set it aside and moved on to the flask. It was a fine piece of silver, tarnished with age, and wrapped in a piece of leather at the bottom. It was exactly the type of vessel I imagined had been used to transport a gentleman's drink discreetly, perhaps even during the Prohibition era. I tried to unscrew the cap, but it was stuck tight. Using a little of my metal magic, I loosened the screw top enough that I could easily spin it off. I tipped the flask over. Something seemed to shift inside, but it made no sound, and nothing fell out when I shook it. Cautiously, I gave the small opening a sniff. The faintest hint of deep oak and alcohol wafted out of the flask. Either someone had done a poor job cleaning the container or it had stored nothing but alcohol for several years. Perhaps both.

I set the flask to the side and picked up the set of keys. They were quaint and old looking. I brushed them with my magic, trying to use it to identify the metal. I'd been experimenting more with my magic since moving to Havenwood to try to see what my limits were. I wasn't as powerful as the Silverthorne siblings. Not by a long shot. But I was getting better at using my magic. From my examination, the keys appeared to be made of solid brass, each with its own unique patina testifying to the passage of time and regular use. There were several in the set, varying in size, length, and the intricacy of their patterns. The teeth of the keys were not the uniform, precise cuts you'd find in modern keys but were instead more irregular, with each one suggesting a handcrafted origin.

The largest key had a round head with an ornate swirling "H" engraved on it. After discovering the keys with Benny O'Rourke's picture, part of me wondered if this might not be the key to his Hearthstone Inn or possibly even the Hideaway itself. But that was probably just pure whimsy. Why would my great-granny have the keys to the town's speakeasy hidden away in a secret compartment in her attic? Was Spellbooks the original site of the speakeasy? It didn't make sense. The chapter on Benny and the Hideaway said that there was currently a new inn being run on the site of Benny's Hearthstone, not a bookshop. But the history book had been old. From the '80s if I remembered right. Maybe the inn mentioned wasn't even an inn anymore. Perhaps it wasn't even standing.

I shook my head at my distracted thoughts and examined the other keys, which were smaller but no less intriguing, with long shanks and different letters inscribed on each. Based on the wear on the metal of each key, someone used these keys a lot. The smallest and most delicate of the keys caught my attention. I traced the swirling letter "C" engraved on the key's head with one fingertip, trying to imagine what it might open. A cabinet perhaps? No, the key looked too fancy to open something so mundane. It reminded me a little of the keys to the box Seraphina, Finn's ex-girlfriend and a talented enchanter elf, had created. Could this key open a safe? Maybe even a jewelry box? I shook my head, my memories of the Christmas Eve Ball and similar keys rising to the surface. Isadora promised me a memorable night, but after jewel thieves, being held at gunpoint, and a devastating betrayal, I wasn't sure I wanted extraordinary evenings anymore. All I wanted at the moment was a little fun with my friends, some peace after the excitement of Christmas, and enough time to read a good book at the end of the day.

With each item I examined, I imagined what role it could've played in order to end up locked away in Granny Bea's attic. Even though it was all in my head, I felt like I was peeling back the layers of Havenwood's history, touching pieces of a past that were as much a part of the town as the cobblestone streets and whispering trees. Today, I wasn't just the owner of a quaint shop; I was an investigator of the past, a keeper of stories, someone who could, perhaps, bring closure to a tale left too long without an ending.

Unseen Threads

My phone rang, interrupting my daydreams of being a detective. Startled by the sudden ringtone slicing through the silent musings of the morning, I glanced at the phone. Mason Forham's name flashed across the screen. "Mason?" I muttered to myself, wondering what could make the dwarf who ran the local auto repair shop call me this early.

I answered the phone curiously. "Hello?"

"Harper, there you are! I've been knocking for a solid five minutes. You planning to let us freeze out here?" Mason's gruff voice came through, tinged with a mock annoyance that couldn't hide his underlying warmth.

"Us?" Suddenly, I remembered I had agreed to meet him today. It was a good thing I hadn't hurried over to Bella's after all. I quickly piled the items I'd been examining together in the middle of my table, returning the photograph to the notebook so it didn't fly away in an errant gust of wind.

"Oh, Mason, I'm so sorry! I forgot you were dropping off Ignatius today!" I quickened my pace, almost tripping over a stray slipper in my hurry to get downstairs. "Hold on a second! I'll be right there!"

I darted down the stairs, all thoughts of Benny O'Rourke and hidden compartments temporarily forgotten. As I opened the door, a gust of cold air burst in, along with Mason, his beard slightly frosted over.

"I was caught up with...something," I explained, faltering over my words but Mason waved my excuses off good-naturedly with a gloved hand.

"It's fine. Make me a cup of coffee, and we'll call it even," he said, his eyes dancing with unspoken mirth.

"Deal," I said, bustling around the counter to get the coffee brewing. I flicked on the kettle and then pulled out all the items I'd need to make Mason the best cup of joe he'd ever had.

"Coffee?" a little voice sounded from inside Mason's coat. A small dragon pushed through the dwarf's bushy beard like it was masking a hidden doorway and looked around eagerly. Either the dwarf, the beard, or the dragon would've surprised most people. But this was Havenwood, and I was not most people.

"Hello Ignatius! Read any good books lately?" I asked, scooping grounds into a small French press before pouring boiling water over the top, giving it a stir.

The tiny dragon worked his way free and fluttered across to me, perching on my shoulder and giving my cheek a nuzzle.

"Many. Good see Harper," he murmured, working hard to enunciate the words around his many teeth. Speaking was difficult for his kind, but he always tried his best.

I stroked his scales. "It's good to see you too." When I'd met Ignatius, he'd been just a little statue. Turns out, it was a spell, which Bella accidentally dissolved and returned him to his uncontrolled, fire-breathing self. He was a good-hearted creature who just got a little overexcited from time to time, especially when he was reading. Then the sparks came out, and he lit things on fire. Accidentally, of course. With some help from Mason, he'd been working on his control with some specially crafted, dwarven jewelry, and he rarely caused any sort of unintentional flare-ups anymore. That made it infinitely easier for him to come around Spellbooks without me fearing he would burn it to the ground. Or Spellbooks locking him out again for that matter. Over the past few months, Ignatius and Mason had struck up an unlikely friendship, and the dragon spent more time at the dwarf's auto body shop than at Spellbooks these days.

"Well, we've been reading up a storm as we were working. I reckon we must've chewed through at least eight audiobooks in the last few days," Mason said as I pressed the plunger down and poured a steaming cup for the dwarf.

"How do you take it?" I asked.

"Black, thanks."

"A pleasure," I said, sliding it carefully over. "Eight books, huh? Anything I should check out?"

"Ignatius has a talent for picking out great reads. I'll make you a list," Mason said with a hearty chuckle.

"List," Ignatius confirmed with a serious nod of his tiny head.

I poured myself a cup of coffee, wrapping my hands around the ceramic mug, savoring the warmth. "And how is Project Fire Control going?" I asked. Mason had been working tirelessly on a creation of emberite and lavastone steel for Ignatius as he learned to manage his fire powers.

"Going well, thanks. Just a few more tweaks on the latest version—trying to balance the emberite better. But I think we're close. I'll grab some more supplies from my kin when I visit this week, and hopefully, we'll have it all sorted," Mason replied, gratefully inhaling the rich scent of freshly brewed coffee.

I nodded thoughtfully. "By the way, what do I owe you for the materials? I know you won't let me pay for your time, but I should at least cover the cost of all that lavastone and emberite."

Mason waved me off with a grin. "You don't need to worry. The Silverthornes already stocked up on enough lavastone and emberite to fill a dwarven mine, thanks to a few...challenges they've been managing."

I raised an eyebrow, catching the subtext. He was talking about Isadora and her difficulty controlling her elemental powers, especially that of fire. "Right. Well, sounds like you've had your hands full lately."

He chuckled. "Let's just say there's never a dull moment."

Before I could respond, Luna stuck her head out of her hutch, her ears twitching. "Wait a hare-hopping moment! Don't tell me the little fire-breather is moving back in permanently."

I shot her a stern look. "*Ignatius* is just staying for a few days while Mason travels."

Luna narrowed her eyes, clearly not convinced. "Are we sure that's safe? You remember October and the Harvest Festival, don't you? Fires, Harper. So. Many. Fires."

"You say that like they were infernos," I said, trying to calm her down even though the reality of discovering a fire-breathing dragon in my newly inherited bookshop hadn't been the easiest on my nerves at the time. "He wasn't responsible for most of them. He just singed a couple of books."

"Yeah, but what happens if he moves back in here full time?" Luna demanded.

Mason chuckled. "Don't you worry your whiskers. Ignatius and I have been working hard and honestly, he's been doing fantastic. Not a single fire incident since we've tweaked his gear again last week. These days, he's as safe as that furry lump you call a cat."

"That isn't reassuring," Luna muttered, glaring at me. "What if the furball and the fire-breather form some sort of coalition? You don't know what they're capable of. Who knows? They could plot to take over the world, and you'd be responsible, hosting world domination parties right here in your cozy little bookshop. No one would suspect a thing until it was too late."

"Ignatius is more than welcome in Spellbooks anytime he wants," I said, forcing confidence into my voice that was as much for Luna's benefit as for the dragon's. A little vibration rolled under my feet, letting me know Spellbooks gave its approval. I ran my fingers along the wall, letting the shop know I understood and also trying to show how grateful I was for not getting locked out again. It was a lot to communicate with a simple gesture, but I hoped Spellbooks understood.

Ignatius made a sound that seemed like an attempt at polite agreement, but with all the teeth and the peculiar dragon anatomy, it came out more as a gurgling growl. "Too kind," he managed, the corners of his mouth turning upwards in a toothy smile.

"But—" Luna started to protest. Her eyes shot open, and I saw a little wiggle of the floorboards under her feet as Spellbooks' communicated its opinion. She huffed. "Fine. I guess I'm outvoted."

Mason looked around in confusion, but I quickly turned my attention back to Ignatius, hoping to distract the dwarf from Luna's unexpected capitulation. I ran my hand over his warm scales. "I'm so glad you're back. I've missed having you around. It seems like we haven't seen much of you recently what with Mason and even Agatha hogging your time."

"Good to have friends," Ignatius managed. One benefit of hanging out with Mason was that the little dragon's language skills were improving, even with the excess teeth.

"It's also good to have breakfast," Luna muttered, nudging her food bowl with a paw.

I rolled my eyes where the rabbit couldn't see and pointed Ignatius toward the stairs. "Why don't you go on up and get yourself settled. I've got a new audiobook I think you'll enjoy." As Ignatius flew up towards my apartment, I set about getting breakfast for Luna and Mr. Wigglesworth.

Mason watched him go with a grin. "He's quite the social butterfly, isn't he? Agatha said she even wants him helping with her garden when the seasons turn. Says he's got a knack for it. Probably the dragon fire. It helps with the weeds."

A surprised laugh escaped me. "I never thought of that, but I'd believe it. I'm just glad he's found his place here in Havenwood and not as part of the décor any longer. It's not every day you get a dragon for a friend, much less one that's part of the family." I glanced up the stairs, making sure Ignatius was out of earshot before turning to Mason and lowering my voice to a whisper. "Is Ignatius really that safe? With his fire, I mean. I don't want him causing any damage to Spellbooks." I wasn't sure what dragon fire could do to the sentient building, and I didn't want to find out. However, I also didn't want to go blabbing the secret of Spellbooks all around town either. To the best of my knowledge, Mason thought Spellbooks was just a bookshop, and I preferred to keep it that way. At least, for the time being.

Mason nodded emphatically as he drained half his coffee in one long slurp. "Of course, he is. I wouldn't have brought him around if he wasn't. His new gear's top-notch, and he's taken to his training like a duck to water. He's about as dangerous as a kitten now."

"That's not reassuring!" Luna said, looking up from her cabbage. "Kittens are just cats in training, and we all know how *cats* are."

"You mean adorably cute and furry?" Mason said with a chuckle as he rubbed Mr. Wigglesworth's back affectionately. The enormous cat barely looked up from his food, but his tail twitched with pleasure.

Unexpectedly, a chilly breeze whispered down the stairs and through the shop, sending a shiver down my spine. I wrapped my arms around myself. "Did you feel that? There's got to be a draft here somewhere. I wonder if Ignatius opened a window up there or something?"

"I didn't feel anything. Are you okay, Harper? You're not coming down with a cold, are you?" Mason asked, his voice tinged with a hint of concern as his gaze briefly swept the room.

"I don't think so. Just a sudden chill. This old bookshop has its quirks, and I'm still getting used to the New England winter," I said, trying to laugh it off, even though I felt the return of the strange tingle at the back of my neck like I was being watched.

Mason gave a soft chuckle, taking another long drink from his mug. He set the ceramic cup on the counter. "You know, places with as much history as Spellbooks often have more...quirks...than you might expect. Sometimes they have stories to tell that you won't find in your books."

I raised an eyebrow, a smile tugging at the corner of my mouth. "Are you talking about ghosts, Mason?" I asked, remembering a town meeting where a story involving Mason, the town vicar, and some mischievous ghosts had been alluded to. I still hadn't heard the full version, but I'll admit, I was curious.

"They've been known to hang around Havenwood. I have a friend or two myself on the other side. Good lads, if a bit insubstantial," Mason said seriously.

I let out a small laugh, finding the idea charmingly absurd that a ghost could be here. In Spellbooks, of all places. I already had a talking rabbit, a pet cat, a guardian gargoyle, and a miniature dragon living inside a sentient bookshop. Adding a ghost seemed completely over the top, even to me. "Well, I can assure you, the only spirits we have here are the literary kind," I said lightly.

"If you say so, lass." Mason clapped his hands, the sharp sound dispelling any creeping doubt about ghosts. "Now, I really must get on my way. Thanks for the coffee and all that. Tell Ignatius he's welcome to come hang out for as long as he likes once I get back."

"Will do," I said, walking the dwarf to the door. "And thank you for taking such good care of him."

"Anytime. He's a decent sort of fellow. Pleasure to spend time with him. You take care now," Mason said, zipping up his jacket and flipping up the collar before braving the late December weather. I waved goodbye as he hurried down Arcadia Avenue, shutting the door quickly behind him to keep out the chill. It might have been my imagination or the talk of ghosts, but the cold seemed to linger long after he'd left.

After Mason departed, I busied myself with some online business coursework I'd been procrastinating on for far too long. When I glanced up at the clock, I realized the morning rush at the Enchanted Oasis was likely dwindling to a trickle, and Bella might be free soon. Before I left, I decided to check on Ignatius. Maybe I could also figure out where that draft was coming from. I headed upstairs, already making plans for what I could carry and what Bella would have to pick up in her car. Despite the chill I'd felt earlier, I couldn't find a crack in a wall or a drafty window. Was

I imagining it all? Maybe Mason was right, and I was fighting a bit of a bug. Getting sick just before Bella's party wasn't my idea of a good time. Neither was returning from the Oasis to find my beautiful apartment charred to a crisp. I scanned the room once more, ensuring everything was safe for a fire-breathing dragon's solo stay.

Satisfied, I packed a small bag of extra decorations, a few of the dresses I'd found in the attic, and the history book. The pile of items I'd pulled out of the attic still looked comically large in the middle of my apartment, a colorful cascade of fabrics and sequins. I couldn't help but chuckle; Bella would love to examine each and every piece, but she definitely needed to bring the car for the rest.

Ignatius watched me curiously. "Harper go?" he asked.

"Yes. I promised Bella I'd help her with her New Year's Eve party," I said, adding a couple of extra pieces of flashy costume jewelry to the bag I thought Bella might like.

"Ignatius come?"

I shook my head. "Not today, I'm afraid. We've got a lot of set up and planning to do. I don't think it's going to be very interesting for you. Why don't I put an audiobook on here instead, and you make yourself at home?"

"Okay." Ignatius yawned, padding around in a circle on one of my many throw pillows in the window seat before settling down and tucking his nose under his tail. He reminded me of a puppy. A scaly puppy, but one with a good heart.

I set up an audiobook for Ignatius, one of his favorites about a knight's quest. "It might be best for you to stay up here until after Luna's had her breakfast," I suggested. "She can be grumpy at the best of times, but when she's hangry, she's a terror." The last thing I needed was a hungry rabbit causing havoc with a dragon in tow. Who knows what I might return to if Luna decided to stir things up with Ignatius?

He nodded and gave another toothy yawn. "Ignatius nap. Thanks lots."

"Anytime buddy," I said, slipping out the door with my heavy bag slung over my shoulder. I shut the door to the apartment behind me. Hopefully that, and her lack of thumbs, would keep Luna from riling up the little dragon.

Just as I reached the top of the stairs, ready to leave, a deafening cacophony erupted from the front of the shop. A clatter that was loud enough to startle the portraits off the walls, followed by a yowl and a hiss. I dashed down, my heart in my throat, imagining all sorts of catastrophic mishaps.

The scene downstairs was a whirlwind of ruffled fur and twitching whiskers, the aftermath of what I could only describe as household anarchy. Luna, with ears flat against her head in unmistakable irritation, had backed Mr. Wigglesworth into a corner. Amidst the chaos, my latest batch of decorative bookmarks lay scattered like autumn leaves on a windy day. And at the epicenter of their dispute? My Bluetooth speaker. It lay face down on the floor, emitting the faintest hint of a pop song.

I sighed. I should never have taught Luna how to change the music. Now, she claimed the remote to be her own personal magical music wand. Mr. Wigglesworth seemed to often disagree with her music choices but, lacking both the ability to communicate verbally and thumbs, hadn't ever learned to select his own tunes. Instead, when Luna put on a song he didn't like, he'd taken to batting the speaker off the shelf. Part of me was glad he was getting the exercise because he really was getting large. I should probably cut back on his treats. But now wasn't the time. Actually, it was moments like this when I wish I could send them to separate rooms.

With a sigh, I scooped up the speaker, clicked it off, and placed it safely on a tall shelf. "You two are worse than siblings," I muttered.

"I can't believe you would even *suggest* I was related to that mangy beast you call a pet," Luna huffed as she hopped away with a dignified snort, while Mr. Wigglesworth slunk off, his poofy tail flicking in annoyance.

"If the shoe fits," I murmured, though I couldn't help the amused smile tugging at the corners of my mouth at their antics now that the storm was abating.

Gathering up the scattered bookmarks, I made a mental note to create a playlist just for the animals, something soothing to keep the peace. Amid the clean-up, a book from a nearby shelf thudded to the floor. I glanced up in surprise. My gaze fell on the spine. *The Enigma of Codes and Secrets.*

"Was that you, Spellbooks?" I asked. Silent stillness met my words. I took that as a negative from the sentient shop. For a moment, I considered the oddity of it. I didn't even remember seeing this book on the shop list. But then again, I didn't have Granny Bea's amazing memory for every item in the shop yet. Maybe one of the animals had unbalanced it their romp, or perhaps it was just the result of an overburdened shelf. I might have to get Grimgor to check out the shelf when he came to look at the seals on the windows. With the morning slipping by, I scooped up the book and shoved it back onto the shelf without a second thought.

"Keep the peace, you two," I admonished, though I doubted they would listen. Luna would likely make snarky remarks all morning that Mr. Wigglesworth would undoubtedly ignore and then nap through, which would prove even more infuriating to the rabbit familiar. Either way, I needed to get to Bella's.

I laid a hand on the wooden doorframe. "Make sure they don't destroy the place, would you?" I whispered to Spellbooks. The wood warmed beneath my fingertips, and I felt the barest hint of a vibration, as if the shop was chuckling silently so as not to add to the drama. I patted the wall. I was a lucky girl. Not only to live in a magical bookshop, but one that was as understanding as Spellbooks.

I slipped out of the shop, making a mental note to investigate the stability of the shelving units later. The cool morning air of Havenwood swirled around me, a greeting made of crisp, icy snow, wood smoke from chimneys, and the faint scent of baked goods from nearby homes. The quaint town was coming to life. I had things to do, people to see, and parties to plan. I tightened my scarf against the chill and hefted the large tote bag more comfortably on my shoulder. My mind was already dancing with the day's agenda as I crunched along the salted sidewalks towards the B&B, the cold seeming to swirl around me every step of the way.

Party Planning

I ENTERED THROUGH THE kitchen door, not wanting to disturb any guests who might still linger over Honey's excellent breakfast. As far as I was concerned, Honey's kitchen was the heart of the Oasis. Bella's mom might have a magical talent for baking, and she also somehow navigated the hustle and bustle of the morning rush without looking frazzled. That was its own kind of magic, in my mind. The rich aromas of cinnamon swirls and vanilla bean pastries suffused the air. Loaves of bread with perfect golden crusts nestled beside bubbling berry tarts, while the air itself seemed to be sweetened with sugar and spices. Here, in Honey's domain, every dish was a masterpiece, imbued with flavors that satisfied the deepest of cravings and warmed the soul.

"Harper! So nice to see you," Honey said, her caramel eyes sparkling with joy. She wiped flour-dusted hands on her pretty pink apron as she hurried around the massive kitchen island to greet me.

"Good morning, Honey. Whatever you're baking smells amazing!" I exclaimed, sniffing at the fragrant air appreciatively.

"Oh, it's just a little of this and that," Honey said, waving a hand. "I know Bella's expecting you. She can't stop talking about this New Year's Eve party she's planning. She's so excited."

"We both are," I said, resettling the heavy bag on my shoulder.

"Well, she's upstairs in her room. You're welcome to go on up. I need to close out a couple of guests, and then I'll bring you both a tray with some goodies," Honey said, expertly balancing several large plates of baked goods.

"Do you need a hand?" I offered.

Honey shook her head. "Oh no. I've got it, and Antonio is around here somewhere. You girls have fun," she said as she backed through the swinging door leading to the breakfast area. Through the crack, I could see that several guests still lingered over coffee and pastries.

I headed up the stairs and knocked on Bella's door. She called out an answer. "Come in!"

As soon as I opened the door, I saw that a veritable explosion of decorations covered her room. Glittering dice, feathered boas, playing chips, and an array of sparkling trinkets covered every available surface.

Bella threw her arms around me in a welcoming squeeze. "I'm so glad you're here. I might have gone a bit overboard."

"A bit?" I echoed, looking around at the chaos in her normally pristine room.

"Well, I thought we could get a jump start on the table decorations or maybe some gift bags for the guests. You know, something small as a memento of the most fabulous night of their lives. Mama has already agreed to bake something delicious, and we're putting a ten percent discount offer on for anyone who wants to stay with us in the next three months. You're welcome to add something to promote Spellbooks as well, if you like."

"That's a great idea. Maybe I will," I said. I looked around at the whirlwind of chaos that had made landfall in Bella's bedroom. "But where do we start?"

"I've got the table décor, if you'll handle the gift bags?" Bella suggested, pointing out the items she wanted included. It didn't take long for me to develop a system. Soon we were laughing as we chatted the morning away, just like we used to do as kids.

A soft knock on the door interrupted our girlish giggles. Isadora breezed into the room a moment later, her cheeks flushed nearly the same shade of pink as her hair.

Bella greeted her with a hug. "So glad you could make it!"

I was next, giving my new friend a warm squeeze. "Me too. Thanks for offering to lend a hand."

Isadora fluffed her pink hair. "When I heard there was a party in the works, how could I refuse? Now, tell me everything. Vegas, I'm guessing?" she asked, gesturing at the décor spread everywhere.

Bella put her hands on her hips, looking around. "Yeah, that was my original plan, but then we found some incredible things in Harper's granny's attic that have me questioning Vegas or Prohibition. You know, with the fringe, speakeasies, amazing headwear, the whole shebang?"

Isadora's eyes lit up. "If I get a say, I'd definitely go with Prohibition. Think of the clothes! And you can repurpose a lot of what you've got already." She waved a hand at the decorations.

Bella nodded emphatically. "That settles it. Prohibition it is." She clapped her hands and did a little excited dance. "Oh! This will be fun!"

I grinned. "Agreed. I can't wait to see what your mama bakes, Bella."

"Knowing her, it'll be something incredible. I wish I had her ingenuity in the kitchen," Bella said with a little sigh.

Isadora flung her arms wide. "Forget the kitchen. This is where your genius lies! I can't believe I've never been to one of your parties before."

Bella surveyed the organized chaos. "I do like planning events. And I'm glad we've gotten to know each other better. I can't believe we never hung out as kids."

"Me too," Isadora agreed, throwing an arm around Bella's shoulders and giving her a squeeze.

Bella smiled ruefully. "I'll be honest, Mama and Papa are equally excited and nervous that a Silverthorne is attending our party this year," Bella said, handing Isadora a pair of scissors as we got to work.

Isadora sighed. "I wish they wouldn't be. We're just people."

"People who own most of the town," Bella pointed out.

"I suppose. When you grow up in my family, that's not what you hear though. Everything is 'for the good of Havenwood,'" she said, deepening her voice and striking a pose. She relaxed and shook her head. "My mother doesn't help with the whole being approachable thing either. If it were up to me, I'd attend every party, event, and festival in Havenwood. I absolutely love them," Isadora said. Her face fell a bit. "Too bad I have to go back to that stuffy school. It's uptight, and everyone is so full of themselves."

"You'll be finished soon, won't you?" I asked, consolingly.

"Another eighteen months," Isadora sighed dramatically, toying with the ring on her finger. I recognized it as the one Mason had given her.

I tipped my head at her hand. "How's it all going? You know, with the..." I trailed off, unsure of how to end my question politely.

Isadora caught my glance. "Oh, you mean with the uncontrollable elemental powers?" She didn't look the least perturbed. A small smile of relief danced across her lips. "It's going much better since I got this ring. No more unexpected fires, for which my furniture thanks you."

I waved away her praise. "Thank Mason. He's the genius behind the ring."

Isadora nodded seriously. "Believe me, I have." She sighed, toying with a stack of playing cards. "I can't believe I have to go back to school soon. I plan on taking in all the excitement here before I have to get locked away with my nose in dusty old books again. No offense, Harper," she said, leaning over and giving my arm a squeeze.

"None taken," I said with a smile at Isadora's antics.

"Speaking of excitement," Bella said, "was that a typical Christmas Eve Ball, or were we just special?"

"What? You mean with the jewel thieves and the blizzard?" Isadora quipped. "No, I ordered that just for you two."

"So kind of you," I said with a laugh covering a barely suppressed shudder.

"Speaking of excitement, what's going on with you and your neighbor? The handsome Mr. Oakheart," Isadora asked me.

I sighed and shook my head. "Honestly, it's all a bit messy right now. Finn's great, but with his ex back in town, I don't want to make things more complicated than they need to be. Things haven't been the same between us since Christmas Eve," I admitted, trying to keep the subject light, though my thoughts flashed briefly to Isadora's brother, Gabriel, and the unforgettable ball. I shook my head, refocusing. "So, until we each figure our own lives out, we're keeping things casual with open lines of communication."

"Sounds like you're prolonging the inevitable," Isadora teased, leaning forward.

Bella immediately came to my defense. "Hey, let her figure out her own heart. These things take time."

Isadora held up her hands in surrender. "Fair enough, fair enough. All I'm saying is maybe Finn's jealous because you had a wonderful evening with a certain someone..."

I felt my face heat up. "You're making it sound way more salacious than it was! It was just...hanging out," I said, though the memories of Gabriel flooded back, making it hard to keep the smile off my face.

Isadora grinned. "Uh-huh, 'just hanging out.' Sure. But don't think I didn't notice how cute you two were at the ball! Dancing and solving mysteries together? How romantic!"

"I'm not sure I'd call getting held at gunpoint 'romantic,'" Bella said.

Isadora's eyes sparkled with mischief. "I just have a vested interest in the outcome, seeing as Gabriel hasn't stopped talking about you since the ball. The two of you looked so charming together when you were dancing! In between catching jewel thieves of course."

I rolled my eyes, laughing. "It's what I do. Multi-talented. Dancing and detective-ing all at once."

"I agree. You're definitely multi-talented," Bella said, handing me some card stock and a tub of glitter. "Which is why I have every confidence you'll be able to decorate these table cards while we figure out your love life."

I chuckled and took the tub of glitter, shaking it at her playfully. "You just don't want to get this in your hair like the time when we were kids."

Bella ran a hand through her wavy locks. "Can you blame me? It didn't come out for months. If the light caught me right, I looked like a walking disco ball."

I grinned, placing the tub of glitter on the table. "Fair enough. I'll handle the glitter—no disco ball reruns this time."

Isadora, refusing to be side-tracked, leaned in with a gleam in her eye. "I don't know, Disco-Ball Bella sounds like a great name for a doll, don't you think?" She smiled mischievously, then abruptly shifted gears, almost giving me conversational whiplash in the process. "But seriously, Harper, if you had to choose between Finn and Gabriel right now, who would you pick?"

"Finn, of course," Bella said instantly.

Isadora tipped her head to the side, studying me. She tapped a finger against her lips and then shook her head. "No, I think she might be leaning towards Gabriel. I'm right, aren't I? Tell me I'm right?"

A gentle knock on the door saved me from answering. "Bella? Can you open the door? Your mama sent up a tray for you and your friends." I recognized the voice as Antonio's, Bella's dad.

She hurried to help him while Isadora and I cleared some space on her desk. Antonio slid a heavily laden tray onto the cleared surface. My mouth watered instantly as I took in the delights on Honey's masterfully prepared tray. At its center lay her famous chai spiced cinnamon rolls, the rising swirls of steam carrying with them the aroma of cardamom and ginger mingled with the sweet scent of vanilla icing. Beside them were three cups and a delicate teapot painted with vines and flowers that steamed with an herbal tea I recognized by scent as one of Aunty Agatha's blends, a unique combination designed for the morning to awaken and soothe the soul in equal measure. Crisp pecan biscotti, drizzled with a maple glaze, promised a satisfying crunch with whispers of nutty sweetness. Tucked neatly to one side of the tray were her typical morning egg tartlets, their flaky pastry cups cradling soft-set eggs topped with a sprinkle of savory herbs. This tray wasn't just brunch-worthy; it was an edible spell for comfort, satiation, and joy.

Antonio brushed Bella's cheek with a kiss. "Everything looks fantastic in here."

"You're being kind. It's chaotic. We decided to switch themes from Vegas to Prohibition this morning. It's a mess right now, but we're getting there," Bella said, brushing a strand of hair out of her eyes.

"Well, why don't you take a break and have some food?" he suggested.

"Great idea!" I exclaimed, relieved to have the attention shifted away from the question I was steadfastly avoiding—not just in front of my friends, who seemed to have a vested interest in my answer, but even in my own mind.

Isadora beat me to the cinnamon rolls, but I filled up my small plate with a heaping selection of the treats. Antonio paused to snag a tartlet from the tray before retreating out of the party-prep zone.

In the happy silence, I suddenly remembered I hadn't told Bella about my discovery last night. "Hey Bella, do you remember how you asked me to investigate the history of Havenwood? I think I might have found something interesting."

Bella's eyes lit up. "Another secret society?" she asked eagerly.

"No, a speakeasy and a mysterious death."

From that point, all discussion surrounding my love life vanished as the girls leaned in eagerly to hear everything about Benny O'Rourke.

"...and they discovered his body in his speakeasy," I finished dramatically.

"That's so sad," Bella sighed.

"I think it's kind of cool," Isadora said, and then hurried to add. "Not the murder part. The speakeasy. I never knew that part of Havenwood's history."

"You too?" Bella asked, surprised. "I thought it was just me."

"There's so much about Havenwood's past that I don't know," Isadora admitted. "Most of it is pretty dull in comparison to this—one town festival turned into another, that kind of thing. But I never imagined a quaint little place like this had its own bootleg enterprise back in the day. If I'd known about the speakeasy, I probably would've modeled the Vault after it."

Bella's brow furrowed. "Wait... what's the Vault?"

"Oh," Isadora said, "It's a place my brothers and I started. It's our own little secret club—kind of a family and friends thing."

Bella's eyes widened. "You have a secret club? In Havenwood?"

Isadora chuckled. "Yeah, but it's not as glamorous as it sounds. We built it ourselves, and it's hidden away. Not many people know about it." She paused, then added with a warm smile, "But now that we're friends, I could take you there sometime."

Bella beamed. "I'd love that! It sounds amazing."

Isadora winked. "Trust me, it's a lot of fun."

I smiled, glad that Isadora had told Bella about the Vault. She'd taken me there earlier, but I didn't want to blab her secrets around town, even if it was to Bella, my best friend and one of the most loyal people I knew.

I spoke up. "There's something exciting about secret places like that. I mean, speakeasies were all about staying hidden, right? The thrill of it. And the magical people I've met in Havenwood seem good at keeping secrets like Isadora's club. I can't help but wonder if Benny's place was just one of many. Who knows how many more we don't know about?"

"Maybe the Hideaway's still out there, under the floor of Benny's barn," Bella mused.

"Well, if it is still out there, it would be cool to find it someday. Imagine the history we'd uncover," I said.

Bella's eyes lit up. "If it still exists, it would be like a capsule of the Prohibition era, wouldn't it? Frozen in time! Could you imagine?"

Isadora twirled a section of her hair thoughtfully. "I don't know. Unless the barn is still standing, I'd imagine the speakeasy was probably dismantled and demolished."

Bella shivered. "You're right. Who would want to own a building where a man had been killed?"

"Wait! I just thought of something!" Isadora said, her voice bright with sudden inspiration. "What if we incorporated a speakeasy theme into your New Year's Eve party? It would be such a cool twist! We could hang a curtain over a doorway to make it look hidden—like it's only for those in the know. Maybe even add a secret password or a handshake for entry."

Bella tilted her head thoughtfully. "I like that. I wouldn't want anyone to feel left out, though. We could hide the password on signs around the Oasis, something subtle but fun for people to figure out. It'd add to the atmosphere without being exclusive."

"That's brilliant!" Isadora said, her grin widening.

"And you know what would be even better?" Bella added, her tone turning more animated. "What if we actually found the Hideaway someday and turned it into a modern-day speakeasy?"

Isadora clasped her hands together, her enthusiasm bubbling over. "Oh, that would be incredible! Imagine the history, the ambiance—it would be perfect!"

I laughed, amused by her boundless energy. "Wouldn't that put the Hideaway in direct competition with the Vault?"

Isadora waved me off, brushing the idea aside with a flick of her hand. "The Vault was more of a hideout for my brothers and me, not a real business venture. But converting the Hideaway? That would be a whole other level of fun!"

"If it exists," I pointed out, keeping her excitement in check. "That's still a pretty big 'if.'"

"And if we could even find it," Bella added with a soft smile.

Isadora leaned forward, undeterred, her eyes sparkling. "Exactly! But how thrilling would it be to re-open a piece of Havenwood's history?"

"What about poor Benny?" I asked, glancing between them. The other girls looked at me in confusion. "I agree with Isadora—if the Hideaway still exists, it's hidden somewhere, maybe under a barn or repurposed into something else. But if it's still out there, don't you think there might be clues left behind? They never solved what really happened to him. What if there's something there that could explain that night?"

As if on cue, an icy chill swept through the room. We exchanged surprised glances.

"You all felt that, right?" I asked. "I've been getting chills all day."

"It is winter in Connecticut and some of these houses are really old," Isadora pointed out, but that didn't stop her from looking around the room with a shiver.

"Probably just a guest not shutting a window," Bella said firmly as she rubbed at her arms. "With all the allure of a speakeasy, the secrets, jazz, drinks, and overall fun, you're the only person I know who would focus on solving a crime roughly a century old."

"She's right. Are you sure you're in the right profession?" Isadora teased. "Especially after the Christmas Eve Ball, it seems like you might be more cut out for detective than demure bookshop owner."

Bella laughed and shot me a playful grin. "Demure? *Harper*? I think you've got her confused with someone else. Maybe a detective-slash-adventurer, but demure? Not in this lifetime!" She gave me an exaggerated wink, clearly poking fun.

"After the excitement of the jewel thieves, I think I'll stick with armchair detective work and my mystery book, thanks," I said with a laugh. "Even so, how cool would it be to solve Havenwood's very own cold case?"

The next few hours passed in a blur of laughter, chatter, and party preparations. Ribbons were tied, signs crafted, and plans were discussed, the room filled with easy camaraderie.

A soft knock at the door sounded, and Honey stuck her head in a moment later. "Sounds like you ladies are having a delightful time. Mind if I interrupt to borrow your tastebuds for a few minutes? I've been trying out some recipes for the party, and Antonio is no help at all. He thinks everything I do is amazing."

"That's because it is," I said without thinking and then blushed as Honey shot me a wide smile.

"Sure, Mama," Bella said with a laugh as she held the door wide for her mother.

Honey bustled in, carrying a sample tray. "I heard from Antonio that you've changed the party theme to Prohibition, so I whipped up a few things to match. I'm not sure they're perfect for the theme, though, so I'd love a second—or rather a third—opinion."

I listened intently as Honey described each dish, my stomach grumbling more with every luxurious detail. The spread before us looked like it belonged at a glamorous 1920s soirée. I could hardly believe she'd managed to whip up all these treats just this morning, though I had a feeling her magical touch might have played a part.

Delicate bite-sized canapés featured smooth pâté on crispy crostinis, each one adorned with a sprig of dill. Mini crab cakes were paired with a tangy remoulade, their golden-brown crusts giving way to tender, flavorful centers. The whiskey-glazed meatballs were a rich, savory delight, each one perfectly caramelized with a sweet and smoky glaze. The perfectly crisp, fresh cucumber sandwiches were all calling my name, a nice contrast in simplicity and elegance, but it was the gleaming, chocolate-topped mini éclairs filled with a velvety vanilla cream that truly tested my patience as I waited for Honey to finish explaining her creations.

"These are delicious!" I exclaimed around a mouthful of éclair. My mother always told me life was short and to eat dessert first. Trisha Sullivan was a wise woman.

"This is incredible," Isadora said, dusting crab cake crumbs from her fingers. "How did you get the time to make all of these?"

"Oh, Antonio took care of the guests checking out, so I had some time to play in the kitchen," Honey said, beaming with pride.

"Speaking of guests, Mama. I think one of them might have left a window open. We just had a draft come through a while ago, but now that I think about it, it might've been after checkout time," Bella said.

Honey's brows knit together briefly, a flicker of surprise crossing her normally cheerful face. "I'll check all the rooms. We can't have windows open with the current cold snap outside. The heating bill for this place is already through the roof this year. But before I go though, any favorites?"

"Éclairs," we all said at once. We looked at each other and giggled.

Honey rolled her eyes good-naturedly. "Of course. I spend all this time on these refined, savory bites, and you girls go straight for the sweets. It's just like when Bella was little—all she ever wanted were the desserts," she said with a loving glance at Bella.

Bella went over and gave Honey a hug. "Speaking of history, Harper discovered something interesting in a book about Havenwood's past. Have you ever heard of a guy named Benny O'Rourke? He ran a speakeasy called the Hideaway back in the 1920s."

"A speakeasy?" Honey thought for a moment and shook her head. "I can't say I've ever heard of something like that around here."

"Do you know of someone who has an old barn? Apparently, this Benny guy tunneled from the inn he ran to his nearby barn and built the speakeasy under that," Isadora said eagerly.

Honey scrunched up her face as she tried to recall anything in town that might fit that description. Finally, she shook her head. "Sorry girls. The only barns I know are the ones on the outskirts of town like the one over on the Moonshadow pumpkin farm. All of that would've happened long before our family even moved to Havenwood. Although now that you mention it..." she trailed off, staring at a memory long in the past that only she could see.

"What is it, Mama?" Bella asked eagerly.

Honey shook her head. "Probably nothing. But something you just said reminded me of when we first moved here."

"To Havenwood?" I asked.

"To the Oasis. You see, Antonio and I bought this place from a nice older couple. They had three grown children, none of whom wanted anything to do with the daily grind of running a B&B full time. Anyway, the older lady liked to talk and told me a lot about the Oasis, much of which I don't remember..." she trailed off, squinting as if trying to pull the memory back from the depths of her mind. I leaned forward, holding my breath.

"But I thought she mentioned that the family who owned the Oasis before hers had an Irish name—"

My heart leaped. This had to be it. A lead! "Irish?" I echoed, almost too eagerly.

She nodded slowly, her brow furrowing in concentration. "I can't remember exactly what she said. Flanagan maybe?"

Flanagan? My excitement fizzled out as quickly as it had surged. That wasn't even close to what we needed. It felt like a balloon deflating with a pathetic squeak.

"Anyway," she added, oblivious to my sinking hope, "something like that. It just struck me as odd that there were two Irish families in the hospitality business in a small place like Havenwood back then. I wonder if they knew each other?" She shrugged, her interest in the matter fading almost as fast as it had arisen. "Anyway, I'd better check for an open window. And make more éclairs," she said with a wink and a smile before she swept out of the room.

I turned to Bella, her eyes mirroring the wheels turning in my mind. "You don't think that's just a coincidence, do you?" I asked, voicing the niggling thought that had taken root.

Bella's frown deepened as she considered the implications. "History has never been Mama's thing," she mused. "And if previous owners called the Oasis something else…"

I picked up where she left off. "The Enchanted Oasis and the Hearthstone could actually be the same place, just passed through different hands and renamed over time?"

Isadora's eyes sparkled as she gave a little wiggle of excitement. "Could it really be the same place?"

A spark of determination lit up Bella's face. "I think there's only one way to find out," she said, darting for the door.

"Where are you going?" I called after her.

"Papa's shed!" she shouted over her shoulder.

Isadora and I exchanged startled glances before scrambling to chase after her, racing out the door.

Paths of Time

THE THREE OF US burst into the woodworking shed, the brisk air doing nothing to quell our excitement. The familiar scent of sawdust and varnish surrounded us as we found Antonio sweeping up wood shavings from a recently finished project, oldies rock playing softly from a nearby speaker.

"Hi Papa," Bella called out, her voice a mix of cheer and curiosity.

Antonio looked up, obviously surprised by the interruption, but not upset. "Oh, hello ladies. Are you looking for more decorations for the party? I'm afraid all you'll find here is some excellent oak, decent maple, and a bit of a mess. But that part will be remedied soon," he said with a flourish of his broom.

"Actually, none of the above. We think we might have discovered something about the history of the Oasis, but Mama wasn't much help," Bella said.

"Your Mama is an amazing woman, an incredible cook, and the most loving partner a man could ever wish for, but she is not a student of history." Antonio leaned on his broom and smiled. "However, you've come to the right place. How can I help?"

"We were wondering who owned the Oasis before you?" Bella asked eagerly.

"That's easy," Antonio said with a shrug. "The Cumberlands. They were a friendly couple, but their kids were all grown up with their own careers and no interest in running a B&B. The Cumberlands didn't want to see the Oasis demolished though. This old place has been a Havenwood staple for over a hundred years. Although, between you and me, I'm not sure how much of it is still the original building. Several adaptions have been made by various owners, and several more made by yours truly."

Cumberlands - not an Irish name. Even though I'd known it was a long shot, my curiosity was still piqued. The idea that the Oasis and Benny's Hearthstone Inn could somehow be connected kept nagging at me. I kept my voice casual, trying not to jump to conclusions. "And before them? Do you know who owned it nearly a century ago?"

Antonio shot me a look. "Now, that is very specific and also a very long time ago. Why do you ask?"

"We think the Enchanted Oasis might have originally belonged to an Irish family before the one that sold it to you," Isadora explained, her words tumbling out in a rush.

"And they had a speakeasy under the barn," Bella added, her eyes sparkling.

"Also, there's a story of the owner meeting an unfortunate end in said speakeasy," I finished.

Antonio scratched his head, his fingers brushing sawdust through his thick hair. "A speakeasy *and* a death, you say? I don't think I've ever heard about anything like that in Havenwood, but you're right about one thing. The family that owned this before the Cumberlands was Irish. The Flanagan family I believe. Before the Flanagans, the family who owned this place was another Irish family...the O'...no, that's not right." He stroked his mustache as he thought. I leaned forward instinctively, hope rising inside me. Suddenly, he snapped his fingers, making me jump. "Now I remember. It was the Kellys."

My hope washed away as disappointment flooded through me. Despite the odds, I'd actually believed for a second that the Oasis and the Hearthstone were the same place. Looking at Bella and Isadora's faces, they must've been going through a similar emotional rollercoaster.

"Oh. Well...." I trailed off, not really knowing what else to say.

Antonio looked up at the ceiling, drumming his fingers on the handle of the broom. "Let's see. And before them was..." he trailed off, searching his memory for the information. "...ah, yes! The O'Rourke family."

"O'Rourke?" I exclaimed, feeling a flicker of excitement spring to life inside of me once more. "As in Benny O'Rourke?"

"Well, now, I'm doing well to remember back that far. The O'Rourkes likely owned this place, what? Eighty years ago? A hundred? They were probably part of the wave of Irish immigrants that moved over here after the Great Famine in Ireland," Antonio said.

"But do you remember the first name of the O'Rourke owner?" Bella asked.

"Or if there was a barn on the property? One with a speakeasy under it?" Isadora added.

"Or if this isn't the inn Benny O'Rourke owned, where might a place called the Hearthstone Inn have been located in Havenwood?" I asked, trying to temper my excitement with logic.

With a hint of a knowing smile, Antonio set aside his broom and wiped his hands on a rag. "I can see you're all quite taken with this mystery. Now, I don't know the answers to any of those questions off the top of my head."

As Antonio's words sank in, I saw the spark in Isadora's eyes flicker and dim. Bella slumped slightly, her shoulders drooping as if the weight of disappointment settled over her. I felt a pang of empathy as our once-promising trail seemed to dissolve with every syllable he uttered.

Antonio put an arm around Bella's shoulders and squeezed with a good-natured chuckle. Antonio's laughter had a way of making even the coldest days feel warmer. "Don't look so downhearted. This old place used to have a veritable trove of buildings and structures long before we came along, all lost to time now. But I've kept the blueprints, some dating back to the Flanagan era, perhaps even older. When we took over the Oasis, we had plans for refurbishing, and I made it my mission to grasp every detail, every nook and cranny of the property and the buildings that survived. There could be a few dusty old ledgers too. Would you like to look at those? Might be something in there worth your detective work." He smiled, and it was like a ray of sunlight piercing through the overcast cloud cover of doubt.

Bella and Isadora's eyes met mine, and we instantly agreed without a word being spoken. "It could be an adventure," I said, a smile tugging at my lips. "Even if this doesn't turn out to be the Hearthstone, maybe we learn something interesting about the Oasis that we can use in your New Year's Eve party," I suggested.

"Sounds good to me," Bella said, her normal optimism returning.

Isadora glanced around the shed thoughtfully. "Wait a second...if there's a hidden speakeasy, wouldn't it make sense for there to be a trapdoor or hatch around here?" Her eyes brightened at the idea.

I caught her excitement and immediately started scanning the floor. "Yeah, especially considering they repurposed the old tunnel that connected the barn to the house. They'd have to have a way to get into the speakeasy or there'd be no point in the tunnel." I knelt down, knocking on the wooden planks, listening for any hollow sounds.

Antonio broke in with a chuckle. "I hate to burst your bubble, but I had this shed built when we bought the B&B. No speakeasy hatches here, unfortunately."

We all laughed, a little embarrassed, but the thrill of the hunt hadn't worn off yet. "Worth a try," I said, getting back to my feet and dusting off the knees of my jeans.

"But if you find any buried treasure elsewhere," Antonio teased, "I owe Honey a new stove, so make sure you set enough aside for that, okay?"

"You've got it, Papa," Bella said as we walked toward the house.

Antonio opened the door off the kitchen to a small room the DeLucas used as an office space. It was more of a cozy alcove than a study, the walls lined with books and stacks of papers crowding the desk, a lone computer station claiming its permanent residence in one corner. He delved into the shelves with the focus of an archaeologist unearthing relics, eventually emerging with a pile of ledgers and a stack of blueprints heaped high in his arms.

"I think it's probably best to look at these on the table. There's not enough room in the office," Antonio suggested, carrying his armful over to the round table where the family ate their meals in privacy away from their guests.

We gathered around the trove, anticipation crackling in the air. The blueprints spread out before us seemed to hold whispers of a hidden past, intricate lines and symbols mapping out a history long forgotten. The old record books showed the day-to-day management of the inn in neat, detailed rows of handwritten numbers. But as minutes stretched until we stopped noticing time passing, with page after page offering no mention of a speakeasy and no hint of a hidden barn, our enthusiasm waned. Honey passed out cups of tea and offered some mini-praline croissants that helped to ease our disappointment, but it seemed some secrets of the past might be determined to remain lost to time.

"It would've been quite the discovery, wouldn't it? Digging up a long-lost puzzle like that? In this day and age, there aren't too many of those forgotten mysteries left. At least, not ones you could solve." Antonio offered his warm smile.

I nodded, appreciating his effort to keep our spirits high. The croissants helped to mitigate the anticlimactic end of our search as well, but neither completely erased my disappointment at the dead end.

Isadora leaned over the table, scanning the documents as she sipped from her mug of tea. "Do you really think an underground speakeasy would survive a century without turning to dust and mold?" she asked curiously.

Honey spoke up. "Well, in the mundane world, plenty of speakeasies and other buildings have survived a century or more, with just good construction and a bit of care. Take the Oasis for example. This place has held up pretty well with the right maintenance." She glanced lovingly at Antonio.

He cleared his throat. "But you're right to be concerned about disrepair. In this region, it's less about dust and more about the damp, weather changes, and neglect. Freezing winters, thawing springs—they can really do a number on places left unchecked."

I twirled a loose strand of hair around a finger. "So, I guess the pressing question—besides where the Hideaway is located, of course—is how well it was preserved."

Isadora spoke up, her voice cheerful. "If there's one thing I've learned, it's that Havenwood is full of surprises. After all, there are so many magical people in this town that you can never really be sure what to expect."

Antonio pointed a finger at her in agreement. "Exactly." He rapped the top of the table with a knuckle. "We found this table in the attic along with some other pieces that are older than some trees outside and still in perfect condition. There's a beautiful desk in the attic. I asked your nonna about it once, Harper. She discovered that there were some enchanted runes carved into the bottom of the furniture which helped to preserve it over the years. See the figure here on the table's edge? Magic has a way of bending the rules of time, you know."

I chewed on his words, thinking about what I had found in Spellbooks. The notebook, the photo, everything I'd discovered in that hidden compartment had been in almost perfect condition, despite how old they seemed. What if the runes on the panel had been not only hiding but also protecting the items inside?

"Could runes on a wall protect something inside?" I asked Antonio.

He shrugged. "Maybe. I don't have the ability to imbue runes with magic, being a normal human with no magical gifts and all that. But I don't see a reason why not. Magic has been used to preserve plenty of things."

Bella leaned forward, running her fingers along the edge of the table. "So, if we find the Hideaway in good shape, someone must've gone through a lot of trouble, either by building it to last or by using magic."

Isadora peered at the runes as well. "Do you really think the speakeasy might have survived a century of neglect? That would be incredible!" she exclaimed, her eyes shining.

My mind whirled with the possibilities. "Imagine the stories those walls could tell if they were preserved by runes. It would be incredible if we could actually find it."

Antonio gave a small smile. "If those walls are still standing, that is. Now, wouldn't that be something?"

Bella furrowed her brow. "Harper, didn't you say that the tunnel leading to the speakeasy was originally used to connect the inn to the barn?"

I nodded. "Yeah. It was."

Bella ran her hand through her hair. "Well, the tunnel couldn't have been that deep then. If it were me, I wouldn't have dug down further than I had to, especially a hundred years ago when they didn't have machinery like we do now."

Antonio pursed his lips. "I think I see what you're getting at. If the tunnel and possibly even the speakeasy itself were close to the surface, both would be more prone to shifts in the ground or even new buildings. To survive this long, every inch would likely need protection—from the support beams to the floorboards. The amount of work and magic that would take is staggering, not to mention the foresight needed. The runes would have to be part of the construction itself."

"I don't know about that," Honey said, finishing her tea. "But what I do know is that these walls are still standing, and there is plenty of work to be done around here without borrowing trouble from years past."

Antonio pressed his hands down on the table and stood. "That's my cue. I wish you three the best of luck, but for now, there are dishes with my name on them. Good luck with your party planning and your mystery."

The Asterisk in the Ledger

Antonio and Honey left us to our detective work, diving back into the B&B's endless to-do list. The three of us stayed put, circling around the puzzle pieces of the inn's past like hawks, but as time dragged on, the lack of concrete clues made me feel as if we were more like puppies chasing our own tails. As far as we could discover, the oldest entry in any of the books went back to when the Flanagan family owned the inn. Even then, it was called the Enchanted Oasis. There was nothing about the O'Rourke's, a speakeasy, or the Hearthstone Inn.

"Maybe we were wrong," Bella said, shutting the book in front of her with a sigh. "There could've been more than one O'Rourke family or perhaps they owned more than one inn. Either way, I don't think there's anything here. Besides, we should get back to organizing things for the party."

I wasn't ready to give up just yet. "I'd really like to see this desk upstairs. You know, the one with the runes on it? If it's been well-preserved, maybe there will be a clue in it about the history of the Oasis."

"Now that you mention it, I'd like to see it too," Isadora chimed in. "I took an exploratory magical studies class last semester. It's the kind of class that's supposed to broaden our horizons and get mages to try new things. There's an entire week dedicated to runes, not that it's enough to master rune-craft, but I have a basic understanding. I'd love to see them in action though. You know, in the real world, not in some stuffy classroom."

"If you want to see runes you should go over to Spellbooks and check out the hidden room we found in the attic," Bella pointed out. "Or even Wildwood Ink. Runes are right up Finn's alley."

I nodded, though I couldn't help but pause for a moment. It still struck me as strange how casually everyone in Havenwood spoke about magic. In most places, people kept these things hidden or, at the very least, whispered about them behind closed doors. Here in Havenwood, magic wasn't just something whispered about in secret—it was woven into the very fabric of life. Openly accepted and naturally entwined with everything from family legacies to casual conversation, magic was simply a way of being. Of course, we kept its more fantastical aspects hidden from the mundane tourists, but after a few months of living here, I'd come to realize what a gift it was to truly be yourself—quirks, magic, and all.

Isadora interrupted my thoughts. "Going up some stairs to look at a desk or bundling up and heading all the way over to Arcadia Avenue?" She held out both palms toward the ceiling and tipped them up and down like they were plates on a scale, plopping dramatically down on the hand representing the upstairs option.

"But we still have so much to do on the party," Bella protested.

"Let's give it a quick look," I said, eyeing the time. "Fifteen minutes, then we jump back into party planner mode."

Bella rolled her eyes good-naturedly. "Fine. You girls win. I suppose we can take a little more time."

Bella unlocked the door to the attic and led us up the narrow staircase. A chill breeze blew past me, making me shiver and wish I'd at least grabbed my scarf before heading into the attic. Maybe the draft we felt earlier came from up here. However, once we were up in the attic, the warm air was stuffy. It smelled like no one but moths and spiders had been up here in months, if not years. It was also dusty, making me sneeze three times in a row, effectively distracting me from the temperature changes.

"Bless you," Isadora murmured.

"Thanks," I said, wiping at my watery eyes.

The attic was a treasure trove of the mundane, a monument to the commonplace rhythms of yesteryear. The dim light from sparsely placed bulbs illuminated the relics of the past, each item whispering a tale that wove through the threads of time. I wished we were trying to unravel this secret back in Spellbooks. Having a sentient shop that had been around for ages would likely have made the searching process so much faster. I could've just asked it about what we were looking for, and Spellbooks would've shown me where it was stored. As it was, we'd have to do this the old-fashioned way and search for it ourselves.

Bella led us past what seemed like mountains of boxes stacked on top of one another and then shoved against the walls to make a narrow pathway. It was like walking through a canyon of cardboard. I don't know what I'd been expecting exactly, but it felt just like an ordinary attic. It was giving off less "vault full of hidden secrets" and more "storage unit" vibes.

I squinted at the towering stacks of mismatched chairs, tables, and shelves piled haphazardly around us, creating a maze of forgotten furniture. It was hard to imagine any sort of rhyme or reason to the chaos.

"I think Dad put all the furniture back here," Bella called from up ahead. "It might not feel like it, but there is a system. At least, I'm pretty sure there's one." She paused, eyeing a precariously stacked tower of boxes. "Probably. Maybe."

Despite her waning confidence, it only took another minute for Bella to prove her memory was correct. Beyond the boxes was an odd assortment of furniture. Everything from old hat racks to a large hope chest to a couple of broken dining room chairs. Ahead of me, Isadora and Bella forged ahead through the wilds of the dusty, forgotten furniture. I followed, sneezing occasionally.

"Here it is!" Bella called.

I peered around the flared horn of an old gramophone to see Bella and Isadora already examining a sturdy-looking desk. It stood solidly against the wall like an old guard at the gates of history, a testament to both craftsmanship and enchantment. Made from what looked like dark, rich mahogany, its surface gleamed with an unnatural luster, untouched by dust or wear. The lack of even a single scratch or speck of dust hinted at powerful magical runes protecting its integrity.

I took a closer look. Despite its age, the wood bore no cracks, no signs of dry rot that plagued the less fortunate furniture of its era. Instead, it possessed a timeless quality and exceptional design work that was both utilitarian and aesthetically pleasing. Each corner post was thick and sturdy, adorned with deeply carved motifs of Celtic knots and spirals. They reminded me of symbols of eternity and continuity I'd seen around Finn's shop. I couldn't help but wonder if those decorations were more than just ornamental—perhaps they served as the focus for the protective spells that kept the desk in such pristine condition.

"Do you think we'll find answers in there?" Isadora asked, hurrying over.

"I don't know, but as long as we're here, let's check it out," Bella said, crouching in front of the desk.

Below the expansive work surface lay an array of drawers, their brass handles aged to a gentle patina that only years of use could achieve. The central drawer was broad and shallow, ideal for storing stationery and writing implements. Flanking it on either side were stacks of narrower drawers, perfect for keeping personal correspondence organized. At the base of the desk stood two large filing drawers.

Bella's eyes were doing that sparkly thing they did when she was onto something. "Who knows? Maybe this desk's got backstories stashed in every nook and cranny." She tugged on the narrow drawer with the ornate keyhole under the flat tabletop. It refused to budge. "But we might need some help to uncover its mysteries," she said with a grunt as she tried pulling again. Despite her best efforts, the door stayed solidly stuck.

"Here, let me," I said. Bella stepped to the side to allow me access to the drawer in question. Normally, I was hesitant to use my magical gifts in front of people. Like most other witches I knew, I had a talent for one specific thing. In my case, it was metal manipulation. Very minor metal manipulation. Nothing big like setting up scaffolding or sculpting statues, but if you lost your keys and got locked out of your house, I was who you wanted on speed dial. Why didn't I advertise my gifts? Well, a couple of reasons. I grew up on Army bases, following my dad's job wherever it took him. Magic and the military don't mix. But mostly, I didn't want people to think I was capable of what I was going to do right now: namely breaking and entering. However, Bella and Isadora weren't only my closest friends in Havenwood, they also both knew about my magic. Trying to hide my abilities from either of them now felt a little silly.

I put my fingers against the ornate brass lock and closed my eyes, concentrating. It wasn't hard. The lock was old and worn, with none of the redundancies of modern tumblers. It gave way easily under the merest brush of my magic and the drawer popped open.

"There you go," I said to Bella with a flourish.

"I knew you were handy to have around," she teased. Together with Isadora, we got to it, tackling the desk like it was the last few pieces in a jigsaw puzzle. If this thing had secrets, we were determined to coax them out, one drawer at a time.

As Bella started on the top drawers, I opened the nearest bottom drawer, revealing about a dozen record books. I lifted out a stack so I could look through them more easily. That's when I noticed intricately carved runes on the edge of the drawer.

"Wait, look at this," I said, drawing the others' attention to the carvings as I pointed them out.

"Oh! Let me have a look at those," Isadora exclaimed, kneeling next to me and running a fingertip along the carvings. "Hmm. Now, my rune-craft isn't great, but these either ensure that the documents within are protected from moisture and mold or possibly mice and cockroaches. Which do you think?"

"You'd know better than I do. Why don't you take a closer look?" I suggested, moving to the side. As Isadora examined drawer after drawer for more runes, I decided to inspect the record books. I opened the one that looked more recent. The date was in 1947, and someone inscribed the name "Kelly" with a flowing hand on the inner front cover. That meant we were on the right track but hadn't gone back far enough yet. Antonio said the family that owned the Oasis just before the Kellys were the O'Rourkes. If I could find conclusive evidence that Benny O'Rourke had been one of the owners of this place in the past, that would mean the Oasis and the Hearthstone really were the same inn.

I set the newer record books aside, opting to examine the older ones as Bella and Isadora conducted their own examinations of the desk and its contents. As I opened one of the dusty volumes, I marveled at the neat rows of entries that filled its ancient pages. The numbers and lists of expenses—provisions, laundering, linen—each one a testament to the inn's bustling history.

The more I flipped through the pages, the more I began to understand. The columns of figures reflected the rhythm of life at the inn. As I scanned down the entries, it was as if the day-to-day operations of the past were breathing again, whispering their narrative in a language I now recognized from my time working at the bookshop.

Excitement fluttered in my chest. Maybe there were clues here, buried in the very fabric of the inn's operations. My fingers tingled as I turned the pages, anticipation building with each rustle. Maybe the clues I had been looking for were buried in the notes of the inn's operations. The inventory lists, the patterns of expenses, the subtle hints that something more was happening beneath the surface. I flipped back to double-check, my heart pounding as the realization solidified: hidden within these mundane records could be the key to the inn's mysteries, waiting to be revealed.

Excited and strangely nervous with anticipation, I paged back to the beginning of the book. There, inscribed on the inside cover, was the clue I'd been hoping to find.

"We were right," I breathed out, my voice barely above a whisper, afraid to shatter the hushed reverence that had fallen upon us.

"What is it?" Bella asked, leaning down curiously.

I held up the book for her to see the name of the inn written in bold letters. "This is the record book for the Hearthstone Inn owned by the O'Rourke family. The Oasis and the Hearthstone...they're the same place. This ledger's detail of all the orders for the Hearthstone clearly shows that both a Liam O'Rourke and his son Benny ran the place," I said, trailing my finger over the handwritten title page.

"Wow!" Isadora breathed, peering over my shoulder.

"See if you can find anything in there about the speakeasy," Bella urged.

"I'll do my best," I said, moving to the side to allow them both easier access to the desk as I perched on a dust-covered chair. I started flipping through the pages as quickly as I dared, scanning for anything that might be a clue.

Minutes passed with only the sound of turning pages and creaking drawers to interrupt the excited search. Bella lifted out a narrow box from the top drawer and started sifting through the odds and ends. With a triumphant smile, she pulled out an old brass key, ornate and heavy. "Aha! What do you suppose this opens?" she asked, turning it over in her hand.

"It's the same style as the keyhole on the desk," Isadora observed.

"Good catch," I said, standing up to get a closer look at both the key and the ornate lock once more. After a moment, I shook my head. "They look similar, but look, the key is too big for the lock."

"Besides, why would anyone lock the key *inside* the desk? Scratch that. *How* would that work? Wouldn't they need it to open or lock the drawer?" Bella added.

"Unless they had magic like Harper's. Then it would be a clever way to make sure your secrets stayed hidden," Isadora pointed out.

"Maybe," Bella allowed. "But then why have the key in the first place? Besides, I can't see much of anything that appears to be a secret in here. Some old stationary and a handful of receipts by the look of it. Did you find anything Isa?" she asked.

"More of the same, but I haven't opened all the drawers yet," Isadora said, moving to the other side.

I retreated to continue my examination of the ledger. Every listing seemed to be the repetitive and mundane necessities for running an inn. Taking a chance, I flipped to the last entry and worked my way in reverse. To my surprise, I discovered what I was looking for on the second-to-last page of records: an entry for "tunnel construction" stood out as a stark anomaly. I traced the letters with my finger, feeling the weight of their implication. If a tunnel was arranged and built, that only seemed to further prove that the Oasis had once been the Hearthstone Inn, complete with a tunnel to the Hideaway.

An asterisk next to the entry caught my eye, and I flicked through the empty pages to the last few, which were reserved for notes. A cramped narrative awaited, penned by someone determined to leave a legacy of explanation. With the mystery beckoning, I read eagerly.

Liam's Story

As I read the words, the voice of one Liam O'Rourke seemed to echo through the decades.

**Appendix: On the Construction of the Subterranean Passage*
In the winter month of January in the year of our Lord 1888, a
calamity of snow and wind unlike any storm before descended
upon Havenwood, so fierce and unyielding that it paralyzed
our town and threatened the very lives of our cherished live-
stock. Our barn, a mere stone's throw from the Hearthstone Inn,
stood isolated, an island amidst the white tempest, our animals
trapped within, besieged by cold and hunger.
As proprietor of the Hearthstone, it is my solemn duty and care
to provide for all under my charge, both man and beast. Yet,
that blizzard rendered me helpless, a feeling I vowed to never
again let grasp my heart.
Thus, with a resolve as unshakable as the ancient hills that
cradle our town, I, Liam O'Rourke, did set upon a venture
most ambitious. In league with the Silverthorne family, whose
roots run as deep in Havenwood soil as the mightiest oaks, we

conceived and constructed a tunnel. This passage, hewn from the earth itself, runs deep beneath the frost line, from the cellar of our humble inn to the very heart of our barn.

This note shall serve as a testament to the undertaking and a guide to any who may find themselves custodians of the Hearthstone and its secrets in future years. The tunnel, reinforced by the Silverthornes' ingenuity and my own determination, stands as a monument to Havenwood's fortitude and community spirit.

We have taken meticulous care to ensure the passage would endure the tests of time and nature. The walls shored up with timber from the thickest pines and the most resilient oaks. They have also been inscribed with runes of preservation—ancient symbols passed down through Silverthorne generations, a blend of their wisdom and the old ways of my Emerald Isle.

Let this record reflect my gratitude: to the land that has borne us, to the community that has embraced us, and to the Silverthornes, without whom this endeavor would have remained but a dream in the winter's shadow. May this tunnel serve as a haven, safeguarding life against the furies of nature for as long as the Hearthstone Inn shall stand.

In faith and in hope for the future,
Liam O'Rourke

"We have a tunnel," I whispered, more to myself than to the others. My heart raced at the thought of such a secret artery lying dormant beneath our feet, feeling even more certain that the Oasis and the Hearthstone were one and the same. Could it have survived over a hundred years? Could it still be there, hidden and waiting?

Isadora's pink head popped up from under the desk. "What was that?"

"You found mention of a tunnel? Benny's tunnel to the Hideaway?" Bella asked excitedly.

"Not exactly," I said, passing over the ledger so she could read Liam's note for herself. "It's written by a guy named Liam O'Rourke. Maybe he was Benny's dad or possibly even his grandfather? Anyway, this Liam guy worked with the Silverthorne family. Do you know anything about that, Isadora?"

She shook her head, sending her pink hair flying. "Not off the top of my head, but I could check it out when I head home. Did you say they worked on a tunnel together?"I shoved my hair back out of my eyes as they peered at the handwritten note in the ledger. "Yeah. According to that, with the help of the Silverthornes, Liam tunneled from the house to the barn to make sure his livestock stayed alive in case there was another blizzard as bad as the one in 1888."

"You think they built more than one tunnel?" Isadora asked, pushing to her feet with a bundle of papers wrapped in a red ribbon in one hand.

"No, I think the tunnel might be one and the same. Think about it. According to what I read, Benny opened his speakeasy relatively quickly after Prohibition hit. How could he manage to dig and reinforce a tunnel that quickly without help? And would the upstanding Silverthorne family be willing to break the law of the land to help the local inn keeper establish an illegal bootleg joint?" I asked excitedly.

"Not a chance if they were anything like my mother," Isadora said without hesitation. "She's never met a rule she didn't want to enforce."

"Exactly," I said, snapping and pointing at her. "It makes more sense that the historian who wrote the book I read made a mistake or possibly never knew that Liam, not Benny, built the tunnel in the first place. Maybe it was an oversight or shoddy research. Think about it. There wasn't another blizzard documented that rivaled the one in 1888."

"At least not one that you have read about yet," Bella said logically.

"Okay, you have a point," I admitted. "There *might* have been another one, but don't you think that would've been mentioned in the chapter about the terrible blizzard? After all, what's more exciting? One blizzard or two?"

"Fair enough. I'll buy that," Bella said.

"So, the tunnel gets built, and either is never used or only used by family. There's no point without a blizzard. Until Prohibition hits and Benny opens a speakeasy. Then the tunnel that no one remembered his dad built roughly thirty years before becomes the ideal secret path to convey people to and from the speakeasy."

"Sounds plausible to me," Isadora said, untying the ribbon and unfolding the top paper in the stack she held.

"So, if we're right, then there really is a hidden speakeasy somewhere on the property. Who knows? Maybe that key even opens the door!" I said, pointing excitedly at the large brass key Bella had found. Suddenly, the key seemed less of an enigma and more of an invitation—perhaps the very means to unlock the path Liam O'Rourke had so desperately forged all those years ago.

"Benny still would've had to build the actual bar, but if he didn't have to worry about the tunnel, that would've saved him a lot of time during construction," Bella mused. "But if the Silverthornes helped Liam rune the tunnel, they wouldn't have necessarily helped Benny do the same for the speakeasy—especially if they were sticklers for the rules. Even if this key unlocks a door that leads to Benny's Hideaway, there might be nothing left of the actual speakeasy but a very well-preserved tunnel."

She paused, considering the other possibilities. "The real concern wouldn't be the tunnel collapsing—it's rune-protected, so that's less likely—but what if the underground speakeasy was torn down or filled in? Or what if it's buried under something else now, covered over by new buildings or underground utilities? The tunnel might still be there, but the speakeasy could be long gone."

"I suppose..." I said. My shoulders slumped slightly, the excitement that had sparked earlier dimming with the weight of reality.

"Wait a second. I think there might be more to it than that," Isadora said suddenly, her voice lifting as she looked up from the stack of letters, several of which now sat open on the desktop.

"What do you mean?" I asked, the flicker of excitement roaring back to life as my curiosity reignited.

"Look at this," Isadora said, spreading the letter flat on the desk. She jabbed a triumphant finger at the elegantly written name at the bottom of the page. Bella and I bent over the desk to get a closer look. It simply read:

Clara

I looked up at Bella. The confused expression on her face mirrored the one on my own. "I feel like we're missing something," I said hesitantly.

"Clara!" Isadora exclaimed. She flipped the letter over to reveal a blob of red wax with a design pressed into it. "Clara *Silverthorne*. That's my family's crest! And this is a love letter from Clara to Benny O'Rourke."

I blinked in surprise and looked closer. Sure enough, it was the same design that had proved so instrumental in solving the jewel heist less than a week before. Prior to the Christmas Eve Ball at the Silverthorne manor, I wouldn't have been able to tell you if the family had a crest, much less what it looked like. However, the wax evinced the impression of the familiar thorn bush, crown, and wolves of the Silverthorne crest.

"Have you ever heard anything about one of your distant relatives getting involved with a bootlegger?" I asked in disbelief.

Isadora shook her head. "No. Never. Otherwise, I might've paid more attention to family history, especially when setting up the Vault."

Bella raised an eyebrow and grinned. "Looks like the apple didn't fall far from the tree, huh? You've got your own speakeasy now, don't you?"

I couldn't resist chiming in, my voice teasing. "Carrying on the family tradition, are we?"

Isadora rolled her eyes and threw her hands up. "Hey, hey! The Vault is completely legal, thank you very much. No bootlegging or smuggling involved. It's just a place to escape mother's scrutiny and have a little fun. That's all!" She shook her head, a thoughtful frown on her face. "No, I never heard about a Silverthorne being involved with anything like this, but I'm not sure I would have. Mother is a stickler for propriety. Even if she'd caught wind of a love affair between Clara and Benny that didn't result in a proper marriage, I very much doubt she would've told us."

I bit my lip. "So, you think that Clara might have helped Benny to rune the speakeasy much like her relative did for Benny's father or grandfather?"

"I think it's a possibility, don't you?" Isadora said excitedly.

"I agree! Besides, even if she didn't, there might be something in those letters that helps us figure out where the entrance to the speakeasy was," Bella said.

"Or in the ledgers," I said, tapping the leather cover of the one I had been reading.

Bella's eyes gleamed with excitement once more. "Right. Isa, you read the letters and see if you can uncover a clue. Harper and I will tackle the ledgers."

"Wait. What about your party planning?" I asked.

Bella waved a hand dismissively. "We're already way ahead of where I hoped to be today and if we do find a speakeasy on the grounds, think of how perfect that will be for our Prohibition theme? For that, we can spare a few more minutes before we get back to work."

I wasn't going to argue with her. Bella took the guest books and reservation lists, her familiarity with the B&B business making her the perfect fit. I dove into the ledgers, poring over them with almost forensic intensity, seeking any inconsistency, a clue left unintentionally by a long-gone hand. At the desk, Isadora searched through old letters, completely enveloped in the intimate world of Clara's handwritten missives. Would she find a whispered secret between the lines of faded ink, or would we? The air was thick with the tension and hope for discovery. Each page turn was a step deeper into the past. Time stretched as we worked in silence, each of us absorbed in our tasks. Minutes blurred into an hour, the quiet rustle of pages and the occasional soft hum from Bella the only sounds in the room. With every turn of a page, my anticipation grew, the weight of history hanging in the air.

Suddenly, Isadora gasped. Wide-eyed, she held up a letter with a trembling hand. "I found something!" she exclaimed, her voice slicing through the musty silence and immediately pulling our attention toward her.

The Lost Love Letter

Isadora fluttered the letter in her hand at us. "Listen to this," she called out, her voice a mixture of triumph and disbelief. We leaned in as she read the letter aloud.

September 30, 1928

Dearest Benny,
In the hush of evening, I sit with pen in hand, heart brimming with thoughts of you. I find solace in our memories: the soft echoes of your laughter bring warmth to my solitary evenings. In those moments, I am reminded of the future we've dreamt of—one painted in the bold hues of our shared hopes.
The world, it seems, is not so fond of dreams, especially those that do not heed the rigid lines of propriety and expectation. My father, with his gaze fixed firmly on the past, cannot see the future that pulses so vividly in my chest when I hold your hand. A future that belongs not to tradition, but to us.

Each day that passes under the weight of his disapproval is a day too long. So, I pen this letter, a vow woven with words, as an emblem of my resolve. Benny, my beloved, we cannot let the world decide our fate. We must clutch it with both hands and run where only the stars can witness our union.
My heart swells with the courage that only love can bestow. I am ready, Benny. Ready to step into the unknown with you, my surest compass, my most trusted friend, my greatest love.

With all that I am,
Clara

Isadora's voice faded away. We digested Clara's words in silence. The letter seemed to dance with hope. She envisaged a plan to escape a life predetermined, an audacious dream to seize control of their destinies together. A dream, it seemed, that time had left unfulfilled with the unfortunate and unexpected death of Benny O'Rourke.

Bella leaned back, her eyes alight with the fire of revelation. "They had plans, big ones. Can you imagine the courage that took? To go against her father and possibly the most influential man in town. Especially at that time," she mused, her gaze drifting to the window as if picturing Clara and Benny's escape plan.

I tapped the top of the letter. "Based on the date, they didn't get to enjoy that dream for long. Benny died less than a month later."

Isadora, ever the romantic, clutched the letter to her chest. "But don't you see? This letter—it's not just a piece of the past. It's a piece of them, a clue. Clara's determination to run away with him meant she truly loved him."

Bella, always the practical one, cut in, "Okay, but if Clara was a Silverthorne, and if she really loved him, then maybe she helped him with more than just emotional support. She could've helped him set up the Hideaway. Think about it—there's a chance that if Clara had a hand in it, the speakeasy might still be there, protected by magic."

Isadora blinked, her dreamy expression fading slightly as the practical side of Bella's idea took root. "You really think so?"

Bella leaned in; her brow furrowed in thought. "Yeah, but I've been giving this some thought. We're pretty sure the Oasis used to be the Hearthstone back in the day, right?"

Isadora and I nodded in agreement.

"And the Oasis is still standing, right? Without the use of magical runes, apart from the odd table or chair," Bella continued, her voice gaining momentum. "So, if the Oasis has lasted this long on its own, why would the tunnel or the Hideaway need to be runed?"

I paused, considering her point. "Preservation, maybe?"

"Yes, but that's exactly it," Bella said. "Things were built to last back then. The Hideaway's structure wouldn't need magical preservation, but what if the runes were meant for something else?"

"Like what?" I asked, curious now.

"To hide it," Bella said, her voice serious. "Think about it. If Benny had a secret speakeasy, he wouldn't just want to protect the structure, he'd want to protect its secrecy. What if the runes were used to keep the tunnel and the Hideaway from being discovered or demolished when everything else around it was changing?"

Isadora's eyes lit up, catching on. "So, the runes weren't just about keeping it standing—they were about keeping it hidden from prying eyes. Like an invisibility spell for the Hideaway."

Bella nodded. "Exactly. And if Clara helped Benny with the runes, then they weren't just trying to preserve a building, they were trying to keep it safe from detection—maybe even from being destroyed as the town grew and changed."

I snapped my fingers and pointed at her. "If Benny was smart enough to use runes to protect the Hideaway back then there's a good chance that it's survived the last hundred years."

Bella's smile widened. "My thoughts exactly."

Isadora bounced on the balls of her feet, letting out a little squeal. "We need to go on a treasure hunt for the Hideaway! Like, right now!"

I couldn't help but grin at her enthusiasm, but I bit my lip and glanced over at Bella. "This is exciting! But we shouldn't get too distracted. Don't forget, we have a fabulous party to plan."

Bella's enthusiasm was a flame in the dim room. "Finding the speakeasy would be a real coup for Havenwood's history, and what a scoop for the Oasis! Just imagine unveiling it at the New Year's Eve bash! I'm even more thrilled we changed the theme now. If it's in good enough condition, we might even be able to unveil it to the public."

I held up a hand, trying to rein her in. "Whoa, slow down. Let's find it first before we start planning any grand reveals."

Bella tipped her head, conceding with a playful grin. "Okay, fine, point taken. But just think about it. Having a restored speakeasy here would bring in so many tourists and locals alike. If we could fix it up, the Oasis would be booked solid for months, maybe even longer." She paused, her cheeks reddening slightly as she glanced between Isadora and me. "Not that it's all about the money, but it would really make a difference for my family."

I squeezed her hand. "Of course it would. If your family and the town can benefit from uncovering the location of the Hideaway, then I'd say that's a win-win."

Isadora's smile was bright. "Exactly! And I love the idea of hosting the New Year's Eve party in an authentic speakeasy."

Bella hesitated for a moment, her brow furrowing. "I mean, I wouldn't want to compete with the Vault, Isa."

Isadora waved the concern away with a flick of her hand. "Oh, please! The Vault is just a private little hideout I've opened up to a few friends. It's not a business—it's my escape from reality, and it's nowhere near as grand as reopening the Hideaway could be. This would be something special for Havenwood and for your family. I'm all for it."

Bella's smile returned, softer but full of appreciation. "Thanks, Isa. That means a lot. I think the Hideaway could be something really great for us."

I paused, organizing my thoughts. "As much as I love where this is heading, let's approach it step by step. We need to find the tunnel, check its condition, and still plan the party—all by New Year's Eve. That's a lot. Should we really focus all our attention on finding the speakeasy right now?"

Bella nodded thoughtfully. "You're right, but how can we pass this up? We have to at least try. If we find it in time, I'd love to unveil the Hideaway during the party. Imagine revealing an authentic speakeasy at a Prohibition-themed event! And maybe at midnight, we could even celebrate the 'end' of Prohibition."

"We'll give it our all then. For Havenwood and the Oasis," I promised, feeling the excitement of our little team buzzing in the air. But even as the words left my mouth, another thought tugged at the edges of my mind—what if the Hideaway held more than just forgotten walls? What if it had clues, buried deep within, about what really happened to Benny O'Rourke? Could we finally uncover the truth behind his untimely death?

I shook my head, trying to push the idea away. It sounded absurd. Sure, I loved a good mystery, but this wasn't some fictional case in one of my beloved books. This was a century-old crime, cold as ice. Did I really think I could solve it?

No. I had to focus on what was within our reach—finding the speakeasy, learning its secrets. Solving Benny's death? That could wait, if it was even possible at all. But something about Clara and Benny's unfinished love story, written in that fragile letter, tugged at my heart. Maybe it wasn't just about the thrill of discovery anymore. Maybe it was about giving them the ending they never got, uncovering whatever truth the Hideaway had held captive all these years.

Isadora, ever the spark that kept us moving, was already on her feet, pulling us forward. "No mystery is going to solve itself while we're standing around talking," she teased, her hand catching mine as she urged me back to the present. "Tunnels don't just appear out of thin air. To the basement we go!

The Key to Secrets

BELLA UNLOCKED THE DOOR leading to the basement, and we hurried down the stairs, hoping to discover more about the Hideaway and Benny's story. There was a chill in the basement air that made me wish I'd thrown on an extra layer this morning or grabbed my jacket before descending the steep staircase.

Looking around, there was no doubt in my mind that we weren't in the early twentieth century. Heavily laden shelves lined the walls, filled with extras for the inn, such as sheets, canned goods, and more cleaning supplies than I'd ever seen outside a big box store. It was just an ordinary basement. Less "epicenter of mysteries" and more "storage unit on steroids."

While Bella and Isadora fanned out across the basement, they tapped their heels against the floor, the steady thumps creating a rhythmic beat that echoed through the room. Each step was purposeful, their ears tuned for the slightest hollow point, a potential clue to the tunnel's entrance. The sound of their stomping became like the ticking of a metronome, setting the pace of my thoughts as I watched them work.

I let the rhythm lull me for a moment, but something tugged at the edge of my memory—something about the barn, about the need for quick access to the animals. It was like a melody out of sync with the beat of their steps, pulling me in a different direction. My gaze wandered, landing not on the walls or the floor, but toward where I imagined the barn once stood outside.

"If I were Benny, where would I hide the entryway?" I murmured to myself. A cool breeze tickled at the hairs on the back of my neck, making me shiver. I spun around instinctively, but there was nothing there. "Wait a second," I muttered, my own footsteps quiet now as I broke from their metronomic search.

Bella stopped mid-stomp and turned to me, brow furrowed. "What is it?"

"The tunnel," I said slowly, piecing it together. "If it really was built to feed the animals during the storm, it wouldn't have been hidden beneath the floor. It would've run straight from here to the barn, wouldn't it?"

"You're guessing it's behind a wall, not under the floor?" Isadora started pressing on the walls and gently tugging on shelves.

"That's what I would do," I said with a shrug. "Why dig more than you have to?"

Isadora rapped her knuckles on a bare wall, listening for a hollow echo. Unfortunately, a solid thump met our ears. She moved down the wall, talking as she knocked. "You know, if it were me, there'd be a hidden latch or a secret button to press," she said.

"Yes, but Papa built all these shelves himself and found nothing like that," Bella pointed out.

"Maybe he built straight over the entrance and never even realized it," Isadora hypothesized.

Another breath of chill air washed over me, making my skin burst out in goose bumps. "It's possible, but..." I trailed off, trying to remember the words Liam had written at the end of the ledger.

Bella glanced in my direction. "Uh oh. I know that look. What's going on in your head?"

I spun around in a circle, trying to get my bearings in the windowless basement. "Where are we? If those are the stairs, then...this must be the front of the house," I said, pointing at the wall to the left.

"Yeah. So?" Bella asked, confused.

I pointed at the wall to the right. "That means that wall faces the woods which leaves us with either the one that points towards Honey's vegetable garden," I jerked a thumb at the rough stone behind me, "or the wall that faces Antonio's shed," I said, hurrying across the room to examine the far wall which looked like someone had once intended to decorate the interior of the basement by putting up paneling but had given up partway through. In front of it, some shelves stood cluttered with items related to the B&B—cleaning supplies and a few old decorations.

"Are you confused why she looks so excited because I'm not following," Isadora loudly whispered to Bella.

"It wasn't a tunnel to a speakeasy. Not originally," I said over my shoulder as I ran my fingers along the unfinished stone beside the shelves. "The tunnel was originally constructed by Liam O'Rourke, Benny's father, to help his animals in the barn should another blizzard ever hit, remember? It wasn't about secrecy. It was about necessity. Here, help me move this," I called to the others.

In short order, Bella, Isadora and I shifted the free-standing shelf to the side, giving us better access to the back wall.

"Okay, I'm with you so far," Isadora said, dusting her hands off as I ran my fingers from rough stone to the smooth wooden panels previously tucked behind the shelving unit

"Well, Liam wouldn't have hidden the tunnel, would he? It would've been unnecessary and probably have gotten in his way while he was trying to haul feed or whatever to his animals in the barn," I said.

"And the other wall looks like it's solid stone," Bella murmured, as she finally understood my reasoning.

I glanced over my shoulder and nodded at her with a small smile. "Exactly. Now, I'm not saying that there couldn't be a century-old enchantment on the wall over there. This is Havenwood after all. But why put in all that magical effort when you could just have a regular door?"

I placed my hands on the paneling, feeling the wood under my fingertips as I ran them along the surface, searching for any hint of metal or something that didn't quite fit. Nothing. The wood seemed solid, smooth.

Isadora joined me, her fingers brushing along the same area. "There has to be a handle or a latch hidden somewhere," she said, her voice full of hope. She pressed harder, trying to feel for any seams or triggers. "But...nothing." She sighed, stepping back. "Why would anyone hide a door so well without leaving a way to open it? This doesn't make any sense."

Her frustration stirred a thought. My eyes darted back to the corner of the panel, where it met the stone wall. "Wait a second. What if it doesn't open with a handle or a latch?"

Isadora and Bella both looked at me, puzzled.

"What do you mean?" Bella asked, her brow furrowed.

I leaned in closer to the corner, my fingers brushing over the edges of the wood again. Instead of just searching at torso height, where one might expect to find a handle to a door, I extended my magic, letting it flow to the edges of the panel, seeking any hint of metal. There! Right at the base and top of the panel was a faint sense of metal. A grin tugged at my lips as I pushed my magic further. The groove ran the entire length of the panel and beyond.

"There's something... something metallic," I whispered. "At the top and bottom. Almost like... a rail."

Bella and Isadora leaned in closer, their eyes bright with curiosity.

I knelt, letting my fingertips brush along the surface, searching for something—anything—that might reveal a secret. Slowly, I traced the edge of the wood, my fingers catching on the faintest hint of metal. Although the dim basement light made it difficult to see, I could feel it—a thin groove, almost imperceptible. My fingers followed the track, exploring its length.

"There's something here," I murmured, my heart beginning to race. "What if it slides?" I said, looking up at my friends.

Isadora's eyes widened. "Oh, that would make sense! If they wanted to keep it really hidden after repurposing the tunnel..."

I took a breath and gave a cautious push. At first, nothing happened. But then, with a soft creak and the grating sound of wood against stone, the panel began to shift. The panel slid open just a few inches along the metal rails, revealing a narrow, weathered door nestled into the wall, its wood darkened with age but preserved against time.

"Whoa," Bella whispered, her voice filled with awe, as if the very air had changed.

Isadora bounced on her toes, her earlier disappointment completely forgotten. "I knew it! I just knew there had to be something!"

I stepped back, staring at the door, still only partially revealed. The room seemed to hold its breath along with us. "We really found it," I said, the weight of the moment settling over us like a heavy, exhilarating blanket. "The tunnel."

Isadora clapped her hands in excitement. "What are we waiting for? Let's open it up!"

I gave it another push, but the door barely budged this time. I grunted and tried again. Nothing. Stepping back, I put my hands on my hips. "It's stuck. It feels like it hasn't been moved in decades."

"Looks like it's going to take a bit more than excitement to open this," Isadora quipped, already stepping forward.

"Let's do it together," Bella suggested, gripping the edge of the panel.

We exchanged nods, and with renewed determination, the three of us braced ourselves. I pushed while Bella and Isadora pulled. With a collective grunt and effort, the panel inched further, groaning as if reluctant to give up its secret.

"Almost there!" Bella gasped, her fingers gripping tight.

The door finally slid open with a harsh creak. Behind it, another door stood, its wood darkened but intact, solid and imposing, the last barrier between us and the secrets hidden within.

The craftsmanship was undeniable. The dark wood appeared almost as rich in color as anything Antonio had made upstairs. Carved into its surface were intricate runes, their lines and curves weaving an elaborate pattern across the grain, suggesting magic had been used to keep it preserved. An ornate escutcheon plate surrounded a hefty brass keyhole, its polished luster gleaming as if it had been buffed only yesterday, untarnished by the passage of decades. It was a beautiful contradiction—brass that should have dulled with age but instead shone with a polished gleam. Whoever had carved the magical designs hadn't wanted time to damage either the wood or the lock.

"Well, this explains why no one found it sooner," I said, wiping the dust from my hands.

Isadora bounced up and down in excitement. "Ready for round two?"

Bella reached out, twisting the knob to open the hidden door. It refused to budge. With determination etched on her face, Bella tried again, her hands gripping the knob with more force this time. The door remained steadfast, the knob wiggling uselessly.

Stepping aside, Bella gave me a nod. "I think this is more up your alley than mine," she said, waving at the locked door.

I stepped forward. Time to see if the minor magic that coursed through my veins was up to the challenge. I closed my eyes and focused, extending my hands towards the brass lock, willing it to click open. A hush fell over us, the kind of silence that's heavy with expectation. I concentrated, yet the lock refused to budge. I focused all my will on the mechanisms, brushing them gently with my magic. The lock was old and held none of the modern elements used to stymy thieves these days. My mundane lock picking skills weren't great, but even I could've gotten this lock open easily. So why wasn't my magic working?

"What's going on?" Isadora whispered, breaking the silence.

"Just…give me a sec," I muttered, refocusing on the lock with my magic, looking for any anomalies. A moment later and I found it. Embedded in a hidden crevice within the lock was a small set of complicated runes pressed deeply into the metal. "That's interesting," I murmured.

"What is it?" Bella asked excitedly.

"Runes inside the lock. It's just a guess, but I'd bet my socks that they keep any intruders without the key from opening the door," I said.

"Key! Of course!" Bella said, slamming the heel of her hand against her forehead. With that, she spun and dashed up the basement stairs, taking them two at a time.

As the echo of Bella's footsteps faded upstairs, Isadora and I blinked at each other in surprise.

"Well then," Isadora said.

"I suppose we just wait and see what all the fuss is about," I suggested.

Isadora nodded and turned her attention back to the door. Together, we examined every inch for further clues. I focused on the lock. The fancy brass design seemed familiar, teasing the edges of my memory. Something niggled at the back of my mind, a fleeting whisper of knowledge I couldn't quite grasp. "I've seen that design before…I just can't shake the feeling that I'm missing something," I confessed, my frustration evident.

Isadora glanced at me. "The key in the desk?" she asked.

"No. Something else."

"We'll figure it out," she assured me.

"I hope so. It would be so exciting to rediscover a long-lost town secret don't you think?" I asked.

"Speaking of discovering things, look!" Isadora exclaimed, pointing at the fancy plate surrounding the keyhole and tipping her head to the side. "The swirling pattern there. If you squint, it forms an 'H', don't you think?"

"An 'H' for Hideaway perhaps?" I asked, feeling excitement swell within me.

Bella dashed back down the stairs, holding onto the wooden rail to keep from tumbling headlong into the basement in her haste. The antique key in her hand seemed to shine with possibility.

"I've got it!" Bella crowed, her voice trembling with excitement. She dangled the key in front of us, a victorious grin stretching across her face.

As she stepped toward the door, Isadora jumped forward, hand outstretched. "Here, give it to me. I can't wait to open this door!"

"Hey! I'm the one who remembered the key. And ran up all the stairs to get it," Bella said with mock seriousness, clutching the key to her chest as if we were trying to steal it.

"Shouldn't I get a say? My family probably built this place," Isadora pointed out.

Bella rolled her eyes playfully, but a small smirk tugged at her lips. "Yet it's my family's building," she shot back.

I cleared my throat, stepping between them with a grin tugging at my lips. "Technically, I pieced together all the clues to get us here. Shouldn't I get a shot at opening the door?"

A brief silence passed before we all broke into giggles.

"Okay, okay. You do the honors, Bella," I relented, stepping back and giving her space.

Bella's fingers trembled slightly as she slid the key into the lock. We all leaned in, breath held as if we were on the edge of some grand discovery. Isadora's hand brushed against mine, and I squeezed it without thinking, holding my breath as Bella gave the key a firm twist and—

Nothing.

Bella's fingers tightened around the key as her shoulders slumped, the soft clink of metal breaking the tense quiet. She glanced at me; her earlier excitement dimmed. "I was so sure this would work. They look like they were made to match," she murmured.

Isadora peered over her shoulder. "Not quite. They look similar, but those swirls on the key look like vines. Look. There are little leaves there and there." She pointed at the key head to show what she had noticed. "The design on the lock is more abstract, with a kind of intricate elegance. Similar, but not the same, see? Were there any more keys up in the desk?" she asked.

Bella shook her head, her voice tinged with frustration. "Nothing. But maybe we missed a second key? That desk wasn't exactly tidy, and we got a little overexcited when we rushed down here."

I slumped against the wall, feeling the coolness of the stone through my shirt, the letdown heavy in my chest. How disappointing would it be to find the door and not be able to go through it?

Isadora squared her shoulders, her optimism undimmed. "Let's take another look. I bet there's another key that fits, just waiting to be found in the attic."

An idea sparked in my thoughts, pulling me from the slump of defeat. "The attic," I said, the realization hitting me.

"Yeah, we were just there, remember?" Bella teased. "Old ledgers, giant desk, love letters?"

"No, not yours. Mine! When we were looking for costumes and decorations at Spellbooks, we found that hidden compartment, remember? Inside was a bunch of things, including a set of brass keys. They might just be what we need!" I said, excitedly.

Bella and Isadora turned to me in surprise. "Okay, team," Isadora said, a new energy in her voice. "Let's go on a key hunt."

Bella waved a hand, responsibility and excitement warring in her expression. "Just remember, we've still got a party to pull off," she said, a note of caution in her voice. She looked torn between her desire to continue the century old treasure hunt and the responsibility to uphold her commitments to her parents and the Oasis.

I reached out, giving Bella's arm a reassuring squeeze. "How about we divide and conquer? I'll run back over to Spellbooks and grab the keys. Isa, you could go through the desk again, and Bella, you can keep the party plans on track here."

Relief washed over Bella's features. "Deal. I really don't want to drop the ball on my first major event at the Oasis."

"I'm in. Especially if it means I don't have to go out in the cold again," Isadora said with a shiver.

With our plan set, I turned to leave, the secret door in the basement already feeling less like a daunting obstacle with our newfound direction. A sudden chill sent a shiver down my spine as I hurried up the basement stairs after Bella and Isadora. An odd sense of being followed niggled at me, a whisper of intuition that I was not entirely alone. I glanced over my shoulder, peering into the dimly lit basement. Nothing moved.

"Are you coming?" Isadora asked from the top of the stairs.

The eerie sensation clung to me for a moment, but I shrugged it off. Maybe Isadora's shivers had gotten to me, like yawns that pass from one person to another. I draped my scarf around my neck and tugged up the collar of my coat against the chill. As I stepped outside, a blast of winter wind slapped my face, numbing the tip of my nose and sending a chill racing down my spine. This Connecticut winter was no joke—definitely harsher than what I was used to. Wrapping my scarf tighter, I flipped up my coat collar higher and braced myself against the cold. Luckily, Spellbooks wasn't far, and with it came the promise of unlocking our speakeasy mystery—hopefully just a key turn away.

The Whispering Portrait

My cheeks flushed, my toes tingled with cold, and every breath puffed into the air like little clouds of smoke. Snow drifted lazily to coat the ground in a light dusting as I hurried back down Arcadia Avenue. I glanced toward Finn's shop as I passed, the idea of asking him about the runes nagging at the back of my mind. His expertise might be helpful, but the thought of seeing him right now, especially with everything still so unresolved between us, made me quicken my pace. The last thing I wanted was another awkward conversation. Not today. At least the snowplow had been through recently to allow for cars to traverse the narrow road. Someone had also thoughtfully cleared most of the sidewalks before it started to snow again.

The bell above the door to Spellbooks chimed my arrival, and the door swung closed behind me, cutting off the biting cold that nipped at my heels. The warm, comforting welcome scent of old leather and ink instantly wrapped around me, a stark contrast to the chill outside. I stamped the snow off my boots as Luna's ears popped up from behind the counter. The elder rabbit hopped into view a moment later, an indignant glare on her whiskered face.

"Radish ruckus! I'm glad you came to your senses. I thought you were joking when you said you were leaving me here alone with that mangy furball and the scaled menace upstairs to spend ages party planning," she exclaimed.

"I was, and I am. Party planning that is. I just need to grab something, and then I'm headed straight back over to Bella's."

"By the pink nose of the right honorable Flufferrump, I can't believe it! That brute of a cat has been causing mayhem all day. If he keeps strutting around like he owns the place, I'm going to lose my patience," Luna grumbled, her voice a scratchy blend of annoyance and authority. The rabbit thumped her back foot in frustration.

I chuckled, glancing over at Mr. Wigglesworth sprawled nonchalantly across a stack of books that I'd forgotten to put away at the foot of the comfy armchair. "I see what you mean. It's utter chaos around here," I said dryly.

Luna's glare was unforgiving. "And don't get me started on that dragon upstairs. The nerve!" Her whiskers twitched with each huff, her fur bristling. "How can you expect me to relax in my old age just knowing he's flapping around up there with a potential bonfire in his mouth?"

"First, I doubt anyone in their right mind would call you old," I said reassuringly. "And second, you heard Mason. With his new jewelry, Ignatius is as harmless as a pussy cat."

"So, an absolute terror that never should have been released upon the world?"

"Okay, Luna, keep your whiskers on," I murmured. The grumpy rabbit always had something to say about Mr. Wigglesworth's latest antics and adding Ignatius back into the mix seemed to have antagonized her even more.

"What was that?" Luna demanded.

"Nothing!" I called.

"No. I heard you. You said something about whiskers." She gasped and clapped her front paws to her chubby white cheeks. "That dragon didn't threaten to singe my whiskers off, did he? Oh, cabbage catastrophe! A rabbit without her whiskers might as well be a cat!"

"Cats have whiskers too," I couldn't help but point out.

"Whose side are you on?" Luna harrumphed.

I couldn't let Luna's gripes delay me, not with the mystery of the brass keys and Benny O'Rourke's past waiting to be unraveled. "Don't worry, I'll sort it all out," I promised as I headed upstairs.

I paused at the entrance to my apartment, pressing my palm against the wall. "Everything good in there?" I asked softly to Spellbooks. The wood beneath my hand seemed to warm slightly, a reassuring affirmation that settled my worries. I opened the door, still half-expecting some sign of magical misadventure despite Spellbooks' reassurances. But the only greeting was the normalcy of the place—no smoke, no ash, nothing amiss. A small, grateful smile tugged at my lips.

At first, I couldn't see Ignatius anywhere. The low hum of the audiobook I'd turned on for him when I left provided a cozy background noise to the apartment. Underneath it, I heard a soft, contented snore from the window seat. I tiptoed over to see Ignatius nestled comfortably among the cushions, his snoring a quiet, rhythmic purr that almost matched the cadence of the narrator's voice. I felt a wave of relief wash over me. There wasn't a single scorch mark in sight. It seemed Mason hadn't been exaggerating. Not that I thought he would've risked letting Ignatius visit Spellbooks if he hadn't been sure the dragon could control himself. Still, it was nice to see the evidence of their hard work firsthand. Seeing Ignatius so at peace was reassuring, a confirmation that the careful balance of chaos and control within Spellbooks was being maintained even in my absence.

With a small, pleased smile, I turned my attention to the task at hand. The pile of objects we'd discovered in the hidden compartment was still on my kitchen table. The brass keys seemed to glitter invitingly at me as I scooped them up, the metal cool against my fingers. A larger key, the one with the swirling "H" seemed to stand out. Now that I'd seen the door in Bella's basement with its decorative motif, there was no doubt in my mind that this was the key that opened it. But how did the key to Benny O'Rourke's Hideaway come to be in a secret compartment in Sullivan's Spellbooks? Curiosity nipped at me, but with no answers offered by the mute metal, I pocketed them.

"One mystery at a time," I reminded myself, even as my mind raced with questions, and I headed back towards the door. On a sudden whim, I grabbed the remaining items I'd found hidden away in Spellbooks' attic. The old flask, its surface telling tales of a time when secrecy was paramount, found a place in the deep pockets of my heavy winter coat. The cryptic notebook was next, with its bewildering array of letters and numbers.

As I lifted the notebook, a slip of paper fluttered out, dancing to the floor. I caught it before it touched the ground, staring into the sepia likeness of Benny O'Rourke. A surprise gust of wind, cool and forceful, swirled around me, causing me to stagger back a step. My magic stirred instinctively at the back of my mind, and I pulled on it without thinking, a self-protective reflex. A faint tingle of magic tickled my fingers, and a barely discernible glow rippled across the surface of the photograph.

"Whoa!" I exclaimed, a shiver running down my spine despite my heavy coat and not entirely from the chill. As quickly as it had appeared, the gust was gone, leaving behind only a faint echo of movement in the otherwise still air. "What just happened?" I asked.

Silence greeted my words.

I carefully held the edges of the picture to prevent any more strange, stray gusts from blowing it out of my hands as I studied Benny O'Rourke. The picture captured a young man in the prime of his life, his hair a slicked-back wave typical of the early 1920s. He wore a confident smile, the kind that said he knew all the secret passcodes and handshakes in the world. His eyes were bright and sharp, a clear window to a soul that thrived on the thrill of running both an inn and a hidden speakeasy. Maybe I was just imagining that last part, but there was a certain charisma about him. The effortless charm of someone who could calm a tense situation with a joke or raise the stakes with a dare. Even in the photo, it was clear he was the kind of man who would never let you have a boring night out. Not on his watch.

In the picture, Benny leaned casually against a richly stained wood bar, his arms crossed, a white apron tied neatly at his waist, leaving a crisp, collared shirt and suspenders fully visible. Behind him was an array of bottles, each with a distinctive label. I focused on Benny once more. His attire was impeccably dapper, complete with sleeve garters holding his shirt sleeves in place, and a tie pin that caught the light just right. A faint, knowing smirk hinted that he was well aware of the excitement—and danger—his line of work entailed.

I straightened up, still gripping the photograph, absently moving to tuck it back into the notebook when a strange shimmer rippled over its surface, almost as if the light bent around the image for a split second.

"That was weird," I murmured, peering more intently at the photograph in my hands.

"You're telling me!"

Haunting Runes

I BLINKED, STARING DUMBLY at the picture. Had Benny O'Rourke just...spoken to me? The photo still rested in my hand, unchanged, yet the sound of his voice lingered in the air. My mind whirled as everything that had happened earlier—the chills, the draft, Mason's cryptic comment this morning about spirits and their stories not recorded in history books—all collided. All of it crashed into one startling clear realization. It wasn't the photo that had talked. It was Benny's ghost conversing with me *through* the photo.

I sat down on the nearby kitchen chair. Hard.

My mind raced to keep up with the unbelievable situation that was unfurling before my very eyes. I still clutched the photo in my hand, and I could see the smirk on Benny's pictured face turning into a grin at my stunned silence as his voice resonated from the scrap of paper with a mixture of amusement and bewilderment. "You can hear me, doll? 'Bout time."

I gaped in amazement, too shocked to formulate words, let alone verbalize them. My heart hammered in the sudden silence as the photograph slipped from my fingers and hit the floor. Slowly, I knelt to pick it up, staring at Benny O'Rourke's face. His smirk in the photo seemed a little too smug now, like he knew something I didn't. My stomach twisted.

"Benny?" I whispered, still half-expecting this to be a hallucination.

Benny gave me a little wave and continued. "Sorry to scare you, but I've been trying to get your attention since you sprung me from that joint upstairs. Been giving you the cold shoulder, literally. Knocking books around, making the hairs stand up on the back of your neck—real haunt-like behavior, see?"

My mouth was dry, but I found my voice. "You've...you've been here all along?" I stammered, still half-convinced this was some elaborate ruse.

"Yeah, I've been tailing ya since you popped open my cozy little pad. Wasn't my plan to spend an eternity in the rafters, but a fella's gotta rest his dogs somewhere, right?" His voice was light, but an undercurrent of relief was there, a hint of gratitude for the conversation after being isolated in silence for so long.

"But...how...I mean, when..." I swallowed, forcing myself to formulate an entire sentence. "What is going on?"

His voice sounded clearer now, like he was standing right next to me. "Listen, doll, I don't have all the answers, but I've been feeling the magic weakening for a while. One night, I managed to break free from this picture, thought I was finally making my big escape. But lemme tell you, getting out of that runed-up room? That was a whole different ballgame. Then, out of nowhere, the door opens, and I'm thinking, 'This is it, I'm free!' Only problem? Nobody could hear me. I've been tailing you, hoping somebody would finally notice. But wouldn't you know it, your magic just locked me right back in."

I frowned, confusion creeping in. "What do you mean, 'locked you back in?'"

Benny sighed, the sound weary and resigned. He pointed downward. "Those runes at the bottom of the photo, sweetheart. They've been keeping me bound here since the day I got stuck. At first, I could move around, mess with things a little... but I've been chipping away at 'em for ages. Wearing 'em down. I figured I was making progress—until you showed up and recharged them all."

I stared at the photograph, my fingers trembling as I held it up to the light. The faint shimmer of runes along the bottom edge caught my eye, barely visible, but unmistakably pulsing with renewed energy. My magic.

"Wait, I recharged the runes?" My heart skipped a beat as the realization settled in. "How? I didn't even know I could do that!"

"Beats me, but there ain't a doubt you did," Benny said, almost cheerfully. "Your magic's got a spark, and I haven't had anyone with that kind of power come 'round in a while. Guess when you touched the photo, you gave the runes a nice little boost. And now, well, I'm stuck inside this picture again."

I swallowed hard, trying to process it all. "So, you're trapped?"

"Only until the magic runs out again, but if last time was anything to go by, that could be a while. Or maybe not." He scratched his head and shrugged.

"That's right. You're trapped because of *my* magic," I murmured, the realization settling in. I hadn't even known that was possible, but then again, what I didn't know about runes could fill all the books in Spellbooks.

"Don't beat yourself up, doll. You didn't know." He paused, then added with a wry chuckle, "But I gotta admit, it's been a while since I've had someone to talk to. So, silver linings, right?"

I tried to shake off the shock, grasping for something, anything, to say. "But... how did you...? Why were you in my attic?" I stammered, still piecing it all together. My mind was racing, trying to comprehend how I was actually speaking to a ghost. I wasn't even sure what to ask first. Part of me wanted to demand every single detail about his life, but another part of me was stuck on the fact that history itself was suddenly talking back. It didn't make sense—yet here we were.

Benny's chuckle came out soft and airy, like a distant melody from a speakeasy jazz band. "Dollface, this yarn's more tangled than last year's Charleston contest. I was on top of the world, the bee's knees, then outta nowhere—curtains for Benny. And just like that—zowie—I'm mixing with the spirits, see? Giving the ol' up-and-over to the pearly gates without an invite." The timbre of his voice was like a scratchy record spinning tales from the days of flappers and bootleggers, making my kitchen feel for a moment like a scene straight out of a Fitzgerald novel.

I shook my head, trying to focus on his words. "You don't know what happened to you?" I asked in disbelief. "If you don't mind me asking, that is. I don't know the etiquette in this situation. I've never really talked to a ghost before. Or a picture. At least, not one that talked back. I don't want to offend, but I don't know the proper protocol here. I should warn you, if it requires a curtsey, I never went to finishing school." I could hear myself start to ramble and shut my mouth with a soft click of my teeth.

Benny's voice carried a twinge of somberness as he recounted his spectral struggles. "I don't rightly know. I never saw the coward that done me in. All I knew was I was wiping down the bar and then bam! Lights out! After taking the big sleep, I spent a good while trying to suss out who'd done me in. It ain't easy, coming to grips with being a ghost. Learning the ropes of the afterlife took some time. Years, maybe decades—time gets all mushy when you're dead."

His words hit me like a punch to the gut. A murder. Not just some accident or unexplained mystery, but a murder. My breath caught in my throat as the reality of it sank in. Benny had been killed, and someone had gotten away with it. All this time, this hidden speakeasy, the secrets of Havenwood—they were tied to an unsolved crime. A shiver ran down my spine, but this time it wasn't the cold. It was the undeniable pull of the mystery, the need to uncover the truth.

I leaned in, intrigued. "Okay, but how did you end up in the attic of Sullivan's Spellbooks?"

He seemed to drift a moment, lost in thought. "Ah, is that where we are? I think I remember hearing that name. It's all a bit fuzzy. I was in a real lather, see, getting all walloped in the belfry. This sweet old dame found me throwing a fit in the graveyard, knocking things over whatnot. Can't seem to recall it all now. She calmed me down and said she'd help. Next thing I know, she's leading me back here, to Spellbooks, is it? And then, after that...it's just this photograph and the dark."

Granny Bea's face flashed in my mind. If Benny ended back here in his ghostly form, she had to be the "sweet old dame" he mentioned, didn't she? Assuming that was true, what prompted her to put him to sleep? And why hide him away in the attic? There were more layers to this story, wrapped in Granny Bea's own mysterious ways. If only she were still alive for me to ask her. At this rate, I'd even settle for talking to *her* ghost if that meant I'd get some answers.

"Sounds like you've had a rough time," I said, still processing.

"Yeah, doll, it's been a real bad time. But you've got moxie, see, and together, we might just straighten out this whole kettle of fish," Benny said with a hint of hope. His voice, combined with a charming smile and the charisma that must have made him a standout figure of the speakeasy world, had me nodding before I fully realized what I was doing. It was clear as day, even without seeing him in the flesh, why he was the cat's pajamas back in his heyday.

"Of course, I'll help you if I can. What else can you tell me about...well, about *that* night?" I asked.

I could see Benny was struggling, like he was trying to sift through a foggy memory. Finally, he shook his head, lifting a sepia-colored shoulder in a shrug.

"So you were at the Hideaway, cleaning the bar. Were you there to meet someone?" I pressed gently, hoping to jog something loose.

"Yeah, someone...I think? Maybe? It's hard to remember. It's like trying to grab ahold of the fog, see. It slips right through your fingers," he said, sounding frustrated.

"And after...well... you know. You woke up. You were angry?" I asked, tiptoeing around the subject of his death with care.

"Not right away. Took me a while to realize what'd happened. When I did, I was boiling over, doll. So hopping mad that I could've made the whole graveyard shake, that's what I was. The details are a bit hazy, but I remember tearing the place up," his voice grew distant, like he was back there, in the thick of his spectral rampage.

"What made you so angry?" I tried to keep my voice even. The last thing I wanted to do was enrage Benny's ghost again. If Luna was upset with me for letting Ignatius nap here, I didn't even want to imagine her reaction to finding an irate ghost haunting the shop.

"If I knew that, we wouldn't be having this chinwag," he groaned. "It's like trying to remember a dream after you've had your morning joe."

I nodded, understanding the difficulty. I tried a different tack. "What about the sweet old lady, the one who calmed you down—what did she tell you?"

Benny's tone softened. "Now that dame was the bee's knees. Told me wrecking tombstones wasn't the way to get answers. She promised to help. There was something about her, reminded me of my nan. Felt right to trust her, so I did. She was the only soul I'd spoken to in a year. Or was it a decade? Time's funny for us ghosts. Gets a little fuzzy 'round the edges. Wait. Did I tell you that already?"

I leaned back, trying to piece together the puzzle Benny presented. How did Granny Bea fit into the story? Why put Benny to sleep, and why here, at Spellbooks? How in the world had anyone managed to trap a ghost, especially if he was strong and volatile enough to tear up a graveyard? That thought made me uneasy. As I shifted in the chair, I felt the brass keys jab against my thigh, a pointed reminder of the speakeasy and the history just waiting to be unearthed. I pulled them out, glancing at the largest one with the swirling "H."

"Say, how'd you get your mitts on the keys to my Hideaway?" Benny demanded, with a mix of surprise and a hint of sly intrigue in his tone.

"Is this the one?" I asked, holding up the large brass key. "The one that unlocks the door to the tunnel?"

Benny paused, as if weighing his options, but his hesitation melted away almost as quickly as it came. It was like he'd decided he had nothing to lose by telling me the truth. "That's the one, dollface. The very key to the kingdom, or the Hideaway, at least," Benny confirmed.

He leaned in, his voice dropping just a little, as if sharing a secret. "But the key ain't enough on its own, see? It's got a trick to it. You gotta know how to turn it just right, or it won't budge."

Benny's words echoed in my mind. Without knowing the trick to unlocking the door, we weren't getting into the Hideaway, and I wasn't leaving until I had some answers. I leaned back in the chair, finally shrugging off my heavy winter coat and draping it over the backrest. As I did, the notebook slipped off the table, landing on the floor with a soft thud. I picked it up and flipped through the cryptic pages before holding it up to Benny. "And this? Does this notebook ring any bells? It doesn't make any sense. Any idea what it means?"

He squinted at it, and then a soft smile stole across his handsome face. "That's mine."

"It looks like it's coded," I said.

He nodded. "That's Clara's touch. The code was all her brainstorm. She had me jot down every transaction the Hideaway ever did in a notebook just like that one. 'For our eyes only,' she'd say, with that knockout smile that always left me reeling. She was the heart and soul of the operation, my Clara—sharp as a tack and twice as fast. But tell me, doll, what's the scoop on her? What happened to my gal after I cashed in my chips?"

I hesitated, my heart pinching at the thought of Clara's unknown fate. "I don't have all the pieces, Benny, but I'm putting them together. I think there might be a way for you to help, if you're interested."

There was a pause, a shift in the air as he considered. "Help, huh? Lay it on me."

"The Hearthstone, your old inn? It's called the Enchanted Oasis now, and it's got new life in it."

"That so? Snazzy name. I like it," Benny remarked, a hint of a smile in his voice.

I nodded. "Yeah. And there's a party coming up for New Year's Eve. We really want to make it the talk of the town. When we stumbled upon the story of the Hideaway, and then found the tunnel, we thought it could be amazing to show off a piece of Havenwood's hidden gems during the bash. If we can pull it off, it'll be legendary."

Benny furrowed his brow, confusion wrinkling his spectral forehead. "Hold your horses, toots. Ain't the bulls gonna raid the joint if you're pouring the giggle water?"

"What?" I asked in confusion. I understood the words, but not the meaning. It was like he was speaking in British English slang to the uncultured American girl. A common language separated us, making communication difficult.

"Prohibition, dollface! You can't just go showing my secret Hideaway off to the whole town."

"Oh, Prohibition?" I chuckled. "That's ancient history. We've been legally able to drink again for, well, decades now," I said carefully, not really knowing how to go about telling Benny it had nearly been a century since the end of that era.

He processed this, a flicker of astonishment passing over his face "Decades, huh? If it's been that long, do you really think you can suss out the skinny on Clara?"

At least he wasn't asking me to *find* Clara. I didn't know what I could say to that. As I was, I said, "I'll do my best to track down her story."

Benny paused, his easy smile fading for a moment as his eyes narrowed. "Here's the deal, dollface. You want the Hideaway, I want answers. Find out what happened to me and Clara—who iced me, and why. You scratch my back, and I'll unlock all the secrets of the Hideaway. No answers, no key. Simple as that."

I swallowed, the weight of his words sinking in. This wasn't just about uncovering a hidden speakeasy. It was the kind of discovery that could put the Oasis on the map, give Bella's family a story that would draw people from miles around. A game-changer. But Benny wasn't handing it over without a price.

"Deal," I said, though uncertainty twisted in my gut. The stakes were set, and there was no turning back now.

Benny's grin returned, but there was an edge to it this time, something that made the air feel heavier. "Good to hear, toots. But let me give you a tip—once you start digging, you might not like what you find. You ready for that?" His voice, low and almost a growl, sent a chill up my spine.

It wasn't a question. It was a warning.

The affable bartender act cracked just enough for me to glimpse the man behind it—the one who ran a dangerous speakeasy, and the ghost who had been stuck here for far too long.

I tucked Benny's photo between the pages of the encoded notebook, ensuring the ghost trapped in the runed picture wouldn't accidentally blow away on my walk back to the Oasis. Ignatius was still fast asleep, the faintest puff of smoke escaping in a snore. All was calm when I tiptoed downstairs. Mr. Wigglesworth lay motionless beside the books, with only an occasional twitch of his tail. Luna had vanished, likely off in one of her moods. I could almost hear her tutting at some minor annoyance or another.

As I crossed the room, a spine on the bookshelf caught my eye. It was the codebook, the one Benny mentioned shoving off the shelf to catch my attention. A shiver ran down my spine—not the ghostly kind, but from a sudden realization. Benny had said his ledger, his secrets, were written in code, and this book might hold the key to deciphering them. I snatched it, adding it to my growing arsenal.

Sure, Benny was friendly now. Cooperative even. But I couldn't shake the feeling that wouldn't last forever. The man had once run an illegal speakeasy, after all, and I wasn't naïve enough to trust that he'd keep playing nice if things didn't go his way. Having this codebook felt like a safeguard. A backup plan. Because great detectives always had a trick up their sleeve in case things went south, didn't they?

History's Heartbeat

SILENCE FILLED THE KITCHEN of the Enchanted Oasis. The kind of eerie quiet that usually follows a lightning strike—electric, tinged with awe. There we all were, circled around the kitchen table and away from the prying eyes of the guests, staring at Benny's photo. It was propped up like a shrine to the improbable. Introductions had been awkward but cordial, given the circumstances. Honey and Antonio took turns with an outpouring of questions about the B&B's history. Bella just sat in stunned silence. Isadora seemed skeptical about Benny's ghost status. She appeared half-convinced that Benny was an illusion and kept trying to trip him up with bizarre requests such as sticking his tongue out or grabbing random items in the photo's background, which he performed with good-natured patience.

Finally, she sat back in her chair and narrowed her eyes. "If he really is an illusion, he's the best one I've ever seen, and that's saying something given that I grew up with Gabriel." Her brother was famous in Havenwood for his impeccable magical illusions.

"Talking to an illusion is easier to reconcile than speaking with a ghost?" I asked in confusion.

"Naturally," Isadora said. Even Antonio nodded.

"Of course it's normal. This is Havenwood, after all," Antonio added with a calm certainty.

I blinked, trying to anchor the moment in some kind of logical framework. "Havenwood? *Normal*? You mean the place where your mechanic is best buds with a bunch of ghosts?" My voice rose just slightly, the absurdity still catching me off guard. "I mean, Mason Forham does hang out with ghosts all the time, doesn't he? That's not just a town myth?"

Antonio's smile didn't waver. "Mason's always been a…unique fellow," he said.

Honey, with a shake of her head, cut in. "Talking with ghosts doesn't happen as often as you might think." She tipped her head, adding thoughtfully, "Although strange things do seem to be happening more frequently lately."

"Yeah, ever since Harper moved to town," Bella chimed in, her tone a mix of teasing and affection, as if my presence alone conjured chaos. I could tell she was only half-joking, and, to be honest, I couldn't really argue the point. Since my arrival in Havenwood a few months ago, weird things had been happening. Stranger than usual, even by Havenwood's standards.

Benny's voice from the picture brought us back from our thoughts. "Well, ain't that the cat's pajamas! Seems I bring the party to life, or afterlife, in this case!" His joke, though met with chuckles, didn't quite dissipate the thick sense of wonder that hung in the air.

Isadora eyed the photo again, arms folded, and her lips pursed in skeptical contemplation. "I'm still not convinced," she said. "My brother's pulled off some wild illusion magic before, so you'll have to forgive me if I'm a little cautious." She flicked her pink hair out of her eyes, still watching Benny closely.

"I'm not an illusion," Benny repeated, sounding a bit annoyed.

She raised an eyebrow. "Which is exactly what any competent illusion would say. Still, I must admit, this is the best one I've ever seen."

I leaned back in my chair, the corners of my mouth twitching upward. "Well, there's one surefire way to test whether Benny is a ghost or an illusion," I suggested. "If he can show us how to get into the tunnel, that would settle it, right?

Bella pointed at me in agreement. "She's got a point. No illusion could accurately tell us how to open a magically locked door that's a hundred years old."

"A hundred years!" Benny exclaimed, his face freezing for a split second before a forced laugh broke the silence. "You're pulling my leg, right? Ain't no way I've been gone that long. I was just running the joint not too long ago." His voice had a nervous edge, but his eyes darted around as if trying to place himself in time.

I shot Bella a quick look, silently willing her to stop talking, but the damage was done. Benny's smirk flickered and faded. The runes around the photo glowed brighter. The air around him rippled, not with his usual cool charm, but with uncertainty.

"Nah," he muttered, shaking his head as if to clear the thought. "It can't have been a hundred years. That's crazy talk." But his voice wavered, the bravado cracking.

The runes brightened further, and I held my breath, wondering if we were about to witness an outburst. But then Benny's shoulders slumped, his hands resting on the bar in the photo. His eyes clouded with something I hadn't seen before—disbelief mixed with fear.

"Guess time doesn't wait for nobody," he said quietly, more to himself than to us. His usual charm was gone, replaced by a hollow look that made my stomach twist.

I kept my voice steady as I replied, "It doesn't. But we can still figure this out together."

As the runes dimmed, I made a mental note to tread carefully. Benny was teetering on the edge, and the last thing I needed was for his mood to shift in a more dangerous direction.

Isadora pursed her lips and gave a curt nod. "Alright, ghost or not, we've come too far to just give up now. Let's go see if we can open that door."

Bella led the way down the steep basement stairs, the rest of us following close behind, with me carefully holding the photograph so Benny could see our progress. I handed Bella the key with the swirling "H," but just as she moved to insert it, Benny's voice cut through the quiet, sharper than before.

"Hold up, dollface," he said, his tone tight. "This ain't just about opening a door. You find out what happened to me and Clara, like you promised." His voice hardened, the frustration of decades creeping through. "Don't even think about welching on the deal, you hear me?"

A chill ran up my spine, my grip on the photograph tightening. I swallowed hard. He didn't have to remind me—I'd already made the promise, and I wasn't about to break it.

I nodded solemnly, holding his gaze. "You have my word. I'll do whatever I can to figure out what happened to you and Clara."

Benny seemed to study me through the photo for a long moment before letting out a slow breath. "Alright then," he said, calmer now. "Let's get this thing open."

He gave Bella precise instructions on how to turn the key—more complicated than I'd imagined. Another layer of protection. We all held our breath as she twisted the key back and forth, following Benny's careful directions. The grating of metal against metal echoed in the cool basement, making the tension nearly unbearable. Finally, after what felt like an eternity, a loud, satisfying click echoed through the room, and with a push, the door creaked open, revealing the gaping entrance to a dark tunnel.

"We found it!" Bella exclaimed.

"There's really a tunnel?!?" Honey gasped.

"I wonder what's inside!" Antonio said, peering excitedly into the dark maw of the tunnel's mouth.

"He really is a ghost," Isadora said at the same time, looking away from the tunnel and back at the picture I held in my hands.

Benny's voice floated from the photo, a touch of pride lacing his words. "Now, for the grand tour," he said. "Watch closely."

He instructed us how to activate the runes that adorned the walls of the tunnel. Bella crouched slightly and reached out a tentative hand, brushing away cobwebs as Isadora held up her phone, using it as a flashlight. Following Benny's instructions, she touched the appropriate runes. A moment later, a warm amber glow emanated from the etchings, illuminating our path with a soft, otherworldly light.

"Da's idea. He didn't want to use a hand for a candle if he needed to deal with the animals or carry feed," Benny explained. "But brightening the whole tunnel? That was my Clara's touch—with a little help from me, of course."

"She runed the whole tunnel?" I asked in awe as I followed Bella through the door, ducking a little so as not to bump my head on the low ceiling.

Benny's voice echoed in the tunnel, carrying that nostalgic tone. "Nah, see, Clara's old man, Clarence Silverthorne, threw up the first bit of razzle-dazzle with my pop, right after the big snow blow of '88. But my Clara? She didn't start out messing with the rune business. Nah, the dame was sharp though. She picked up her old man's tricks real quick, and with a little study, jazzed 'em up better than he ever could. By the time we got around to fixing the Hideaway, she was cooking with gas, outshining her old man's work in nearly every way. Her magic? That's what made this joint the cat's pajamas, no two ways about it."

He paused for a moment, and his tone shifted slightly. "But there was something else Clara figured out early on. This place—the Hideaway—it's got some kinda natural magic to it, y'know? Like the ground itself has a pulse, humming with energy. Clara used to say there were spots in Havenwood that were stronger, like they had a mind of their own, just boosting whatever magic you threw at 'em. It's why we never needed much to keep the runes going. The place always had a way of juicing 'em up, like it was built on something special. Clara understood that better than I ever could. I wasn't no good with magic, but she was sharp. She worked with what was already here, knew how to tap into it. Smart dame, my Clara."

As we ventured through the tunnel single file, its walls seemed to whisper with hushed secrets. The sturdy stone, shaped and set in the late 1800s, bore the marks of practicality, widened and reinforced in places, likely around the time of the roaring '20s, for the transport of more than just livestock feed. Magic runes, dormant for decades, now thrummed with an energy that brushed the air like velvet, casting amber hues that danced across the surface of each stone, awakening the corridor to its former glory. Except for the gentle hum of magic, the air was cool and still, making the space seem less like a relic and more like a passageway frozen in time, shielded from decay by the same spells that now glowed softly in the narrow space.

At the end of the tunnel, another stout door barred our way, its wood darkened with age but unmarred by rot, the brass fixtures gleaming dully in the rune light. Benny described the correct key to Bella, who was in the lead. It was the key we'd found in the desk which she'd prudently brought with her. She inserted it into the lock, her hand steady. A series of turns following Benny's instructions, a pause, and then the telltale click before the door swung open, revealing the Hideaway for the first time in nearly a century.

Stepping across the threshold was like being initiated into a secret society. Benny showed us how to activate the illumination runes, and my breath caught in my throat as I took it all in. The paneled walls were painted a deep forest green and lined with oak wainscoting that met a low ceiling, giving the space a cozy rather than cramped feel. The floor, a checkered pattern of black-and-white tiles, had only the faintest layer of dust, a testament to the magic preserving the space and holding back the worst of time's effects.

Bella stepped forward cautiously, her eyes wide, taking in the room. "This is incredible," she whispered, as if speaking too loudly might disturb the delicate balance of magic and time.

I spun around slowly, trying to take everything in. The bar, a handsome affair of polished mahogany, now covered in a layer of dust, still bore glasses upside down over a drying rack, each waiting for a pour that would never come. On either side of a dusty mirror, two modest shelves displayed a sparse collection of bottles, their labels faded and peeling, yet the liquid inside gleamed untouched. Every so often, an amber glow from the runes hidden along the edges of the bar flickered to life, casting a soft glimmer that hinted at the protective enchantments still clinging to the place.

Isadora, unable to resist, brushed her hand along one of the glowing runes, her face lighting up with curiosity. "Look at this place!" she whispered, her voice filled with wonder.

The furniture—round tables and velvet-cushioned chairs—was sparse but functional, the dark upholstery only slightly worn beneath a thin veil of neglect. Scratches and dents marred their surfaces, signs of use long ago.

Honey ran her fingers over the velvet of one chair, her voice soft and wistful. "Imagine the stories this place could tell," she murmured.

Antonio examined the bar, tracing a finger over the smooth wood. "I can't believe this place is still standing after all this time," he said, a mix of admiration and excitement in his voice. "And in such good condition!" He ran a hand along the bar's edge, clearly eager to explore the craftsmanship.

I drifted to the far corner where a piano sat silent, its keys hidden beneath a heavy cover, waiting for the touch of a pianist's hand to spring back to life. The soft echoes of long-forgotten jazz seemed to reverberate faintly through the air as if conjured by the room's aura.

As we all stood within the long-abandoned speakeasy, the air seemed to hum with echoes of raucous nights past. It wasn't hard to imagine the Hideaway as a monument to the rebellion against the dry dictates of Prohibition—a hush-hush haven where spirits soared as freely as the booze flowed.

"It was Clara's idea, really," Benny's voice drifting up from the photo I held, drawing our attention. "She's the one who planned it all out from the tunnel to the secret escape behind the paneling in case the coppers caught wind of what we were doing. The night we opened, it was the berries! Clara was the belle of the ball. The dame who could turn any frown upside down with just a glance. I knew then that she'd been born for this, not the repressive life her father had planned for her. She was the fizz in the gin, the life of the party."

Bella, with a sparkle of excitement in her eyes, asked, "What was the opening night like?"

Benny's voice carried the warmth of the memory. "Like it came straight outta a picture show. Clara wore a gown that shimmered like the night sky, and when she smiled, it was as if the stars themselves had settled in our little nook of joy to reflect her radiance. We were rebels with a cause, and that cause was to keep the spirit of freedom alive and well. Living the high life and defying those dry laws."

Isadora, leaning against a bar stool, chimed in with a curious tilt of her head. "And the patrons? What were they like?"

"Eclectic, electric, effervescent," Benny said. "Actors, flappers, writers, and those who just wanted a break from the everyday humdrum. This place," he paused, the sentiment thick in his ethereal tone, "it wasn't just an escape, doll. It was our hidden cabaret, a secret shared in whispers and sealed with a wink. A canvas, and every night was a masterpiece painted with laughter, dance, and a dash of devilry."

"And the runes...they protected all of this?" I asked, motioning to the glowing symbols still lighting the Hideaway.

"Like I said, they were old man Silverthorne's doing. At least the ones in the tunnel. But my dame had moxie. Once Clara worked them out, it was her who made them sing. She had a way with magic that was pure artistry. The runes weren't just protection though—they were part of the show, a spectacle that started the moment someone stepped into that tunnel. You knew, down to your bones, that this place was going to be special the second you set foot in the tunnel."

My curiosity piqued as I glanced at the covered piano in the corner. "Was there music here? Did Clara play?"

Benny laughed, a sound that seemed to dust off the weight of the decades. "Did she ever! Sure, we had a pianist, but sometimes, on a quiet night, she'd sit there, tickling the ivories, and the entire world seemed to hold its breath. As far as I was concerned, she was the heart of the Hideaway. She turned simple drinks into potions, conversations into confessions, and evenings into legends."

"She sounds like a special lady," I observed.

His smile turned wistful. "She was the cat's meow," Benny confirmed, his voice softening. "My job was to run the place and find the finest giggle water this side of the Atlantic. But Clara? She *made* this place. Her flair for the dramatic found its way into the Hideaway's very bones. She added her own touches—a swing band on Saturdays, tapping into the magical hotspots for some swinging good times, and those rugs...oh, those rugs from faraway lands, where your feet sank into them like they were clouds. But her masterpiece? Those runed keys. They kept our haven locked tight, just us and the revelers, no busybodies allowed. She and I had the only copies. No one else could get in without our say-so. Not even her stick-up-the-arse father or his cop buddies."

I glanced at Benny's photo, his voice still carrying that nostalgic warmth. "Her father," I started cautiously, "he didn't approve of this place, did he? You think maybe he knew what was going on? Or worse—maybe he had something to do with what happened to you?"

Benny's image flickered slightly, a shift in the photograph like a momentary static charge. The amber light from the runes dimmed, and his tone hardened. "Watch your step, dollface. Clara's old man was a stiff, but no killer."

I pressed, my mind racing with the possibilities. "But if he didn't like you two together—maybe he concocted a plan to get you out of the way?"

The runes along the walls flared, as if reacting to Benny's growing agitation. His voice came back, lower, more dangerous this time. "Don't push it, sweetheart. He wouldn't have done nothing. But those cop buddies of his? I wouldn't put it past one of them."

I leapt at the idea. "Well, maybe one of the cops had it out for you. Perhaps they didn't like the idea of a speakeasy in Havenwood?"

Benny's image flickered, but this time, his voice didn't hold that nostalgic warmth. "Yeah, those flatfoots were always sniffing around. But they couldn't touch us, not with Clara in the mix. Not without proof and lots of it. Besides, they couldn't find a way in. There were only two ways in or outta the Hideaway, and as far as I knew, both were kept secret. Tight. Ain't no way they stumbled on this joint without help."

My breath caught in my chest. "So there *was* a beef with the cops then? What kind of trouble were you—"

Before I could finish, the runes along the walls flared brighter, and Benny's voice grew darker, more ragged, almost like a storm brewing in the photograph. "Beef? You could say that. But those mugs couldn't touch me. Not a chance. I had them locked out tight. Only Clara and I had the keys. No one could get in without us knowing. No one."

My pulse quickened, and I asked. "But what if someone found out? What if—"

The photograph in my hand seemed to pulse with energy, and Benny's voice came out in a harsh growl. "Watch your mouth, doll! You're talking like I didn't know how to run a tight operation. No cop got in here, ya hear me? Not unless me or Clara showed 'em the tunnels, and we'd never do that, ya hear?"

The tunnel walls seemed to hum with the rising tension, the runes glowing fiercely. I could feel Benny slipping, losing his grip. Antonio must have sensed it too, because he quickly cut in, voice calm but curious. "Tunnels? Plural? There's a second way in, huh? Now that's interesting, Benny. You said there were two ways in or out. What was the other one?"

The sudden shift in the conversation made Benny pause, his anger cooling, but the photograph still held a faint glow. He hesitated, then answered, almost begrudgingly. "The other way wasn't for just anybody. Clara and I set it up as a backup, a way to disappear if things got too hot."

Antonio's eyes sparkled in the light from the runes. "I'd love to see it. This whole place is fascinating. I can't wait to study the construction more. You really had an amazing thing going, didn't you?"

The photograph flickered once more, the light dimming as Benny's voice softened again, his temper reined in. "Ah, this place has heard more secrets than a priest in a confessional, and it would only be right to share that one with you now given that you own the Hearthstone—sorry, the Oasis."

Antonio smiled broadly, rubbing his hands together. "I can't believe it. A real speakeasy with a real escape hatch. Right under our feet all these years!"

Benny's chuckle reverberated through the photo in my hand, and I relaxed slightly although my heart still raced from the tension. Antonio had bought us some time, but it was clear that pushing too hard would only make Benny more volatile. We'd have to be careful from here on out, especially when it came to prying into the darker corners of his past.

Benny spoke to Antonio. "That was one of the Hideaway's best-kept secrets. Back then, you see, a speakeasy wasn't worth its salt without a slick exit strategy. Clara wanted our joint to be the cat's pajamas with a backdoor, just in case the bulls came a-knocking."

"She designed it herself?" I asked, surprised.

"Indeed, she did. Clara had a real knack for secret chambers and who-dunits. See, she got the idea from this old dumbwaiter system that used to connect to the barn up top," Benny began, his tone matter-of-fact. "Back in the day, it was used to haul feed or supplies up and down without break-ing your back. Once we built the Hideaway, me and Clara sealed it off, though—didn't want anyone sneaking in that way. Too risky, with folks poking around the barn. We figured if someone wanted in bad enough, they'd come through the front like everyone else."

Isadora traced the edge of the bar, her fingers brushing over the dust-coated surface. "So you blocked off the dumbwaiter?"

"Tighter than a drum," Benny confirmed, his voice carrying a hint of pride. "We wanted complete control. Just two ways in or out. We weren't taking any chances with Johnny Law sniffing around."

Bella looked around the bar skeptically. "Where's this escape tunnel? I don't see anything that looks like a hidden door."

Benny's voice lightened with a hint of nostalgia. "Ah, now that was Clara's stroke of genius. She had a real flair for keeping things under wraps. Those nifty cubbies behind the bar for the regulars' bottles? That was all her, too. Each one locked up with brass locks that only the ones that owned it, or Clara and I, could crack open." He paused for a beat, then added, "Right. The escape tunnel. Go on, look under the bar. You'll find a brass lever. Give it a pull."

Antonio reached under the bar, his hand gripping the sturdy wood for balance. After a moment, he ducked low and scouted beneath it. "Found something!" he announced.

With a faint click, a rectangular section of the paneled wainscoting next to the bar popped ajar. Together, we tugged it open, revealing a narrow, darkened passageway hidden behind the panel.

Benny's voice swelled with pride. "Clara wanted a joint where folks could feel snug but vanish in a second if Johnny Law came knocking. That hidden tunnel's the cat's pajamas, ain't it?"

The escape tunnel was nothing like the rune-lit entrance we had come through. It was stark, utilitarian, with walls roughly cut from the earth and held together by timber beams. The passage was narrow enough that I could easily touch both sides without stretching, and we all had to crouch slightly to fit, though not so low as to crawl. Antonio, with his broader shoulder span, nearly had to turn sideways just to maneuver through the gap. The floor beneath us was packed dirt, rough and uneven, with a musty scent of long-buried secrets hanging in the air.

Honey called out, her tone slightly apprehensive. "It might be better if someone stays behind, you know? Just in case."

Antonio gave a nod, stepping further into the tunnel as the rest of us lingered in the Hideaway. "I'll take a quick look," he offered. "If anything's off, I'll let you know."

"This is incredible," I whispered, half to myself.

Isadora spoke up. "This is like something out of a movie. Did anyone ever have to use the tunnel to escape, Benny?"

Benny's voice grew soft and serious. "We thought we'd have to here and there, but the coppers never found this place. Me and Clara ran a tight ship."

While Antonio cautiously ventured ahead, I glanced down at the floor, and something caught my eye. Two distinct tracks, half-obscured but unmistakable, ran parallel to each other. One set was smaller, with a pointed toe—likely from a woman's shoe—and the other was slightly larger and square toed. A brief smile tugged at my lips as I realized how much smaller people's feet were back then, especially compared to my own. Suddenly, something struck me as odd about their placement.

"Benny," I said, pointing down at the ground and twisting the photo so he could see. "There are tracks going the wrong way. They're leading from the tunnel into the Hideaway."

"That's strange. Although, there was a time or two Clara would slip in through the escape tunnel to avoid her da's watchful gaze."

Before I could give voice to my curiosity and ask any more questions, Antonio reappeared, his broad shoulders brushing the walls as he backed out of the tunnel. "Everything looks secure as far as I can tell," he reported. "But it's tight in there. No way more than one person can get through comfortably at a time."

Bella glanced around, hands on her hips. "Well, it's not going to collapse on us, is it?"

Antonio shook his head with a confident grin. "I don't think so. The tunnel's solid, and if it's lasted this long, I'd say we're safe for now. I'd like to get a professional out to look at it though. Just to be sure the construction has held up over the years."

Benny chimed in, his voice sounding almost proud. "It ain't just good construction. Remember, this place sits on a magical hotspot. The magic in the runes will keep this joint standing stronger than any concrete could."

Honey glanced at her wristwatch and gasped. "Gracious, look at the time!" she exclaimed. "I hadn't realized we'd been gone so long. Antonio! We have guests coming in less than an hour, and their room isn't ready yet!"

Antonio wiped his hands on his jeans. "I hate to leave, but we can't have the McCarthys thinking the Oasis isn't a top-notch place." His voice echoed slightly as he turned to follow his wife out of the warmth of the Hideaway's embrace.

Bella stood as well. "Do you need some help?" she asked.

Honey waved away her offer. "We'll be just fine. You stay here and explore with your friends. Supper will be ready in a couple of hours. Is everyone okay with spaghetti and meatballs?"

Isadora and I answered in the affirmative.

Antonio turned and winked at us. "Have fun and let us know what you discover," he said before following Honey back down the tunnel leading to the Oasis.

As soon as they were gone, Bella turned to Isadora and me, eyes gleaming with excitement. "Now, where do we start?"

Ghosts of Doubt

I'm not sure how long we were down in the Hideaway. Without daylight penetrating the underground speakeasy, time became a nebulous thing as we explored, with Benny pointing out some of the more unique features that he was especially proud of.

He pointed out the carved mahogany bar, the centerpiece of many raucous nights. My gaze fell on a dent and crack along the bar's edge, like something hard had struck it. I remembered the note from the book speculating on Benny's death—whether it had been an accident or a crime. Could this be where Benny hit his head? The damage didn't prove anything, but it seemed worth noting. Of course, the dent could have been caused by any number of things over the years. Still, I filed the possible clue away for later, just in case.

Behind the bar, there were a series of locked cabinets, still boasting tarnish-free brass locks. Benny explained that patrons of the Hideaway could purchase a bottle of their favorite booze and stash it in their locked cubby for their own personal consumption. I glanced around. The entire bar seemed to pulse with secrets, as if trust and suspicion had once intertwined in every corner. The silence now felt eerie compared to the lively jazz and laughter that must have filled the room in its heyday, a stark contrast that left me wondering just how many hidden stories were left untold.

Benny's voice grew more animated, cutting through our quiet exploration. "Hey, doll, take a look over there," he directed. His eyes seemed to light up—which was remarkable for a ghost in a photo—as he guided our gaze to a corner where a roulette wheel once spun fortunes. He chuckled, recounting stories of high rollers and lucky streaks. "And over there," he said with a wistful tone, "is where we kept the good stuff—top-shelf hooch that could make a bishop kick a hole in a stained-glass window."

Benny paused, letting the memories of the Hideaway wash over him once more. In the stillness, we perched at the bar on worn, high stools, their wood polished smooth by time and use. I propped Benny's photograph against a forgotten glass, his gaze fixed on the scene before him, as though reliving every moment he had spent in this place. The weight of untold stories hung in the air until Benny finally broke the silence.

"I showed you the Hideaway like I promised. Now, what say you keep your word to me?" he asked, pointing seriously in my direction. The runes at the bottom of the photo glowed a little brighter.

Bella's eyes flicked up to meet mine. "What's he talking about?" she asked.

"I told him I'd do my best to find out what happened to him," I explained.

Benny's voice had a hopeful note as it came from the photograph. "And don't forget Clara. We need to know about her too. It's been eating at me, not knowing."

"That should be easy enough," Isadora said, whipping out her phone, her thumbs poised to conduct a digital séance to summon the past. "Oh wait, I don't have a signal down here," she said, frowning at the screen, her frustration clear as she tried waving her phone in the air as if to catch a stray whisper of Wi-Fi from the world above.

"What is that thing?" Benny asked, leaning forward curiously.

"It's a cell phone," I explained. He looked confused, so I tried to explain in words he might understand. "Think of it like a telegraph, a talking phone, a cinema, and a newspaper all rolled into one handy package."

Benny let out a little whistle. "Whooee. Times sure have changed since I was around."

Isadora continued to wave her phone around. "I really can't get even the faintest signal. You know what? Let me just run upstairs. I'll do a quick Google search. Failing that, I'll try giving my mother a call to see if she knows anything about an ancestor named Clara. I bet I have answers faster than you can say your own name."

"Benjamin Sean O'Rourke," the ghost in the picture said promptly.

Isadora rolled her eyes. "You know what I meant. I'll be right back." With that, she hurried down the tunnel.

Silence settled back over the Hideaway as the echoes of her footsteps faded. A thought occurred to me. This could be the perfect opportunity to get Benny to tell his side of the story. Maybe there was a clue in his version the police back then had never discovered because he was, well, a ghost. I took a deep breath, reminding myself to approach the matter of his death as tactfully as possible.

I cleared my throat. "I know you're worried about what happened to Clara, but what about you? From what I read, your death is still an unsolved mystery."

"As much to me as it is to you, dollface," Benny said with a shrug, but this time, his voice cracked, betraying the emotions simmering beneath the surface.

I quickly opened my phone's note app, jotting down a few key points. "Maybe if you can tell us what you remember, we can figure out something that got overlooked which will point us in the direction of whoever was behind what happened to you."

Bella jumped in, obviously interpreting what I was trying to do and helping me in the hopes of unearthing a clue. "Yeah. Maybe someone was jealous of your success. What about rivalries? Did anyone hold a grudge against you?" she asked.

The photo of Benny seemed to darken, his eyes reflecting a past riddled with tension. "Oh, I had rivals aplenty," his voice emerged from the picture, laced with a tinge of bitterness. "There were a couple of big shots who would've given their eyeteeth to claim the Hearthstone. And the coppers," he scoffed, "they kept sniffing around, trying to find the Hideaway, but Clara and I were always a step ahead. As for Old Man Silverthorne, that fella didn't take kindly to his daughter consorting with an Irish upstart like me. And let's not speak of the stuffed shirts and the town elders. I reckon there were more than a few in Havenwood who'd have liked to see me disappear."

I exhaled slowly, feeling the weight of the long list of potential suspects press down on my hopes for a quick solution to the cold case. I tapped on my phone, jotting down what Benny had said. A suspect list was starting to form in my mind. Rival business owners, disgruntled customers, the coppers Benny had mentioned, or maybe even Clara's father. The list seemed to stretch on forever, and I hesitated, my thumb hovering over the screen as doubt gnawed at me. Too many suspects, too many motives. Where did I even start?

"That's...a lot to consider," Bella said as I tapped on my phone.

"Do you have any gut instinct on who might've been behind it? A business rival? Someone who wanted Clara? One of those, um, stuffed shirts?" I asked.

"Maybe," Benny admitted. "But I don't know who might've had a big enough grudge to kill me."

"It's like piecing together a puzzle with half the pieces missing," Bella murmured, her eyes narrowing in thought.

I nodded, feeling the dense shroud of mystery enveloping us. "Yeah, every suspect seems viable, but without more information, it's all just hypothetical. Like we're just chasing ghosts—no offense, Benny."

"None taken," the ghost said with a charming smile and a little twitch of his shoulders. "I just appreciate you trying to help me make sense of everything that happened."

"Speaking of that, we need details, Benny," I urged. "Can you walk us through what happened that night you...well, when it all ended for you?"

Benny's image frowned deeply, as if disturbed by the memory. "I'd left a deck of cards down here and one of the guests at the Hearthstone wanted to pass the time, so I said I'd run fetch it. I let myself in, grabbed the deck, but then something caught my eye behind the bar. There were some bottles out. I thought I'd cleaned up everything the night before, but I must've missed a few. I went back there, to put 'em all away and wipe down the bar again. That's when I heard the footsteps—stealthy, like they were trying to be quiet. I only got halfway turned before the lights went out for good," his voice grew distant.

"That's not much to go on. What did you see? Anything unusual before...you know?" I pressed, trying to dig deeper.

Benny's face scrunched up as he tried to concentrate, and the edges of the photo shimmered slightly in the glow from the illumination runes. "Blurry...it's all so...blurry...but there was something."

I leaned forward eagerly. "What was it?"

"Clara and I—we kept a master set of keys tucked behind that vase. For the Hideaway, for the cabinets, for everything in this place, just in case. We couldn't just let any Tom, Dick, or Harry stash whatever without some oversight. I think...I thought I was onto something shady. I remember seeing...something..." He trailed off, his eyes going distant.

"What did you see?" I asked softly.

He shook his head and looked up at us. "Something around the bar, I think. I can't remember exactly. Then nothing but sharp pain on the back of my head, a second thump on my noggin, and a darkness that never went away."

"I'm sorry," I murmured.

"Me too," Bella echoed.

"What's done is done. Not much we can do about it now anyway except find out who was behind it all," Benny said with a shrug.

I paused, feeling awkward about pressing Benny for more details. However, if he wanted answers, this was the only way. I cleared my throat again. "I'm sorry to ask, but do you remember anything else? A sound? A smell maybe? Perhaps you caught a glimpse of your attacker when you turned? Any little detail might be the clue we need to solve the case."

Benny's gaze went distant, and a heartbeat of silence filled the room as he tried to remember. Finally, he shook his head. "I don't think so, doll. At least, I can't remember nothing like that."

The hope that had been rising within me deflated like a balloon. "Oh. Well. That's okay," I muttered, but frustration gnawed at me. There was something we were missing, something key—literally. Then it hit me.

I sat up straighter, my heart racing. "Wait, Benny—you said you and Clara had the only two sets of keys to the Hideaway, right?"

The runes below Benny's image flickered. "Yeah, that's right. Nobody else had access to the Hideaway. Just us and the regulars when we let 'em in."

"But you also mentioned a backup set of keys kept here in the Hideaway, didn't you?" I asked, my voice rising with urgency.

Benny paused, then nodded slowly. "Yeah, we kept a spare set, just in case.

Bella crossed her arms, a small frown on her face. "And you're sure no one ever tried? To get the keys I mean. Maybe to sneak into the Hideaway after hours?"

"No...no, I don't think..." Benny trailed off.

"Are you sure?" Bella pressed. "No regulars with sticky fingers? No trouble?"

Benny seemed to bristle at that, his voice growing defensive. "I ran a tight ship, toots. No one was getting near those keys without me noticing."

I leaned forward, trying to stay calm, knowing I needed to push just a bit harder. "Benny, think. Was there ever a time, right before you died, when something happened? Something that made you step out from behind the bar for a couple of minutes?"

For a moment, the photo remained silent, Benny's expression growing distant. I glanced at Bella, who raised an eyebrow, urging me to keep going.

I took a deep breath. "I know it's hard, but was there anything unusual that happened? Anything that could've given someone a chance to get their hands on those keys?"

Benny's image flickered again, and this time he seemed almost...unsettled. "There was a ruckus the night before," he muttered. "A couple of fellas had too much giggle water, started roughhousing by the piano. They crashed into Clara, almost knocking her over. I had to step in, toss 'em out on their ears."

Bella straightened up. "Could someone have used the fight as a cover?"

Benny let out a slow sigh, his voice low and uncertain. "I thought it was just a couple of clowns going at it, but... now that you mention it... there was a lot of shoving, a lot of movement. It was chaos for a minute. Someone could've made their way behind the bar while I was dealing with those mugs."

I nodded, my heart rate picking up. "And the extra keys? Did you check for them after the fight?"

Benny was silent for a moment, then his voice came back, softer now. "No. Didn't think I needed to. Figured everything was in its place, like always. But now..." His voice trailed off, and the runes at the bottom the photo flickered again. "Maybe someone swiped 'em. And I didn't even notice. How could I not have remembered?"

I felt a flicker of excitement as I latched on to what felt like a solid lead. "Let's look for them. If they're missing, maybe that's how the perpetrator entered the Hideaway."

"But how would they know the secret way to turn the key?" Bella asked.

I shrugged. "I'm not sure, but if they are missing, that gives us a clue, don't you think?"

Bella didn't look convinced but joined in the search as Benny directed us where to look. When the original hiding place for the spare keys was empty, we quickly searched the rest of the bar in case they'd been moved. My hands skimmed over surfaces and checked obvious spots, but the shadows and time-worn corners of the Hideaway felt like they were working against me.

The more we searched, the heavier my chest felt. Every empty corner and fruitless glance sent frustration curling through me, but it wasn't just that—it was the overwhelming sense of history here, of loss.

After a while, I stepped back and exhaled. "Nothing. There's no sign of them."

"They were here," he said, more to himself than to me.

Benny didn't say anything else for a long moment, his face clouding with frustration. "It's all a blur. I should know, but I just... don't." His voice wavered, unsure and full of regret, and I couldn't help but feel a pang of guilt for not finding anything that might help him.

"Do you remember anything else?" I asked, glancing around. The room seemed impossibly large now, full of potential places where the keys could be—or had been.

"Yeah," Bella added. "Maybe something else will come back to you now that you're back in the Hideaway," she said gently, trying to lift the tension.

I nodded in agreement, setting Benny's photograph down near the dented section of the bar, hoping for a spark of memory. Nothing.

We tried a few other spots—the piano, the roulette wheel—but no matter where we placed him, Benny's image stayed still, his voice quiet.

Bella sighed. "Well, it was worth a shot."

The photograph flickered briefly, and Benny's voice came back, low and soft. "Don't sweat it, doll. Some things just don't come back so easy."

"Keep trying," Bella encouraged. "There might be something here that jogs a memory for you."

Benny glanced over at Bella, a small grateful smile twisting his lips. His gaze shifted to the ring of keys Bella left on the bar, a spark of recognition igniting in his eyes. "Where'd you get those, doll? Those keys are Clara's. The keys to the kingdom, so to speak."

"Are they for these cabinets behind the bar?" Bella asked, picking up the photograph so he could see where she was looking.

"Exactly," Benny confirmed with a nod that seemed to make the photo ripple.

"I have an idea," I said as I beckoned for Bella to hand the keys over. She did with a confused look on her face. I jumped off my stool and went to the row of cabinets that stood like silent sentinels behind the bar. "Maybe the answer's been waiting here all along," I murmured, looking at the locked cabinets.

Bella was beside me in an instant. "You think there might be a clue in one of the cabinets?" she asked in disbelief.

"Only one way to find out," I said, twisting the first key in the lock of the nearest cabinet.

We worked through the cabinets systematically, the tension ratcheting higher with each turn of the key. Some yielded treasures from a time long past—bottles with labels that whispered of a forbidden era. But others were empty, gaping voids that seemed to be filled with more questions than answers. I snapped photographs of every cubby before carrying each item to the bar, using an old bar rag to lift them and make sure I didn't leave any fingerprints behind. Eventually, we opened all that we could find and lined the fruits of our labor up on the bar. A dusty row of half empty liquor bottles was the sum total of our efforts.

Benny's spectral chuckle was dry, almost hollow. "Ran a tight ship, didn't we? Like I said, we only kept booze for our best clients. Nothing amiss here. Not for a speakeasy at least."

"But why wouldn't someone take all the alcohol?" Bella asked. "Wouldn't that have been worth a lot of money back in the day?"

"It'd be awfully hard to move," Benny said. "Lots of trips. Hard to do that without drawing attention."

"Whoever it was obviously wasn't interested in the liquor," I mused. A darker thought occurred to me. "Maybe they wanted something else. Maybe whoever was responsible cleared out the evidence after they...after they dealt with Benny," I suggested. "Maybe we can figure out who the empty cabinets belong to and see if any of those people held a grudge."

"We kept all that in our coded books, but I don't know where those got to after my death," Benny said.

"With no evidence, it circles back to motive," Bella concluded. "Who had the most to gain from silencing you?"

"It could have been a rival bootlegger," I suggested. "Jealousy and the pursuit of money makes people do crazy things."

Benny was quiet for a moment, his ghostly image flickering slightly. "Rival bootlegger? Sure, we had competition, no doubt. But none of 'em had the guts to make a play like that. We were good at what we did, too good. Ain't nobody dumb enough to come at us head-on."

Bella nodded, mulling over the possibilities. "Or a jilted lover, maybe?"

"Hey now! I don't like what you're insinuating! I might've run a gin mill, but I was always a gentleman with the ladies, and I'd *never* do anything to hurt Clara," Benny protested.

"Well, maybe it wasn't about you. Perhaps someone who couldn't stand to see Clara with anyone else," Bella ventured.

Benny's visage in the photo scowled with irritation. "The lads knew better than to cross me, and, as for love rivals, Clara wouldn't give them the time of day. No, it's not that."

"Okay, if it's not a business or personal rival, then what about someone else?" I asked.

Bella tapped her fingers thoughtfully against her lips. "What about Clara's father?" she asked carefully. "Clarence, right?"

Benny's scowl deepened, and the runes in the photo flared with a faint, angry glow. "Yeah," he snapped. "That big-shot blowhard thought he ran this town. Always strutting around like he was some kinda king. You think he didn't try to muscle me out? He sent plenty of warnings, all dressed up in polite words, but the message was clear: I wasn't good enough for his little princess. Like I didn't already know he hated my guts."

Bella hesitated, glancing at me, but pressed on. "Well, he had motive, didn't he?"

I followed her train of thought. "A man of his stature in this town might not have approved of his daughter seeing the local speakeasy owner. Maybe he couldn't stand the possible scandal," I hypothesized.

Benny let out a harsh laugh, quick and biting. "That stiff wouldn't dirty his own hands. Nah, that wasn't his racket. But would he bankroll a couple of palookas to rough me up? Sure. I wouldn't put it past him to send some goons to give me the business."

The runes glowed brighter as Benny's voice rose, tinged with frustration. "And you're sitting here, playing detective, like I shoulda done something different! How was I supposed to see it coming, huh? You think I didn't keep my eyes peeled? It still happened!"

"Benny," I said gently, stepping closer to the photograph. "No one's blaming you. We're just trying to put the pieces together. We don't have much to go on—just your memories. If Clarence or someone else had it in for you, you'd know better than anyone."

The light around him flickered, and he exhaled, his voice softening, though it still carried a sharp edge. "Yeah, yeah, you're just trying to help. I get it, doll. But I'm stuck here, playing this scene over and over. You don't know what that does to a guy."

Bella nodded, trying to move things along. "What about some of those other stuffed shirts you mentioned before? Could one of them have had it out for you? Maybe even a lawman who didn't like the idea of a speakeasy operating right under their noses?"

Benny clicked his tongue and scrunched up his face, thinking hard. Finally, he shook his head. "Nah, those bulls were on the level, see? Sure, they might've thrown a stink eye towards our little operation now and again, but as long as I wasn't interfering with their business, they kept their noses out of mine. And we kept it all quiet like at the Hideaway. No beef with the law, that was our motto."

Unease prickled at the back of my mind. Benny sounded sure about the cops, but frustration and bitterness laced his words. Memories—especially ones tied to a life of secrets—had a way of playing tricks, and a hundred years was a long time for facts to get hazy.

On the surface, the Hideaway's existence might've been a secret, but secrets have a way of slipping out. If the local cops did know, they could've stayed quiet for a reason. Maybe someone higher up—someone like the Silverthornes—had leaned on them to look the other way. It made sense they'd want to keep the most powerful family in Havenwood happy, especially if busting the Hideaway meant crossing Clarence's daughter, Clara.

On the other hand, what if some of those cops weren't so clean? If the Hideaway's crew hadn't greased any palms, resentment could've been brewing beneath the surface—no booze, no bribes, no payoffs, no glory. A place like the Hideaway managing to stay untouched for so long might've made someone desperate enough to act. Benny might not have seen trouble coming, but that didn't mean it wasn't there. It could've led someone to do something drastic.

I made a note in my phone to check out the police when I had internet access again.

When I finished, I glanced over at Bella. There was still one suspect I hadn't wanted to voice. As if she could read my mind, Bella nodded. I took a deep breath, steeled my nerves, and revisited my previous questions, "What about Clara?"

The runes flickered violently, and his voice, once steady, grew rough. "Watch it, dollface. You're walking on thin ice there."

"Well, she had the keys, the access, the know-how. Could she have...I don't know...wanted a different life? Maybe...without you?" I had to force myself to finish as storm clouds covered Benny's face.

The reaction from Benny was immediate and violent. A fierce wind whipped through the Hideaway, rattling bottles and knocking over chairs. The lights above us flickered wildly, casting jagged shadows as his voice roared with fury.

"*Don't you dare!*" Benny bellowed, the runes on his picture flaring brightly. A glass tumbled off the bar, shattering on the floor. His rage felt like a living thing, crackling in the air. "Clara was true! True as the North Star! We were gonna be hitched!" His voice cracked with a guttural shout, almost incoherent. "She was everything to me!"

Bella and I flinched, the chaos around us deafening.

"Benny, stop!" I shouted, trying to break through the storm.

"Please!" Bella's voice wavered. "We believe you!"

The fury swelled, but then, just as suddenly, it collapsed. The room stilled. His voice, once booming, dropped to a broken whisper.

"I bought her a ring. Hid it under the bar. I was going to ask her when the time was right, but..." The silence that followed was thick with sadness, the shattered glass glittering like tears on the floor.

Bella cautiously reached out to touch the edge of the photo, her face softening. "We're just trying to consider all angles, Benny. Nothing more."

A heavy sigh seemed to emanate from the picture, and Benny's voice softened. "I know, I know, but she ain't behind this. She can't be. I won't believe it. I can't believe it."

My eyes widened, a possibility dawning on me. "Hold on, maybe this isn't about old grudges or secret rivalries. Perhaps it's just plain old greed. What if someone was after the ring? They slipped in, thinking they'd have a moment to snatch it, but you were here. They panicked. A robbery gone wrong."

"Could be, could be," Benny mused, "But that rock was tucked away tight. You'd have to know exactly where to look and have the keys besides. See, Clara and I each had our own cabinets hidden under the bar. Hers was hidden under a panel set with a carved sun and mine was under a matching moon."

Bella and I shot each other a glance, heavy with meaning, and then rushed behind the bar.

Bella, with an anticipatory tremble in her fingers, found the cabinet Benny described. Following his directions, she slid the wooden panels to the side, revealing a pair of matching locks. She tried several keys before finding the right one. With a twist and a click, Benny's hidden compartment opened with an aged creak, revealing a velvet box that symbolized the promise of what could have been, a sealed bottle of whiskey, and a photograph of Clara standing next to Benny, her image smiling out at us across the years.

I picked up the picture, scrutinizing it closely. "Look at this," I said, pointing at the photo. "Clara couldn't have done it. She's petite. You practically tower over her, Benny. It would've been quite the task for her to land a blow on the back of your head that would've taken you down without dragging over a chair or something to stand on."

"That's what I've been trying to tell ya! Clara wouldn't and couldn't have been behind this," he said.

Bella set the bottle of whiskey on the bar. "Was this your favorite bottle or something?" she asked.

Benny shook his head. "I was always more of a gin man, myself. Clara fancied the whiskey. I set that aside for her, hoping to raise a toast to our life together after I proposed."

"That's sweet," Bella said sincerely.

I crouched to retrieve the last item in the cabinet. I flicked open the velvet box. My eyes shot wide as I took in the gorgeous ring sparkling against the rich velvet. The engagement ring Benny had chosen for Clara was a timeless piece, featuring a dazzling emerald-cut diamond set in a band of intricate gold filigree, symbolizing their enduring love amidst the clandestine glamour of the speakeasy era.

"That's a stunning ring, Benny," I breathed.

"Gorgeous," Bella echoed as I passed it over to her.

"It's still there?" he asked, his voice filled with a strange mix of disappointment and joy.

"Were you hoping someone took it?" I asked.

"No...well, yes. Clara. I was laying a bet she'd find the sparkler after I took the big sleep. Then at least she'd know what she meant to me. What I wanted our life to be."

My gaze drifted and caught the sight of the other small door next to Benny's. "This one over here is Clara's, right? Do you mind if we open it?" I asked, nodding towards the locked cabinet.

"That's the one," Benny confirmed. "Our personal stashes. We respected each other's privacy—never pried into one another's cabinets. But I suppose that now...well, go ahead."

A silent exchange passed between Bella and me, one of shared suspicions and unsaid plans. I reached for the key on the brass ring that matched the cabinet. The lock clicked, surrendering to our inquiry, and the door swung open to reveal Clara's personal effects.

Map to a Broken Heart

I paused, taking a steady breath as I leaned in, peering inside Clara's cupboard. Was this it? Would there be some sort of clue here? Would we find the answers we sought? I didn't know, but the surge of hope mixed with excitement running through me was undeniable.

Carefully, using my phone's flashlight to make sure I didn't miss anything, I retrieved all the items from inside the small storage space. There were only three. The first was a sealed bottle of gin. A thin layer of dust covered the bottle, likely because of being locked in the cabinet for such a long time. I drew it out and blew lightly on the label, revealing an intricate looking red design and the production date. 1928. The date on it the same year Benny died, but it wasn't a brand I recognized, not that I was a big gin drinker. The label was bold, done in a bright scarlet and the bottle looked like it hadn't ever been opened. I wasn't an expert when it came to this type of thing, but surely a sealed bottle in this good of condition, much like the whiskey we'd found in Benny's cabinet, had to be worth a lot of money.

"It looks like Clara knew you as well as you knew her. She put aside a bottle of gin for you," I said as I set it on the bar carefully to make sure I couldn't accidentally knock it off.

Benny's eyes lit up. "That was from our latest shipment. It was remarkably good stuff. Everybody was talking about it."

"It's sweet that she set aside a bottle of your favorite," Bella said gently. Benny nodded, a sad expression stealing the joy from his face as the reason why they never got to share the drink settled in.

Looking for a distraction, I examined the other things I'd retrieved from Clara's cabinet. The next item was a small notebook, nearly identical to the one I'd discovered in the attic at Spellbooks. As I flipped through it, I realized the handwriting was different from Benny's, but still coded. Clara wrote in a much more feminine, flowing script, but her messages were still unintelligible. She had also included strange symbols and doodles at the bottom of every page that I hadn't seen on Benny's.

I tipped the open notebook towards Benny. "Hey Benny, I found a nearly identical notebook in the attic where your picture was."

"You found Clara's notebook!" Benny exclaimed.

Excitement sprang to life inside me. Maybe there was a clue hidden in either Clara's or Benny's encrypted notebooks. "Any idea how to break the code?" I asked.

"Sure, dollface," he shrugged. "It's a Caesar cipher."

"A what?" Bella asked, leaning forward eagerly.

"It's a simple switcheroo of letters, a substitution game. You swap each letter for another—like A becomes M, see? At first, it was all Greek to me, but once you get in the swing, you can suss out the lowdown without scribbling it all out. Kept the Hideaway's books on the hush-hush that way. Clara was the brains behind it. She loved all those secret things. Spy novels and mystery stories. That's how we kept our little operation completely under wraps."

"These don't look like records," Bella observed. "Look, there's no order to them. Some pages are full, and others are nearly empty."

"And what about the strange symbols at the bottom of each page?" I asked, running a finger along the bizarre collection of shapes and doodles which never looked like they repeated from one page to the next.

Benny squinted at the small notebook and finally shook his head. "Beats me, doll. Clara must've cooked up this batch of secret sauce solo. It's not the same code I used. And these extra doodads? They got me stumped. It's like she's talking in tongues—way out of my league," he said with another shake of his head. The lights in the Hideaway flickered slightly as Benny's frustration mounted. I found myself glad that I'd accidentally activated the runes on the photo. Not that I wanted Benny trapped, but my gut told me if he'd been able to go where he wanted, he might get into trouble. Or cause trouble. I wasn't sure and didn't really want to risk either one.

Sensing I wouldn't get anything more from him, I set the notebook to the side with a mental vow to examine it in more detail later. I picked up the last item, which was perhaps the most interesting of the three. It was a crumpled map of what looked like Havenwood. There were some handwritten notes on the back, but before I could examine them further, Isadora burst back into the speakeasy, waving her phone at us.

Benny perked up, looking her way. "Did you find something?" he asked hopefully.

"No and then a possible yes," Isadora said. She sank onto a stool, her expression softening. "I did a quick search, and, well, I'm so sorry to tell you this, but Clara passed away the same year you did." Her voice was gentle, trying to cushion the blow. "I didn't find much else, but...I thought you should know."

His face fell. "She was so young! Barely had a spin on the dance floor of life. I'd been banking on her living a full and happy life."

"We're so sorry for your loss, Benny," I said. Bella and Isadora murmured their condolences as well. Benny nodded, acknowledging our words before swiping at his eyes with the back of his hand, staring glumly into space, no doubt lost in his memories of Clara.

Giving Benny a moment to compose himself, I took a few steps away from the bar, pulling Isadora and Bella with me. "Did you find out what happened?" I asked, lowering my voice to a hushed tone, careful not to let Benny hear too much just yet.

Isadora nodded slightly, her voice soft. "Not at first. Every site said the same thing—Clara Silverthorne, only daughter of Clarence and Victoria Silverthorne, passed away unexpectedly on November 9th, 1928, leaving behind her parents and two older brothers."

My heart skipped a beat as I did the math. "That's only a couple of weeks after Benny died," I whispered, casting a glance over at the photo of Benny propped up on the bar.

Bella leaned in; her brow furrowed. "Do you think their deaths are related?"

Isadora shrugged, keeping her voice hushed. "Maybe. But that's where the trail goes cold. The usual records don't say much."

Bella pressed gently, "So why did you say the 'possible yes' earlier?"

Isadora glanced briefly toward Benny, dropping her voice. "Because she was a Silverthorne. I tried calling my mother first, but when I couldn't get through to her, I got in touch with Gabriel. He's digging through the family records right now. They're well-organized, and he's pretty sure he found something about Clara and her father already, but he wants to deliver the news to Benny personally."

From the photo, Benny's voice cut through, sharp with tension. "What news?" His eyes narrowed, his ghostly form almost leaning forward, as though testing the limits of the runes that held him inside the photograph. If not for the magic trapping him, I had no doubt he'd be floating in front of us, demanding answers.

Isadora shot us a look and then quickly summed up the situation. "My brother Gabriel has been digging through the Silverthorne records. He thinks he's found something about Clara and her father, but he wants to tell you himself."

Benny eyed Isadora skeptically, still caught between the past and the strange present he found himself in. "You told him I'm a ghost, right?" he asked, a hint of anxiety in his spectral tone. "Otherwise, he's in for quite the shocker."

Isadora nodded. "Yeah, he knows. But Gabriel's not the kind to spook easily."

"I sure hope not," Benny muttered. "Wouldn't want to be causing any gent a case of the heebie-jeebies with my chattering portrait."

"You underestimate us modern folk," Isadora said with a chuckle. "We've seen it all. Ever heard of Hogwarts?"

Benny looked puzzled. "Hogwash-what-now? What's he got to do with me?"

"Never mind," I jumped in, keen to avoid a long explanation that would only confuse him further. "It's just a movie thing—moving pictures. Don't worry about it."

The subject change was welcome, but the playful banter could only momentarily ease the tension hanging in the air, a tension that snapped back into sharp focus as Benny's face darkened, reflecting his shift in mood. He was no longer just a quaint relic from another time, but a man wronged, a spirit unresolved. The edges of the photograph holding his likeness quivered and shook, the ambient light from the runes catching the tremble of the paper.

"What's wrong, Benny?" I asked.

"Clarence Silverthorne, that's what. The nerve of that man, thinking he could control us like his own personal chess pieces! Especially when Clara had so little time on God's green earth! Why couldn't he have just let us be to find our own happiness?!" Benny's voice crackled with a sudden edge of fury. The shadows in the speakeasy seemed to draw in closer, circling around us as if his anger stirred them into action.

Bella quickly interjected, sliding the map toward the photo, hoping to break through the rising storm of his wrath by distracting him. "Look, Benny, Clara left something behind. It looks like a map. But to where?" she asked as she opened the scrap of paper I'd found in Clara's cabinet.

Benny seemed to calm down as he examined the map. "It looks like Havenwood. There's the forest surrounding the town. It's a little rough, but I can see it."

I took the map from her and flipped it over to reveal a list written in a delicate hand. "What do you think this means?" I asked. "She made a list on the back here. Clothes, some money, Benny's locket, and...a heartwood tree? What's a heartwood tree?"

"*The* heartwood tree," Benny murmured, his voice softening. He sounded wistful, the violence in his voice giving way to something like wonder.

"Is that the location that's marked on the map?" Isadora asked.

"I've never heard of it. What is it?" I asked, mostly to distract Benny. I might not know what the heartwood tree was, but I understood completely what it signified. The items Clara had listed told a story of hope and escape. She'd made her choice between her love for Benny and her father's overbearing protection.

Benny's photo glimmered as he peered closer. "Indeed, it is, doll. That's no ordinary timber—it's *the* heartwood tree. Stands proud and tall, a sentinel of passion, sweethearts, and star-crossed lovers. Been around since forever, its roots twined with the very soul of Havenwood's enchantment."

"What does that mean?" Isadora asked.

Benny shrugged. "Not sure, myself. Just what everyone used to say, you know?"

Bella leaned in, her fingers tracing the heart on the map. "What makes it so special?"

Benny chuckled, a nostalgic sound. "Word on the street is, it's got a knack for granting love's wishes. But more than that, it's the real McCoy when it comes to true love's promises. Sweethearts pledge their love beneath its canopy, and their love's said to be stitched into the very soul of the tree—like it's part of its magic."

My eyes danced with curiosity. "Are you saying this tree gives them some sort of magical blessing?"

"That's the rumor," Benny continued, his voice laced with a warm recollection. "Not only that, but also any pair speaking their vows of love near its trunk feels the earth's own heart beating with theirs. That's the tree tipping its hat, so to speak—sealing the deal. Though, considering we're talking about Havenwood, who's to say it's just a tall tale?"

"And the wishes?" Bella pressed on, clearly intrigued.

"If your heart is in the right place, that tree has got an ear for ya. True-hearted lovers bask in a warmth like no other. If your love's the genuine article," Benny's tone dropped to a whisper, "the leaves themselves will carry your joys, weaving a spell of happiness to weather any storm life throws your way. At least, so the legend goes."

I smiled, imagining the scene. "Sounds like the perfect place to run to if you're in love and need a blessing."

Benny's image softened around the edges. "That's the very spot I told Clara about, the night we first met. She told me that if the stars aligned for us, she'd meet me there one day, at the heart of all our dreams."

The realization of Clara's intentions dawned on him as it had on me moments before. The spectral image in the photo gaining a look of tender remembrance. "She must've planned this all along, ever since that day..." Benny's voice broke with emotion. He took a shuddering breath. "She was going to run away with me to the heartwood tree, to start a new life together. Away from her father's heavy hand..." His anger had dissipated completely, replaced by a bittersweet longing for what could have been.

The room fell into a hushed silence, filled only by the warm ambiance of the rune lights, casting long shadows that danced around us. Benny's ghostly countenance was still within the picture, the mirth and anger that had animated him moments before now replaced by a quiet sorrow. "So many plans, so many dreams," he murmured bitterly.

Bella, Isadora, and I exchanged a glance, a shared understanding passing between us. History surrounded us. A love story cut short and the tangible remnants of lives that once burned brightly but were now nothing but whispers in the dark.

"I wish we could change the past," Bella murmured, her voice barely above the sound of our collective breathing.

Benny's spectral image looked up, his eyes meeting mine with a depth of emotion that no mere photograph should hold. "But we can't, can we?

As we stood there, in the Hideaway's silence, I placed the map gently on the table, smoothing out its creases as if in doing so, I could smooth out the wrinkles in time. "We'll find the truth, Benny. For Clara. For both of you."

Locket of Shadows

BENNY'S IMAGE IN THE photograph seemed to retreat into the dark shadows of the future he'd been robbed of experiencing. Guilt gnawed at me as I looked at the picture. Trapping him in a runed photo had never been my intention, but now it felt like I'd taken even more from him. The hard glint of unshed tears in his eyes was a stark reminder of all he'd lost, of the life he should have lived but he was somehow bound to this place instead. I held on to the fragile hope that if I could solve the mystery of his death, maybe he'd finally be able to move on. But how was I supposed to crack a century-old cold case? And even if I did, would the runed photo let him leave, or would he remain trapped until the magic drained away—whenever that might be?

The silence weighed heavily in the room until Isadora finally spoke, her voice cutting through the stillness. "Benny, you said you talked about going to the heartwood tree before. How were you and Clara going to make your escape? There must've been a plan, right?"

His gaze seemed to sharpen, and he straightened slightly within the confines of his two-dimensional world. "Ah, the escape. The grand skedaddle," he began, a hint of the old fire returning to his voice. "That was Clara's genius. We were going to pack a bag with the necessities. Just some clothes and the money we'd made from the Hideaway and leave it in the escape tunnel. Then, one night after we closed, we'd just walk away. She even devised a trick with the tunnel door—a snazzy trick to open or close it from the outside, a real humdinger. We also used it a time or two when we were feeling lazy and forgot to grab the keys. It was plum invisible unless you were in the know."

With renewed curiosity driving us, we urged him to guide us, and he directed us to carry his photograph into the escape tunnel. "Shut the door," he directed.

Bella held up a hand. "Hold up. Shouldn't one of us stay behind? You know, just in case something goes wrong?"

She had a point. Could we really trust this old mechanism? Who knew what could happen? I nodded. "Good call. You stay here in the Hideaway, Bella. If anything happens, you can get help."

Bella lingered near the bar, her fingers drumming on the polished wood as her foot tapped anxiously on the floor. Isadora and I wedged ourselves into the narrow tunnel, following Benny's instructions. As Isadora shone her phone's flashlight over my shoulder, I held up the photograph, allowing Benny to guide me. I fumbled along the rough wood until my fingers stumbled upon the hidden catch. Holding my breath, I pressed it. With a soft click, the door swung closed with a muted creak, a testament to the ingenuity that had gone into every detail of the Hideaway. I pressed it again and the door swung open. I let out the breath I'd been holding in a whoosh and stepped back into the speakeasy, the light from the rune-inscribed walls offered a comforting return to the familiar.

Bella took Benny's photo, propping it up on the bar. "Well, we know that works now."

Isadora bounced over with her usual enthusiasm. "Do you suppose that's how the killer snuck in?"

Benny let out a sharp laugh. "Not a chance, sweetheart. Nobody knew about that escape tunnel. Not a soul. Clara and I made sure of it."

"Maybe someone was watching without you realizing?" Bella suggested, frowning thoughtfully.

Benny scoffed. "Did you see the size of that escape tunnel? Who could rightly sneak down there without us noticing? A mouse?"

But what Isadora said had ignited a spark of curiosity in me. Despite Benny's protests, the killer either had stolen the spare set of keys or entered through the escape tunnel. I swung my phone's flashlight back into the darkened maw of the escape route. "I wonder..." I trailed off, carefully picking my way over the uneven dirt floor of the passage.

"Hey! Where ya going, doll?" Benny's voice came from behind me.

"Just checking something out," I called over my shoulder, already crouching as the tunnel narrowed.

The escape passage was much tighter and less welcoming than the main entrance. The ceiling pressed low, forcing me to hunch over as I shuffled forward. The rough, packed dirt walls, held together by weathered beams, added to the claustrophobic feel. This wasn't built for show; it was designed for quick exits, not comfort. The soft amber glow from the speakeasy barely reached me now, casting long shadows. The tunnel took a sharp turn to the right, plunging into complete darkness.

Behind me, I heard Bella's hesitant footsteps catching up. "You're crazy if you think I'm letting you go in there alone," she muttered, her voice bouncing off the walls.

The escape tunnel stretched on longer than I expected, the walls pressing close as the path narrowed. The dirt beneath my feet felt uneven, forcing me to crouch as I made my way forward. The air was heavy, stale, with a faint, earthy scent. As I continued, the passage took a barely noticeable curve to the right, and soon, the faint light from the Hideaway behind me was completely cut off. I glanced back, realizing that the warmth of the speakeasy had disappeared entirely, swallowed by the dark turn of the tunnel.

Bella looked up when I paused. "What is it?" she asked.

"Nothing. I just hadn't realized that this went so far. Where do you think it comes out?"

Bella shrugged, a difficult gesture given her crouched posture. "My guess would be the forest behind the Oasis somewhere. We should go back. I don't think Papa checked the tunnel this far. It might be dangerous."

"We have to be close to the exit," I pointed out. "Just two minutes more."

"Two minutes," Bella said, half in agreement and half in warning.

I swung my flashlight back to the tunnel in front of me and the beam caught something unexpected on the dirt floor. I caught my breath as I hurried forward. Faded garments, brittle with age, were strewn about, their colors leeched by time. A small suitcase sat open, its contents ravaged by the elements. Cautiously, I crouched next to the case, using my phone to snap some photos before carefully poking through it. I wanted to disrupt as little as possible but wanted to get pictures of everything. Surprisingly, there was nothing else in the case but tattered clothes.

"That doesn't make sense," I murmured out loud, feeling the puzzle pieces shifting and rearranging in my mind.

Bella's voice carried a hint of excitement tinged with concern as she approached. "What did you find?"

"I think I found Clara's suitcase," I said, the beam from my phone highlighting the forlorn array. "But if she packed it for an escape with Benny, why is it here, all scattered around the escape tunnel?"

"I don't know," Bella murmured, pressing up next to me in the narrow confines to examine the case.

Another thought struck me as I moved to the side so she could get a better look. "There's just clothes in there, right?"

"That's what I see," Bella confirmed. "Why?"

"Well, if I was a wealthy Silverthorne running away from my family, I'd pack money. Jewels. Something valuable and transportable to make setting up in a new place easier."

Bella shifted a tattered skirt to the side. "There's nothing like that here."

"But why? Why wouldn't she pack money at the very least?" I said.

"She would have. It doesn't make sense," Bella said.

"Unless...someone else was here before us and took it," I said, swinging my light back and forth across the dirt floor searching for a clue. Maybe there was a footprint or a...

Something caught the illumination from the flashlight and glittered in the darkness. I paused and swept the light back over the spot until I found what had caught my eye. A glimmer of gold against the dark earth. I hurried ahead to get a better look.

My fingers brushed away loose dirt from the cool metal of a slender gold chain. Carefully, I tugged on it. More dirt fell away, revealing a heart-shaped locket that seemed to glow in the light of my flashlight as it spun on its chain from my fingertips.

"Do you think that's Clara's?" Bella asked softly.

"Only one way to find out," I said, gesturing back down the escape tunnel toward the Hideaway.

Bella and I burst through the escape tunnel door and into the speakeasy, breathless from the rush. Benny's photo still sat propped up on the bar next to where Isadora perched on a stool, his expression frozen in the same distant contemplation as before, but it shifted the moment we entered. His ghostly form stirred, his gaze sharpening as he noticed our urgency. Bella picked up the photo, turning it towards me. I held the locket up, letting it dangle from my fingers. The heart-shaped charm glinted under the soft, amber light.

"Benny," I said quietly, "is this Clara's?"

Benny sucked in a gasp. "That's...that's her locket!" he exclaimed. "The one I gave her. Put a little picture of me on one side and one of her on the other. She swore she'd never take it off."

"So why is it here?" Bella asked.

"And why is it covered in blood? That is blood, isn't it?" Isadora whispered as the locket rotated, giving all of us a clear look at the reddish-brown discoloration that was embedded in the swirling details of the locket. The unmistakable color stood out starkly against the glittering gold.

The room fell into a suffocating silence, the air thick and still.

I swallowed, my mind racing. Too many questions. No answers.

But one thing was certain—Clara hadn't made her escape as planned. At least, not unharmed.

The Escape into the Woods

As we stared in silence at the locket, each lost in our own thoughts, Honey stuck her head through the doorway leading into the basement of the Oasis.

"Oh! There you all are. Time to come upstairs. Dinner is ready," she said, wiping her hands on her bright floral apron.

"Coming, Mama," Bella said dutifully, heading towards the opposite tunnel and still holding Benny's photograph.

Isadora and I exchanged a glance, both of us reluctant to leave the mysteries of the Hideaway behind. There was still so much to uncover, but when Honey's cooking was involved, there was no contest. We shrugged in silent agreement and hurried after her, the promise of a meal too tempting to resist.

As we hurried up the stairs, the rich scent of tomato sauce and succulent meatballs floated through the air. It surprised me to see Antonio, instead of Honey, standing at the stove, stirring a large pot. "Ah, you found them. Good, just in time," he said.

"You're in for a treat," Bella said to us as she set Benny's picture safely on the window ledge next to the table and helped her mother fill water glasses. "Papa usually leaves the cooking to Mama, or 'the professional' as he calls her. But you haven't *lived* until you've had his homemade spaghetti and meatballs."

"With my nonna's secret sauce recipe," Antonio said, bending over the pot and wafting the scent of oregano and roasted tomatoes towards his nose. He nodded with a smile and dipped the tip of a clean spoon in the red sauce, tasting it. "And this is the best one I've ever made!" he declared, whisking it off the burner.

"You say that every time," Honey chuckled, dancing around her husband to pull a steaming loaf of garlic bread dripping with butter out of the oven. She generously sprinkled flaky sea salt over the top before placing it next to the richly scented sauce.

Antonio put his hands on his hips, surveying the countertop. "There. I think we're all set. It's buffet style as I'm afraid our table won't fit us and all this food, but there's plenty of spaghetti and meatballs to go around, and my lovely wife made us a salad if you want a token vegetable on your plate," he said, wrapping an arm around Honey's shoulders and pressing a kiss to her temple.

She leaned into him with a smile but spoke to us. "Make sure you leave room for dessert though. I whipped up a tiramisu last night that luckily matches Antonio's whole Italian dinner theme."

"And if you're too full for dessert, I'd be happy to eat your share," Antonio said with a smile as he patted his belly.

"Oh, stop it, you," Honey said in mock exasperation, swatting playfully at him.

"What? I can't appreciate my beautiful wife's amazing talent for baking?" He leaned down and placed a kiss on her cheek before waving us forward. "Come on, now. Don't be shy. Dig in!" Bella handed us each a plate just as the doorbell rang.

Honey shooed us towards the food. "You girls need your energy. I'll get the door."

With the smells coming from the counter, I didn't need to be told twice. As we all busied ourselves piling our plates, I couldn't help but add an extra scoop of the bright, tangy salad topped with fresh, juicy cherry tomatoes, feta cheese, and a generous amount of what looked like homemade croutons. Who knew you could work up such an appetite digging into the past? Just as a slice of Honey's sumptuous garlic bread found a precarious purchase atop my mound of food, Honey reentered the kitchen.

"Look who it is!" she exclaimed.

Gabriel Silverthorne, all effortless charm and affable grace, followed Honey back into the kitchen. Gabriel was Isadora's older brother and the middle child of the magically gifted family. I felt my pulse quicken, a ripple of warmth spreading through me as unexpected memories fluttered through my brain of a dance at the Christmas Eve Ball, the thrill of unmasking a pair of notorious jewel thieves, and the end of the evening kiss from the very man whose attractive smile grew wider as his gaze landed on me.

He hesitated on the threshold. "I didn't mean to interrupt your dinner. My sister called about some information, so I thought I'd drop it off rather than text," he said, lifting a book covered in worn green leather.

But Honey, ever the hostess, swept away his protests with a cheery command. "Our motto is the more the merrier around here. There's plenty of food. When Antonio cooks, he cooks for an army."

"It would be a sin to send anyone away from our table hungry," Antonio protested, passing Gabriel a clean plate.

"You'll be doing us a favor, really," Honey said, waving him forward. "Saving us from all the leftovers."

"Well, if you're sure," Gabriel said, setting the book down so he could accept the plate.

"I'm sure. We insist," Antonio said with a grin. "Here, let me help you."

The kitchen was a hustle and bustle for the next few minutes. Honey and Bella quickly rearranged the table settings to accommodate one more guest while Antonio pressed the plate into Gabriel's hands and loaded it with a mountain of spaghetti. There was a shifting and sliding of chairs and tableware until every fork and glass found its new place. The kitchen was a symphony of clattering cutlery and good-natured banter as everyone settled into their new seats. Isadora, with a mischievous twinkle in her eye, had orchestrated the seating in such a way that left me right next to Gabriel. There we were, side by side, our knees occasionally brushing under the table, sending tiny shocks of awareness through me, as we indulged in Antonio's delicious pasta dinner.

Gabriel's attention shifted to the photograph of Benny on the nearby window ledge when Isadora brought up our spectral guest. "Is this the ghost? Mr. Benny O'Rourke?" he asked, not missing a beat as he swirled spaghetti onto his fork. He gave the photo a courteous nod. "Nice to meet you, Benny."

Benny, who'd been quiet for a spell, seemed to straighten up at the attention. "Likewise, kid," he replied with a hint of a smile, continuing to make small talk that came surprisingly easily to someone who'd been out of the game for a century.

The conversation turned to the mystery at hand. Isadora leaned forward, her curiosity clear. "Gabriel, what did you learn about Clara Silverthorne?"

He hesitated, his fork midway to his mouth, and his gaze flickered to Benny's image before settling back on his sister. "I'm not sure this is appropriate dinner discussion..."

Antonio, always the embodiment of warmth and hospitality, waved away the concern. "We aren't ones to stand on ceremony and have all been swept away in the excitement of uncovering the mysteries of history. Here, we feast on curiosity as much as we do on food," he declared, to a round of chuckles.

As if he physically felt the weight of everyone's anticipation, Gabriel let out a slow breath, set his fork down, and began. "Well, Clara Silverthorne's death was indeed sudden. From what I gather, it was a shock to the whole family. To the whole town, in fact. I found hints, whispers of her less-than-lawful ventures, but I couldn't find anything concrete. She was the jewel of the family, especially to her father. It seems he turned a somewhat blind eye to her...entrepreneurial spirit."

Benny's image leaned forward, almost as if trying to edge closer. "There's got to be more. What aren't you saying?"

Gabriel shifted uncomfortably, an uncharacteristic hesitation in his posture. "It's just...," he started, then paused, looking directly at Benny, "...it's not easy to speak ill of the departed, especially when..."

I found myself hanging onto his every word, the proximity to Gabriel making the air seem charged with electricity. Benny craned toward us, his voice tinged with a mix of anxiety and desperation. "You've got to have more, lad. What happened to my Clara after I was gone?"

Gabriel took a deep breath, and in the quiet that settled over the room, his voice was almost a whisper. "From what I could uncover in our family archives, she became a shadow of herself, aimless and heartbroken. It was as if she'd lost her anchor to the world when you...when you passed, Benny."

The room was still, the air thick with empathy and sorrow. Gabriel continued, "Her father found her bed empty one night. In a panic, he called the police. They combed the town, examining every street and path until dawn. It wasn't until the first light crept over the horizon that Clara emerged from the Hearthstone's basement, disoriented and dazed as though she'd lost part of herself in those dark passages."

"Oh no," Honey murmured, completely engrossed by the heartrending story. We all were.

Gabriel continued, "It's recorded that after the keys were taken from her, Clara still returned to the Hideaway, although they couldn't figure out how."

I glanced at Bella, and I could tell we were thinking the same thing. That explained Clara's footprints headed into the Hideaway. But what about the other print?

Gabriel cleared his throat. "Every morning, she'd be found sitting in the same spot, an empty glass in hand, staring off into the distance, lost in her own thoughts. Her father would escort her home, but she'd return the next night like clockwork." Benny's presence in the photo wavered as if the revelations rocked him to his very core.

"Wait a second," I said, a thought popping in my head. "There's a trick to open the Hideaway door, one that only Benny and Clara knew, right? How did they get in?"

Gabriel shrugged, but Isadora jumped in. "Maybe she told them?"

"But why? After they'd gone to all that trouble to keep the Hideaway a secret," Bella said, following my train of thought.

"Perhaps she let them in as part of the police investigation?" Isadora suggested.

"Maybe," I allowed.

"It sounds plausible, but I guess we'll never know the full details," Bella said.

"What if—" I started to say

Benny cut me off. "What happened to her, lad? What became of my Clara?" he asked, his voice strained.

Gabriel hesitated, his eyes flicking to me and then Isadora for a brief moment, as if seeking silent encouragement. When she gave him a small nod, he continued, "The details are sparse, but from what I could gather quickly, it seems that one night, Clara decided she couldn't bear it any longer. They found an unfinished note in her diary hinting at plans to run away. But a storm tore through Havenwood that evening. She was found in the forest, bleeding from a head wound, apparently struck by a falling tree limb in the raging wind."

A collective gasp filled the room. Gabriel looked down, his tone soft and sorrowful. "They took her back to her father's house. She never regained consciousness and passed quietly in her sleep two days later."

The silence that followed was a respectful tribute to the tragedy of Clara Silverthorne, broken only by soft sobs from Benny's portrait.

Sleepless Nights and Secret Codes

Despite the anticipation I'd initially felt for Antonio's dinner and Honey's light and creamy dessert, faced with what Gabriel had just shared, I couldn't really remember eating either. Yet when I looked down, all that remained of my food was a smear of rich tomato sauce, crumbs of garlic bread, and an empty dessert bowl dusted with chocolate.

As Bella and her parents cleared away the plates, I heard Benny's small voice whisper, "Please. Take me back to the Hideaway."

"Anything you want," I murmured, picking up the picture and heading towards the stairs leading to the basement. I brushed my fingers along the runes in the tunnel to turn on the magical glowing lights before heading into the Hideaway. The air felt heavier now, laden with the sorrow of the story Gabriel had shared at the dinner table. I clutched Benny's photo, his image virtually motionless and his usual vibrant countenance now a mask of utter despair.

I set the picture gently on the bar, the same spot where Clara might have spent all those sleepless nights, lost in her vigil. Seeing the locket where we'd left it on the bar, I opened it up, positioning the locket so Benny could see her picture inside. "I'll come back and see you in the morning," I promised, though Benny's eyes didn't lift to meet mine. Clara's notebook sat on the bar next to him, along with the map. On a whim, I asked, "Would it be okay if I take these with me? Maybe I can figure out the code."

"Take whatever you want, doll," Benny said, his voice listless.

I nodded and backed out of the room, deciding to leave the lights in the tunnel glowing in case it helped comfort Benny in this dark moment. Upstairs, the clinking of dishes and indistinct murmur of familial conversation drifted through the hall leading to the kitchen as Bella and her parents tackled the post-dinner chaos. I stepped back, reluctant to intrude on the intimate family scene that had nothing to do with ghosts or long-lost love stories.

Instead, I turned down the hall, heading to the front room to gather my belongings. But as I reached for the doorway leading to the foyer, a low voice stopped me.

It was Gabriel, his tone laced with concern as he cautioned Isadora, "...all I'm saying is that you need to be careful with spirits like Benny. They're often...unpredictable."

"What do you mean by unpredictable?" Isadora asked, her voice hushed.

"When ghosts have unresolved issues combined with intense feelings, they lash out in sudden, unexpected, and sometimes violent ways. I think it's admirable what you and your friends are doing, trying to help Benny find his peace, but you'd better be ready for his reaction if you uncover something that makes him angry."

"Are you saying he's dangerous?" Isadora asked, her voice rising.

"Perhaps. Perhaps not. It's hard to tell with ghosts. But it would be prudent to tread carefully."

Isadora's response was a quiet murmur, but I felt the weight of Gabriel's warning settle in my stomach. Spirits. Unpredictable. Violent, even? The notion was like cold water down my back. What was Benny capable of?

I turned, not wanting to intrude on the Silverthorne siblings either. However, other than returning to the kitchen or the basement, there was nowhere else for me to go. I quickly grabbed my coat, intent on heading back to the kitchen and saying my goodbyes when Gabriel caught the movement out of the corner of his eye. "Harper! Sorry, I didn't see you there. Are you heading out? Perhaps I can give you a ride home?" he offered.

I looked down at my coat, the cool fabric in my hands. Riding with him made sense—it was already dark outside, and the thought of braving the cold alone was less than appealing. Gabriel's offer was practical. Sensible, even. Still, the thought of getting more involved, of accepting his help, made me hesitate. I didn't want to send the wrong signal or lead him on.

But then again, it was cold, and walking home alone wasn't exactly inviting.

Without really realizing it, I found myself nodding. "I'd like that. Just let me say goodbye to Bella and her parents first, okay?"

"Take your time," Gabriel said easily, turning to grab his scarf from the hook. Behind his back, Isadora gave me a giant grin and a double thumbs up. She'd never hidden her opinion that I should go out with Gabriel. I rolled my eyes and stuck my head into the kitchen.

"Hey! I'm heading back to Spellbooks. Thanks again for the dinner," I said.

"Oh, you're more than welcome. Here, I packed up a little bag for you," Honey said, bustling over, and handing me a paper bag with some to-go containers. "Just some meatballs with sauce and a slice of tiramisu."

"We appreciate all you did today to help Bella," Antonio said, coming over to wrap his arm around his wife's shoulders.

"I'm afraid we didn't do as much as we could've, what with getting distracted by Benny and the Hideaway," I said.

"What they mean is this is a down payment on all the work you're going to do tomorrow. I'll see you at nine," Bella said, coming over and giving me a big hug.

I chuckled and hugged her back. "If you throw in a cup of coffee, I'll be here at eight thirty."

"Deal. I'll see you tomorrow," Bella said, returning to finish the dishes.

I added the rest of my things to the bag Honey had given me and headed back to Gabriel, who was waiting by the door. He held my coat as I slipped it on, his easy-going nature making everything feel relaxed. Outside, the frosty night air hit me like a shock after the warmth of the house. Gabriel led the way to his car, and once we were inside, the hum of the engine provided a comforting backdrop as we began to chat.

"Are you okay?" he asked as we pulled away from the Oasis, glancing my way with concern. "Isadora filled me in on what happened today.

Finding a ghost in your attic and then opening the speakeasy presumably for the first time in decades, not to mention hearing about what happened to Benny and Clara?" He blew out a breath and shook his head. "What a day."

"Yeah," I murmured, "Just a lot to process, you know?"

He nodded with a small smile. "Ghosts and mysteries can get under your skin, but hey, at least we got tiramisu, right?" His lighthearted comment worked, pulling a tired but genuine smile from me.

As the car rolled down Havenwood's quiet streets, Gabriel glanced over. "Harper, if you ever need someone to take a little of this off your plate, or just unwind...you know where to find me."

His offer was casual, no pressure, yet thoughtful. I tucked a loose strand of hair behind my ear, glancing over at him. The passing streetlights painted soft shadows on his face. "Thanks, Gabriel. I'll keep that in mind."

He smiled—a genuine, soft expression that made my heart do a peculiar little flippity flop. "And just to make sure I've set the record straight," he continued, "I'm not just offering because Isadora says so. I...I want to. Be there for you, I mean."

The car slowed to a stop outside of Spellbooks, and he turned to look at me, his eyes earnest. "I realize we haven't known each other very long, but I think you're an incredible person. And after all that excitement with jewel thieves and the Christmas Eve Ball..." he trailed off, chuckling, "I think we make a good team, in more ways than one."

My cheeks warmed at his words, and the sweetness of the moment settled around us like a soft blanket. Before I could respond, Gabriel put the car into park and, to my surprise, hurried around to open the door for me—a gesture that caught me off guard, something I'd never experienced in my dating life. We walked together toward the front door of Spellbooks, the soft crunch of snow underfoot the only sound in the still night.

Standing outside the shop door, he looked down at me, his expression open and warm. "For what it's worth, Harper, I think there's something here. Something I'd like to explore if you're interested. But Isadora's filled me in. I know there's also something between you and your neighbor. Don't get upset with her. I noticed something at the ball and tend to be pretty determined when I want answers. As far as I'm concerned, we all have history, but I'd like the chance to get to know you better, if that's still okay with you."

I swallowed, fiddling with the strap of my bag. "Gabriel, I'm not...I'm not great at this. This is all unfamiliar territory for me," I said, my voice barely above a whisper. I'd rarely had time to settle in one place long enough to establish roots, let alone date for any significant amount of time. Now, to be setting up a life in Havenwood and have not one, but two men interested in me? It was overwhelming. However, my current strategy, namely, to ignore the situation as much as possible in the hopes it would resolve itself, wasn't working. I needed to act. I just wasn't sure what action to take.

Gabriel nodded, his smile never wavering. "That's okay. Most people don't like to admit it, but we're all just figuring it out as we go. If you ever want to figure it out together..." He trailed off, leaving the invitation hanging between us like a gently cast lifeline.

I smiled, my heart squeezing at his kindness. "I'll keep that in mind. Thank you. For the ride, for the talk, and for understanding," I said, feeling a sense of comfort despite also sensing that I was approaching an inevitable crossroads.

"Anytime," he said, stepping back as I opened the door. "Goodnight, Harper."

"Goodnight, Gabriel," I replied with a small smile, turning to enter the darkened shop, the warmth of the moment lingering like the afterglow of a sunset as I closed the door.

I locked the door of Spellbooks behind me, waving through the window at Gabriel as he drove away. The gargoyle, Gideon, who was a stone statue above the door during the day and my night watchman when the sun went down, was gone from his post. I assumed he must be on patrol or something. Mr. Wigglesworth blinked sleepily at me from his cat bed in the window before yawning widely and rolling over to go back to sleep. In the other window, Luna's long white ears poked up, twitching in my direction.

"Where were you? Who was that? Why were you out so late?" She paused the barrage of questions and sniffed loudly, sending her whiskers twitching. "Is that tiramisu I smell?"

"How did you get that scent past the meatballs and sauce?" I asked with a surprised laugh.

"Hey! I'm the one asking the questions here. Where? Who? Why? And are you going to share the tiramisu, or do I have to wake up the cat and sic him on you?"

"Hush!" I whispered urgently, throwing out a placating hand. "You know what he's like when he doesn't get his twenty naps a day!"

"So...tiramisu?" Luna said, tipping her head to the side imperiously.

I rolled my eyes. "Fine. But come upstairs."

How Luna ate so much and stayed so skinny was beyond me. In fact, I still didn't understand how she ate so much human food at all, but I supposed it must be one benefit of being a witch's familiar. Whatever magic was behind her appetite, her diet never seemed to cause her any problems. I wish I could say the same.

I tiptoed up the stairs, Luna padding along behind me. Ignatius fluttered up from reading a book in his nest of pillows on the window seat when we entered. I was pleased to see there were still no scorch marks anywhere. As if reading my mind, the little dragon smiled proudly at me. I shot him a thumbs up and reminded myself I really needed to thank Mason again for helping Ignatius find his way.

I set the bag on the counter and started to unpack it to get to the tiramisu. On top of Benny's notebook, the flask, and the code breaking book, I set Clara's notebook before busying myself with feeding two hungry, talking animals. As I set the food on plates for Luna and Ignatius, tiramisu for the rabbit and meatballs for the dragon, I filled them in on everything that we'd discovered both at the Oasis, under it in the Hideaway, and what had happened to Benny and Clara.

Settling down at the kitchen table with a cup of tea, I finished my story as Luna and Ignatius devoured their snacks. I sighed at the end, the weight of unresolved histories and mysteries pressing down on me. "One question that's still bugging me is how did Benny end up in Spellbooks in the first place? Granny Bea left a whole heap of puzzles for me to uncover when she left me this place, didn't she?" I murmured, half to myself.

Luna hopped onto the chair next to me, brushing a stray morsel of sweet mascarpone from her whiskers. "Beatrice was never one to sit on her tail, that's for sure. She was always digging into the past, sniffing out stories like a bloodhound. She believed that understanding people, even ghosts such as Benny, was key to something bigger. Like it would give her an insight into some grand design. She often said, 'Luna, we're all threads in the same tapestry, woven tightly together, even if we can't see the pattern.'"

"So, you remember Benny?" I pressed, eager for any fragment that could piece together the fractured narrative of his and Clara's final few days.

"I didn't until just now. Not from when he was alive, mind you. I'm not *that* old. But yes, I remember him now. The ghost version of him, at least," Luna said.

"How did he get stuck in the attic?" I asked.

"Beatrice found him in a graveyard, smashing everything in sight, which is quite a feat for a ghost. He was furious, lost, confused—and somehow that gave him more power over the physical world. Before you ask, I'm not exactly sure how it works with ghosts, but Beatrice mentioned something about the old runes carved into the gravestones. She thinks they might've amplified his abilities somehow. Once she got him out of there, he calmed down and lost a lot of that intensity. She promised to help him and convinced him to come back here while she tried to figure out his story."

"And did she?" I asked eagerly.

Luna lifted a shoulder, daintily licking a smear of tiramisu from the back of her paw. "No. Much like Ignatius, she didn't find all the answers she wanted. I was surprised when she managed to convince Benny to have a little, magically induced nap upstairs until she found the answers he wanted. I didn't think he'd go for it. But it's been so long since then that I'd honestly forgotten he was up there. You must have released him in your searching," Luna said, her ears twitching.

"This place should really come with warning labels," I muttered with a half-smile, despite the gravity of the situation. A sudden thought occurred to me, and I laid a hand on the wall, raising my voice. "Hey Spellbooks? Next time I'm about to release a temperamental ghost from his magical coma, one who might prove violent, stop me, okay?"

The shop stayed stoically silent and still.

I rapped a knuckle on the wall. "Spellbooks? Did you hear me?"

"Fluff and furballs, of course it heard you," Luna said with a roll of her eyes. "Spellbooks just likes to stir the pot. Always seeking out a bit of excitement and when that doesn't happen, creating it."

The wood of the wall warmed under my fingers at the rabbit's words. I shot the shop a surprised glance. For a moment, I marveled at how easy it was to talk to the shop just like I would any other person. At least, when it decided to answer. A year ago, if you'd told me I'd be having conversations with a building, I would've thought you were crazy. Now, this was my new normal. Well, as normal as things got in Havenwood.

I spoke to Spellbooks. "Okay, but next time, I could do with a little less excitement please."

Luna let out a small sound I interpreted as agreement, but Spellbooks stayed silent. I was about to press the point with Spellbooks when Luna cleared her throat, halting me before I could formulate the words. Her serious gaze captured mine, reflecting a wisdom that seemed to stretch beyond her years—or at least her species. "Your gran brought Benny here because she knew he was more than just a remnant of the past. She understood ghosts like him are stories that haven't found their endings. Beatrice believed in giving those stories a chance to unfold, to finish."

I pulled a blanket around my shoulders, feeling the chill of the evening creeping in. "And you think I should help Benny find his ending," I murmured. Luna nodded firmly. "Do you think Granny Bea had a plan? Any idea what it might have been?" I asked, half-hoping the shop would give up one of its secrets or Luna might recall something she'd forgotten about earlier.

"Probably and no," Luna replied, passing Ignatius a paper napkin with a sniff as the dragon messily buried his snout in the last of Antonio's sauce, licking up every drop but smearing it across his nose in the process. "Knowing Beatrice, the plan was all up here," she tapped her temple with a paw. "Unless she met him during one of her journaling phases. However, now it's up to you to figure out how to give the ghost his peace."

"Why *me*? Why not *us*?" I asked.

"Because I am a rabbit who takes my need for beauty sleep seriously. Thank you for the tiramisu and goodnight," Luna said with a haughty sniff before hopping towards the door.

I leaned back in my chair, looking around the room as if something in my apartment might give me an insight into Granny Bea's master plan. Unsurprisingly, nothing jumped out at me. I don't know how long I sat there after Luna left. Ignatius curled up on my couch and went to sleep. I pondered the situation as I sipped my rapidly cooling tea.

The past had a way of reaching out, intertwining with the present, insisting on being heard. Benny's outburst still echoed in my mind, the raw emotion of it rattling me more than I'd expected. As the night deepened, wrapping Havenwood in its quiet embrace, it was nice to escape the weight of everything for a moment, to step away from the intensity of the Oasis and find a little calm. But I couldn't ignore the truth—I wanted to finish what Granny Bea had started. To give Benny the closure he needed, to make sure his story didn't end in anger and confusion. History was repeating itself, but this time, I'd make sure the story had an ending. It had to.

Code Breaker

I TRIED TO SLEEP. I really did. But thoughts of Benny and Clara kept replaying on a continuous loop in my mind. Unable to shut off my brain, I padded past the snoring dragon and made myself another cup of tea. I looked longingly at the coffee on the counter. Tea wasn't my preferred beverage of choice, but if I gave in to the lure of richly brewed coffee, I'd never sleep. The notebooks on the counter just beyond the coffee caught my eye, distracting me. If I couldn't sleep, at least I could be productive.

Balancing the books, my steaming mug of tea, and the coziest blanket I could snag without waking Ignatius, I settled into the window seat and got to work. I started with Benny's notebook, but after the laborious effort of decoding three pages of sales records, I skipped ahead, picking pages at random. Each time, it was more of the same. Records of sales, inventory, and other items necessary for running a speakeasy. I couldn't find any hidden messages among the lists, but I kept at it until my patience ran out. Finally, I flipped to the end, decoding the last pages using the substitution code he'd given me. That's when I discovered something that gave me more of a jolt of energy than any cup of coffee ever had. Instead of more lists of inventory and prices, the final page was filled with names. Next to each was a number. Could this be the list of people who'd used the cabinets in the Hideaway? If so, maybe there was a clue here. Perhaps one of the empty cabinets had been used to store something dangerous or valuable, and the person using it killed Benny when he came to retrieve it. I made a mental note to ask Benny about it tomorrow and see if we couldn't start to compile a suspect list.

Having exhausted the coded pages, I set Benny's notebook to the side. Maybe Clara's would reveal something just as exciting. I grabbed her notebook, opening it to the first page. Like Benny had said, the encoded text wasn't the same one he used. Also, I noted the mysterious symbols drawn on the bottom of each page. The symbols became a riddle within the riddle, another layer to the mystery of Clara's code. My fingertips brushed over the sketched images as if they could impart some hidden knowledge through touch. Unfortunately, I had no such luck.

I set my jaw and got to work. I assumed Clara had opted for another substitution cipher, but it took me a lot of trial and error to work out the code she'd used. However, with time and determination, I cracked it eventually, and I was glad I did. What she'd put in her notebook was infinitely more interesting than the inventory lists in Benny's.

Within the pages, Clara had recorded tidbits, gossip, and overheard secrets. These snippets of life from a bygone era offered a colorful glimpse into a world where propriety battled with passion. These glimpses into the past painted a vivid tableau of the speakeasy Clara navigated. Here, a note about a bashful suitor's blunders; there, a wry observation of clandestine meetings over illegal drinks. It was like peering through a window into a world that spun on an axis of whispered secrets and unspoken yearnings.

As I delved deeper, the entries became more personal, revealing the burden of Clara's double life. On one hand, there was the weight of her father's expectations—the pressure to make a respectable match and settle into the traditional role of housewife and mother. On the other, the exhilaration of defying those very expectations, of secretly forging a path that was all her own.

Obviously, she wanted something more for herself than what her father had planned for her. Her words were a silent rebellion against the predetermined path that had been planned for her since her birth. Each sentence hinted at her inner conflict—a woman torn between familial duty and desire for something more.

Then there was a shift. The frivolity of gossip faded almost entirely, replaced by solemnity and hope. Clara had begun to write of a future, one that danced on the edge of something great.

"Beneath the heartwood tree…" the entry began, the rest of the sentence trailing off into a dreamy ellipsis, as though the allure of that sacred place had interrupted her mid-thought.

A few pages later, the mention of the heartwood tree in Clara's flowing script caught my eye once again. It was more than a mere nod this time; she wrote of it with reverence, a hushed awe reserved for the most sacred of secrets. I could tell that the tree wasn't just a landmark to Clara. It was a symbol, a beacon of enduring love in an age of temporary thrills. It was a poignant reminder that the heart of her story—her love for Benny—was as timeless as the legend she believed in.

My heart filled with the bittersweet realization of what they once had and what might have been. I turned the page, and my breath caught as I decoded the next entry. Clara's words were almost frantic, the script tighter, as if written with a shaking hand. Here, Clara detailed a close call—a night the speakeasy nearly got raided and the dread that followed. Yet, in this retelling, I could sense the unwritten exhilaration. A defiant note that seemed to say, '*We survived. We're alive.*'

From that entry onwards, her notes seemed to shift again. On October 18th, a week before Benny's murder, she wrote starkly about her father's anger,

"Father's temper has taken a dark turn; I've seen that look before, and it chills me to the core. I must tread lightly."

A shiver ran down my spine. Based on what I'd read so far, Clarence Silverthorne had jumped to the top of my otherwise very thin suspect list. I could imagine him, motivated by his twisted version of family honor, forcing Clara into a life she didn't want. I nodded to myself; only half-aware I was doing it.

My pulse quickened as I flipped to the next page, anticipation building. Maybe the answers I needed were buried right here, waiting to tie Clarence to Benny's death. I scanned the text eagerly, my fingers moving just a little too fast as I started decoding Clara's words, eager to uncover the truth.

This entry detailed increasing police interest in the Hideaway. It was significantly longer than previous ones and an Officer Crowley's name appeared with an ominous frequency.

"Crowley's eyes are prying, following me whenever I walk around town. I've even heard whispers and rumors of a raid. I feel the walls closing in."

Was the law after Benny and the Hideaway as part of a crackdown? I wondered if I should add Officer Crowley's name to my short suspect list.

However, as far as I was concerned, he was still a distant second to Clarence Silverthorne. I turned the page, this entry as long as the previous one.

Clara wrote, *"A new bootlegger has turned up on the scene. He goes by the name 'Driftwood Sam' which is obviously an alias. Since our regular gin distributor got pinched last month, a mutual connection suggested we work with Sam. I'm not sure we should be associating with anyone new just now, given our brush with the law. It was a near thing, and I'm still on edge. Benny says we need to though, and gin is always a good seller in the Hideaway. Against my better judgment, we have accepted a trial shipment from this Sam—just a few bottles to evaluate the quality of the product. But it makes me nervous that he showed up at precisely the right time. I can't help it. It's too convenient. Isn't it? Could he be a copper in disguise, trying to catch us in the act? Or maybe he's trying to horn in on our business? Either way, I don't like it. I am grateful that our intermediary ensures our identities remain concealed. There is no possible way this Sam knows who we are, just as we would be unable to identify him."*

The mention of Driftwood Sam sent a shiver down my spine. Clara's suspicions lingered in every word, and she was right to be cautious. A figure like Sam—whether a rival or someone with ulterior motives—had plenty to gain from Benny's demise. Could it have been a raid gone wrong? A deal that ended badly? But if Benny had died during a police raid, surely there would be a record of it. Why was there no mention of any raid in the history book?

Excited by the prospect of a lead, I set the notebook aside and opened my journal to a blank page. I started a suspect list with Clarence Silverthorne at the top, followed by Officer Crowley and Driftwood Sam, with a note next to his name: "bootlegger, possibly a cop?". Lastly, I added "intermediary" with a question mark—someone in that role might have known where the keys were kept and used them to slip into the Hideaway that fateful night.

Eager to see if I could uncover more details about a potential raid on the Hideaway, I pulled out my phone. However, my detour into the digitized town records online revealed nothing new related to police raids in Havenwood in the 1920s or Benny's speakeasy.

The lack of news, while not entirely unexpected, dampened my mood. I set the phone down and returned my attention to Clara's notebook, hoping I could discover some new tidbit that could crack this case wide open. With increasing urgency, I flipped ahead until I found the date of

Benny's untimely death. However, there was nothing in Clara's code about his demise. As I continued to decode her words, I noticed the entries dated just after his death grew ever more frantic.

"The feeling of being watched never fades. Are the walls listening, too?"

Clara's fear was palpable, seeping through each carefully penned word. As I translated her journal, I found my own handwriting growing shakier, the dread leeching from the page into me. My pulse quickened, an unsettling empathy with Clara's mounting anxiety washing over me, as if her terror had crossed time to take root in my chest.

If I hadn't known Spellbooks was utterly unique, I would've been tempted to return to the Hideaway right now and try talking to the walls in hopes that they might have the answers I sought. However, I knew better and returned my attention to Clara's notebook with a feverish intensity.

One of her last entries was almost a plea, scrawled in a desperate hand. *"I think I've uncovered who is behind Benny's death. But confronting him? He's so powerful! What if it's my undoing?"*

The last page was a jarring juxtaposition to the rest. When decoded, all it said was, *"I know who it is."*

The short sentence was a stark, abrupt end to Clara's thoughts and fears. My pulse quickened, and I snapped the journal shut, rising from my seat and pacing across the room. The runes at the bottom of the page—a circle, a spiral, and a triangle—stayed with me, etched in my mind. Why did she include them here, on some pages but not others? Were they spells? Clues? I paused by the window, pressing my fingertips against the cold glass, and my thoughts spiraled like Clara's sketch.

Was she hiding from something more sinister? A conspiracy, maybe? A police cover-up? Or was it her father, intent on controlling her, forcing her into a life she didn't want? My head buzzed with a hundred possibilities. Maybe Driftwood Sam wasn't just some bootlegger—was he a pawn in something larger? A threat she didn't see coming until it was too late? I needed answers, but they felt impossibly out of reach. Taking a deep breath, I returned to the journal, resting my hands on the cover.

Calm down. Think logically, I told myself. But Clara's words had set me on edge, and now I felt like I was racing the clock, solving a century-old puzzle before it slipped through my fingers entirely.

The nature of Clara's last few entries kept racing through my mind. She'd known something crucial, something perilous. Was that what kept her returning to the Hideaway, where whispers of the past still clung to the air like cobwebs? Had there been some clue there? Something she uncovered? A dangerous truth, one that perhaps led to her own untimely demise?

I closed the book, her words still echoing in my head, and yet, my task remained simple. I had to delve into the pasts of Clarence, Officer Crowley, and this new bootlegger, Driftwood Sam. Not to mention tracking down any leads from the owners of the cabinets after I talked to Benny tomorrow. Maybe someone unexpected would jump to the top of my suspect list. Someone wanted Benny out of the way, for one reason or another, and I was determined to find out who. If I couldn't get answers from Benny or historical records, maybe I could return to the speakeasy to uncover whatever Clara had found on the nights when she went there following Benny's death.

I would unearth the truth—not just for Benny and Clara, but for Havenwood. Benny's outburst in the Hideaway had shaken me more than I'd like to admit. His trapped spirit was becoming more unpredictable, and if I didn't act soon, I feared what turmoil might be unleashed—not just on the speakeasy, but on the Oasis itself.

Full of energy, I pulled out my computer and got to work. Hopefully, I'd be able to turn up some answers in the vast informational swamplands of the internet. I spent what felt like hours trawling through one website after another but to no avail. There was no mention of a Driftwood Sam linked to Havenwood as far as I could tell. A significant amount of information existed about Clarence Silverthorne, as one might expect of a prominent town leader, but none of which I felt applied to the case. There were several photos of him and other town officials at ribbon-cutting ceremonies or posing in front of town landmarks, but nothing that directly linked him to the Hideaway.

Eventually, I even found a single photo of Officer Crowley. He was shaking hands with the new mayor of Havenwood while a man and a woman stood in the background. It was dated the year after Benny and Clara had died. I zoomed in, scrutinizing the grainy black-and-white image for any clue about Officer Crowley and his motives. Other than an impressive handlebar moustache and a formidable stare, there didn't appear to be any other defining elements to the stoic-looking police officer. I glanced at the caption. It read:

Newly elected Mayor J. Featherfoot and Sheriff O. Crowley.

Joining them are the sheriff's wife, M. Crowley, and mayor's brother, S. Featherfoot.

March 5th, 1929.

"Huh." The grunt of surprise escaped me, echoing loudly in the otherwise silent room. The current mayor of Havenwood was also a Featherfoot. Flavian Featherfoot. I wondered if the two were family. They had to be, right? It wasn't a terribly common name. Maybe I'd ask the mayor when I saw him at the next town meeting. Hopefully by then, I'd have solved Benny O'Rourke's murder and could focus on more mundane mysteries like genealogy and Havenwood family trees.

I turned my attention back to Officer, now Sheriff Crowley. When I entered his new title in the search engine, more information appeared. I retreated down a rabbit hole of online research, scrolling through page after page. When I finally looked up, my eyes were gritty, my shoulders hurt from hunching over my keyboard, and I still didn't have any concrete answers for Benny.

The night deepened around me. As the silence of Spellbooks closed in, a certainty I couldn't articulate settled over me. The answers lay somewhere between the lines of Clara's coded writing or were hidden in the speakeasy. I could feel it in my bones. They had to be there. Because hours online had turned up next to nothing. For now, though, answers remained frustratingly out of reach, as elusive as the shadows at midnight.

I sat in the window seat, staring out into the frosty night and trying to imagine Clara Silverthorne searching for clues as to the identity of her love's killer. It must've been terrifying for her to return to the Hideaway night after night. To the scene of Benny's murder. The emotional trauma alone would've made it almost impossible for me to function had I been in her shoes. I wondered what clue or epiphany Clara stumbled upon that caused her to write the final entry in her notebook, the one claiming she knew the killer's identity.

Thinking of Clara's journal and her time after Benny's death, a slow, creeping realization began to form in my mind. What if Clara's death wasn't an accident after all? Gabriel said someone found her out in the woods. Most people likely assumed she was running away, and the suitcase we found in the escape tunnel seemed to confirm that suspicion. I suppose, given her obvious interest in the heartwood tree, one might also guess that she was trying to find that landmark to reminisce about her lost love. But why in a storm? Why would she have chosen that moment to run away or reminisce? It didn't make any sense. And speaking of things that didn't make sense, why was her bloodstained locket in the tunnel and not with her when they found her?

The initial supposition settled into a chilling understanding the more I contemplated it. What if someone noticed her nightly excursions to the Hideaway after Benny's death? Not just her father, but perhaps also the killer? He might've thought Clara was closing in or feared she'd discovered some clue. He decided to take advantage of her nightly isolation in the Hideaway. If her father confiscated the keys to the Hideaway, the only way in or out would've been through the escape tunnel. The hidden latch Benny showed us easily explained Clara's mysterious nightly sojourns to the locked Hideaway. Maybe the killer watched her, followed her to the escape tunnel, and attacked her there. In the struggle, her necklace broke. The idea that the killer wanted Clara's body found, carefully staged to look like a tragic accident, sent a chill down my spine. If they had truly wanted her to disappear forever, the secret escape tunnel would've been the perfect hiding place—undisturbed for nearly a century. But no, they wanted her discovered. The location in the woods, the head wound... it was all too convenient. If Clarence was behind this, surely, he would've wanted to bury his daughter's secrets along with her, preserving the Silverthorne name. Or maybe someone else feared the consequences of leaving a Silverthorne missing, knowing the family would never stop searching.

It was possible. The limited facts of the case supported my conclusions. However, what if I'd just read too many mystery novels and was forcing the sparse facts to fit my theories instead of searching for the truth?

Resting my forehead against the cool glass, I let the puzzle pieces of Clara's last days scatter and reform in my mind. The locket, the storm, the secrets she witnessed and took part in—all woven into a tale of love, loss, and potential treachery. Every angle I considered seemed to lead to more uncertainty. There were still too many unanswered questions.

Why did Clara feel compelled to return to the Hideaway night after night? What exactly did she hope to find? Had she found anything? And how did Granny Bea come into possession of the keys to the Hideaway years after the tragic deaths of Clara and Benny?

The locket remained a mystery of its own. How did it end up in the tunnel, half-buried and stained with blood? Was it merely a trinket, or did it hold some deeper significance in Clara and Benny's story? And what about the storm that fateful night? Had it precipitated the unfortunate accident that led to Clara's demise, or was there something more sinister at play, like I suspected?

As I sat there, lost in thought, I imagined that night playing out in Clara's home. It wasn't the first time her father had found her bed empty, nor the first time he'd searched for her in the shadows of Havenwood. But that night, something was different. The storm had raged, winds howling through the trees and rain hammering against the windows. Panic must have gripped Clarence as he realized she wasn't in the Hideaway. Then, after hours of searching, someone had brought her home—cold and unconscious from a head wound, destined never to wake again.

The questions persisted, gnawing at the edges of my mind. What secrets did Clara take to her grave? Could those secrets have been dangerous enough to make her a target? Was there someone out there, even now, who knew the full truth of what happened?

Sleep, when it finally claimed me, was fitful. Half-seen figures lurking in shadowed tunnels haunted my dreams with whispered secrets and the poignant echo of a tragic love song played only for ghosts.

The Rune Reader's Revelation

THE SUN WAS ALREADY shining brightly, making the snow glitter in the morning light when a gentle but persistent tapping at my window stirred me from the tangle of my dreams. Rubbing sleep from my eyes, I groggily blinked away the blur to find Finn standing below, lobbing pebbles upward. He hoisted a cardboard coffee cup with a pantomime of drinking, his silent invitation clear.

"Just a sec," I mouthed, signaling him to hold on. I shook the remnants of sleep from my mind and tried to focus, shoving my hair into the sanctuary of a messy bun as I glanced at the clock. It was five to eight. Still enough time to figure out what Finn wanted and get to Bella's by eight thirty if I hurried. I clattered down the stairs as quickly as I could. Mr. Wigglesworth looked up from his empty food bowl piteously. I swear, that cat could do puppy dog eyes better than any pooch I'd ever seen.

"I'll feed you, I promise. Just let me open the door for Finn," I told the cat as I flicked open the lock.

"Sorry for the wake-up call," Finn said, offering the coffee as a peace treaty as he entered. "You're usually up by now. I saw Bella this morning, and she said you're getting together, so I thought…" His voice trailed off as he took in my disheveled state.

"It's fine, really," I replied, shutting the door behind him to keep out the chill. I accepted the warm cup gratefully, letting the aroma of strong coffee anchor me back to reality. "Just one of those nights, you know?"

Finn nodded, the morning light casting a soft halo around him. "One of those nights that turns into one of those mornings. I've been there before, and coffee always helps," he said, a gentle teasing in his voice that made the corner of my mouth twitch into a smile.

I snorted a laugh. "Not exactly."

He leaned a hip against the counter, raising an eyebrow. "So, what? You were drinking with Bella? Or by yourself? You should've given me a call. I would've come over."

"No, nothing like that," I said, shaking my head. "I was just reading."

"Ah, now it makes sense." He grinned. "A good mystery, I take it?"

"Something like that." I took a sip of the coffee, letting the warmth seep into my bones. "Thanks for grabbing this, by the way. Definitely needed it."

Finn raised an eyebrow. "Oh? Sounds like this might be a story worth telling."

"You can say that again." As quickly as I could, I explained about Bella's party, finding Benny, the Hideaway, Clara, everything. There was no reason to hold anything back from Finn. Living in Havenwood, he knew about the paranormal world. He even had a little magic himself. Though he never finished his full druid training, his connection to nature and magical bindings had come in handy over the past few months. He chose to live quietly in Havenwood now, with less magic but far less risk.

Finn's casual posture against the counter morphed into intent focus as I recounted yesterday's adventures, his eyebrows arching higher with each revelation. People in Havenwood embraced the odd and the arcane, but last night's escapade had its own unique flavor of weird. I wasn't sure how Finn would respond and watched him anxiously as I concluded my retelling of events.

"I'm impressed," he admitted after I'd finished. "You seem to have a knack for creating excitement wherever you go."

His attempt at levity had the desired effect, and I found myself smiling despite the heavy thoughts about Clara and Benny that weighed on my mind. "I'm not so sure 'creating' is the right word. 'Discovering' perhaps?

Although you're giving me too much credit. Most of this adventure rests solely on…" I paused, catching myself before I gave away the secret of Spellbooks. I felt the faintest of vibrations tickle my toes before I hurriedly said, "…Granny Bea's shoulders. That's how we got started. We found this secret cubby in the attic with all Benny's things in it. Granny Bea sure loved history and a mystery."

Finn shifted uneasily. I wondered if he'd caught my hesitation and was going to press me on it. A bead of sweat formed between my shoulder blades. I wasn't a very good liar at the best of times, and my brain was still fuzzy from the lack of sleep. I just knew that I'd mess things up somehow if he started asking questions.

Finn's gaze became more serious. "Speaking of history, there's something else I wanted to tell you. Seraphina is coming back this weekend."

The mention of his ex brought a flicker of relief with a distinct undertone of discomfort. I struggled to respond as nonchalantly as possible. "Oh?"

He nodded, his fingers drumming on the side of his cup. "Yeah, she's got business with Vivienne Silverthorne. Something about the details of moving her company here. I didn't want you to be blindsided by her showing up in town again."

"Oh. Um. Right."

"Sorry. I didn't know how to bring it up more tactfully, but this is me trying for open and honest communication, as promised," Finn said, shifting awkwardly from foot to foot.

He was referencing when Seraphina appeared for the first time in years, just before Christmas. I'd assumed, incorrectly, that they were getting back together. I still felt that reigniting a spark with Finn was exactly Seraphina's goal. Especially now that she was relocating to Havenwood permanently. Finn didn't seem eager to dive back into the past, but there was something in the way he looked at me—like I was standing on the other side of a door half-open, and he wasn't quite ready to close it. Besides, I wasn't sure I could justify my jealousy, given that we'd never declared any sort of exclusivity when it came to our own relationship. In fact, after the events surrounding Seraphina's reappearance, we'd agreed to open and honest communication, which was less clear than one might expect. Regardless, I tried to mask the tightness in my chest by putting on a bright smile. "Thanks for telling me." And then because I couldn't help myself. "Does she have anyone to celebrate the New Year with?"

I nearly facepalmed myself. *Why did I ask that?*

"Not that I know of. She's just here for business, she said."

Something about the idea of Seraphina spending New Year's Eve alone struck a chord with me. Perhaps it reminded me too much of Clara sitting alone in the empty Hideaway after Benny's passing. Before I could consider it, I blurted out, "She should come to Bella's party, then. No one should be alone on New Year's Eve."

Finn's surprise was evident, but it shifted quickly into a warm smile. "That's very kind of you, Harper. I'll let her know."

"Okay." I nodded, affirming the impromptu invitation. My stomach twisted. What was I doing? Did I really want Seraphina there? Maybe not. It would put her and Finn in close proximity on the third most romantic holiday of the year. No, it definitely wasn't a good idea, but it was too late to back out gracefully now.

Finn leaned back slightly, his smile fading as he studied my face. "Are you okay? You seem distracted."

"Bella really wants this to be the talk of the town," I admitted with a shrug, "but it wasn't the party prep that wore me out. It was everything else. It's...a lot to take in. The ghost and the murder and, well, everything."

Finn's expression softened. "You're doing a good thing, you know. Helping everybody else. Bella. Seraphina. Benny. Clara. Just don't forget to let someone look after you."

"Well, if you want to help, I wouldn't say no." I blushed hotly when I realized what I'd said and hurried to add, "Um...with the party that is! I doubt Bella would turn down an extra set of hands. We got distracted yesterday, what with all the ghost turmoil and discovering the speakeasy. It was fascinating but didn't help put up decorations."

"Done," Finn said instantly, graciously not commenting on the pink burning my cheeks. "I've got a client coming for a tattoo in about twenty minutes, but unless I have a walk-in, I should be free this afternoon. Should I just come over to the Oasis?"

I nodded quickly, feeling a little bit like a manic bobble head figurine. "If it works out that would be awesome. I'd really like...I mean, I'm sure she'll appreciate the help."

"Well then, I'll be sure to come over," Finn said with a warm smile that let me know exactly who he was showing up for, and it wasn't for Bella. An unexpected tingly feeling raced straight down to my toes and right back up to my heart again.

An idea occurred to me, and I couldn't believe I hadn't thought of it the second Finn walked through the door. I must not have gotten much sleep if it took me this long to put together the pieces that were literally right in front of my face. Excitement chased away my embarrassment almost instantly.

"Although if you want to help me with something right now, I know a way you can. I decoded and read Clara's notebook last night. That's what really kept me up so late. She included some strange symbols at the bottom of each page. They look kind of like the runes that are in the tunnel, but not as complex. You know a lot about runes, right?"

Finn chuckled and nodded. "As a druid, I kind of have to, but I don't know as much as some. I stopped my training early, remember?"

"Well, you know more than I do. Will you do me a favor and take a look? See if you recognize anything?" I asked hopefully.

"Sure. I'd be happy to."

"Great. Let me go grab the notebook," I said, setting my coffee down and dashing back upstairs. Ignatius twitched on the couch but didn't wake as I rummaged through the pillows on the window seat, eventually finding Clara's book tucked under a cushy floral one.

I brought it back downstairs, handing it over to Finn excitedly.

Finn peered at Clara's notebook with a practitioner's keen eye. Maybe it was just my imagination or anticipation, but the very atmosphere in the room seemed to respond to his focused attention, a subtle shift in the air that made the hairs on my arms stand up.

"These aren't runes, but I don't think they're just random doodles either," Finn murmured, tracing the symbols with the tip of his finger. "They're specific. Intentional."

I hovered over his shoulder, trying not to let my eagerness overwhelm his concentration. "What do they mean?"

"I'm not sure, but I think they might be a code within a code. See? Look here," he said, pointing to the bottom of the page where Clara's journal lay open, my translation notes sitting beside it in a separate notebook. "According to your notes, this entry is about Benny. At the bottom of the page, she's drawn a fancy heart. Like the kind you'd find on a Claddagh Ring." He flipped forward a few pages. "Here's the heart again, and again. Each time, it looks like she's talking about Benny."

Realization sunk in. "So maybe the drawings are a quick categorization system? Even with her proficiency with codes, it might've taken her time to figure out what she'd previously written."

"And the symbols give her a quick clue who she's talking about on each page," Finn finished.

I grabbed the notebook in excitement. "If we're right, then she didn't keep the killer's identity a secret. She wrote it down. Right here," I said, flipping to Clara's last entry and jabbing my finger at the three symbols triumphantly.

Finn peered down at the drawings and then shook his head. "If these are meant to tell us who Benny's killer is, I don't know how to unravel the meaning."

"Why?"

"I think that specific combination probably only had meaning to Clara," Finn said. He frowned, his brow furrowing as if recalling a long-forgotten memory. "Although..."

"Although what? What do you think they might stand for?" I asked, feeling anticipation swell inside me.

He pointed at the symbols in the notebook. "In my experience with magic and runic lore, a circle is about eternity. It's often used in protective charms. The triangle symbolizes ambition. A rising up. The foundation of strength and leadership." Finn's hand hovered over the spiral. "And this one, the spiral, it speaks of progress and expansion outward. It's a hopeful sign, showing growth and influence."

"But you said you didn't think these were runes."

"Maybe they are, maybe they aren't. I don't know how much runic lore Clara knew. Runes are usually more complex than simple shapes, interweaving two or more to make some sort of a pattern. Something more than a child could draw. However, if Clara Silverthorne was a mage, it stands to reason that she had at least a rudimentary understanding of runes. Perhaps she used these in her code to point towards a magic user?"

I hit the heel of my hand against my head. "Magic! I forgot about magic entirely."

"What do you mean?"

"Maybe magic was the reason Benny didn't hear or see his assailant. Here I am, living in Havenwood, and I didn't even consider *magic* as a possible means, motive, or opportunity."

Finn scratched his cheek and shook his head at me. "Are you sure you're only a bookstore owner?"

"Pretty sure. Why?"

"Because it seems every time I see you, you're becoming more of a detective," Finn said, his charming smile removing any potential sting from his words.

"I wouldn't say that. I'm just...curious. Do you think Clara understood the meaning of the symbols? From a runic point of view, I mean?"

Finn hesitated and then nodded. "More than likely. However, I don't know if she was referring to magic here or perhaps the full moon over a mountain near a whirlpool," he said, tracing his finger along the symbols once more. "Without more context, it's hard to know what she was trying to tell us with these designs."

His words sank in, and my initial excitement waned. It was all so...broad. I had hoped for a secret message, a hidden plea, or a clear accusation from Clara herself. Something that would crack the case wide open. But what Finn described was more like an overarching theme that could apply to almost any family with deep roots in a community or possibly something else entirely.

My shoulders slumped. "So, no secret messages then? No finger pointing towards Bob or Fred?"

Finn closed the notebook gently, handing it back to me. "Doesn't seem like it. But if what you've told me about Clara is true, there's a reason for every word and drawing she put in this notebook. We just have to figure out what she meant."

I accepted the notebook, the weight of the unsolved mysteries resting heavily in my hands. "Thank you for the help, Finn. Really."

He smiled that easy, comforting smile of his. "Anytime. I just wish I could've given you the answers you wanted. But don't get discouraged. You've got a real knack for unraveling mysteries. This is just another puzzle piece."

His optimism did little to lift my spirits, but I forced a smile. "Yeah, another piece of a very, *very* complicated puzzle."

With a final supportive squeeze on my shoulder, Finn excused himself, citing the need to get set up for his client. Left alone with the notebooks, the runes, and the lingering echoes of a story, my frustration began to mount. Picking up Clara's notebook, I idly flipped through the pages. I wanted a neat resolution, a clear-cut solution to the mystery, just like in the detective books I read. But being the detective was far harder than reading about one. I'd solved mysteries before, but none of them had ever been this terrifying or filled with stakes this high. Murder wasn't just a puzzle—it was something much darker, and the weight of that reality settled heavily on my chest.

As I glanced down at the final pages, something caught my eye—a small crown sketched delicately in the margins of an adjacent page. I'd seen it before, scattered throughout Clara's writings, usually when her father was mentioned. Maybe it was a symbol she used for him, or perhaps it hinted at the power he held over her life and choices. I quickly jotted a note in my journal: *Figure out what the crown means.* If her father had a hand in what happened to Benny, I wasn't about to let it stay hidden.

This mystery was a challenge—a scary yet tantalizing one. And I couldn't, wouldn't, walk away from it. Clara, Benny, and even the Hide-away itself still had secrets to tell. And I was determined to listen.

Specters and Sentiments

I GLANCED AT THE time as Finn left and nearly spat out my coffee. I was running later than I'd imagined. Finn's unexpected visit, while beneficial, hadn't helped my promptness. The morning sun was already climbing higher as I dashed into the shower, the hot water rushing over me in a haste that mirrored my thoughts. Who could be behind the circle, triangle, spiral in Clara's notebook? I had barely dried off and thrown on some clothes before I was out the door, keys in hand and decoded clues in my bag, heading back to the Oasis. Every step was brisk, a silent prayer repeating in my mind: *Let Bella not be mad, let Bella not be mad.*

I skidded to a stop in front of the Oasis, took a deep breath, and pushed the door open. The aroma of freshly brewed coffee immediately enveloped me, a soothing balm to my frazzled nerves. As I stepped into the kitchen, I found Bella, Isadora, Gabriel, and Bella's boyfriend, Alex, sitting around the kitchen table with steaming mugs and a plateful of freshly baked scones in the middle of the table. Their laughter and conversation punctuated by the soft sounds of Honey shaping bread dough at the counter. Antonio waved at me as he carried another tray of food out to the B&B guests lounging in the breakfast nook I'd seen on my way in.

"Sorry I'm late," I gasped out, sliding into the chair Bella pointed at.

Bella waved off my apology and passed me a plate. "Don't worry about it. You're here now, and that's what matters. Besides," she added with a wink, "Finn made a peace offering on your behalf. Texted to say he'd come by later to lend a hand, which was all your idea."

"And we'll happily put him to work!" Alex said cheerfully, raising his mug. He and Finn had always gotten on well.

I let out a sigh of relief and gave an appreciative nod. Finn always knew how to smooth things over. "Thanks, and I'm sorry again. I'll make it up to you, I promise. In fact, I may have already done that. At least partially," I said, digging into my bag and passing over the decoded notebooks.

Bella flipped through Benny's while Isadora looked at Clara's. Gabriel peered over his sister's shoulder. He paused and gave me an impressed look. "You decoded all this last night? That's no small feat."

"It's really impressive," Bella said.

"I think I found—"

"Look at this! She did the entire book," Isadora said, nudging Bella and showing her Clara's notebook.

"No way! That's incredible!" Bella said.

I shrugged modestly, feeling my cheeks heat a little under their praise. "Well, I had a bit of help. Luna and Ignatius were just as interested as I was," I fibbed, uncomfortable with the amount of attention I was receiving.

Honey set the dough aside to rest and chuckled. "Help or not, you've got a knack for this kind of thing, Harper. We're lucky you moved here." She pointed a flour-coated finger at the scones on the table in front of me. "Eat up, dear. We've got a busy day ahead, and you'll need your strength."

I didn't need a second invitation, plucking the nearest scone from the plate and slathering it with a dollop of Honey's homemade strawberry jam. From the crumb-covered plates in front of the others, it looked like everyone else had already indulged in Honey's baking.

"You know, the more I think about it, the more I love the idea of incorporating the Hideaway into the New Year's Eve party," Bella said, leaning forward eagerly as Antonio pushed back into the kitchen, carrying some dirty dishes. "We talked about it before, but it would be such a great way to showcase a hidden piece of Havenwood's history. Imagine unveiling it with a Prohibition theme—it could be incredible."

"I'm glad you're still thinking about it!" Isadora exclaimed. "I think it's an excellent idea! And I have the perfect bead curtain we could hang in front of the basement stairs to give it even more of a secretive vibe."

Before I could swallow my bite of scone and add my own enthusiasm, Antonio interrupted. "Not to rain on your parade, cara mia, but before we host a party down there, we need to make sure the place is secure. Are those magic runes holding everything up going to give out? We need to be one hundred and ten percent sure it's safe for guests before we even consider this," he said, his serious expression adding weight to his words, a stark contrast to his usual easygoing nature.

"And we'd need to give the basement and the Hideaway a thorough clean," Honey added, nodding. "I don't want people thinking I host parties in cobwebs and dust. What would that say about the reputation of the Oasis?"

"Still, if we could pull it off, wouldn't that be incredible?" Bella said, her excitement undimmed. Behind her back, neither of her parents looked convinced, but I wasn't about to tell her that.

Gabriel must've noticed the same thing I did because he spoke up. "I'd be happy to double check the protective runes for you. Isadora gave me a brief overview of what you found last night and how they work. Rune-work is something I covered extensively in my magical training, and I know more than my fair share about protective spells. With a little work, I'll be able to tell you if it's safe to host anything down there. If not, I could make some suggestions on how to fix the magically weak areas."

"That sounds perfect!" Isadora practically bounced on her feet. "I'm going to call my friend who's a party planner—she might have some Prohibition-themed decorations we could borrow!" Without waiting for a reply, she dashed out of the room, already dialing her phone.

Gabriel chuckled and shook his head. "Isadora never was one to sit still."

"And neither am I," Bella declared. "What do you say Papa? Mama? Can we have the party in the speakeasy?"

"There's a sentence I never thought I'd hear," Antonio said with a bemused shake of his head. He stroked his moustache contemplatively. "Well, if Gabriel doesn't mind checking out the runes and making sure everything is safe—"

"And we make everything presentable," Honey added. "By that, I mean guest-worthy cleaning. Not a cobweb in sight."

"Wait." I hesitated, glancing around the room. "Before we dive into cleaning, does anyone else remember that this place is technically still a crime scene? I mean, Benny was killed down there, and we haven't exactly gone over every inch of it yet. What if there's evidence that was missed?"

Honey and Antonio exchanged a glance.

"That's a fair point," Bella added. "The cops must have gone through it at the time, but we'd better make sure before we launch an all-out cleaning frenzy."

I nodded, a sense of urgency building in me. "I'll head down now and take photos, just to make sure we didn't overlook anything. Gabriel, would you mind coming with me? You could check the runes while we're there."

Gabriel set down his coffee mug and nodded. "I'm in."

"Assuming you don't find anything, I suppose I don't see why we couldn't re-open the Hideaway," Antonio finished, offering a small smile.

Gabriel pushed to his feet and offered me his hand. "Sounds like we've got a lot to do. We'd better get to work."

I took his hand, my mind already whirling, wanting to see if the discoveries I'd made last night led to any more clues. "Absolutely. I need to have a word with Benny about a couple of things too," I said.

Descending the stairs into the basement with Gabriel close behind, the cool air wrapped around us like a shroud, a stark contrast to the warmth of the kitchen above.

"So," Gabriel broke the silence as I reached the last step, "I couldn't help but notice you started to say something about what you found before my overly excited sister cut you off. Did you uncover anything new about Clara?" His voice echoed slightly off the stone walls.

I paused outside of the doorway leading to the Hideaway. If Benny was unstable, gauging Gabriel's response to the news might help me figure out how I should approach the matter with him. As quickly as I could, I recounted the revelations from Clara's journal, watching Gabriel's face closely for his reaction as I wrapped up.

"I think those symbols at the bottom of her pages might be the key to finding Benny's killer and maybe hers as well. They're not just random drawings. At least, I'm pretty sure they aren't. F..." I hesitated, not sure of how Gabriel would react knowing I'd discussed the matter with Finn. However, he was a friend and my neighbor. Gabriel's sharp gaze snapped up to me. Internally, I sighed. It was too late to stop now so I continued. "Finn suggested they might be a kind of personal code Clara came up with and I agree. They might point us towards who did it. If we can decode them, that is."

Gabriel stopped in his tracks, the notebook open in his hands. He studied the pages, his finger tracing the delicate, looping symbols. "That's clever," he murmured. "Her way of leaving a trail without tipping off the wrong person. Finn's right—it has that feel. But cracking it won't be easy. Do you have any leads on how she structured the code?"

I blinked, momentarily surprised by his calm acceptance. I'd worried, even briefly, that bringing up Finn might stir something—jealousy, maybe, or irritation. Not that Gabriel had ever given me any reason to think he'd feel that way. Sometimes I worried anyway. Not about him, exactly, but about the awkwardness of navigating a world where everyone in Havenwood had some connection to one another.

"Not yet," I admitted, meeting Gabriel's gaze, "but I think Clara left the key hidden in her writing style. Finn said she might've used recurring patterns or phrases as part of the code. We just need to connect the dots."

Gabriel nodded, his expression thoughtful and focused. "Then we've got something to work with. Between your observations, Finn's suggestions, and what we can figure out, we might be able to break this."

"Do you think Benny will know what the symbols mean?" I asked, keeping my voice soft.

Gabriel shrugged, handing the notebook back to me. "He would have the best chance out of all of us but be careful. Ghosts, especially those with unresolved pasts, can be temperamental at best."

I thought back to the story of how and where Granny Bea had first found Benny and nodded seriously. The last thing I wanted was to unleash an angry ghost on the DeLucas' B&B.

I brushed my fingers along the wall of the tunnel and the runes responded instantly, glowing brighter under my touch. Gabriel followed me into the main room, examining the runes as he went. The speakeasy was unnervingly quiet as I approached Benny's photograph on the bar. His ghostly figure flickered with an unsettling intensity, as if barely containing his anger. The edges of his form seemed to blur, and the runes surrounding the image pulsed rhythmically, almost like a heartbeat in sync with his barely contained fury.

A low hum filled the room, vibrating through the floor beneath us. Gabriel muttered under his breath, tracing one of the runes on the wall. "Something's off..."

The lights overhead flickered violently. Without warning, a chair shot across the room, slamming into the wall with a deafening crash. I gasped, stumbling back as the pulse of the runes grew more frantic. Benny's figure writhed within the photograph, the air around him distorting as if his anger was tearing at the seams of the speakeasy itself.

The air in the speakeasy was growing heavier by the second. Gabriel moved quickly, stepping in front of me, his arm pushing me gently but firmly behind him. His eyes flickered between the photograph and the runes on the walls. "Stay back," he murmured, his tone protective, "this could get worse."

I peeked around him, my heart pounding. "Benny!" I called out, trying to keep my voice steady. "Benny, listen to me!"

The lights above us flickered even more violently, the furniture rattling ominously. Another chair wobbled, and I braced myself for it to fly across the room. But just as the tension seemed ready to snap, Benny's ghostly figure paused. His blurry form twisted, as if he was trying to focus. His gaze locked onto mine.

"Benny, it's me—Harper," I said softly. "I'm trying to help you. We all are."

The lights flickered one last time before steadying, the buzzing hum slowly fading. The air in the room calmed, the oppressive weight lifting. Benny blinked, his figure in the photograph stilling as recognition washed over him. He glanced at the locket on the bar, his gaze softening for a moment.

I stepped around Gabriel. "Harper!" he hissed.

I ignored him, focusing on keeping my voice steady as I addressed the angry ghost. "We're doing everything we can to uncover the truth, but I've hit a snag. I was hoping you could help me with some things I found in your notebooks."

Benny's form flickered slightly, his gaze still intense. "Notebooks?" he muttered, his voice tinged with frustration. "You wanna talk about notebooks while I've been stuck here all night, right next to Clara's locket, see?" His eyes shifted from the photograph of him and Clara to the locket, his expression going from wistful to something darker—sadness mixing with fury. The soft glow around the portraits in the golden locket caught my eye again—a glow that seemed to underscore the depth of their bond, even in the stillness.

"I gave her that locket," Benny said, his voice sounding harsh with barely restrained emotion. "I never saw her without it. The more I stew here, the hotter under the collar I get. I'm raring to do my bit, doll. We gotta nose out the mug responsible for this mess."

"I know," I said. "Look, I've decoded both your notebooks. At the end of yours, I found a list of names. Were these the people who used the cabinets behind the bar?" I flipped to the correct page and showed him the decoded list.

Benny leaned closer to the page, his ghostly lips mouthing the names. "Yeah, these are the folks. Each cabinet was assigned to one of them."

I double checked the list against the empty cabinets we discovered yesterday. "What about the ones that didn't have anything stored?" I tested out a theory. "Could it be one of them emptied out their cabinet to protect a secret? Maybe you were in the wrong place at the wrong time when they came back to retrieve it."

Benny shook his head adamantly, his image flickering slightly. "Nah, none of these folks could've done such a thing. I ran a tight ship at the Hideaway. I never would've given a cabinet to someone I didn't trust. This list proves it. Everyone here was loyal. Besides, they'd have to be a special kind of stupid to hide anything here, knowing I had an extra key to each of their cabinets."

"I have to admit, it doesn't really seem like a sensible option," Gabriel said from across the room where he was double-checking runes.

"I guess not," I said with a sigh, feeling a bit deflated. I closed Benny's notebook and picked up Clara's. "I don't want to upset you, Benny, but I think you might be the only one who can help me figure out what Clara wrote in her journal."

Benny's eyes lit with a mixture of fierce determination and overwhelming sorrow. "Lay it on me, doll."

I flipped through the pages. "There are tidbits and gossip in here that Clara collected. She had information on pretty much everyone. Do you think she was gathering this for a reason?"

Benny's image softened slightly. "Clara wasn't interested in stirring up trouble or holding grudges. She was all about keeping the good times rolling and the music playing. She wrote things down to keep track of the nights that sparked her interest, not to cause mischief. And it's not like she needed any kind of leverage—she was a Silverthorne, and they never lacked for anything. Her heart was in the Hideaway."

"But what if *that* was the issue?" I mused, biting my lip and wondering how to gently approach the symbols under that ominous line of text on the last page. "Maybe someone wanted the Hideaway closed for good. Perhaps when Clara kept coming back after you passed, maybe they worried she'd take up your mantle. She did mention there was a new bootlegger on the scene. Someone named Driftwood Sam?"

Benny's figure twitched, his ghostly form seeming to bristle at the name. "Yeah, I remember him. Slick fella, that one. Sent over some high-class hooch when the cops took down our regular supplier. Just a few bottles to test the waters, but it went down smooth with the crowd. I was thinking about bringing him on as our steady giggle juice guy."

Gabriel shifted slightly, shooting me a look from across the room. I could feel his skepticism, but he didn't say anything. I pressed on, sensing Benny's lingering frustration. "But what if that was all a front? What if he was using the opportunity to scope out the Hideaway for a hostile takeover?"

Benny's expression darkened, his image flickering more erratically. "Maybe. But I don't think that sap had the guts to pull something like that. Not with the Silverthornes involved. Anyone smart enough knew not to cross that family."

I glanced at Gabriel, who crossed his arms, his face thoughtful but guarded. "It could've been more than just the bootlegger," I said softly to him, weighing my words. "Maybe someone else—someone with real influence—wanted the Hideaway gone. Clara's father, for instance. He had power and connections. Maybe he found someone who would get rid of Benny for him."

Gabriel's brow furrowed slightly, his jaw tightening. "Her father? You really think he would've...?"

"Maybe not directly," I admitted, "but what if he set things in motion? Maybe he found a suitor for Clara, someone who didn't like Benny standing in the way. That might explain why Clara packed a suitcase. Perhaps she was in a rush to leave."

Gabriel didn't respond right away, his gaze slipping to Benny's figure, flickering as if caught between anger and desperation. "I suppose it's possible," he said finally, his tone soft but cautious.

Benny's figure twisted slightly in the photo, his ghostly form almost vibrating with tension. "Trust me, if someone was sniffing around my Clara, I'd know. I'd have been wise to it. I had eyes on every nook and cranny of the Hideaway, and more than a few spots in Havenwood, too. Smart business, y'know, especially for a fella running a juice joint on the sly."

I frowned, thinking back on my list of suspects from the night before. "If it wasn't Driftwood Sam, Clara's father, or some jealous suitor, what about law enforcement? I read about an Officer Crowley who became sheriff after you...well, after you died. Could what happened have been a raid that went sideways? Maybe Clara's father had a quiet word with the cops to put a stop to all of it, or they were tired of you running a speakeasy right under their noses."

Benny's form flickered again, his voice filled with a mixture of frustration and doubt. "Maybe, but Crowley was a decent sort. He was the type of guy who just wanted calm waters, see? If I didn't disrupt the town's official business, Crowley seemed happy enough to turn a blind eye."

I glanced at Gabriel, then back to Benny, the question forming before I could stop it. "Wasn't that...unusual? I mean, back then, didn't most people in his position expect some kind of...kickback?" I asked, my voice hesitant but curious.

Gabriel's expression darkened slightly, but he stayed quiet, watching Benny's reaction closely.

Benny's ghostly figure twisted, his tone sharpening. "Yeah, well, most coppers might've expected a little something to keep things smooth, sure. But I didn't pay Crowley off. Thought if I kept my nose clean, didn't rile him up, we could both just go about our business." He paused, his form flickering as if struggling to contain his emotion. "Guess maybe that was a mistake, huh? Maybe he thought I was trying to pull one over on him."

"Maybe Crowley saw the existence of the Hideaway as a black mark against him. Especially since he was running for sheriff," I suggested.

Benny shrugged. "Now I ain't never heard nothing about that. Must've happened after I took the big sleep."

I tried not to look at Gabriel when I spoke next. "Which brings us back to Clarence Silverthorne. He might've been Clara's father, but are we sure he's not behind this somehow?" I asked.

"Maybe he was the guy who snuck up on me that night. Or paid that guy, whoever he was," Benny said, the edges of his picture starting to glow and blur with his rising anger. "He never did like me with Clara. Thought I wasn't good enough for her. Maybe he was behind it. Forced Crowley to raid the joint."

Gabriel spoke up from where he was inspecting more of the runes. "Doubtful. If it had been a raid, there likely would've been some record of it. Either in the town records or in the Silverthornes'," he said, echoing my own thoughts from the night before.

"Unless..." I said, biting my lip, "unless the raid was a favor to Clarence or done behind his back. Then there definitely wouldn't be a record. Especially if it resulted in a death—they'd cover that up in a heartbeat."

Gabriel didn't look convinced. "Perhaps, but I don't see it. I don't think Clara was the type of woman to just accept the story handed to her. If her father was behind Benny's death, even unwittingly, I have a feeling she would've found out one way or another."

I raised an eyebrow. "She did find out, Gabriel. Maybe not right away, but she clearly pieced together enough to know something was off and even claimed she knew who was responsible in her notebook."

Benny's gaze suddenly sharpened. "Hold up there, toots. Run that by me again. What'd you just say?"

I took a breath, flipping open Clara's notebook to the page I'd found the night before. "Clara figured it out," I began, holding the notebook out for him to see. "She wrote a note in here, saying she'd uncovered the truth behind your death. But there's more. There are symbols at the bottom of these pages—here, look," I pointed to the delicate drawings scattered beneath her words. "We think they represent different people. See this heart? She always uses it when she's talking about you."

Benny's ghostly form flickered, a low hum of frustration vibrating through his voice. "A symbol for me, huh? And these others?" His tone softened, tinged with something deeper—sadness, perhaps—as I traced the remaining symbols, carefully laying out what I'd already pieced together.

"I think Clara used symbols to represent people," I explained, my voice calm as I flipped through the notebook. "It's not conclusive proof, but it could tell us who she suspected."

"Or at least who she wanted to point us toward," Gabriel added, his tone steady but cautious.

I nodded and placed Clara's notebook and my notes on the bar. Flipping to a section I'd already matched up, I gestured for them to look. "Here. Every time Clara writes about her father, there's a little crown sketched at the bottom of the page. Finn and I noticed it when we went through this earlier—it's consistent. See? Here it is again, and here." I turned a few more pages, pointing out the repeating crown symbol.

Benny leaned in, his form flickering with a mix of hope and tension. "A crown for her father. Makes sense."

My fingers skimmed over the lines, this time focusing on pointing out what I'd already pieced together. "Now look here. This is what I was talking about. There's no crown on this page. Instead, she used a circle, a spiral, and a triangle." I tapped the symbols lightly. "If the crown always represented Clarence, then it means it wasn't him she suspected."

Benny's figure flickered sharply, his frustration buzzing through his voice. "Not Clarence?" His form vibrated violently, the runes around him flaring faintly as his anger bubbled over. "That high-hat? That puffed-up blowhard who thought he owned the whole town? You're telling me it wasn't him behind all this? The guy hated my guts, made it his mission to throw a wrench into my life any chance he got! Always strutting around like he was king of the hill, like I wasn't fit to shine his shoes."

His voice grew louder, sharper, the frustration spilling out like a dam breaking. "The man was a real four-flusher, all bluster and no heart. You expect me to believe he didn't have the gall to pull the strings? If it wasn't that stuffed shirt, then who?! Who else had it out for me like that?"

I hesitated, watching his form waver, caught between his fury and something deeper—betrayal, maybe, or the overwhelming realization that his long-held suspicions might have been wrong. It was the kind of resentment that came from years of carrying the weight of blame, of being sure he'd pinned the right person. And now, that certainty was unraveling.

I hesitated, watching his flickering form and the raw emotion etched into his face. This wasn't just about solving a mystery for Benny—it was about finally giving him some kind of closure. The weight of his century-old grief pressed down on me, heavy and unrelenting. Whatever the truth was, we had to uncover it, no matter how tangled or painful it turned out to be.

I let out a long breath, my fingers tracing the unfamiliar symbols. "It's not over yet. Clara left these for a reason. We just need to figure out what they mean." The one lead that had felt solid—Clarence's involvement—was slipping away. I looked down at the notebook, deflated. "I don't know. I thought it all fit."

Benny's form seemed to sag, his ghostly energy flickering with a deep sadness. "Me too, dollface."

Gabriel, who had been silent for a moment, exhaled softly. "Well, if nothing else, it means my ancestor wasn't responsible for all of this." Relief flickered across his face, though it was tempered with caution. "That's...something. That's...something, but I get it. It's not the answer we hoped for."

I nodded, but the weight of frustration was still heavy on my shoulders. "But then who? If it wasn't Clara's father...we're back to square one." The defeat in my voice echoed in the quiet of the room.

The air seemed to still, Benny's frustration palpable as his form flickered in and out of focus. "Back to square one," he muttered bitterly. "Just when I thought we were getting somewhere..." His voice wavered, thick with frustration and something deeper. "All I want is the truth, y'know? After all these years, still stuck here, no answers, no peace."

I could feel his despair pulling at me, but I wasn't about to let either of us lose hope. I stepped forward, refocusing the energy. "We're not done yet, Benny. Gabriel's right. We've ruled out one suspect, but that just means we're closer to the truth. Clara left these symbols for a reason, and we're going to figure out what they mean."

"How?" Benny asked almost plaintively.

I pulled out my phone. "First things first, I'm going to search the Hideaway from top to bottom. I'll take photos, check for anything we might've missed. There's still something here, I can feel it."

Benny's flickering eased slightly, though his frustration remained. "You really think you'll find something? I feel like I've been staring at this place for eternity."

I offered him a reassuring smile. "I won't leave a single stone unturned. You've been waiting long enough. You deserve answers."

Gabriel shifted beside me, his expression thoughtful as I focused on snapping photos of the room, documenting every corner. "She's right, Benny. We're not giving up."

I moved through the room, eyes darting over the dimly lit space, searching for anything out of place—a flicker of light, a hidden compartment, something we'd missed. There had to be something here. There had to be. Some clue we missed before that would lead us to the truth.

The stillness thickened the air around me, and the runes, normally steady, began to pulse with erratic energy. Their soft glow dimmed, then flared, casting wild shadows along the walls. Benny's presence flickered with the lights, his frustration radiating through the room. The runes trapping him in the photograph hummed louder, their vibrations prickling the air, sending an uneasy shiver down my spine.

Suddenly, one of the runes on the wall sputtered, its light faltering. A chair scraped the floor behind me, the sound sharp in the silence. I spun, heart hammering in my chest, but there was nothing—just the shifting glow of the runes casting eerie, distorted shadows across the bar.

Benny's form crackled with energy, his restless figure flickering with a force that rattled the walls. I could feel his growing agitation, his desperation to break free.

"Benny, calm down," I whispered, though my voice felt too small, too fragile in the charged air.

The runes flared again, the pulse quickening, like the heartbeat of the room itself was syncing with Benny's anger. The glow twisted unnervingly, flickering in sync with his frustration.

Everything around me vibrated with a barely contained energy, the runes, the room—everything holding its breath, teetering on the edge.

And then, in an instant, it stilled—but the runes didn't go quiet. They pulsed steadily now, their hum deep and ominous, like a warning.

Something was happening to Benny. Despite the runes that trapped him in the photograph, it felt like he was growing stronger. The air hummed with his presence, charged and electric. I shook my head, the thought too bizarre, too impossible. And yet...it was there. I could feel it—his energy building, pressing against the boundaries of the magic trapping him.

The lights flickered again, the runes dimming in and out of sync. A cold sensation crept up my spine, the certainty settling in my bones like an unspoken truth. We were running out of time.

Collapse of Dreams

Suddenly, Gabriel's voice echoed through the room, pulling me away from my thoughts of Benny. "Harper, you need to see this!"

I looked around, surprised to notice he'd vanished from the speakeasy. I hadn't even seen him go. "Gabriel? Where are you?"

"In the escape tunnel. Come here!" he called, his voice bouncing off the narrow walls.

I flipped on the flashlight app on my phone and hurried through the secret door we'd left open. That was probably foolish. It led to an escape tunnel, after all. One that supposedly exited into the woods where anyone could find the entrance and sneak into the Hideaway. Was that what Gabriel had found? An intruder? He hadn't sounded worried, but maybe I just didn't know his vocal inflections well enough.

With a surge of adrenaline, I rushed over the uneven ground, past the tattered remnants of Clara's suitcase and around a slight bend a few yards further on. I hadn't come this far in my first exploration of the escape tunnel. As I rounded the bend, I skidded to a halt. In front of me, the tunnel had collapsed, completely blocking the escape route. Gabriel knelt in the dirt, running his hand along an exposed but broken support beam that lay splintered among the ruins.

"Look," he said, his voice grim, "this wasn't just decay. See how the runes are scratched out? And the wood near the top? It's been cut. Not all the way, but enough that, without the magic in the runes, it was only a matter of time before it collapsed."

My heart skipped. "Sabotage?" I whispered.

He nodded. "Someone did this deliberately. They didn't even have to risk being here when it happened—they just set it up and waited."

The pieces of a dark puzzle slotted together in my mind. "Could it have been Clara's father?" I wondered aloud. "After he confiscated the keys, he could have discovered this tunnel, tried to collapse it to stop her coming here. Making it look like an accident would mean he'd have plausible deniability."

"But I thought we just eliminated him as a suspect. You know, from the lack of a crown in Clara's journal," Gabriel pointed out.

"Okay, well, if not Clarence, maybe one of his lackeys? A police officer? Maybe even Officer Crowley," I said.

Gabriel pondered the idea. "Okay, so maybe this Crowley scratched out the runes. What if Clara was caught in the collapse? Could that be how she was injured?" He shook his head. "I don't think either Clarence or someone who worked for him would've risked Clara's life like that."

"Okay, so let's assume it was someone else. Another bootlegger perhaps. Maybe Clara caught him sneaking in one night when she was mourning Benny. They struggled, and she lost her necklace in the fight. Is it possible that the killer staged the accident in the woods to cover his tracks?" I asked, thinking through the possibilities.

"Maybe," Gabriel replied slowly, "but why would he come back to the Hideaway? If he had already taken care of her in the woods, wouldn't he want to stay as far away as possible?"

I frowned, realizing his point. "Unless...unless he needed to come back for something. The runes, maybe? To destroy evidence or sabotage something?"

Gabriel's eyes narrowed in thought. "You're saying he might have returned to tamper with the runes, causing the collapse? To make sure no one uncovered whatever secret he was hiding?"

"Maybe?" I bit my lip, considering alternative theories. "Or maybe her father sent someone to scare her? Maybe to get her to stop coming here? Perhaps she ran away from the hypothetical intruder and into the woods, getting hit on the head in the storm as she ran?"

"It's a possibility," Gabriel allowed, tracing his fingers over the destroyed runes. "But if I were Clarence in that scenario, I'd be consumed by guilt, even if I hadn't been the one to physically destroy the runes."

"I keep circling back to this police officer. She didn't write about him in a flattering way. Maybe Crowley took it upon himself to put her on the straight and narrow, but instead of scaring her off, she died, and he never said a word," I finished, the weight of the tragedy settling in.

"This is all just supposition at the moment and too many nebulous suspects. We need some real evidence," Gabriel said.

I ran a hand through my hair. "Yeah, but evidence that is a hundred years old? Where could we find something like that other than Clara's belongings which I assume have been undisturbed until I found them."

"I'm not sure." Gabriel frowned, running his light along the beam. "Whoever was behind this had to be at least somewhat knowledgeable about magic to deface the runes. In this town, that means it could've been just about anyone. They wouldn't even have to have magic, just enough knowledge to disrupt the runes. Besides, once the tunnel collapsed, why not just exit through the door, go get help when Clara didn't show up, and 'discover' the collapse when the inevitable search party came hunting for her? That seems like a more logical scenario to me."

"I suppose that makes more sense than someone carrying her through the speakeasy, down the tunnel, up the stairs, through the inn, and out into the woods to stage an accident," I agreed. Thoughts of Driftwood Sam entered my head. "Okay, let's assume for a second Clarence had nothing to do with any of this, either firsthand or through the police or a lackey. What about a rival? Someone who wants Benny and the Hideaway out of the way. But he comes back, maybe to steal the booze or ransack the place. He thinks no one is down here and is surprised when he sees Clara. They struggle, she runs away. He catches her in the tunnel, and she loses her necklace in her rush to escape. Maybe he hits her, maybe she just gets unlucky in the storm. Either way, he doesn't want to be tied to the scene of an attack on Clarence Silverthorne's daughter, so he collapses the tunnel to hide any evidence," I said.

Gabriel kicked at a rock, his brow furrowed. "Okay, but why take the risk of coming back just to scratch out a few runes? If he wanted the scene covered up, why not just collapse the tunnel himself? Seems like a half-measure to rely on the tunnel falling eventually instead of making sure it collapsed right away."

I bit my lip, considering his point. "Maybe he didn't want to draw too much attention. If the tunnel collapsed suddenly, it might've raised suspicions, especially with Clara missing. Scratching out a rune or two could make it seem like an accident—a slow, natural collapse instead of something more deliberate."

Gabriel looked thoughtful but still unsure. "I guess...but it still feels like a risky move. If he wanted the whole place buried, you'd think he'd make sure it happened."

"Perhaps it was the attack? Maybe that messed up his plans?" I guessed. "After all, if we hadn't found her bloodstained locket, we might have assumed, as everyone else did, that she was just a victim of a tragic accident in the woods and the magic in the runes gave out, collapsing the tunnel sometime after her death."

"Maybe," Gabriel said, drawing the word out. I could tell by his tone that he didn't believe the scenario. I wasn't sure I did either, but there was little else to go on.

"We're not getting anywhere by making up theories about what happened or the motive behind it," I said with a sigh. "Maybe it's time to focus on the how. For example, how did someone else know about this escape tunnel? Benny said it was a secret only the two of them shared."

"And how did whoever it was know about the runes?" Gabriel added.

"Let's search for more clues. Maybe Clara left something behind. Or perhaps the saboteur did," I suggested.

"Good idea," Gabriel said, looking more excited by that prospect.

Together, we examined every inch of the ruined support beam, careful not to touch it lest we trigger another collapse, this time with us as the victims. My phone's flashlight swept over the area, but the dim light didn't reveal anything out of place. Frustration started to bubble up as I realized how easy it would be to miss something important, buried beneath layers of dirt and debris.

Then it hit me.

I had another way to search.

I straightened up, taking a steadying breath and closed my eyes. I tapped into the familiar hum of my magic, letting it spread through the tunnel, instantly aware of the nails in the support beams, and other metals woven into the structure. There was a lot to sift through, but I focused, filtering out the familiar metallic hum until only the abnormal remained.

Something small and out of place pulsed back.

I followed the thread of energy, letting it guide my hand down toward the ground. I frowned and crouched down, bringing my light closer to see what had triggered my magical senses. My fingers brushed against a cool metallic surface, half-buried in the dirt. With a surge of energy, I focused, drawing the object toward me with a delicate touch of magic.

"Did you find something? What is it?" Gabriel asked.

"I'm not sure," I said, brushing the loose dirt away. It didn't take long to unearth the item. It was a piece of jewelry that appeared to be crafted from gold. I tested it with my metal magic, surprised to find that it was a high-karat gold composition. This was not some cheap decoration. Its surface gleamed with a polished finish that reflected light with an almost liquid shimmer. At its heart was an intricate spiral, meticulously etched and nestled within a perfect ring embellished with some sort of swirling design. Dirt caked the item and settled into the grooves, making it hard to see the design clearly. An equilateral triangle framed the entire circle, its edges subtly scalloped and the gold catching the light from my phone in a dance of shadow and brilliance.

Gabriel peered over my shoulder as I pulled the small object from the dirt. "What is that? A tie clip?"

I squinted at it, rubbing off some of the grime with my thumb. "I think so, but it's filthy." I handed it to Gabriel, who pulled a cloth from his pocket and carefully began wiping away the layers of dirt.

As the design came into view, I gasped. My heart raced. "Wait—those symbols!" I snatched my phone from my pocket and pulled up the photo of Clara's notebook. "Look at this. Do you recognize them?"

Gabriel cleaned off the last bit of grime, revealing a spiral, a circle, and a triangle etched into the metal. His eyes widened as I shoved the screen in his face. "These are the same symbols Clara drew when she said she knew who was behind everything," I exclaimed, barely able to contain my excitement.

Gabriel studied the tie clip, turning it over in his hand, then compared it to the photo on my phone. "You're right. It's the exact same pattern."

I grinned, feeling a rush of excitement. "We just have to figure out who it belonged to."

But then Gabriel frowned as he inspected the back of the tie clip. "No name or initials," he said, turning it around. "The back is just covered in grime."

My excitement faltered for a moment, but then an idea struck me. "Maybe we just need to clean it properly. There's no way this is a coincidence—let's get back to the Hideaway. We can wash it off there and get a clearer look. Maybe Benny might recognize it. Perhaps one of the Hideaway's patrons wore it."

Gabriel nodded, but his expression darkened with worry. "Good idea. But remember, Benny's been growing more volatile. Ghosts in his situation can lose control, and I'm concerned he's getting worse. Do what you can to keep him calm."

"I will," I promised, trying to steady my nerves as we made our way back through the escape tunnel.

Gabriel's warning lingered in my mind as I walked into the Hideaway, gripping the tie clip in my hand. I tried to appear calm, but the tension was hard to shake. Benny's image in the photograph pulsed slightly, the runes glowing in sync with his ghostly presence.

As I approached the bar, I cleared my throat. "Benny, we were going through the escape tunnel, and..." I hesitated, choosing my words carefully. "Well, part of it has collapsed. Looks like it's been that way for a long time."

Benny's form flickered, and the runes dimmed briefly. "Collapsed?" he echoed, his voice tight, almost disbelieving. "What do you mean, collapsed? That tunnel was solid. Sturdy as the day it was built!"

I raised a hand, trying to distract him. "We found something buried in the dirt near the blockage." I stepped forward, holding up the tie clip, keeping my tone light. "Thought it might be worth checking out. Do you recognize this?"

Benny's form flickered more violently now, the runes dimming as a low hum filled the room. A chair slid sharply across the floor with a screech, and I flinched, stepping back instinctively as Gabriel moved in front of me, his arm outstretched protectively.

"That—!" Benny's voice surged with excitement, his form brightening. "That might be—"

But just as quickly, everything stilled. The runes brightened again, the chair settled, and Benny's form dimmed as though his energy had been drained. He shook his head slowly, his voice deflated. "Nah...No, I don't know it," he muttered. "Never seen it before."

Gabriel let out a breath, lowering his arm. I straightened, my heart still racing, and exchanged a glance with him. "We'll figure this out, Benny," I said softly, though the uncertainty in my voice betrayed me.

Gabriel stepped forward, his expression tense, and wiped the tie clip carefully with a cloth he dampened with his tongue. After a few moments of silence, he shook his head. "This isn't working. I'd need to wash it to be sure, but I can't see any initials or other markings. Nothing else to go on," he said, his frustration clear.

Benny's fingers reached out as if to touch the tie clip, a futile gesture, but his gaze was intense, searching. "It's mighty fine though, ain't it?" he remarked, the tie clip gleaming in the light from the glowing runes. "But how did the tunnel collapse? Clara's magic was powerful."

Gabriel shot a look at me and cleared his throat. "She was definitely gifted with runes. From what we could see, we think someone sabotaged the support beam in the tunnel. The tie clip might have belonged to the person responsible for...well, for what happened."

"Those symbols are the same ones as what Clara drew in her notebook," I added.

A shadow crossed Benny's visage. His frustration was palpable. "I don't understand why anyone would sabotage the tunnel unless it was Clara's old man," Benny said, shaking his head. "But I ain't never seen him wear a tie pin like that."

"Given the situation, we don't think it was Clarence either," Gabriel said.

"Don't worry. We'll keep looking, Benny," I reassured him. "We'll find the truth."

Gabriel placed a hand on my shoulder, a silent gesture of support. "We should go upstairs and let the DeLucas know about the tunnel's condition," he suggested. "I'm not sure its sensible to have a party down here until we are confident the rest of the escape tunnel is shored up and won't collapse."

I nodded, sparing a last glance at Benny, who seemed anchored to his spot, caught in a tempest of past and present. "Would you like to come with us?"

"No," Benny's voice was a whisper, "I reckon I'll stay here a bit longer. You know, think on things. See if I can remember anything else."

"Okay. We'll leave the lights on for you," I murmured, following Gabriel out of the speakeasy.

As we stepped into the cool air of the Oasis' basement, Gabriel's brow furrowed. "So...Benny. Was he some kind of powerful magic user? He shouldn't be able to do all that—" Gabriel waved a hand down the tunnel towards the Hideaway. "Most ghosts don't have that kind of strength."

I glanced back at the door behind us, unease settling in my chest. "I don't know. I was trained not to ask people about their magical abilities. A habit from growing up on military bases. Benny did mention this place being a magical hotspot, but I'm not sure what that means. Do you?"

Gabriel's steps slowed, and he stopped, staring ahead for a moment before turning to me with a serious expression. "A magical hotspot isn't just a place where magic is stronger—it's where magic from the natural world gathers. Havenwood being what it is, there are several around town, but I didn't realize one was here."

"What does a magical hotspot do exactly?" I asked.

Gabriel ran a hand through his hair. "It's a place where excess magical energy pools. Generally, it seeps back down into the earth, into the magic of the natural world. Sometimes, it can soak into objects, places, occasionally even people. That's how the runes are powered, by ambient energy." He glanced at the tunnel behind us. "That actually explains a lot. How the runes have lasted so long and are still so strong."

I tilted my head, intrigued. "Okay, so... the runes draw energy from the magic around them. But you said people could soak up this magic too? Could someone—like Benny—be gaining power from the runes or the magic in the hotspot?"

Gabriel hesitated, his jaw tightening. "Yes, he could, but it would be dangerous. If Benny's trapped down there, and his connection to the runes is growing stronger... it's possible he's been slowly draining the energy meant to contain him or the runes in the Hideaway. The more power he takes, the more control he loses over himself. It would explain why he's becoming more volatile."

The weight of his words settled over me like a cold fog. "So, the longer he's down there, the stronger he gets, but also the less control he has?"

"Exactly. And if he keeps feeding off the magic...the runes around him, even the ones protecting the Hideaway, could eventually fail."

My heart raced as the pieces began to fall into place. "Then we're running out of time. If Benny keeps pulling power from those runes..."

"We might lose more than just a ghost," Gabriel finished gravely.

"How bad is it?" I asked, my voice barely above a whisper.

Gabriel's expression was grim. "If the runes in the Hideaway collapse, the entire Oasis could suffer major structural damage and given how much power he's likely siphoned...the impact very well could spread beyond the building itself. We could be looking at something far bigger, possibly stretching to other parts of Havenwood."

Without a second thought, I turned back toward the tunnel. "We need to get him out of there before he gets any stronger," I said, my voice tight with urgency as I started down the path.

Before I could take another step, Gabriel grabbed my arm, stopping me. His grip was firm, a warning in his eyes. "Harper, wait. Dealing with unstable ghosts isn't my forte, but I fear he might already be too strong. If we try to move him against his will... that might be the trigger we're hoping to avoid."

A chill ran down my spine as the reality of his words sank in. I glanced back at the speakeasy, the glowing runes flickering in the distance, and felt a growing sense of dread clawing at me. Gabriel was right—one wrong move could set off a chain reaction we couldn't control.

"Well, my great-granny figured out a way to keep him calm and shut away in a hidden compartment of Spellbooks for who knows how long. Do you think we can get him to come with us back there?" I asked, the idea forming as I spoke.

Gabriel shook his head, his expression serious. "Moving him to Spellbooks would be incredibly risky. If he's unstable now, transporting him could set him off—and then you'd be putting Spellbooks and everyone in the surrounding area in danger. We need to keep things as calm and steady as possible down here. Any sudden change could cause him to lose control. The key is to not upset the balance."

I frowned, anxiety gnawing at me. "But what about the party? Won't that make things worse? We should cancel, right? Especially if it's not safe."

Gabriel sighed. "I thought about that, and I think it has to go forward as planned. If we cancel or even change things too much, Benny might notice. With the power he's siphoning, he could get suspicious and use it to lash out. As long as everything feels normal, we might avoid triggering him. But we can't take any chances."

My stomach twisted at the thought of the Oasis, the DeLucas, and the party guests being at risk. "What about Honey and Antonio? The guests? Are they safe?"

Gabriel gave me a steady look. "I'm not going to let anything happen to them. Or to you. But we'll need help." He paused before continuing, "I'm going to call in Lucas and my mother."

My eyes widened. "Lucas? And your mother?" Vivienne Silverthorne was no one to mess around with. She was a powerful mage and if anyone could handle Benny, it would be her. But there was a little part of me that responded to the thought of Vivienne showing up to the party tomorrow night with the same trepidation as getting called to the principal's office.

"Trust me, if anyone can make sure Benny doesn't get out of control, it's my mother. He won't know what hit him," Gabriel said grimly.

I didn't have an answer to that. Part of me was glad Gabriel had already thought of a contingency plan to keep everyone safe. However, I didn't like the idea of Vivienne forcing Benny into compliance when all he wanted was answers.

Gabriel took my hand, his grip gentle but firm. "They're powerful mages, Harper. If anyone can help protect the Oasis and contain the magic, it's Lucas and my mother. We'll set up wards around the Hideaway, make sure nothing gets out of hand. I'll ask for their opinions of course and for the consent of the DeLucas, but I'm pretty sure this is the safest option given the current situation."

I swallowed hard, the weight of his words settling in. My fingers curled around his, searching for some kind of anchor. "Okay," I whispered, though the tension coiled inside me didn't ease. The thought of Vivienne and Lucas stepping in made sense, but it also felt like handing the situation over to forces beyond my control.

Upstairs, the Oasis hummed with the bustle of the party setup, a stark contrast to the haunted quiet below. Gabriel gave my hand a reassuring squeeze. "Let me check in with Honey and Antonio first," he said. "Then I'll call Lucas. Be right back"

I nodded, watching as he stepped out of the room and went in search of the DeLucas.

Left alone, I paced the room, my gaze flicking between the elegant, Prohibition-themed decorations—gold accents, deep velvet curtains, soft lighting meant to transport guests back to the Roaring Twenties, but my thoughts drifted back to the photograph of Benny resting on the bar in the Hideaway.

Would bringing Lucas into this help, or was I just piling more complications onto an already tangled mess? I couldn't shake the feeling that Benny's situation was already volatile, and adding more magic, more opinions, might make things worse. But what other choice did we have? Gabriel was right—Benny's growing instability was a risk none of us could afford to ignore.

And then there was Clara. Every piece of this puzzle seemed to circle back to her and the secrets she'd left behind. If we could find her truth, maybe that would be enough to ease Benny's restlessness. Or maybe it would shatter him completely.

I sighed, rubbing my temples. Every solution felt like a gamble, but we were running out of time to choose.

Gabriel returned a few minutes later, his expression calm but resolute. "It's sorted," he said. "Honey and Antonio are on board, and Lucas is on his way as soon as he can. He'll be here later to evaluate the situation and help me set up wards."

I nodded, still uneasy but grateful for the added protection. "Thank you."

He gave me a reassuring smile. "We've got this. Now, let's focus on keeping everything calm and steady."

My stomach twisted again. Even though Honey and Antonio were already in the loop, the weight of what was happening beneath our feet made my skin prickle. How could we smile, toast, and celebrate upstairs while an unstable ghost simmered with growing power below?

And yet, any sudden change in the atmosphere could alert Benny, tipping the delicate balance and turning a tense situation into a full-blown crisis.

All we had to do was make it through the night. Keep Benny calm. Keep everyone safe. And, hopefully, step into the New Year without unleashing chaos.

Phantoms at the Crossroads

THE REST OF THE day blurred into a whirlwind of activity as we prepared for the party. Gabriel and I met with Bella, Honey, and Antonio, laying out the risks and explaining the plan to involve Lucas. Their concern was palpable, but they agreed, and we all swore to keep the situation quiet. The fewer people who knew about Benny's growing instability, the better—for everyone's safety and the success of the night.

The Oasis buzzed with excitement, its energy a sharp contrast to the tension simmering beneath the surface. Every corner of the space transformed into a glamorous nod to the Prohibition era. Isadora, Bella, and I moved between tables, arranging makeshift gambling spots, adjusting decorations, and adding final touches of gold and silver. Streamers fluttered above us, catching the soft glow of the lights, their beauty at odds with the unease gnawing at my stomach.

Benny lingered in the back of my mind, a restless presence I couldn't ignore. Knowing he was trapped and growing more volatile below us cast a shadow over the sparkling decorations and excited chatter. Honey passed by occasionally with trays of her freshly baked pastries, their sweet scent cutting through my worry. For a fleeting moment, when I bit into one of her creations, I let myself believe this was just another party, another celebration to enjoy.

But the illusion never lasted. The weight of the truth pressed against me, refusing to let me forget the situation that lurked in the basement and the growing threat beneath our feet. There was a delicate balance we were trying to maintain—keeping the illusion of a party going, even as something terrifyingly dangerous simmered below the surface.

Every moment felt like it stretched thin, as if the festive atmosphere could snap at any second. I tried to focus on the bright streamers, on the laughter and the delicious treats, but it all felt like a countdown. We were running out of time.

Gabriel helped with the setup for a while before his phone buzzed with an incoming call. After a quick glance at the screen, he excused himself, his expression shifting to something more focused. He left not long after, his brisk, purposeful stride hinting at something important. I watched him go, feeling a surge of hope. Maybe whatever he was chasing down would bring us the answers that might finally lay old furious ghosts to rest.

Finn arrived in the early afternoon, looking a bit weary from his appointment, which had clearly taken longer than expected. But when he stepped into the Oasis and saw the organized chaos of party preparations, his smile didn't falter. If anything, it brightened, as though the whirlwind of activity was exactly the kind of energy he needed to shake off the day.

What he didn't know—what none of the guests could know—was the unspoken tension beneath the surface. We'd all been sworn to secrecy, the growing threat of Benny's instability kept tightly under wraps. With Lucas and Vivienne set to arrive and their powerful magic protecting the Oasis, we had to believe Benny would be contained. But still, it lingered in the back of my mind like an unsettling whisper: what if it wasn't enough?

Finn had been tasked with creating custom signs for the night, painting abstract hints to the secret passwords guests would need to use to enter the speakeasy-themed sections of the party. He rolled up his sleeves and dove into the tasks Bella assigned him, his hands as deft with paintbrushes as they were with his tattoo machine. Each stroke of his brush brought a sense of authenticity to the Prohibition-era setting.

Bella meticulously worked on setting up the silent auction for charity. Her table was neatly arranged with promotions from local businesses, including a spa day, a gourmet dinner, and a weekend stay at the Oasis, plus some vouchers for discounts at Spellbooks and other local businesses.

I couldn't help but notice the attention to detail in every corner. The centerpieces Isadora arranged were stunning, with black feathers, pearls, and vintage-style flasks adding a touch of 1920s elegance. Meanwhile, I worked on setting up the exchange bank, where guests would swap chips for tickets and prizes.

The hours slipped by almost unnoticed. The B&B's common areas had been transformed into a dazzling kaleidoscope of light, color, and sound, ready to welcome the guests. But even with the glitz and glamour on full display, there was a tension we couldn't ignore. It hovered just below the surface, a constant reminder that despite the festivities above, a growing threat lurked beneath our feet in the Hideaway.

My mind kept wandering back to the tragedies of Clara and Benny. The pieces of their unsolved puzzle were in my hands, but they just wouldn't fit together. Something crucial was missing, a detail or a moment lost in time that held the key to the whole sorrowful mystery. It was a splinter in my mind, a niggling doubt that refused to be brushed away. I couldn't shake the disquiet that clung to me. The feeling that somewhere, in the labyrinth of the past, lay a truth that had been waiting patiently in the dark for someone to find it. I knew, despite the excitement and the surrounding bustle of party preparation, that I wouldn't be able to let it go. Not until the ghosts of Benny and Clara found the peace their all-too-brief lives denied them.

I had just over a day before dozens of people flooded the Oasis to ring in the New Year, and the weight of responsibility rested heavily on my shoulders. The party would go on as planned, but I couldn't shake the gnawing guilt. I'd released Benny from Spellbooks and, even if it wasn't intentional, trapped him in the photo. Then I'd brought him to the Oasis. Now, the danger he posed wasn't just to me—it was to Bella's family, their guests, and maybe all of Havenwood. I needed to keep him calm, needed to figure out what happened, maybe then he'd find peace and disappear before he could harm anyone.

That's why I found myself walking back down to the Hideaway, the dim glow of the runes casting eerie shadows along the walls. My steps echoed in the silence, each one a reminder that time was slipping away. Maybe Benny had remembered something else. If I could just help him solve the mystery, maybe then he'd move on and leave the Oasis in peace.

When I reached the bar, Benny was still there, waiting, his spectral form pacing within the confines of the photograph and shooting dark looks between the photograph of him and Clara in her locket. He didn't say anything at first, just stared at her image, his presence flickering like an old film reel. I hesitated for a moment before stepping closer.

"Benny," I started, keeping my voice soft. "I came back to check on you. I thought maybe—maybe you'd remembered something. Anything that could help us figure out what happened."

Benny continued to pace, seemingly oblivious to my words, as he stared grimly at the photograph of Clara in the open locket I'd set up for him. Perhaps that had been a mistake.

"Benny? Can you hear me?" I asked, leaning closer.

He blinked in surprise, but an urgency in his words sent a chill down my spine. "It's Clara, I tell ya. She's caught in that locket, chained to the memories, see? Just like I'm stuck here, unable to cross the great divide. It's wracking her something fierce. I can't bear it, no ma'am!" His voice, usually so full of old-time charm, now cracked with a mixture of rage and sorrow.

I tried to keep my voice calm, even though shock rocketed through me. Clara was *here*? Trapped in her own locket and unable to move on even after all this time, much like Benny? Did that mean I potentially had two upset ghosts on my hands?

"What do you mean? How can Clara be here?" I asked.

He didn't answer right away. Instead, the air around him seemed to buzz with tension, the runes on the walls dimming as if reacting to his growing anger. His form crackled with energy, flickering in and out of focus like he was struggling to keep control.

"I don't know how. But I feel it, deep in my bones. Like I've always known but couldn't remember 'til now," Benny said, his voice a harsh whisper. "And I'm not waiting much longer to get justice. For Clara. Look at her. My gal." His voice broke on the last words.

I stepped closer, studying the locket. That's when Benny spoke again, his tone grim. "Look closer at the edges," he whispered, his voice low and dark. "Runes. Didn't see 'em at first, but they're there. I think she added them after I gave her that there locket."

My eyes narrowed, and I leaned in, squinting at the metal edges of the locket. Sure enough, faint but unmistakable, I could see tiny runes etched into the gold frame, so small that I'd missed them entirely until he pointed them out.

"Why would she do that?" I asked.

"I don't know, but she did it on purpose, I'll tell you that for certain," Benny muttered. "No way she did it on accident. No sir. She knew what she was doing. Almost like...like she expected it and didn't want to move on."

"But how could she have known? Why would she do that?" I asked. My heart raced as Benny's countenance darkened.

His voice dropped to a growl. "I don't know, dollface. All I know is those runes trapped her just like the ones on this photograph trapped me," he hissed. His form flickered dangerously, frustration thickening the air and sending a chill down my spine. The temperature dropped as his energy buzzed with intensity, and I could feel the familiar hum of the runes on the walls falter, dimming in response to his rising anger.

I swallowed hard, backing up a step. "Benny, listen to me. I'm going to find out who did this to you—to both of you. I swear I will. But you have to give me more time."

His form shuddered, the flicker more erratic now, his face twisted with rage. "More time? More time!" His voice climbed, and with it, the runes pulsed faster, casting jagged, eerie shadows across the room. "I've been waiting a century! I'm not waiting much longer. I can't bear it!"

The bar groaned under an unseen weight, the wood creaking, splitting as if crushed by an invisible hand. My pulse spiked, and I instinctively skittered away from the bar, the energy in the room twisting dangerously, like a coiled spring ready to snap.

"I'll find out who did this," I promised, my voice unsteady. "I will. But please, Benny, stay calm."

His spectral form turned toward me, eyes burning with fury. "You better find out," he hissed, his voice low and menacing, "or I will. And when I do, there won't be any mercy."

The room suddenly shuddered. I flinched as the floor trembled beneath me. The runes flared wildly, their light flickering like the onset of a storm and a sharp crack echoed through the space as a chair skidded across the room and slammed into the bar. My heart raced, panic clawing at my chest.

I stumbled back, heart pounding like a drum, my mind racing to keep up. Benny was growing stronger—more dangerous with each flicker of his form. The air around me vibrated with his fury. My breath hitched as the cold sank deeper into my bones, making it harder to think, harder to breathe. I took another step back, mind spinning. Benny's rage was close to erupting—becoming more volatile with each passing second. If I didn't solve this soon, if I didn't find a way to calm him—there was no telling what he'd do next.

Needle in a Haystack

As soon as I went upstairs, I found Bella, my heart still racing from the encounter with Benny. The tension from what had just happened lingered, making it hard to find the right words. I spotted her near the dessert table, adjusting a tray of Honey's pastries.

"Harper!" she called. She stepped closer, lowering her voice. "Gabriel said Lucas just arrived. They're outside setting up the wards right now."

Relief flooded through me for a moment, but it did little to quell the unease coiled in my chest. "Good," I said, glancing toward the doorway. "We're going to need them."

Her expression had lighted up briefly before falling into something more serious as she caught sight of my face. "Why? What is it? What happened?"

I tugged her gently aside, lowering my voice even further. "Bella, we've got a serious problem. It's not just Benny we're dealing with down there. Clara... she's trapped too. In that locket."

Bella's eyes widened, alarm flashing across her face. "Clara? Trapped?" she whispered, glancing nervously around the room as if expecting someone to overhear.

"And Benny's losing control," I continued, my voice steady despite the nerves threatening to rise. "He's growing more powerful—more dangerous."

Bella's usual cheer vanished entirely. "Harper, what are we going to do?"

I swallowed hard, trying to focus. "You said Lucas is here, right? He and Gabriel are already working on the wards, and Vivienne will be here tomorrow. We just have to hold things together until then. You need to stay focused on keeping Benny calm—making sure nothing upsets him or makes him think anything's off. Business as usual."

Bella paled slightly at the mention of Vivienne's name but squared her shoulders, nodding. "I'll tell my parents. We'll do whatever we have to."

I placed a hand on her arm, giving it a reassuring squeeze. "As for me? I'm going to solve this case—figure out what happened to him and to Clara. I think that's the only way we can end this without it spiraling into chaos."

Bella nodded, determination settling into her expression, though the worry in her eyes didn't fade. "Just...be careful, okay?"

I nodded back, though unease still gnawed at me. "It's our best shot. If Benny snaps, we're all at risk."

Bella cast a nervous glance toward the basement door, her smile faltering. "We'll handle it."

I shrugged on my coat and headed outside, walking around the perimeter of the Oasis until I found Gabriel setting magical wards. His expression darkened the moment I mentioned that I'd gone down to the Hideaway alone. "You shouldn't have done that," he muttered, worry flickering behind his stern tone. "Benny's not stable, Harper. I told you we needed to keep things calm."

"I know," I sighed, running a hand through my hair. "I just thought...maybe I could help."

Gabriel's eyes softened. "Your heart was in the right place, but I'd never forgive myself if something happened to you." He reached up, gently tucking a stray lock of hair behind my ear, his touch warm and steady in the cool night air. "Next time you decide to chat with an unstable ghost, take me with you, okay? Backup wouldn't hurt."

I managed a small smile despite the lingering anxiety in my chest. "You're right."

Lucas' voice rang out from across the yard, shattering the moment.

Gabriel sighed. "I have to finish these wards. Lucas and I will make sure the place is secure."

I nodded. "Thanks, Gabriel."

Gabriel gave me a long, steady look, his brow creased with concern. For a moment, the world seemed to slow, and the tension between us hung heavy in the air. Without a word, he stepped closer, and before I could even register the warmth in his eyes, he leaned down and pressed a soft kiss to my forehead. The touch was featherlight, sending a pleasant shiver through me that had nothing to do with the cold night air.

"Be careful," he murmured, his voice low, his gaze lingering on mine for just a beat longer than necessary. Then he turned back to his brother, leaving me standing in the quiet chill of the evening, my heart racing for reasons that had nothing to do with Benny.

The cold air rushed in, and I gave my head a slight shake, trying to snap myself back to the present.

Focus, Harper. There's too much at stake to get distracted now.

I pulled my coat tighter around me, forcing my mind back to the puzzle at hand. Benny was growing more unstable by the minute. There had to be more—something I'd missed about Benny, the tie clip, or this whole haunting. If I was going to stop Benny from unraveling, I needed answers, and I needed them fast.

As soon as I got back to my apartment, I brewed an entire pot of coffee, not caring that it was already dark outside. Time was ticking away, and I needed to find answers before Benny did something stupid. As if sensing my urgency, Ignatius, Luna, and Mr. Wigglesworth all kept to themselves despite me having spent almost the entire day at the Oasis setting up for the party tomorrow.

I exhausted every search term I could think of online but turned up nothing. I stuck with it for another hour, spiraling into more obscure searches. Unfortunately, I still couldn't find any further information on Benny, Clara, the Hideaway, or the strange symbols on the tie clip.

With my ideas running dry and my coffee already cold, I reexamined the items I'd discovered in the attic along with Benny's photograph. Maybe there was a clue hidden in the pages of the notebook I had yet to discover.

Another hour of boring inventory decoding convinced me that was not the case. Benny's notebook was a complete, if somewhat dry, day-to-day log of everything necessary for running the Hideaway. With a sigh, I set the book to the side, looking once more at the flask I'd found in the attic. The metal body was snugly nestled in a well-worn holder stamped with Benny's initials. I shook the flask again, hearing the telltale rattle. Something was inside, but I couldn't get it out. Curious, I opened the lid and tried to use my flashlight from my phone to peer inside. Despite my best efforts, I couldn't see anything and nothing fell out, even when I turned the flask completely upside-down.

I frowned. I should be able to see something, even if it was just movement inside the flask. However, there was nothing there. Then, a thought struck me—what if the item wasn't inside the flask at all? Maybe it was tucked between the flask and the holder. The fit was snug on the sides, but the bottom felt looser, leaving just enough space for something small to rattle around. If that was the case, whatever it was, couldn't be very large.

It took more effort than I would've imagined to wriggle the flask free of the worn holder, and by the time I managed to separate the two, a fine sheen of sweat covered my brow. However, when they eventually popped free from one another, a small object flew across the tabletop. I scrambled to slam my hand over it before it fell. Something round and hard pressed into my palm.

I lifted my hand to reveal a tiny round pin that laid quietly on the wooden surface, the tumult of its escape from the flask's holder settling into a heavy silence. I examined the intricate piece of jewelry from every angle. The small artifact seemed to be a tantalizing clue. It was no larger than a thumbnail, its face a miniature canvas for a sigil I'd never seen before. It was an artful intertwining of musical notes and a discreetly hidden pair of cocktail glasses that hinted at the underground world of jazz and gin. I wondered if it held some special significance. It had to, being hidden away like that, didn't it? I promised myself to take it to Benny in the morning, hoping it would ignite a spark of recognition.

I tucked the pin carefully into my purse and turned my attention to the other items I'd discovered in the hidden alcove. Perhaps there was a clue there I'd missed. I hadn't made time to examine them before, so I gave them my full attention now.

The first was a faded pack of playing cards with the corners bent from too much play. I examined each one, but nothing appeared out of the ordinary. Just a normal deck of well-used cards. Next was a rusted tin box containing a single, moth-eaten velvet glove—its partner likely lost to time—and a stack of yellowed receipts from various suppliers. Neither revealed any secrets, but they spoke to the everyday commerce that kept either the Hideaway or the Hearthstone alive. Tucked beneath them was a tattered dance card, its once-elegant lace edging now frayed and discolored, the names inside barely legible.

I sighed and slumped back in my chair. I don't know what I'd been hoping for. A signed confession from a hundred years ago was probably too much to ask for, but I wouldn't have turned it down at this point in time if it meant keeping Benny's volatile ghost calm.

Luna poked her head into my apartment. "Fluff and furballs, from all the sighing I heard up here, I thought I'd find you halfway through a Jane Austen novel. What's going on?"

I blew out a breath and shook my head, explaining everything as quickly as I could. "...and now, if I don't figure out who was behind Benny and Clara's untimely demise, I don't know what Benny will do. Not to mention the fact that he claims Clara's spirit is trapped within her locket. What am I going to do with two unsettled ghosts?"

"If you're anything like Beatrice, lock them up in the attic until you can get some answers," Luna said dryly.

"The attic! Of course! I can't believe I forgot about the alcove entirely. Oh, I could kiss you, Luna," I said in a rush.

"Please don't," the rabbit muttered, waving me off. I dashed past her and hurried towards the attic, where Spellbooks thoughtfully swung the door wide for me. I nearly tripped twice in my haste to get back to the hidden alcove where Granny Bea had stashed Benny, but I made it without breaking an ankle.

However, that's where my luck dried up. Nothing remained in the shallow recess. I ran my fingertips along every crack and even examined the surrounding wall in case Granny Bea had more hidden compartments, but there was nothing except cobwebs and dust. Still, I wasn't ready to give up just yet. I shifted the boxes aside and asked, "Spellbooks, anything else you're hiding?"

For a moment, I swore the air grew thicker, the faintest vibration of floorboards somewhere far off. But just as quickly, it faded, leaving me to wonder if I was pushing my luck. Spellbooks had already stirred the pot by releasing Benny in the first place—maybe it was wise not to dig too deep right now. After all, the last time one of Granny Bea's secrets was uncovered, it nearly tore the town apart.

I let out a sigh. "Okay, okay. You're right. Let's not make things worse. One disaster at a time." Dusty and drained from the sudden burst of excitement, I headed back to my apartment. Luna looked up curiously.

"Well?" she asked.

I shook my head. "Nothing. At least, nothing to do with Benny."

Luna's ears flattened in disappointment as she processed the news. "Well, that's a cabbage catastrophe if ever I heard one," she said, her voice tinged with the weariness that seemed to mirror my own. "The thought of Benny running wild around town again doesn't inspire much hope for a calm new year. He's got too much unfinished business, especially if he's convinced Clara never moved on from this existence. That could make things infinitely worse, emotionally speaking."

I nodded, wiping at the grime on my face with a less-than-clean hand. Despite my well-intentioned effort, I think I only managed to leave an extra streak of dirt across my cheek. "I know. He's on edge, Luna. He wants answers, and he wants them yesterday."

With a hop, Luna landed on the table, her enormous eyes narrowing in my direction. "Can't say I blame him," she said, her tone thoughtful but sharp. "Being stuck in limbo is no way to exist. But this?" She tilted her head, ears twitching. "Fluff and furballs, this isn't the way a respectable ghost should behave."

"What is a way a respectable—you know what? Don't answer that. I can't afford to get distracted." I shook my head. "It's the hotspot that's the problem. The magic is amplifying him somehow."

Luna's nose twitched, and she fixed me with a knowing look. "That's a dangerous game, Harper. When you mess around with ghosts and magic, things tend to get out of hand."

"I didn't mean for any of this to happen," I protested, dropping my head into my hands.

She paused and I looked up at her. Luna's gaze softened for a moment before hardening again. "I'll tell you what I don't like even more than you poking around—someone messing with *you*. Or Havenwood. You know what? I need to go get my ninja headband."

I smiled at her fierce protectiveness. "I appreciate the sentiment, but he's getting more volatile. I don't think going full-ninja on him will convince him to stop."

Luna sniffed. "And that shows just how little you understand about the true might of the ninja-rabbit."

"I have no idea," I said honestly. "But what I do know is if we don't find answers soon, Benny might—"

Luna's little paws darted up shadow boxing the air as she bounced on her back paws. "No more messing around, Harper. You'll figure this out. And if anyone else tries to cause trouble—well," she smirked, "they'll have to deal with me."

I let out a breath, feeling a mix of relief and determination. "Thanks, Luna. I just wish I had more to go on. A century-old mystery isn't exactly easy to crack."

Luna's whiskers twitched. "Well, you're like your granny. You both had more than your fair share of moxie. If anyone can crack this caper, it's you," she said, purposefully adding a hint of a 1920s New York accent to her words. Her ears flicked, and she added with her usual sass, "Just don't go getting yourself turned into a ghost. I can only handle so much supernatural drama in one week."

I sighed, moving towards the bathroom to clean up. "I hope you're right. For everyone's sake."

A hot shower felt good, but, unfortunately, I didn't find any answers among the suds and lather. When steam filled the bathroom, I gave up and turned off the water, towel drying my hair quickly before throwing on some pjs. I trudged to bed, my mind spinning with the puzzle pieces of a jigsaw that seemed to have a few too many missing.

As I lay in the dark, staring at the ceiling, the day's discoveries and dead ends replayed in my mind. Benny's increasing agitation, the tantalizing clues that seemed to lead nowhere, and the weight of responsibility to give some peace to two lost souls.

Eventually, exhaustion dragged me under, but my sleep was anything but peaceful. The sounds of the speakeasy haunted my dreams—faint laughter, clinking glasses, the distant hum of jazz. Benny and Clara appeared, spinning together in a slow, eerie dance, their faces hollow, eyes desperate. My chest tightened as I watched, feeling helpless, trapped in the m oment.

I jolted awake, heart pounding. Cold sweat clung to my skin as the shadows of the dream faded, leaving behind a stifling dread. The room was silent, but I couldn't shake the feeling that time was slipping through my fingers.

I lay there, staring into the darkness, my thoughts racing. If I didn't figure this out soon—if I didn't solve this mystery—there was no telling what Benny might do next.

Eve of Revelations

A NEW DAY DAWNED, one that passed in a blur of final touches and preparation. We spent hours ensuring that the party wouldn't disturb the other guests, triple-checking noise-cancellation spells, and finalizing the timeline. Between that and learning how to man the gambling tables for the night's festivities, there was hardly a moment to catch my breath.

But the real fun began as the afternoon drifted into evening. Bella, Isadora, and I holed up in one of the Oasis's rooms, surrounded by makeup palettes, shimmering dresses, and shoes that were both glamorous and impractical for Havenwood's winter weather. Laughter echoed as we primped and preened, turning the room into a flurry of glitter, fabric, and curls. For a little while, it was just us—three friends, getting ready for a night of fun, even as the ghostly storm still brewed in the basement.

"Here, let me help," Bella said, smoothing a stray piece of my hair into place before handing me a pair of dangling crystal earrings. "You're going to look stunning tonight."

Isadora, lounging nearby in a robe with a face mask, added with a grin, "And those shoes! If you don't trip over them at least once, I'll be genuinely impressed."

I rolled my eyes, but secretly appreciated their help. The silver gown I'd picked out from Spellbooks was breathtaking—backless and slinky, something straight out of a Roaring Twenties dream. But those heels? Well, let's just say I wasn't exactly confident about my chances of surviving the evening in them either.

Bella's dress was pure old Hollywood glamour—a deep emerald number that hugged her curves before flaring into a mermaid silhouette. Her hair was in loose waves, pinned back with a jeweled clip that sparkled every time she moved. She looked like she'd stepped off a movie set.

Once she finished getting ready, Isadora was impossible to miss. Her gold dress shimmered with every movement, the fringe and sequins catching the light and reflecting it in dazzling patterns. With a glittery headband nestled in her pink hair, she was a walking invitation to the dance floor, ready to dazzle the night away.

When we finally descended the stairs, all dressed to the nines, the transformation of the Oasis took my breath away. Despite having spent the entire weekend helping to prepare, seeing the final result was something else. The Oasis had been turned into a luxurious speakeasy from the Roaring Twenties, dripping with glamour and mystery. Rich velvet drapes hung from the walls, casting shadows in the flickering candlelight, while crystal decanters filled with amber-colored spirits glittered like hidden jewels. Every corner was adorned with art deco touches, making the space feel like it had been lifted straight from a hidden club of the era.

A makeshift bar lined one wall, its rows of glassware gleaming, ready for the evening's festivities. The whole place exuded the charm and allure of an underground jazz club, where secrets were shared in whispers over clinking glasses. Twinkling lights cast a warm, golden glow over the room, making the entire space shimmer as though the party had been kissed by Gatsby himself. It was hard to believe we had been part of creating something so magical.

Excitement rose in me. I wondered if this is what Benny had felt like in the Hideaway, welcoming guests in to escape the monotony of their everyday lives. It was hard to believe we had all helped create this. For a moment, it almost made me forget the danger lurking beneath our feet.

Almost.

I fingered the pin I'd found in the hidden compartment of the flask thoughtfully. Somehow, I needed to slip away and ask him about it, but I didn't want Bella to think I was deserting her.

Guests arrived, dressed to the nines and ready to celebrate New Year's Eve in style. They mingled, laughter blending with the clink of glass and the rustle of silk. The women were visions of glamor, their gowns flowing and sparkling, beads and costume jewelry catching the light. The men were no less impressive in their crisp suits, adding a touch of sophistication to the whole affair. If there was anything this town did well apart from magic, it was a costume party. Given the sheer number and scope of town events throughout the year, it seemed like everyone had their own extensive costume closet with clothes for almost every conceivable occasion. I was just glad that I'd been able to fit in the dresses I'd found in Spellbooks' attic, or I'd have been at a loss. There weren't many costumed events on the Army bases where I spent much of my childhood, and I never had a chance to amass a closet of outlandish outfits.

"This party is shaping up to be a tremendous success, Bella," I whispered as more guests flooded in, surrendering coats and scarves and revealing their glittering party attire.

"You think so?" she asked nervously, looking around.

"I know so. You've done a remarkable job," I said, linking my arm through hers and giving her a little squeeze.

"I would've loved to open up the Hideaway, but with that tunnel collapse, it's probably for the best that we didn't," Bella said, chewing nervously on her lip.

I patted her hand comfortingly. "Think of it this way; it gives you an entire year to prep for your speakeasy theme for next year's party."

Bella's eyes lit up, her energy returning. "Yes! Or even better—what about St. Patrick's Day? A grand opening of an Irish speakeasy on St. Patty's would be perfect!" She was already imagining it, a smile spreading across her face. "It would really put the Oasis on the map of Havenwood's events. We could make it a party to remember."

"One thing at a time," I said with a chuckle. "Let's focus on enjoying this one first, and then we can figure out what the future holds."

"Speaking of figuring things out, did you have any epiphanies regarding the situation with Clara and Benny?" Bella asked.

I shook my head, hesitant to tell her my fears about Benny's escalating unrest. That was the last thing Bella needed. I didn't want to spoil her night, but if I didn't figure out an answer that would satisfy the ghost in the basement, then we'd have to lock him away somehow again. Hopefully, it wouldn't come to that. I didn't want to see him locked up, but he might not give me much of a choice.

Isadora came over. "Fabulous party, Bella! I can't believe I've never been here for your family's New Year's Eve bash before."

"Speaking of never having been here before, look who just came in," Bella said, dropping her voice and jerking her chin towards the door.

I glanced up to see Seraphina Everbright, Finn's ex, shrugging out of a beautiful, white wool coat to reveal a stunning ice blue silk dress. Finn hurried over and took her coat giving her a little smile of welcome as he waved her into the party.

"What's she doing *here*?" Isadora breathed.

"I invited her," I said, my smile feeling a little forced. Although inviting Seraphina had been a spur-of-the-moment thing based on the kindest of intentions, I was mentally kicking myself now. How could I possibly measure up to the beautiful enchanter elf who was fluttering her eyelashes at Finn?

"You did *what*?" Bella asked in disbelief. "What about Finn?"

"What about him?" I asked with a shrug I hoped was nonchalant. "Look, he told me she was coming back to town for a business meeting and was going to be alone on New Year's Eve. Maybe I was being a little emotional, but all I could think about was Clara. Would things have worked out differently for her if she'd had a friend? If she hadn't spent every evening alone in the Hideaway after Benny passed? Besides, no one should have to welcome in the new year alone."

"That is...incredibly sweet of you," Bella admitted.

"What does that mean for you and Finn? Or have you surrendered Finn to Seraphina because you only have eyes for my brother?" Isadora teased.

"Hey, isn't this a speakeasy party? Shouldn't we be bidding on something at the silent auction or maybe trying our luck with some 'bootleg bucks?'" I said, steering the conversation away from my love life.

Before anyone could respond, Honey popped her head out of the kitchen, her voice bright with excitement. "Bella? Could you give me a hand for a moment?"

"Coming, Mama," Bella said. She shot me a wink. "And don't think I'm letting you off the hook that easy. I expect to see some serious bidding on our silent auction—and I'll be expecting answers later. It's for charity, after all," she teased.

I rolled my eyes, playing along. "The auction or me fueling your gossip obsession?"

"What? Now that Alex and I are back together, I have to live vicariously through someone," Bella grinned.

I brushed away her words. "Whatever. I'm totally bidding on that spa day and taking Isadora with me instead of you."

"Yes!" Isadora said, fist-pumping the air.

"Yeah, right," Bella called over her shoulder as she headed toward the kitchen.

Just then, Isadora nudged me. "Speaking of mothers, I think I see mine," she muttered, nodding toward the entrance where her mom, Vivienne Silverthorne, had just swept in, Lucas and Gabriel close behind.

I grinned at Isadora. "Uh-oh. Time to be on your best behavior?"

Isadora scoffed. "Please. Like I could ever live up to my mom's 'best behavior' standard."

I bumped her shoulder. "Good luck."

I caught Gabriel's questioning gaze as he helped Vivienne slip out of her long, stylish coat, revealing a stunning black dress adorned with sparkling crystals. She nearly gave Isadora a run for her money when it came to being eye-catching but in a more sophisticated way, not that I'd ever tell Isadora that. Regardless, I didn't need words to understand the question in Gabriel's eyes. He was asking if I'd reached a solution with Benny. Slowly, I shook my head. Gabriel's mouth set in a grim line. He turned away, whispering to his mother and brother, no doubt updating them on the situation. I didn't need him to tell me what would happen if Benny lost control. If we didn't find a solution, the only option left would be to ask Vivienne Silverthorne for her help and then who knows what might happen to Benny? I fingered the small pin again, glancing around the room. With more guests filling up the place, this might be the perfect opportunity to slip away and ask Benny about it.

I lifted the hem of my long skirt and silently backed out of the room, unnoticed by anyone caught up in the party's excitement. Moving quickly, I made my way toward the basement stairs. Guests were already trickling in through the front doors, a steady stream of laughter and chatter filling the air, and I knew I didn't have much time before slipping away would become impossible.

Cautiously, I descended the stairs, my fingers brushing over the runes on the walls as I went. A soft glow of magic responded, lighting the tunnel that led to the speakeasy.

The floorboards creaked beneath my feet as I neared Benny, the tiny pin clutched in my hand like a lifeline. The very air seemed to ripple with tension, vibrating faintly with each step I took. Benny's spectral form shimmered, his energy erratic, like static crackling through the air. The runes lining the walls flickered in response to his agitation, their once steady glow now pulsing irregularly, casting jagged shadows across the room.

The temperature dropped sharply, and the wooden beams overhead groaned, a long, low sound that made my skin crawl. A picture frame rattled against the wall, the glass shaking in its frame before cracking with a sharp snap. Dust began to drift from the ceiling, stirred by the vibrations Benny was sending through the very structure of the room.

His voice, when it came, was a low, fraught rumble, vibrating through the air with enough force that the floorboards beneath me seemed to tremble in sympathy. One of the stools near the bar tipped over and crashed to the floor, the sound echoing ominously in the otherwise-silent room.

"I can't take this no more, doll. Clara's trapped, and I feel her slipping further away every day. I gotta get her free, you dig? I don't know how much longer we can last like this." His form flickered, the desperation in his voice growing.

"I know," I said gently, my pulse quickening at the sight of his growing instability. "And the best way to help her—both of you—is to figure out what happened to you two. We have to get to the truth." I took a deep breath, showing him the pin. "Benny, I found this hidden in an old flask, and I was wondering if it might mean anything." I held it out for him to see

.

He peered at it and then shook his head. "That pin?" he scoffed, his laugh hollow. "Clara designed it as a token of our grand adventure. A memento, nothing more. A symbol of the Hideaway and her hope that we might be able to take this place out in the open one day. But what's the worth of adventure when it ends like this?" Benny's voice cracked with a sadness that sent a shiver down my spine.

I bit my lip, the pin falling short of the case-breaking clue I hoped it would be. But I couldn't give up now. Desperation gnawed at me, but there was still more to dig into. "Benny, how many pins did she make? Who else had one?"

His form flickered as he mulled over my words, the runes pulsing faintly as his frustration seeped into the air. "There weren't many. Clara made 'em for a few of us—me, her, a couple of others who were part of the crew. People we trusted." He paused, and the floor creaked under the strain of his growing agitation, his form becoming more transparent, like he was unraveling. "But that doesn't mean anything now. What good is it if she's... gone?"

I took a breath, pressing gently but firmly. "But Benny, why was this one hidden in your flask? If it didn't matter, why tuck it away? Who else had one?"

His face twisted, his form flickering like a candle struggling to stay lit. "I...I don't know! Maybe I was trying to protect it. Maybe it was Clara's and I was keeping it safe. I...I can't remember! Too many memories, you know? They're all blurring together."

His form grew fuzzy at the edges, the effort of trying to remember clearly taking its toll. "The longer I'm here...the harder it gets. Memories—what's real and what's not—start mixing together. Sometimes I can almost feel it, like I'm about to remember, but it slips away. I know there's something more to this, something important. It's just... out of reach."

I stepped closer, my heart racing. "You're holding on to these pieces for a reason, Benny. Please," I begged. "There has to be something. Maybe you heard something that night or saw some people acting suspiciously in town? Anything could help. Something you saw. A noise or maybe even a smell? Anything? Anything at all."

The runes on his photograph flared. "No! Nothing! I can't remember anything!"

I took a breath, forcing my voice to convey a calm I didn't feel. "Sometimes, when I'm stuck on a problem, I like to walk through it," I said softly. "It helps me see things from a different angle, sometimes helps me notice something I missed. Why don't we try that? You were here, at the bar, working that night, right? Let's walk through it together."

Benny's form flickered, but I could tell he was listening. Slowly, I started talking him through the scene. "You walk into the Hideaway after closing. It's quiet. What do you remember hearing?"

His eyes narrowed as if focusing. "I remember...it was late, all the folks had already cleared out. The music had stopped, and it was just me and the bottles. I could hear the sound of glasses clinking as I cleaned up." His voice grew quieter as if the memory was pulling him in.

I pressed gently. "Okay, now close your eyes. Try to focus on what you felt. Not what you saw or heard, but the little things. Smells, textures, things like that."

Benny's form wavered, but he closed his eyes in concentration. A few moments passed, the silence stretching. Then, suddenly, his eyes snapped open, wide and startled. "Gin," he said. "I remember the smell of gin. Strong. Real strong."

I blinked. "Gin?"

He nodded, the memory slowly returning. "Yeah, I was wiping down the bar, but then I remember the smell hit me hard, right before something else did."

My heart raced. "What hit you, Benny? Do you remember?"

His brow furrowed. "It wasn't a fist. I've been hit by plenty of those in my time. This was different—hard, but smooth. Cold."

I looked around the room, searching for clues. My eyes landed on a bottle of gin sitting on the bar, and an idea sparked. "Benny, could it have been a bottle? Maybe something like this?"

He stared at the bottle for a moment, his form flickering again. "Yeah... yeah, maybe. I was hit with a bottle. I smelled the gin right before it smashed, must've spilled all over the place."

Excitement bubbled up inside me. "A bottle! That's what the killer used—a weapon of convenience. They grabbed the nearest thing and hit you with it. And as you went down, you knocked your head on the bar, right?"

Benny's form shimmered, flickering as if caught between the past and present. "Yeah... yeah, that's it. The smell of gin...the wetness on my face...and then...nothing."

I suddenly crouched down under the damaged section of the bar where I assumed Benny had hit his head. Benny watched me curiously.

"What are you doing?" Benny asked.

"Searching for more clues," I replied, my voice muffled as I peered into the shadows.

Benny's voice drifted down to me. "It was a hundred years ago. Surely someone tidied up, be it the coppers or maybe even Clara herself."

"I know," I said, a touch of stubbornness in my voice, "but it doesn't hurt to look." I pulled my phone out of my small handbag and turned on the flashlight, sweeping the beam under the bar.

Under a slight overhang, I caught a glint of something in the flashlight's beam. My heart skipped a beat. Carefully, I stretched my hand out. My fingers barely fit under the narrow gap. I strained, stretching as far as I could, my hand jammed against the hard wood of the bar. There! The tip of my finger brushed a hard surface. Carefully, I nudged it out with my fingers, revealing a shard of glass with an aged bit of a red and white label still attached to it. Lifting it cautiously by the edges, I held it up for Benny to see

"Look at this!" I exclaimed.

"What is it, doll?"

"I think it's a piece of glass from a bottle, and part of the label's still on it. This confirms our bottle-as-a-weapon theory."

Benny stared at the shard, his spectral form trembling with a mix of anger and frustration. His eyes narrowed, and I could see the torment of memories flashing behind them. The reality of his murder, the helplessness he felt, all seemed to resurface in an overwhelming wave.

"That's it then," he muttered, more to himself than to me. "A bottle. Just a durn bottle."

His voice grew louder, edged with bitterness. "Clara's life ruined, my life taken, all with one swing of a bottle!" The air around him began to crackle with his rising fury.

"Benny, please," I implored, taking an involuntary step back as the bottles on the shelf behind the bar rattled ominously. "You need to calm down."

"Calm? Calm!" he bellowed. The gin bottle on the bar fell on its side and rolled towards the edge. I barely caught it in time before it crashed to the ground. "While *she's* trapped, while *I'm* trapped, you tell me to be calm?" Benny roared. The rest of the dusty bottles on the bar shook, and the glasses in their rack behind the bar rattled ominously.

I stepped closer, feeling a cold draft as the surrounding temperature dropped, a physical manifestation of his spiraling emotions. "Benny, please," I coaxed, reaching out as if I could physically calm the storm within him. It looked like my plan to calm the ghost by finding clues to his murder was backfiring on an epic level. I was grateful that Gabriel and Lucas had already worked so hard on wards around the Oasis or there might've been damage to the building from the ghost's outburst. "Benny! You need to stay in control. Please!"

"Control?" his voice broke and there was the snap of breaking glass. Instinctively, I threw my arms up to protect myself, feeling a sting across my forearm. I ducked and covered my head with my hands, somehow still maintaining my grip on the bottle of gin.

At that moment, Bella's voice floated down from upstairs, pulling me from the brink of chaos. "Harper! Are you downstairs? We need you!"

The urgency in her tone snapped Benny back to some semblance of reason, and the room stilled. Broken glass from the nearby tumblers covered the floor. I felt a drip of something warm and wet dribble down my arm. Glancing down, I realized I must've deflected a shard with my forearm, but not without getting cut. I held out my arm to keep the blood from my beautiful dress as I examined the cut. It stung, but at least it looked relatively small and shallow.

Benny looked at me, remorse replacing the rage for just a moment as he saw the blood on my arm. "I—I didn't mean to..."

"I know," I whispered. "It's okay." My heart hammered with a cocktail of empathy and fear as I stared in shock at the broken glass on the floor. I hadn't realized a ghost could do that kind of damage.

"You should go. Before I do something else to hurt you," Benny said, his voice low.

I bit my lip but set the gin bottle back on the bar next to the shard of glass I'd found, backing away without another word. As I retreated, the chill from Benny's outburst clung to my skin like a warning.

Climbing back to the warmth and light of the party, I sucked in a shuddering breath. The stakes had never been clearer. Benny's grip on his restraint was fraying, unraveling with every passing second. And the worst part? He didn't even want to hurt anyone. He was stuck in his own torment, his own unresolved pain, and I knew with gut-wrenching certainty that if I didn't find a resolution—fast—it wouldn't just be the Hideaway at risk. The entire Oasis, the party, maybe even the town, could be caught in the crossfire if Benny's power kept growing.

I paused at the top of the stairs, casting one last glance down into the dark basement. He was too dangerous to contain much longer. If I didn't figure out what happened that night, Benny would destroy everything—whether he meant to or not.

The Watch and the Whisper

BELLA'S EYES WENT WIDE as I climbed the stairs, carefully holding my arm out to keep the scrape from dripping on my silver gown.

"What happened?" Bella demanded, hurrying to grab a kitchen towel.

I held out my arm as she wrapped it around the superficial injury. "Benny," I said by way of explanation. "He's getting more unstable."

"What are we going to do?" Bella whispered, her dark eyes shimmering with worry. "Mama and Papa are depending on this party running smoothly, especially with Vivienne Silverthorne here. If she thinks we're not keeping magic a secret or that the Oasis isn't safe, it could spell disaster for us in Havenwood. More than that, bad reviews could sink the business. My parents have worked so hard to make this place successful. And if word gets out that the Oasis might not be safe..."

Her voice wavered, and I could see the weight of her concerns piling up. But while she was focused on the social and business pressure of the evening, my thoughts were tangled in the threat growing just beneath our feet.

Bella sighed, brushing back a loose curl as she dug out a bandage, wiping my arm dry before sticking it in place. She set her jaw and nodded in determination. "What we need to do is seal the Hideaway. The wards will keep him contained, and we'll deal with Benny in the morning when things are calmer. Right now, we need to keep the focus on the party and make sure no one suspects anything."

I bit my lip, my pulse quickening. *Morning?* Benny's grip on control was slipping fast. I wasn't sure we had until midnight, let alone morning. But before I could voice my worry, Honey burst through the kitchen door.

"Oh good. I was wondering where the two of you had disappeared to." Her eyes sharpened as they landed on the bandage on my forearm. Her expression shifted, furrowing with concern. "What's happened here?"

Before I could reply, Bella interjected with a quick summary. "Just a minor accident, nothing to worry about, Mama."

I winced inwardly at the understatement. But Honey's expression shifted from concern to resolve. "Okay, but let's not have any more 'little accidents,' alright? I don't want people to think the Oasis is a dangerous place."

"We'll be careful," I promised, glancing towards the counter where the towel lay discarded, a grim reminder of the ghost's growing unrest. I shifted my position to block it from Honey's view.

Honey's gaze softened. "I'm glad you are okay, Harper. Bella, we need all hands on deck." She gestured to the bustling room beyond. "The guests are enjoying themselves, but they've really attacked the snacks. Can you help me with some more trays?"

"Sure, Mama," Bella said, instantly springing into action.

I moved to help as well, but Honey reached out a hand to stop me. "If you're injured, I don't think it's the best idea to be hauling around trays of food."

"I agree," Bella said, expertly balancing a full platter of small bites. "Harper can take over the roulette wheel for Papa until she's feeling better."

I opened my mouth to protest that I was fine, but Bella shot me a look that clearly said to just go along with the plan. I swallowed back my words. She obviously didn't want to upset her mother or answer any further questions about my injury. Rather than argue, I nodded mutely and hurried off to find Antonio.

Bella's suggestion turned out to be quite astute. A card game like poker or blackjack required shuffling and dealing, which might have aggravated my cut. As it turned out, I ended up enjoying myself more than I would've thought possible, given the circumstances. My table was popular because so many people could play at once. Luckily, because everyone was playing with fake money, no one cared if they won or lost. In fact, the guests celebrated the dramatic losses almost more enthusiastically than the wins. Laughter and banter flowed easily as party guests drifted between games. For a while, I even forgot about the ghost in the basement, losing myself in the rhythm of the spinning wheel and helping Bella create the most fantastic event the Oasis had ever seen.

Antonio's voice boomed jovially through the room. "Friends, guests! Our very own illustrious Vivienne Silverthorne has just told me she brought along a case of champagne that she cannot drink all by herself. Is there anyone willing to help the lady out of this dire predicament?"

A cheer rose to greet his words, and the crowd swept towards the hall and the promise of free spirits. I wondered if that was what the Hideaway would've been like back in the day. Most of the guests had filed into the adjoining room, lured by the promise of Vivienne Silverthorne's finest bubbly, leaving the gaming tables in a rare state of quiet.

The only person who remained was Mayor Featherfoot, his expression distant, contemplative, as he spun the roulette wheel idly. He didn't seem interested in joining the others for the toast, and I sensed an opportunity.

I'd been turning over the mystery in my mind ever since I sat down at the roulette table. I'd exhausted every clue I could dig up from Spellbooks, and going back downstairs to Benny in his increasingly agitated state didn't feel like a safe option. But Mayor Featherfoot...his family had been part of Havenwood for generations, dating back to at least when Benny was alive, perhaps even before. Maybe he held some untapped knowledge that could help piece things together.

"Not joining the toast, Mayor?" I asked, sidling up to him, trying to keep my tone light.

He offered a small, polite smile. "No, it's not quite my cup of tea. We Featherfoots have always erred on the side of abstaining while in office. Old family traditions and whatnot. I find it keeps the head clear," he said, tapping his temple with a finger.

I smiled, feigning interest beyond the surface. "That sounds admirable. Family traditions are important. You must have a lot of history here in

Havenwood," I said, edging the conversation towards where I wanted it to go.

He chuckled softly, clearly enjoying the attention. "Indeed. Our roots run deep—almost as deep as the Silverthornes'. Did you know my family has produced seven mayors? All Featherfoots. The first of which, my great-grandfather, Joseph Featherfoot, guided Havenwood through Prohibition."

I perked up, the name striking a familiar chord. Joseph Featherfoot—wasn't that the same mayor whose picture I'd found? He had been elected shortly after Benny's death. Could Mayor Featherfoot's great-grandfather have known about the speakeasy? If so, would he have supported it—or turned a blind eye? The thought sent a spark of curiosity through me. I pushed for more information, keeping my tone light. "Wow, I had no idea. That's an incredible legacy. Joseph Featherfoot sounds like he was a remarkable leader. And during Prohibition too? That must have been a wild time."

"A complicated time, to be sure, but my great-grandfather was a good man." he said, his chest puffing slightly with pride. "A principled leader who established our legacy. He even left behind this watch." Mayor Featherfoot pulled out an antique pocket watch, flicking it open to reveal an inscription inside the cover.

I leaned in, trying not to look too eager. "It's beautiful," I murmured, my eyes catching on the delicate etching of words inside. Mayor Featherfoot twisted the watch so I could read the inscription. It read:

To Mayor Featherfoot, for his steadfast vigilance and unyielding dedication to Havenwood.

As Mayor Featherfoot proudly flashed the back of the watch, a faint design under the inscription caught my eye. I squinted, trying to make it out as the light played across the design. "What's that? At the bottom?" I asked.

Mayor Featherfoot drew a finger over the design. "Oh this? It's just an old family emblem. My family never had a crest or anything like that, and I think my ancestors were a bit jealous of some of the other "symbolled" pre-eminent families in Havenwood, so they designed this. It's stuck with my family for generations.

I leaned forward to get a better look. As I did so, a woman's voice called from the other room.

"Flavian? Mayor Featherfoot? Could you join us please?"

I looked up to see Vivienne Silverthorne beckoning the mayor with one manicured finger.

He snapped the lid of the pocket watch closed. "Excuse me. When a Silverthorne calls, a Featherfoot answers," he said with a slight, self-deprecating chuckle.

Seeing the rest of the gaming tables were empty, I followed, pausing at the edge of the crowd and trying to organize my thoughts. Could that symbol mean something? Why did it look so familiar? But I'd lost my chance for a closer look. I sighed in frustration and glanced around. To my surprise, I recognized the man standing next to me.

"Hello Sheriff Jackson," I murmured.

"Miss Sullivan." The stern sheriff acknowledged me with a dip of his chin. "Apprehend any more jewel thieves lately?" he asked, his voice low as the noise from the gathering crowd kept our conversation relatively private.

"Not recently," I said with a shiver, remembering the close call I had at Christmas time. I tipped my head towards the flutes of champagne being circulated. "Aren't you partaking?"

The sheriff shook his head. "Election season is coming up. Vivienne has a lot of influence in these matters, and I find it's better to keep a clear head and a conservative reputation at town events. But don't you worry about me. I'll raise a glass with my wife at home tonight."

"Oh," I said lamely. I hadn't realized the sheriff was married. To me, he'd always been the sheriff, and I'd never really thought about what he did when not on duty. Before I could wonder more about Sheriff Jackson and his personal life, Vivienne called out above the noise of the crowd, drawing everyone's attention toward her.

Once the noise quieted somewhat, Vivienne lifted her voice, introducing Antonio and Honey as the hosts of the evening. She led the polite round of applause, stepping to the side as Antonio raised his glass, thanking everyone for coming.

My attention wandered as he spoke. Several empty green glass bottles lining the table in the room's corner distracted me from focusing on his words. Something about seeing the bottles niggled at me. Benny's killer had used something like that to strike him when he wasn't looking. Except the glass shard had been clear, not green and the liquor was gin, not champagne.

I bit my lip, a question forming in my mind. How did Benny and Clara get their stash into the Hideaway without raising suspicion? They couldn't just carry bottles through the inn without someone noticing, right? And all those empty bottles—where did they go? If they used the escape tunnel, it might have been more private, but even sneaking bottles into the woods would've attracted attention sooner or later. So how did they keep it all hidden?

Slipping quietly through the scattered crowd, I slipped down the hall that led down to the basement. As I passed, I noticed Sheriff Jackson standing near the entrance, his sharp gaze sweeping over the room. I couldn't help but think of the old sheriff from Benny's time. Surely, someone in his position would've known about the hidden stash. Maybe the law had caught up with Benny and Clara after all. Or worse—maybe those in power had turned a blind eye to the speakeasy's existence...or the truth about what happened to Benny. My gaze flicked toward the mayor, standing just across the room with Vivienne. The descendants of Havenwood's old elite, still pulling the strings. Could their ancestors have been involved?

I hesitated, my heart thudding louder in my chest. The bandage on my arm felt suddenly tight as the memory of Benny's growing power hit me. What if I went downstairs and riled him up again? Would I disturb Bella's perfect night? Or worse—disrupt the party entirely? The thought of the Silverthornes witnessing chaos at the Oasis sent a shiver down my spine.

But then, as if in answer, the floor beneath me gave a faint tremor. Something—a shift and shudder that reminded me of Spellbooks—vibrated under my shoes. It was just a hint and, if I hadn't become so attuned to communicating with my shop, I probably wouldn't have even noticed. There was no doubt in my mind. It was Benny. His restlessness wouldn't fade. It was only getting worse.

I swallowed hard, my heart thundering in my chest. Would the wards hold? If I was feeling Benny shake the building, I doubted it. If I didn't act now—if I didn't find a way to calm him—who knew what would happen before the night was through?

Behind the Shadows

A HAND GRABBED MY arm as I silently eased the basement door open. I spun to see Gabriel's concerned face mere inches from mine.

"Harper? What are you doing?" he hissed.

"I felt the floorboards shaking and think Benny might be causing it. I just thought of something, and I need to ask him—"

"Not by yourself, you don't," Gabriel replied instantly, cutting me off. Worry lit his dark eyes. "Like I said before, an upset ghost is nothing to mess around with."

Gabriel's gaze shifted to my arm. His brow furrowed as he reached out, gently brushing his fingers against the bandage wrapped around my forearm. "What happened here?" he asked, his tone softening as he examined the wound with a tenderness that caught me off guard.

I rubbed my thumb over my arm instinctively. "It's nothing," I said quickly, trying to downplay the injury. "Just a scratch."

"Harper," he said quietly, his fingers lingering for a second longer than necessary. "You're not going back down there alone. Not after this."

I quickly grabbed his arm. "Bella wants to seal the Hideaway off for the night and deal with Benny in the morning, but I just felt the floorboards shake. He's growing more powerful. Please, we need to do something now. Strengthen the wards, calm him down—anything."

Gabriel's eyes flickered with understanding and concern as he looked down at where my hand gripped his arm. "You're really sure about this?" he asked, his voice softer now, as if weighing the gravity of the situation.

I nodded, my voice barely a whisper. "I am. I don't think he's going to make it until morning without something...happening."

For a moment, Gabriel was quiet, processing what I'd said. His jaw tightened before he finally nodded. "Okay. We'll figure something out. But we do it together."

I silently accepted his protective presence, grateful not to face Benny's restless spirit on my own again. The chill of the basement greeted us as we made our way through the narrow corridor, the air thick with the tension of unresolved pasts. Each footstep echoed, a countdown to the impending confrontation.

Finally, we stood before Benny, his spectral photo flickering with agitation like a candle in the wind. His face, usually so full of mischief and charm, was now twisted with frustration and pain. "They're not just going to let me rest, are they? Neither of us," he murmured, and it was clear he wasn't speaking to us. "Don't worry, my love. I'll make them. You'll see."

"Hey, Benny," I said gently, coaxing his gaze to meet mine. "We're trying to help, to find the truth, but I need you to calm down and—"

"Calm! How do you expect me to be calm?" Benny's voice rose and cracked as a gust of wind swirled through the Hideaway, making me squint and cover my eyes at the unexpected ferocity. I felt Gabriel take my free hand and shield me with his body, but as suddenly as it came, it died away.

I peeked through my fingers at Benny. "You can't keep lashing out like that," I said, channeling my dad, the stalwart Master Sergeant. "Sending mini-tornados through the Hideaway or making chairs skid on the floor won't get you answers. Help me help you. How did you and Clara keep your stash hidden from the authorities?"

He blinked and, with difficulty, pulled his eyes away from the locket, finally focusing on me. Gabriel gave my fingers an encouraging squeeze. A hint of Benny's usual charm resurfaced as he puffed up slightly with pride at his own cleverness. "That's easy. I'd drive it around back of the Hearthstone at the end of the day, covered in blankets to keep out the prying eyes. Then, under cover of night, I'd carry the crates into the basement, through the tunnel and stash them back there," he said, nodding at an almost empty shelf stretching from floor to ceiling. "We could take what we wanted out of the storeroom before the guests came in. I'd only have to restock once every month or so if I planned it right."

My eyes went wide. "Wait a second. You said 'storeroom' not shelf. Are you implying that there is a secret room back there?" I asked.

"Behind the shelf?" Gabriel asked in astonishment

Benny nodded, looking smug and more than a little pleased with himself. "Absolutely. The bottles are just decoration. Clara fixed them to the shelf with a bit of magic so no one would suspect where we kept the stash. As far as anyone knew, what you see is what you get." He waved an arm at the bar and then laid a finger alongside his nose and winked. "Except it wasn't quite."

Gabriel and I exchanged a glance, then moved to where Benny had indicated. With concerted effort and some direction from Benny, we found a hidden brass lock tucked under a carved panel of wood.

I hurried to grab the key ring from where we'd left it on the bar. "Which key is it?" I demanded, showing them to Benny.

He frowned and shook his head. "I don't see it. Strange. It should be there."

"Would Clara have taken it?" Gabriel asked.

Benny shook his head. "I was the only one who moved bottles in or out of there. I couldn't be asking my Clara to do all that heavy lifting."

Thinking that maybe Benny had just missed the key in his quick glance at the keyring, I tried each one methodically. None of them worked. Not to be deterred, I put my hand on the lock, hoping against hope that it was a mundane lock instead of one of the runed ones. I reached out with my magic, but luck wasn't on my side. The lock refused to give way even under my magical touch. I huffed out a sigh and stepped back, frowning at the wall in frustration.

"What is it?" Gabriel asked.

"I can't get it to open with my magic. The lock is runed," I explained.

"Can you describe what you see to me? Maybe I can use my illusion magic on one of the other keys to trick the enchantment," Gabriel offered.

"That's a good idea. Let me see," I said, focusing on the magic inside the lock. The runes glinted in my mind, stubborn and mocking in their complexity. "The first one is like..." I squinted, struggling to find the words. "A squashed rectangle—but incomplete, sort of unraveling? And there's a pair of lines jutting out the side."

I traced the air with my fingers, trying to match the rune in my mind. "Then there's this...zigzag pattern. It's repeated three times, like lightning striking the same place over and over."

I glanced at Gabriel, hoping my halting description made sense. His brow furrowed in concentration, his hands moving as if sketching the images in the space between us. "Anything else?"

"The last one is a diamond, I think. Maybe a square on its endpoint? But its lines are doubled, almost like it's been shadowed," I continued, frustration seeping into my voice. "Perhaps there's some hatch marks in the space between the diamonds? Sideways squares? Whatever they are?" The descriptions were lackluster, to say the least. I bit my lip as Gabriel attempted to use his illusion magic to recreate the runes I saw in my head.

"Like this?" he said, drawing the runes in the air with a glowing fingertip. They hovered there between us. He'd followed my descriptions as best he could, yet his glowing symbols looked almost nothing like what I saw in my mind's eye with my magic.

I shook my head in frustration. "This won't work," I admitted. "We need someone who knows runes and can translate them accurately." A thought popped into my head. "I know just the guy. You wait right here. I'll be back in a flash." I didn't wait for Gabriel to answer before hiking up my skirts and taking off down the tunnel.

Dashing up the basement stairs, I looked for my red-headed neighbor. If there was anyone who could translate my jumbled description of runes into something meaningful, it was Finn. I saw him in the corner, laughing and talking with Seraphina. I froze mid-step, not sure how to feel about seeing the two of them together. True, I had invited her, but I hadn't exactly anticipated the fallout of my altruistic gesture in the moment. I shook my head. This was no time to be silly or descend into jealousy. For all I knew, the answers to Benny's and Clara's deaths lay just beyond that downstairs wall, and I needed to work with Finn to get inside that storeroom. My feelings about him and his possibly-ex-possibly-again-girlfriend couldn't be the priority right now.

Finn looked up as I hurried over. "Harper? Are you okay?" His eyes flicked from my face to my arm and back again.

"You look as if you've seen a ghost," Seraphina said, concern lighting her beautiful features.

"Funny you should say that," I murmured. Keeping my voice low, I filled them in as quickly as I could. "So, you see, I need your help, Finn. I think with your knowledge of runes, Gabriel's illusion magic, and my own gifts, we should be able to make this work."

Finn, to his credit, mentioned nothing about Gabriel, but I could see a hint of flatness enter his eyes and a slight stiffening to his posture when I mentioned the Silverthorne. But just as now wasn't the time for me to hesitate over Seraphina, Finn seemed to realize his jealousy of Gabriel could wait as well.

"Sounds like we don't have much time. Lead the way," he said, determination lighting his features.

I didn't hesitate but hurried through the crowd back to the basement stairs. It spoke to my urgency that I didn't even protest as Seraphina followed us silently into the basement. Finn, however, stopped dead in his tracks when we reached the end of the tunnel, his eyes widening as they swept over the speakeasy and Benny's shimmering form.

"What the...?" Finn murmured, clearly taken aback. Seraphina gasped softly beside him, her gaze fixed on the eerie glow of the runes.

"Is this...?" she started, her voice trailing off in awe.

Gabriel shot me a look, one eyebrow raised in a silent question as they entered.

I ignored them all, pressing forward. Quickly, I explained my idea to Finn, Gabriel, and Benny. Seraphina watched intently from the side but didn't interrupt.

"Okay, I'm going to reshape one key to fit this lock. Finn, I need you to help Gabriel figure out which runes to make so that the key will work. I'll describe them to you based on what I can sense inside the lock, but we are going to need your knowledge of runes to guide Gabriel's illusion magic so he can create the appearance of the runes on the key. Hopefully, by working together, we can pull off a miracle," I said, selecting one key from the now empty cabinets behind the bar.

We got to work. Much of the initial load fell on my shoulders as I was the only one who could see inside the lock with my magic. I described the runes to Finn, who sketched them on a blank piece of paper Benny had directed us to behind the bar. I double-checked them to make sure they matched what I saw inside the lock and gave Finn a thumbs up. He and Gabriel worked together on translating the sketches into glowing magical sigils while I labored on reshaping one of the brass keys on the keyring.

Sweat broke out on my brow as I concentrated all my magic on the key in my hands. Thank goodness brass was a relatively malleable metal and one that was resistant to corrosion, or I might have had even more trouble. As it was, the metal itself was fine, but after a few minutes, I wasn't sure my magic was up to the task. My gift for metal magic was small. I could easily handle dents in a car, fixing a bent earring, and, yes, even picking a lock. But big magic had always been beyond my reach. In the magical world, it was like I was in the stands, cheering on the professional athletes on the field. I knew enough to make it to the game and even appreciate it while I was there, but there wasn't a chance in this century or the next that I would be the one playing down on that field.

Still, I tried. Slowly, the metal shifted under the magical pressure. I tried not to let that small victory distract me and break my focus. Instead, I bore down even harder. The metal responded sluggishly to my mental commands, but it was responding! At what seemed to me to be a glacial pace but, in reality, was probably only a few minutes, I reshaped the key into a form that I was confident would open the runed lock.

Sweat dribbled down my temple as I passed the key over to Finn and Gabriel. I dabbed at the perspiration carefully with the back of my hand, hoping I didn't have pit stains darkening my silver dress.

"Well done, Harper! This is amazing work," Gabriel said, taking the key from me.

"It's really incredible," Finn said, shooting me an encouraging smile. I tried to nod, but my energy was gone as fatigue dragged at every muscle in my body.

Seraphina drifted over to get a closer look at what we were doing. She was an enchanter elf and was probably just interested in what Gabriel was going to do next. It surprised me when she turned to me instead. "This is no small feat of magic, and the craftsmanship looks excellent," she said sincerely. "If you ever want to switch professions, I think you'd have a bright future in jewelry crafting."

"Really?" The word escaped my lips, but it was more out of surprise than interest.

"Absolutely," Seraphina said, nodding with a warm smile. "I know plenty of jewelers who'd love to have someone with your skill as an apprentice."

I blinked, surprised. "It's really not that special," I mumbled, trying to downplay it.

Seraphina shook her head, her eyes soft. "It is. Trust me, Harper, your magic is something to be proud of. You're more talented than you realize."

I hesitated, feeling a flicker of warmth at her words. Every time I thought I could resort to the comforting and age-old familiarity of being jealous of Finn's ex-girlfriend, Seraphina went and said something like this. The problem was, she *meant* it, too. From every interaction I'd ever had with her, she was genuinely a *nice* person. Thoughtful, warm, welcoming, generous, kind, the list went on. Tell me, how could I descend to the pits of jealousy every teenage movie told me I should be feeling when it was *Seraphina* who was my apparent rival? At this rate, I was more likely to become friends with her than fight her for a guy, even if the guy was Finn.

"Oh. Well. Thanks," I murmured, tucking a loose strand of hair behind one ear. "I'll, umm, keep that it mind."

"You should. You have a gift that could take you far in my world," Seraphina said sincerely.

"I think we've got it," Gabriel said, saving me from having to further contemplate the enchanter elf's offer. He held up the reshaped key, glowing with runes he'd illusioned into place, not having access to metal carving tools.

Finn peered over his shoulder, nodding at the magically inscribed runes on the reformed key. "I think you're right. If those are the runes in the lock, they're as close to perfect as I've ever seen. Good work."

"I told you I wasn't bad at rune-craft, but my illusion magic was always better," Gabriel said with a small smirk. He passed the key to me. "If you don't mind doing the honors?"

I took a deep breath and inserted it in the hidden lock in the wall. I closed my eyes, surreptitiously crossing the fingers of my other hand for luck as I turned the key.

There was a scrape deep within the lock and a snag of resistance. I held my breath, putting more pressure on the key. With a grating sound, it slowly turned until I heard the telltale click of the lock giving way.

"We did it!" I said, excitement bubbling up.

Finn grinned. "Worked like a charm."

Gabriel shot me a warm look. "I never had a doubt."

From the corner of my eye, I saw Finn's jaw tighten slightly, and his eyes flickering a momentary glance toward Gabriel. Seraphina, oblivious, blinked between us, her head tilted in slight confusion, sensing an undercurrent she couldn't quite place.

"What's inside?" Seraphina asked, looking between the three of us.

"Let's find out," I said, gripping the door and pushing it open. Darkness yawned beyond.

Envy's Brew

GABRIEL PLAYED THE LIGHT from his phone along the wall of the secret storeroom until he found the familiar runes to illuminate the space. When he brushed his fingers across the carved designs, a dim glow from the runes etched into the ceiling and walls cast long shadows across the room. The air was cool and musty, filled with the faint, heady scent of aged spirits.

I followed Gabriel into the storeroom, Finn close on my heels. Seraphina stuck her head in the door, but there wasn't much space for her in the already crowded room. I peered at the bottles as I tried not to tread on anyone else's toes in the enclosed space. Narrow shelves lined the walls, some still holding bottles of various shapes, colors, and sizes. The bottles, dusty and labeled with faded, elegant script, held the relics of clandestine celebrations long past. A few wooden crates, lying haphazardly in one corner, appeared as though someone emptied them and tossed them to the side in a hurry. The floor was a patchwork of old, creaky, wooden planks that echoed softly with each step I took. Cobwebs clung to the darker corners of the room, and dust motes danced in the light from the runes.

"What's going on in there?" Benny asked, his ghostly voice breaking through the stillness of the cramped room. "Did you find anything? Any clues?"

Seraphina ducked out of the doorway and returned a moment later, holding Benny's picture.

"Well? Did you?" the ghost prompted again as soon as he came into sight.

I shook my head and waved an arm at the storeroom. "You'd know better than us if there was anything missing. It doesn't look like anyone's been in here in ages. Do you see anything that looks out of place?"

There was a slight shuffle as we passed Benny's photograph around so he could get a better look at the bottles on the shelves. When I held the photo up to the empty crates, Benny called out, "Hold on just a tick!"

I froze, looking at the empty wooden crates. "What is it?"

"This doesn't add up," Benny muttered, sounding more confused than angry. "These crates should be packed. We'd just switched bootleggers. The new guy was the bee's knees, and I put in a full order right before...well, you know."

"Driftwood Sam, right?" I asked, dredging his name from my memory. "He was your new supplier?"

"Yes, but I ain't never met the fella. A mutual contact put us in touch. Assuming the product was quality, he would've set up a regular buy from Driftwood Sam. It was all through a pal who knew a guy. If the hooch was as smooth as the sample, we'd have made it a regular gig. And let me tell ya, that gin was the real McCoy. But we barely broke open that crate. Only a couple of bottles, three or four tops, should be gone."

Gabriel and Finn both moved towards the crates Benny indicated, crouching down to examine the wooden container and nearly knocking their knees together as they did so. The two men engaged in what felt like the world's quietest but most intense staring contest. The air between them bristled with testosterone, and I wished there was something I could do to dispel the tension coiling inside me. Having both of them here, in such close quarters, was fraying my nerves.

"Do you think Clara might have taken some of the gin out?" I asked, breaking the tense silence.

"Nah, dollface. Clara was a whiskey dame, right to her core. Gin? That was my racket. And let me tell ya, the stuff this Sam brought in? It was the cat's pajamas, absolutely top shelf," Benny said.

"Well, if you and Clara were the only ones with the keys, how did the rest of the gin go missing?" Gabriel asked.

"Maybe it's all behind the bar?" I ventured.

"I'll have a look," Seraphina offered, disappearing from the doorway once more.

"Someone had to pass the keys down through the years. I mean, they ended up in Spellbooks' attic," I said logically. "But maybe this key wasn't meant to be passed down with the others. Maybe someone took it specifically and took the gin?"

"But left the rest of the liquor?" Finn asked, his voice skeptical. "If they were sealed properly, which it looks like they have been, they would've fetched a pretty penny. For sure back in the '20s, but even more so now. They've been undisturbed for nearly one hundred years, after all. They must be worth at least a couple of thousand dollars apiece now."

"At least that. Probably more if the liquor was distilled well," Gabriel chimed in, shifting the lid of the crate to the side to get a better look.

"There's no gin except the one bottle that was on the bar," Seraphina reported back, perplexed. I glanced over my shoulder to see Seraphina holding the bottle we'd discovered in Clara's hidden cabinet.

Behind me, the lid from the crate clattered to the floor, the rattle of wood-on-wood reverberating in the enclosed space loudly enough to make me jump.

"Sorry about that," Gabriel muttered.

I pressed my hand to my racing heart as the lid wobbled to a stop on the floor. My eyes sharpened as I spied something on the lid.

"Wait. What's that?" I said, crouching between Gabriel and Finn to get a closer look at the top of the lid. When Gabriel had knocked it to the floor, he'd revealed a symbol burned into the wood on one corner of the lid. "Look at this!" I called, my voice urgent. Both Gabriel and Finn leaned in. I heard the click of heels behind me as Seraphina pressed forward and peered over my shoulder.

I traced a finger around the design. There wasn't a doubt in my mind. It was the same one that we'd discovered on the tie clip. A spiral enclosed in a circle and framed in a triangle. Except this one seemed to be much simpler than the glittering golden element. Just to be sure, I nudged Gabriel.

"It's the same one, isn't it? The symbol on the tie clip?" I said excitedly.

He nodded as he dug into his pocket. "I think so. Here." He pulled it out.

Even in the weak illumination from the runes in the storeroom, it was obvious. They were a match.

"So, whoever produced the liquor in this crate must've been the one in the tunnel," I gasped.

"Maybe it was the delivery guy, not the distiller," Gabriel said cautiously.

"Nah, that's the new rum runner's sign. At least, I'm pretty sure," Benny piped up from his photograph.

"I think Harper's right. It's definitely the bootlegger's symbol," Seraphina said from behind me. We all looked up at her in surprise.

"How can you be so sure?" Finn asked.

"Because the bottle of gin I found on the bar is marked with the same mysterious symbol," Seraphina said, twisting the bottle so we could see the prominent red design emblazoned across the label.

I froze, my mind racing. The shard of glass I had discovered under the bar flashed in my memory, the bit of label still attached to it showing part of a similar design. I dashed out to the bar, carefully lifting the fragment and holding it against the label on the gin bottle Seraphina cradled. There wasn't a doubt in anyone's mind. The shard had come from one of Driftwood Sam's gin bottles. No one seemed to breathe, the implications dawning on us. The storeroom felt suddenly colder, the shadows deeper.

"You mean to tell us this symbol links the gin, the bootlegger, the tie pin, and the tunnel collapse?" Gabriel asked, his voice tense.

"And the murder weapon," I added, pointing to the bottle.

"It sure looks that way," Finn said.

I bit my lip and nodded slowly, the significance of our discoveries settling over me as another piece of the puzzle clicked into place. "Not only that, but those are the three symbols I found in Clara's notebook when she wrote she knew who was responsible for what happened to Benny. Which means whoever supplied this gin might be the murderer after all."

As the others discussed the possibility of a conspiracy, my mind whirred in the background. Something about it didn't sit right. This murder hadn't been calculated or carefully planned. Benny's death—Clara's too—it all felt too rushed, too panicked. My instincts told me this wasn't some grand conspiracy. I just couldn't see it.

The floor gave another faint shudder beneath my feet, and a chill ran through me. Time was running out, and Benny's agitation was growing stronger. I was close. So close I could almost taste it. But if I didn't put the pieces together soon, we might not get another chance.

Gambits and Glances

My mind buzzed with theories and half-formed ideas as everyone else tried to make sense of the clues spread out across the top of the bar.

"So, we're thinking this mysterious bootlegger killed Benny and came after Clara?" I asked, trying to piece everything together.

"This Driftwood Sam?" Seraphina said, glancing from the bottle of gin to Benny's photograph which was once more next to Clara's locket.

"It doesn't make sense," Finn remarked, rubbing his chin thoughtfully. "Besides a name, which definitely sounds like an alias, we can't confirm that Benny and Sam knew each other, right?"

"Besides, Sam had just taken a colossal risk and was on the brink of making an enormous commitment to working with Benny. If his gin was as top-notch as Benny claimed, why would he break in and kill the owner just to steal it back?" Gabriel asked.

"Maybe there was something off with that batch?" Seraphina suggested, her brow furrowed.

"The gin was poisoned or something?" Finn asked.

Seraphina bit her lip. "Or maybe it was just badly distilled and could've made people sick?" She shrugged, obviously searching for a solution that made sense in this situation.

Benny spoke up. "No dice, toots. That gin? I swear to you, it was smooth as silk from dusk till dawn. I should know. I was one of the ones doing the drinking."

"And if it had been poisoned, Benny would've died from that instead of getting hit on the head," Gabriel pointed out.

I shook my head, trying to organize the whirlwind of thoughts swirling through my mind. It felt like piecing together a structure in the middle of a storm, but eventually, two fragments seemed to click into place. "Maybe it wasn't about the gin at all. Let's go back to the basics. Most crimes boil down to a few key motives: anger, jealousy, revenge. At the start, we thought it could've been a business rivalry, which covers most of those, especially with something as secretive as bootlegging. What if Sam wanted to edge in on the Hideaway? He could've used the middleman, tracked him back to Benny, figured out who he was, then killed him to take over the business or run his own speakeasy without any competition."

"That dirty, rotten scoundrel!" Benny growled.

"Maybe that's why he collapsed the tunnel on Clara? To get her out of the way as well so he could take over the Hideaway," I mused aloud.

Finn crossed his arms, looking skeptical. "Except no one took over the business. They couldn't without Clara and her keys. Remember? And then, her father took her keys. How would Sam have gotten his hands on them? I hardly think a town leader like Clarence Silverthorne would've continued to turn a blind eye to the Hideaway if his daughter was no longer involved."

"If he was anything like my mother, not a chance," Gabriel muttered.

"Was there another speakeasy in town back then?" I asked. "Maybe this was about eliminating the competition."

Gabriel shook his head slowly and then shrugged. "Maybe? But nothing we've turned up so far suggests there was another speakeasy. Back then, Havenwood wasn't as big as it is now. Two speakeasies in one town might've been pushing it."

"I ain't heard of no other gin joint. Least, not while I was alive," Benny chimed in.

"Besides, why destroy the place if he wanted to run it?" Seraphina mused. All eyes shifted to her, and she blushed prettily. "What I mean is, an escape tunnel seems like an essential part of an underground speakeasy. If Sam wanted this place, why would he collapse the tunnel instead of dealing with Clara in another way?"

Gabriel glanced at me. "She has a point. The collapse was deliberate sabotage. A potential new owner wouldn't do that."

"Maybe he had another location ready and didn't want the competition. Or perhaps it wasn't about the Hideaway at all. There could be another reason Sam might have been driven to such extremes," I speculated, feeling a twist in my gut as the thought took shape. I tried not to look between Finn and Gabriel.

"And what might that be?" Seraphina prompted.

I swallowed hard, trying to keep my tone neutral. "Jealousy. Maybe this was all about Clara. Sam wanted her, figured out her ties to Benny and the Hideaway. He tries to position himself in her life where he can fill both the bootlegger and boyfriend roles," I theorized, piecing together the human motives that might drive such drastic actions.

"Except she rejects him," Seraphina added, catching on to the narrative thread.

"Maybe the killer sabotages the tunnel in a fit of rage?" Finn suggested.

I held up a finger. "One problem though. It wasn't a fit of rage. The sabotage in the tunnel was deliberate. Meticulous. Premeditated."

Gabriel chimed in. "But the attack on Benny wasn't. That was a crime of opportunity, remember? Benny walked back into the bar unexpectedly. He was hit on the back of the head. Unless someone was lying in wait for him, that couldn't have been premeditated."

"And I wasn't supposed to be down here anyway," Benny pointed out.

I twirled the bottle on the bar, tracing the red design with a finger. On a whim, I opened Clara's notebook to the page where she'd written the similar symbols.

"Okay, let's back up. We're speculating that the escape tunnel collapse, the bootlegger, and the killer are all linked through this symbol," I said, pointing at the recurring emblem on the tie clip, the gin bottle, and the symbols in Clara's notebook. "She must've hidden this bottle in her secret cabinet before someone broke in to take the rest. Maybe she figured out there was something off about Driftwood Sam's gin."

"And who would break into the Hideaway to steal the rest of it?" Seraphina asked, gracefully gesturing toward the open door of the storeroom.

Silence settled over the room as each of us weighed the suspects in our minds. I felt like I was grasping at straws in the dark while wearing a blindfold. We were too far removed from the time. We didn't know the players. Why did I think I could solve this? Gabriel had been right all along. We needed to go to Vivienne Silverthorne and beg her to help us deal with Benny before he became an unchained menace to the town. But what would that mean for him? I doubted Vivienne's method of dealing with spirits was exactly...gentle. If we asked her to step in, Benny might be trapped, likely condemned to spend eternity as a tormented ghost. No closure. No moving on. He'd never find Clara again, and we might never get the answers we needed. Could I really do that to him?

I held up my hand. "You're right, Seraphina. Maybe we missed something. Are there any possible suspects?"

Finn spoke up. "What about Clarence? We keep coming back to him. Could he be the one behind all this? The constant tarnishing of his family's reputation just grew to be too much for him?"

Gabriel slowly shook his head. "I don't think he was involved, and it's not just because he's my ancestor. It just doesn't make sense. We have established that he turned a blind eye, likely put in a word with the local police to do the same, all to protect his daughter's image?" My mind flashed to Officer Crowley as Gabriel continued speaking. "Even if he was behind it, why would he return and only take the gin? Surely, he would've taken all the alcohol in the place and tried to erase any sign his daughter was linked to a speakeasy at all. What really makes me think Clarence wasn't involved is the sabotage in the tunnel. Why would he do something that might hurt his daughter, who was supposedly his pride and joy?"

"Besides, Clara didn't write the same crown symbol she used for Clarence on this page where she claimed to know the killer," I pointed out.

"Are you sure it was sabotage and not an accident?" Seraphina spoke up. "After all, only Clara and her killer would know, and neither are with us any longer."

Benny pointed at the locket next to him. "Not exactly on the level. Clara's around, see. She's tied to that locket, but her spirit ain't as robust as mine." The locket seemed to glow a little brighter for a moment before the light faded,

A spark of hope lit in my chest. Because she hadn't or couldn't contribute to the conversation, I'd forgotten Clara's spirit was here. I leaned forward, speaking to the locket. "Clara? We are so close to answers, but we need your help to put the last few pieces together. Can you help us?"

The locket glowed weakly.

"Step on it, she's losing her grip. You might have time for only a pair of questions before she's out," Benny urged.

"How long would it take her to recover?" Seraphina asked softly.

"I'm on the ropes here. Can't be sure," Benny said, pacing in agitation within the confines of his photograph.

I took a deep breath, trying to focus my thoughts and distill the information we'd uncovered so far into a question or two that could uncover the killer. However, they'd have to be "yes" or "no" questions given that Clara didn't seem to have enough energy to form words.

I cleared my throat and spoke to the spirit in the locket. "Clara, was Driftwood Sam responsible for what happened to you and Benny?" I asked, trying out my best theory. I held my breath as soon as the last syllable left my lips. All eyes focused intently on the locket. Was that the answer? Had we found our killer?

But to my dismay, the locket remained dark.

Disappointment rushed through me, and I sat heavily on the nearest bar stool. Finn started pacing back and forth while Seraphina let out a little sigh of frustration. Despite all the conversation and theories, a tiny part of me really wanted to believe Sam had been behind it all. It just fit.

Except it didn't.

Gabriel took my place, leaning forward with a mix of eagerness and dread on his face. "Was it your father, Clara? Was he behind it?"

On impulse, I cupped the locket in my palm, feeling the cool metal hum faintly under my touch. The vibration was soft, like a whisper just barely verbalized. My connection to metal sparked—weak, but there. Clara was still lingering, barely, as if she was too far away to be heard.

I closed my eyes, concentrating. Gently, I let a thread of my magic pour into the locket, like a quiet reassurance. The hum grew, just a little, the faint pulse beneath my fingertips becoming steadier before fading to a faint thrum once more.

"I can feel her slipping away," Benny whispered. "She's giving it all to stay here. To stay real. But she's fading fast. You've got maybe one more question if you make it snappy."

Finn leaned back, rubbing a hand through his long hair in frustration. "Those were our two best suspects, even if not all the pieces fit exactly. Now we're back to square one."

Benny's expression darkened. "Which means the low-down on what happened to me or to Clara might forever be up in smoke." The photograph trembled like a leaf before a gale and the lights from the runes flickered in response to Benny's rising anger.

I threw out a hand. "Wait!"

Benny froze, and all eyes turned to me. "You have an answer for me, dollface?" he whispered, his voice raw with barely suppressed emotion.

"Just...let me think a minute," I said, trying to buy some time. I needed to keep Benny from exploding, especially with Bella's party going on upstairs. However, Clara was fading and there wasn't time to be had.

"That's not an answer," Benny growled.

Something Finn said tickled at my brain. "Not who. *Why*," I murmured.

"What was that?" Benny demanded.

"We've been so focused on the who. We need to go back to the why," I said, gaining confidence as I spoke. "*Why* would someone do all this? Not for jealousy. From what Benny's told us and what I read in her notebook, Clara never entertained even the merest flirtation from anyone else. Greed? Unlikely. No one took over the speakeasy, and there wasn't a long-term plan to profit from it. So, what other motives could there be? What would drive someone to steal, kill, and leave such a tangled mess behind?"

"Revenge?" Finn guessed.

I shook my head. "It doesn't fit."

"Fear," Seraphina suggested. "They'd discovered something someone didn't want to come out."

I drummed my fingers on the bar. "Maybe. But what was it? And who didn't want this thing seeing the light of day?" Absently, I picked up the golden tie clip, spinning it between my fingers as my thoughts whirled through possibilities.

"Someone who had something to lose," Gabriel said instantly. "Somehow, whatever Clara and Benny knew was a threat. One big enough to kill for."

"But what kind of threat could be linked to a gin bootlegger?" Seraphina asked, pointing at the bottle.

I glanced from the tie clip in my hands to the bottle. Something caught my eye. I blinked in surprise. How had I missed this? Excitedly, I leaned forward, holding the tie clip up to the red design on the bottle.

"Harper? What is it?" Gabriel asked.

"I think I know who the murderer is!"

The Secret of the Speakeasy

I HITCHED MY SKIRT up to my knees once again as I bolted up the stairs, feeling the wooden steps creak under my feet. My pulse pounded against my ribs, partly from the sprint, but mostly from the enormity of what we were about to face. Reaching the upper hallway, I whipped out my phone, frantically scanning for the last critical bit of evidence.

Gabriel was right behind me, his brow furrowed as he tried to anticipate my next move. "Harper, what are you doing?"

"Just give me a second..." I muttered, my thumbs flying across the screen. An old newspaper article popped up on the screen. I scrolled through it, my eyes flicking over the text, searching for the answer I hoped was there. It had to be there. I just needed to find the proof. And then suddenly, there it was. A captioned photograph, moving my theory from mere speculation to circumstantial proof.

My breath caught as the screen lit up, revealing the connection I'd been searching for. I turned to Gabriel, holding the phone out for him to see. "Look at this. Do you see it? The symbol, the bootlegger, they're all connected, and this is the proof. It's the brother."

"Whose brother?" Gabriel asked.

"The mayor's brother. It has to be," I said, swiping my fingers across the screen to zoom in.

Gabriel studied the picture, his brow furrowed. "You really think this ties everything together?"

"I do," I said, but even as the words left my mouth, I knew I needed more. "We're missing something."

"Then who's got the answers?" Gabriel asked, leaning in as if to share the weight of the mystery.

I swallowed, gripping the phone tighter. "I think one of our current town leaders knows more than he's letting on. We need to talk to him."

Finn and Seraphina finally caught up to us, peering quizzically at the phone in Gabriel's hand.

"What proof?" Seraphina asked.

"What do you need, Harper?" Finn added.

I set my shoulders as I met his gaze. "I need you to get Bella and tell her we've solved the case. Someone needs to stay up here with the guests, but she'll want to hear this."

"On it," Finn said instantly, turning and hurrying down the hall. Seraphina shot me a confused look before following him.

Gabriel sighed deeply and flicked his thumb and forefinger over the screen, zooming in on the photo. It wasn't the reaction I'd expected. I thought he would be as excited as I was, but even if he wasn't, did that mean my conclusions were wrong?

"Do you think this will help Benny find peace?" I whispered.

Gabriel studied the screen for a moment before meeting my gaze, his expression unreadable. "Maybe, but it's still a stretch. It's hard to tell how an unstable ghost will respond. Benny's been doing remarkably well so far, but who knows how he'll react to this news."

I bit my lip, my thoughts churning. The weight of my discovery was overwhelming, and I felt my resolve crumbling. Yet, the ticking of the hallway clock was a stark reminder that time was slipping away from us. Benny's control was fraying faster with every passing minute. If we didn't figure this out soon, the fallout would be far worse than just missing a clue.

I squeezed Gabriel's arm. "I think you need to talk to your mother. She should be there with us. You know, as a backup plan. Just in case," I said, trying to keep my voice steady.

"Are you sure?" he asked.

"Yes," I admitted, looking down. "But we're running out of options."

"What about you?" Gabriel asked.

"I need to find someone else. Hopefully he hasn't left yet."

To my surprise, Gabriel reached out and took my hand, squeezing it encouragingly. "I think you're amazing to have tracked down so many clues from so long ago. You're incredible."

"Umm, thanks," I said, a blush creeping up to my cheeks.

Gabriel smiled and gave my fingers one last squeeze before disappearing down the hallway to find his mother. Gathering my courage, I headed back into the party, searching for one face that I hoped would help to set Benny and Clara free from their agony of unknowing.

It took longer than I would've liked to gather the necessary people in the Hideaway, but Bella was insistent that the guests remain undisturbed so they could enjoy the party while we dealt with the ghosts in the basement. I didn't blame her. Now that I had a moment to think about it, cramming prominent members of the Havenwood community into the speakeasy with an unstable Benny didn't seem like a sensible idea. Not by a long shot. But what choice did I have?

My nerves were on edge by the time we gathered the necessary people. Gabriel, Finn, Bella, Isadora, and a few other key figures joined me downstairs, while the rest, including Honey, Lucas, and other responsible adults, remained upstairs to maintain control of the party—and to evacuate the guests if things went sideways or worse.

I took a deep breath and then another, trying to steady my nerves. Gabriel touched the small of my back. I glanced up at him, and he nodded encouragingly. "You've got this," he murmured. I dipped my chin in return. Hearing his confidence in me gave me the courage I needed.

As I stepped into the center of the Hideaway, the murmur of voices died down, and all eyes turned toward me. The weight of their gazes churned my stomach, but I pushed the nerves down. We were out of time. "I know this is unexpected for most of you," I began, my voice steady but tight. "But there've been some discoveries this week, and it's time to unveil the truth—dark as it may be."

I quickly recapped the story, reminding some and explaining to others the Hideaway's secrets—Benny and Clara's ill-fated love, the tragic deaths that followed, and the mystery that had festered in Havenwood ever since. I kept glancing at Benny, his photo trembling slightly as if his ghostly form was barely containing itself within the frame. I didn't have long.

I took a deep breath and caught Benny's gaze across the bar. His ghostly eyes flickered with a determined glint that mirrored my own feelings. We had to get through this. For Clara. For the DeLucas. For Havenwood.

And, although I wouldn't admit it out loud, a little bit for me, too. I'd become so wrapped up in the mystery that I needed answers almost as badly as Benny.

"I'm game," Benny said, gruffly. His voice held a desperate edge now, rougher than before. "If it means getting answers and helping Clara rest, then count me in, see?"

I caught a few people exchanging nervous glances—Vivienne Silverthorne, Sheriff Jackson, and Mayor Featherfoot included—but none of them interrupted. And thank the stars for that, because Benny was growing more erratic by the moment. I had a feeling only precious minutes remained before he finally lost control of himself. The lights flickered as the runes pulsed faintly along the walls. The building trembled subtly underfoot. The entire room felt as though it was holding its breath.

I took another step toward the bar, clutching the last bottle of Driftwood Sam's gin. "The evidence we've found all points to Driftwood Sam," I said, my voice steadying, though the knot in my stomach tightened with each word. "But that's not the whole story."

I glanced at Benny—his spectral form was still, but his tension hung heavy in the air, thickening it with the promise of violence. I needed to move fast.

"This symbol," I continued, holding up the bottle and pointing to the design on the label, "isn't just a bootlegger's mark. It's a family crest—a letter 'F,' wound into a spiral. The same crest that's etched on this tie clip we found in the collapsed tunnel." I produced the clip and began circling the room, showing the symbol to each person in turn.

I paused before Mayor Featherfoot, raising the tie clip higher for everyone to see. "And it matches the design on the watch you carry, doesn't it, Mayor?"

Gasps rippled through the crowd as Featherfoot's face drained of color. His trembling hands reached for the watch in his pocket, fumbling to flick it open. As the mayor stared at the matching symbol, he shook his head, muttering under his breath, "No...it can't be."

Behind me, the tension reached a fever pitch. Benny's form flickered erratically, the lights dimming further as the building groaned. A picture frame fell from the wall with a crash, the shaking more violent now. I couldn't wait any longer.

"It wasn't Driftwood Sam. It was your ancestor, Mayor," I said, my voice cutting through the rising tension. "Joseph Featherfoot—he killed Benny and sabotaged the escape tunnel." The words felt like stones dropping into the silence.

Benny's image crackled, the lights flickering wildly as his ghostly form shimmered with anger. "That coward!"

I held his gaze, trying to keep him calm. "That's not the whole story, Benny. I think Joseph recognized his family's logo on the bottles, realized his brother Sam was supplying Benny with illegal liquor, and knew he couldn't afford a scandal. He was running for mayor on a platform of family values. He couldn't be linked to illegal booze."

Vivienne Silverthorne's eyes narrowed. "So he cleared the evidence?"

I nodded. "I think he broke into the Hideaway to reclaim the gin. But then Benny showed up, and Joseph panicked. He hit Benny with one of the very bottles he'd come to steal." My voice softened. "Maybe he didn't mean to kill him. But Benny died."

The room went still, everyone hanging on my words.

I pressed on, "Joseph needed to cover up not just the bootlegging, but Benny's death, too. He had to access the Hideaway, and somehow, he got the keys—maybe from Clarence Silverthorne or his friend, Officer Crowley."

Sheriff Jackson tensed at the mention of his predecessor's name.

"He took what evidence he could from the speakeasy, but when Clara started asking questions, Joseph sabotaged the tunnel to stop her from finding out about his brother."

I turned to Mayor Featherfoot, whose face had gone ashen. "Joseph did all this to protect his political future. But now, the truth is out."

"No!" Mayor Featherfoot's voice cracked, his pale face stark against the dark wood paneling. His eyes were wide, wild with denial. Vivienne laid a hand on his shoulder, steadying him.

The ground gave a sudden lurch, sending everyone in the entire room stumbling to maintain their balance. A low rumbling sounded from beneath us, the runes flaring with a sickly light. Benny's image was flickering wildly now, and with a sudden roar, he bellowed, "It wasn't supposed to be like this!" His voice echoed with anger, grief, and years of pent-up frustration, shaking the very walls of the Hideaway.

I staggered, grabbing the edge of the bar for support as the rumbling intensified. The ceiling above us cracked, sending a few bits of plaster tumbling down. Vivienne Silverthorne raised her hands, muttering incantations to shield us, while Mayor Featherfoot stood frozen, his hands trembling around his watch.

"Benny!" I shouted over the chaos, my voice barely cutting through the noise. "It wasn't *this* Featherfoot! You've got your answer—now stop!"

But Benny wasn't listening. The runes on the walls flickered like a dying heartbeat, and the air grew thick with magic gone wrong. The power of the Hideaway itself threatened to collapse in on us. I could feel it, the raw magic of the speakeasy, woven into every beam and brick, starting to unravel.

"Mother! Now!" Gabriel's voice rang out, cutting through the din as he rushed to my side, his eyes darting between me and the barrier Vivienne was struggling to maintain. His hands flickered with illusion magic, but there was little he could do. Benny's volatile energy was overwhelming.

Sheriff Jackson sprang into action, his face set with determination as he herded the remaining guests toward the far end of the room. "Everyone move! Get to the tunnel!" he bellowed, his authoritative voice slicing through the chaos.

The lights flickered violently, and Benny's roar shook the room again, this time louder, more furious. "It wasn't supposed to end like this!"

The ceiling above us gave a deep groan, cracks widening, sending chunks of debris raining down. Vivienne, sweat beading on her forehead, shouted, "I can't hold it much longer!" Her hands trembled as the violet barrier flickered dangerously. "Everyone, get out!" Her voice broke with the strain of holding the collapsing room together.

Gabriel tried to tug me towards the tunnel, but I turned, my gaze locking onto the locket sitting on the bar—Clara's locket. My magic stirred, instinctively pulling me toward it. Desperation clawed at me as I grabbed the locket, feeling the cool metal hum under my fingers. There was energy here—faint, but steady. Clara was still here.

Without thinking, I poured my magic into the locket, letting my metal magic seek out the runes carved into the gold, hoping—no, praying—that it would be enough to bolster them, the way my magic had done for Benny's photo. The strain hit me hard, my legs trembling, knees buckling under the weight of it. My vision blurred as the pressure mounted.

Gabriel's arms were around me in an instant, steadying me just as I started t
o fall.

"Harper, what are you doing?" he shouted, panic edging his voice. "We need to go!"

"I'm...buying us time," I gasped, the locket pulsing weakly under my fingertips. "Clara... she's trying to help."

Just when I thought it was too late, when the weight of the collapsing magic was about to crush us all, a voice rang through the chaos, calm, clear, and commanding.

"Benny! Stop this NOW!"

The rumbling halted. The shaking ceased. Benny's flickering image froze, mid-fury, mid-roar. The very air around us stilled, as if the entire Hideaway was holding its breath.

I stared down at the locket in my hand, and as I did, the ghostly figure of Clara began to materialize next to Benny's picture. Her form shimmered with ethereal light, her eyes filled with a mixture of love and sorrow as she gazed at him.

"Benny," she repeated, her voice soft but firm. "It's over. You don't have to fight anymore."

Benny's form froze. His rage, which had been shaking the very walls, seemed to evaporate as his ghostly eyes locked onto hers. The wild anger in his voice vanished, leaving only a raw whisper, filled with emotion. "Clara...?"

"Yes, Benny. It's me," she said, moving closer, her light glowing brighter as she reached the photograph. She extended her hand, her shimmering figure radiating peace.

The room seemed to still, as if everyone was holding their breath, caught in the powerful moment between them.

I spoke quietly but firmly. "Ultimately, Benny, you asked for answers, which we've found. But in the end, all the players have passed on, and we must assume that whatever is waiting for us beyond this life will punish and reward as justice demands."

Mayor Featherfoot, recovering slightly, shot me a grateful look. Vivienne nodded at me regally, a thoughtful expression crossing her face as she considered my words—a considerate diversion from the potential political implications for the current mayor, despite being removed from Joseph Featherfoot's crimes by a hundred years. One never knew just how far back memories stretched in the supernatural town where some people lived for centuries instead of decades.

I looked back at the bar to where there seemed to be an ethereal light surrounding both the photograph and the locket. "Benny and Clara can finally be reunited for eternity, even if it's not the way they'd planned," I continued, my voice soft but carrying throughout the room.

Benny, his spectral form shimmering slightly in the photo, looked around, meeting each of our eyes. "Considering all the circumstances, this is the best ending I could've hoped for, by a long shot. Will you all do me a solid? Crack open that there bottle of whiskey I squirreled away under the bar and raise a toast to Clara and me, just like I planned for the day I would've popped the question." His voice was a wistful echo of his former l ife.

We obliged, and as Antonio uncorked the old bottle, a rich, peaty aroma filled the room. We passed glasses around, and as the amber liquid poured, the anticipation grew.

Benny looked fondly at the picture of Clara, which glowed slightly with her spirit, as I set a token glass of whiskey in front of each of them. "To you, my love. It was always you. And it will always be you."

"To Benny and Clara," everyone said in unison, raising their glasses.

My heart skipped as I realized this was it—the final moment. But the runes holding Benny to the photograph remained intact, flickering faintly. Without thinking, I lunged forward, dragging my thumbnail over the intricate lines. It wasn't elegant, but it was apparently enough to disrupt the magic. A faint crackling sound followed, and the runes' glow sputtered out. Benny and Clara's spirits rose and hovered above the bar, two glowing lights floating in midair. For a brief, breathtaking moment, their forms became clear—Benny's trademark grin and Clara's radiant smile—before they turned to each other with a look of pure joy. The moment their fingers touched, their forms began to merge, the light surrounding them growing brighter and warmer, filling the room with a golden glow that seemed to chase away every shadow. I had to shield my eyes as the light flared brilliantly, and when it faded, they were gone—leaving behind nothing but a lingering warmth, a soft, almost imperceptible hum of peace

Finally, after all these years, Benny and Clara were together - forever.

Echoes of the Past

ANTONIO CLAPPED HIS HANDS together with a grin, his voice carrying over the small crowd. "I'm glad everything is resolved, and I'd like to commend you intrepid young people for your determination to help Benny and Clara find their eternal peace. I'm already looking forward to having our party here next year and officially reopening the Hideaway, with a special tribute to its founders, Benny O'Rourke and Clara Silverthorne," he announced, with a glance towards Vivienne for her nod of approval. The matriarch of the Silverthorne family dipped her head graciously in return.

Bella, ever the pragmatic one, interjected with a laugh, "Speaking of a party, there's one upstairs that we really need to get back to. Charities to support, champagne to drink, and fireworks to light!"

A small cheer rose at her words, and everyone headed back upstairs, Bella, Isadora, and Antonio leading the charge with a newfound energy. I, however, hung back. There were items at the bar that I couldn't bear to leave unattended—not just yet. The photo of Benny and Clara's locket, symbols of the night's revelations, deserved a moment of respect. Even though the spirits of Benny and Clara had moved on, the artifacts that remained held a new significance. I gently gathered them, whispering a quiet wish for their peace in whatever place they found themselves beyond the walls of the Hideaway.

Across the room, Vivienne was speaking in low, soothing tones to Mayor Flavian Featherfoot as they walked towards the tunnel. Although I was sure I wasn't meant to overhear, I caught her measured words that were obviously meant to reassure the distraught mayor. "Everything between us is just as it was before, Flavian. The actions of your ancestor do not change my opinion of your upstanding nature." Her affirmation seemed to bring some color back to his cheeks as they disappeared into the tunnel. Vivienne leaned back into the Hideaway, looking for her son. "Gabriel? A word if you will?"

Gabriel shot me a look that spoke volumes even as he hurried after his mother. I knew in that instant he would've chosen to stay with me if he could. I gave him a little smile and a nod, silently indicating a promise to meet up with him later.

Seraphina and Finn followed them to the tunnel. I noticed she was clutching tightly to Finn's arm and looked paler than normal. Was talking to ghosts an abnormality for the elf? Or perhaps there was some sort of cultural taboo in the elf culture? Or was it something else entirely? I admitted to myself that I didn't know enough about elves, enchanter or otherwise, and mentally added "elf inquiry" to my future to-be-researched list.

Sheriff Jackson lingered near the doorway, his eyes scanning the room with a wary look. "You sure you're good down here?" he asked, his tone casual but edged with concern.

"I'm fine," I reassured him. "But someone should probably make sure everything stays calm upstairs."

The sheriff gave me a nod, but he hesitated for a moment longer. Finally, he turned and ushered the last stragglers toward the tunnel entrance. "Don't stay too long," he called back.

Alone for a moment in the suddenly empty Hideaway, I looked around the once-secret speakeasy. Its walls, if they could talk, would tell stories of prohibition, hidden loves, family torment, and spectral mysteries now laid to rest. As glad as I was that Benny and Clara had found the resolution they'd sought, part of me wished they could've stayed a little longer. Without the pressure of Benny losing his cool, I would've found it fascinating to talk with either or both of them about their experiences in the Hideaway and in Havenwood. But it wasn't to be. I sighed and ran a hand over the wood of the bar. At least I could imagine the stories that might have filled this place so long ago. Who knows? I might even be inspired to write my own version of events one day.

With the photo and locket securely in my grasp, I felt a bridge form between the past and the present, ready to usher these echoes into the light of the new day. On a sudden whim, I tipped a little more of the whiskey into my glass and raised it to the Hideaway.

"The best secrets are the ones we share," I murmured, inspired by the quote from the back of Benny's photo. It might have been my imagination, but I could have sworn the lights brightened for just a moment as I lifted my glass and tossed back the toast. The whiskey burned pleasantly on the way down, warming me despite the chill in the basement.

As I prepared to leave the Hideaway, the air behind the bar shimmered slightly, and Benny's ghost materialized one last time. His spectral form had a gentle luminosity that seemed both comforting and sad.

"Kid, I gotta hand it to ya, you've done me and Clara a solid tonight. I didn't think I'd ever find her again, but thanks to you we're together and...well, I can't tell you all the details but trust me. It's a happy ending for us both," Benny said.

I nodded, clutching the locket and the photograph a little closer to my chest. "I'm glad I could help, Benny. It feels good to know you and Clara are finally together after all this time."

Benny's form flickered like an old film reel, but his smile was warm and genuine. "Clara wanted me to pass along a little message, seeing as she didn't have the juice to make one more trip back herself. She said to tell ya, 'Don't you forget, you're the one holding the pen to your own story now.'"

He winked at me, his infectious charm bridging the ages. "I'd say maybe you oughta mosey on down to that heartwood tree, see? There's power in those old branches. I think they worked to bring me and Clara back together after all this time. If you ever want to find your way there, Clara said to tell you that she left a riddle on her map to the heartwood tree. A place like that might clear the cobwebs, give you a nudge in the right direction—if you catch my drift." He tipped his head towards the door, where both Finn and Gabriel had exited.

But before I could respond, Benny gave a knowing smirk and tapped the old bar. "Oh, and one last thing. Take a look under here," he said.

I reached under the bar and found an old leather-bound book, the cover worn from decades of use. Benny's eyes twinkled as I lifted it out. "That there's all the rune work and secrets to reopen and run the Hideaway. A gift for the DeLucas, so they can keep the magic alive." He gave me one last wink before his form flickered and slowly faded away, leaving the room in peaceful silence.

I looked around the empty Hideaway, the weight of the book in my hands. Benny was right. While some stories had ended, others were still waiting to be written.

As I walked down the tunnel, the muted cadence of voices became clearer. Instinctively, I halted just inside the tunnel doorway, unwilling to intrude on what sounded like a very private moment.

Seraphina's voice drifted through the basement to me. "...and I've been doing a lot of thinking. About us. About everything. I'm proud of what I've built. My business, the positive impact I've made, the work I've done. It's more than I ever dreamed of. But despite all this...I miss you." Her voice cracked slightly, filled with a mix of determination and vulnerability. "I miss *us*. What we had."

There was a pause, and I could almost picture Finn's hesitance, the way his brow might furrow in thought.

"Seraphina, I—"

"No, let me finish," Seraphina interjected, her voice sounding stronger. "Tonight, hearing about Benny and Clara, seeing how everything unfolded for them. It made me realize I don't want to let love slip through my fingers. Not without a fight. I love you, Finnegan Oakheart. And I want a second chance. Not out of loneliness or fear, but because you're still the one who understands me better than anyone else. Because I believe in us."

The silence that followed was palpable. I held my breath, feeling like an intruder on this deeply personal moment, yet unable to tear myself away.

Finn's reply was soft, almost lost beneath the muffled sounds of the party. "Seraphina, you know how much I care about you. But everything that happened...it's a lot to just step back into a relationship. I need time to think about what you've said."

"Okay, I understand," Seraphina's voice was filled with a resigned hope. "Take your time. Just know I'm here, and I'm not going anywhere."

Their footsteps eventually moved toward the stairs. As I waited until the sound of their departure to fade completely, I thought of Benny's advice. Was he right? Did I need to take action instead of wallowing in indecision? Undoubtedly. But my problem was I didn't know what action to take. Seraphina's courage in the face of love was what I wanted too. She didn't wait. She spoke up on her own behalf, and perhaps she was right. Yet, my own heart was a tangle of feelings—between Finn's supportive presence and Gabriel's enticing smiles, I felt lost in a maze of what-ifs.

Whichever path I decided to take, the first step needed to be exiting the tunnel. Cautiously, I peeked out into the basement. It was empty. I took a deep breath, squaring my shoulders. I still had time to figure out what I wanted and which path to walk. As I left the tunnel, my fingers brushed over the runes that lined the walls, now glowing steadily, back to perfect working order after everything they had witnessed. Havenwood's hidden tale had found resolution, but mine was still unfolding.

A Spark of Hope

As I climbed the stairs from the tunnel, the weight of the evening still pressed on me. The long-hidden truths, the unexpected use of my magic, the farewell to Benny and Clara—it had drained me. I was ready for peace, to let the emotions settle in the quiet. But as I reached the top, the contrast of normal life hit me with surprising force.

Laughter and the clinking of glasses filled the air, a celebration continuing as though the events below hadn't just unfolded. The joy and warmth radiated through the room, so at odds with everything I had just witnessed. It was impossible not to smile, feeling the music of life start to lift my spirits again, a reminder that even through all the chaos, life moved on.

As soon as I emerged from the basement, Bella was waiting for me at the top of the stairs. Her eyes sparkled with curiosity as I handed her the old leather-bound book Benny had given me.

"This is for you," I said softly. "Benny wanted your family to have it. It's got all the secrets to running the Hideaway."

Bella's eyes widened in surprise, then softened with a grateful smile. She clutched the book to her chest before giving me a knowing look. "We've worked too hard tonight. Let's lock this up and deal with it tomorrow. Tonight, we party."

With a playful wink, she tucked the book safely away. Then, as if on cue, Isadora grabbed my hand, pulling me back into the fold of the party, which had transformed the Oasis into a whirlwind of excited fun. I let myself be swept up in the moment. Bella and Alex joined us, and together we made the rounds to the tables, gambling our fake money away. Each loss came with overly dramatic groans of despair, and every win was met with shouts of joy. It felt good to let loose, to let the tension of the night melt away.

Eventually, we took our "winnings" to the prize table to trade our chips in for real prizes. I opted for a candy ring with a gemstone made of pure sugar that I immediately slipped on my finger. Had the sparkly blue candy been a real sapphire instead of a sweet treat, I would have been set for life. As it was, I contented myself with turning my tongue blue and the slight sugar rush.

Antonio gathered the crowd, announcing the winners of the silent auction and declaring that all the proceeds would go to charity. Cheers met both announcements, and he had to hold up both his hands and wait for several minutes as the crowd finally quieted.

"We've had quite the night! My family and I want to thank each and every one of you for welcoming in the new year with us," he said, wrapping his arm around Honey's shoulders as they beamed at the gathered guests in tandem. Antonio's eyes sparkled. "And now, if you will all grab your coats and gloves, we have a little surprise set up for you outside."

"A brilliant display of fireworks!" Honey exclaimed, clapping her hands.

Antonio chuckled good naturedly along with the rest of the crowd, shook his head, and pulled his wife in closer to his side with an affectionate smile. "My apologies, friends. I misspoke. My surprise is not a surprise but, in fact, fireworks. We hope you'll join us!" he finished with a flourish towards the door.

The excited energy was infectious as everyone trooped outside for the promised sparkling display. The night air was crisp, and the sky was speckled with a brilliant dusting of stars, making it the perfect backdrop for the bursts of color that would soon light up the sky. I headed outside and found a spot to stand with Bella and Isadora.

"How are fireworks even legal in this part of town?" I asked, genuinely curious amid the excitement.

Bella responded with a quick grin, "They're made by a local coven. Magical fireworks present all of the awe but none of the hazards that normal fireworks do."

Isadora chimed in, her eyes twinkling with excitement, "That's not to take anything away from how awesome they look. If you didn't know, you'd swear they were the real thing."

I spotted Antonio disappearing with a couple of women who were bundled up against the cold, presumably the firework witches. Mentally, I added that to my list of future jobs with a chuckle. Then, all thoughts of the future and past faded as I just enjoyed the present with my two best friends.

The witches, or Antonio, timed the display perfectly. Brilliant bursts of color lit the sky in a breathtaking display, culminating in a glittering countdown leading us into the new year. When a large "Happy New Year" appeared across the sky followed by a big finale, couples kissed and hugged, Bella and Alex being among them. Then Bella, Isadora, and I hugged all around, exchanging congratulations and well wishes with those close to us

.

On the other side of the yard, Finn caught my eye. He was standing with Seraphina. Maybe it was my imagination, but there was a stiffness to his posture that hadn't been there previously. Before he could catch me staring, I turned away. I needed to figure out my feelings for him, but this wasn't the moment.

Across the clearing, Gabriel stood with his mother and Mayor Feather-foot, who still looked quite distressed. Gabriel looked as if he were searching for someone. His eyes combed the crowd, and when he finally spotted me, a warm, dazzling smile spread across his face, matching the brilliance of the fireworks overhead. My heart fluttered, and I couldn't help but smile back.

Not far from him, Finn caught my eye, giving me his own small, quiet smile. I returned it, feeling a sense of comfort and calm wash over me.

Maybe Benny was right. The heartwood tree might hold the answers I needed—if I could find it. Clara's map just might be the key to unlocking that mystery.

Bella interlinked her arm with mine, interrupting my thoughts. The fading luster of the fireworks glowed in her eyes as she said, "You know what? If you'd asked me what this year would bring last January, I never could have anticipated how it would've unfolded." She looked between

Isadora and me. "Yet, here I am, so grateful to be standing with the two of you, and eager for whatever comes next."

I nodded, the warmth of her words seeping deep into my heart. "I couldn't have said it better," I responded, my gaze drifting over the joyful faces around us, lit by the glittering stars above. "This year taught us that no matter how unpredictable life may seem, there's always a golden thread of friendship weaving through the darkness, leading us to moments like these."

As we watched the crowd welcome in the new year with hope and celebration, I felt a profound sense of anticipation. This wasn't just another chapter waiting to be written—it was a promise of endless possibilities, of love and mystery, of new adventures with those who matter most. I couldn't wait to get started.

Thank you!

So, if my stories have made you smile, laugh, or brought a little magic into your life, please let me know. Your support and feedback mean everything to me, and they help keep this writing dream alive for me.

Thank you for being a part of my story, for believing in my characters, and for sharing this journey with me.

With all my gratitude and a heart full of hope,

L. L. Gray

Want more Havenwood?

Don't forget your free book!

Do you want a free book? Of course you do, what madness could possess someone to **not** want free books?

There's no catch - you do sign-up for my mailing list but you can unsubscribe at any time.

There's also no spam.

Ever.

Sign up here to get your free book!

https://www.subscribepage.io/havenwood

Also By

Havenwood Paranormal Cozy Mysteries

The Mystery in the Margins
The Chaos in the Chronicles (exclusive novella)
The Puzzle in the Pumpkin Patch
The Secret of the Silver Serpent
The Riddle at the Revelry
The Manuscript in the Moonlight (exclusive novella)
The Heist of the Hidden Heart
The Mayhem in the Masquerade
The Legend of the Leaf
The Conspiracy on the Cruise (coming soon!)
The Curse at the Carnival (coming soon!)

Smoke and Shadows Series

Shadows and Relics
Pixie Pranks (exclusive novella)
Felons and Fangs
Bones and Blades
Tempest and Treason
Daggers and Deception
Sleuths and Scoundrels
Legacy and Lies
Crossroads and Curses

Children's Books

The Secret About Mistakes
Corner of the Sky
To Mom. Love, Me□
To Dad. Love, Me□
To Grandma. Love, Me□
To Grandpa. Love, Me

About the Author

L.L. Gray writes captivating, fast-paced fantasy full of wit, warmth, and magic. Her books transport readers to charming, cozy worlds brimming with lovable characters and whimsical adventures. A lifelong enthusiast of fantasy and myths, L.L. Gray blends humor and heart, inviting readers to escape into her spellbinding stories that feel like home—cozy, magical, and impossible to put down.

Psst, it's me—L.L. Gray!

I love connecting with fellow story lovers and adventure seekers. If that sounds like your cup of tea (or coffee, or whatever magical potion you prefer), come say hello! Visit my website www.llgray.com to join my newsletter, where you'll find exclusive goodies, or join us in my Facebook readers group. And if email is more your style, feel free to drop me a line anytime at info@llgray.com.

I hope you stay in touch!

Acknowledgments

To you, the reader: thank you for stepping into this world with me. I hope you felt the magic, warmth, and wonder woven into these pages. If you'd like to stay up to date with new releases and special content, head over to my website. And if you're looking to connect with a welcoming, book-loving community, join us on Facebook—there's always room for another story lover.

To my fabulous ARC and Street teams: you've become like a second family to me, cheering me on through every twist, turn, and chapter. Your unwavering support, encouragement, and excitement fuel my creative fire—I truly couldn't do this without each of you. Thank you for believing in these stories as much as I do.

Lastly, to my wonderful husband: your support is the foundation of every story I write. Thank you for believing in me, for being my rock, and for making all of this possible. I'm endlessly grateful to have you by my side.